THE LIBRARIAN

PHILIP WILSON

ISBN

978-1-77370-029-8 (paperback)

978-0-9947753-2-0 (ebook)

978-0-9947753-1-3 (hardcover)

Published in Canada.

First Edition

CHAPTER 1

TAKING THE SUBWAY AT NIGHT ALWAYS FRIGHTENED HER. Looking around anxiously, Sarah boarded one of the middle cars. It was empty except for a tall, white-haired man staring out the window into the darkness. As the train pulled out of the station, she chose a seat not far from the man and took a book from her purse.

While seemingly unaware of Sarah's presence, the man had watched her reflection in the window from the moment she had entered the car. Early thirties, he guessed. Thick raven hair hung to her shoulders. Horn-rimmed glasses partially hid her dark eyes and clear features. She was dressed inexpensively in dark grey slacks, a plain white blouse and well-worn loafers. No jewelry except for small earrings and a simple watch. Attractive. Yet from the glasses and the way she dressed, he sensed she was unaware of her appearance.

Three stops later, two young men entered the car, talking loudly. Dressed almost identically in black jeans and T-shirts, one had a shaved head and the other wore a bandana. They looked around the train, first noticing the white-haired man, then focusing on Sarah. The one with the shaved head sat down beside her and the other sat across from her. Sarah pretended to be engrossed in her book.

"My name's Carlos," began the man next to her. "And my friend here is Raul. What's your name?"

Not wanting to encourage them, nor give them reason to take offense, Sarah hesitated. "Sarah," she whispered finally.

"Sarah. Pretty name," commented Raul.

"Did you know you were riding in our subway car?" Carlos continued.

Sarah shook her head.

"Well, you are. And there's an extra charge for taking this car."

"Please. I don't have much money," Sarah replied.

Raul put his hand on her thigh and grinned. "Then we'll just have to discuss some other means of payment."

Sarah looked around desperately for help, but saw only the white-haired man, still looking out the window, seemingly oblivious to her plight.

"Nice purse," Carlos commented.

Sarah clutched her purse more tightly.

"I just want to look at it."

"Please leave me alone."

"You're not being very friendly." Carlos grabbed the strap and was about to yank it from her grasp when he heard a voice behind them.

"Really doesn't go with your shoes."

Startled at the interruption, the two men looked up to see the white-haired man standing beside them. They had not noticed him leave his seat.

"If I were you, Pops," said Carlos, "I'd catch another train."

Raul laughed.

The man remained where he was. "I'd like you to leave her alone."

Annoyed by his nonchalance, Carlos stood and faced the man, momentarily surprised at his height.

"For the last time, Grandpa, get lost!" Carlos cocked his fist.

The man still made no move to back away and Carlos suddenly became conscious of the man's complete lack of fear. He saw the cold blue eyes studying him with contempt and, for the first time, he sensed the lithe and powerful body that belied the white hair—too late. In an instant, he found himself jammed against the window, face smashed into the glass, his arm forced far up his back, his shoulder searing with pain. Suddenly there was an audible crack and Carlos crumpled to the floor, cradling his broken arm. Startled at seeing his friend so quickly incapacitated, Raul pulled a knife. "Big mistake, Gramps."

The white-haired man simply shrugged.

Raul feinted to the left and then lashed out, a tactic that invariably gave him an opening. But the man easily read his intent, grabbed his wrist and twisted it backwards. Yelping with pain, Raul dropped the knife. Before he could recover, he felt a savage blow to his stomach, sending him to the ground beside his friend, gasping for breath.

The man reached for Sarah's hand. "I think we'd better catch another train."

· · · · · · ·

Numbly, Sarah took his hand and let him lead her out of the subway car onto the platform. They waited for the next train and boarded. The man guided her to a seat and sat opposite her. "Are you all right?"

Sarah could manage only a nod.

The man smiled sympathetically. "Take some deep breaths."

She complied, and found herself becoming a bit steadier.

"Better?"

"A little," Sarah managed to reply, her voice weak and tremulous. "Thank you for what you did."

"It was nothing."

"Shouldn't we phone the police?"

"There's really no point."

Sarah nodded uncertainly. She didn't want to inconvenience the man after what he'd done for her. She looked at him more carefully, struck by his startlingly blue eyes and easy smile. From a distance, the white hair made him look older, but seeing him up close she guessed he was in his mid-forties. He smiled at her. Realizing that he knew she was appraising him, Sarah looked away shyly.

He could see that she was still shaken. She seemed hesitant, even timid, although perhaps it was just a reaction to what had happened. "What station do you get off at?"

"Eastgate. I live a few blocks from the station."

"I go past Eastgate. I'd be happy to walk you home."

"I'll be fine. Thank you again," Sarah replied, her voice firmer.

For a few minutes they sat in silence, neither of them knowing quite what to say. Finally, he asked, "What do you do?"

"I'm a librarian—at the Glenwood Library."

"Do you like it?"

Sarah brightened slightly. "I know it sounds boring, but I do enjoy it."

"With computers and the internet, I would have thought that libraries would be obsolete?"

"You'd think so." Sarah became more animated discussing a subject she was familiar with. "But there's so much published that hasn't been converted to electronic form."

"Interesting. It seems odd, still having hard copy books stacked on shelves when the world is going online."

"It keeps me employed."

He laughed. Despite her apparent shyness, she had a sense of humor. "I haven't been in a library since I was a kid."

"You should try it. They've changed a lot. Computers, Internet access, a DVD section. We even have a coffee bar."

"Cappuccino?"

"Even cappuccino."

"I'll have to try it," he replied with a grin. "My name's Paul Taylor."

"Sarah Andrews."

"Well, Sarah. How come you're riding the subway at night?"

"I was visiting my father. He's in a nursing home. I try to visit him most nights after work. My mother died a year ago," she added, not sure why she had.

"I'm sorry."

"Do you live in the city?" asked Sarah, changing the subject.

"No. I'm just in today to meet a friend. I live in the country on a lake. My car's at the end of the subway line. It's about a two-hour drive."

"Sounds nice."

"It is," replied Paul. "And peaceful. I don't think I could live in the city."

"What do you do?" Sarah asked, curious.

"Nothing."

Sarah looked at him quizzically.

"I retired recently," he went on to explain. "So I just sail, read and listen to the birds. It's a tough life."

Sarah smiled. "Sounds okay to me."

"I think I'll survive it. I noticed you reading before you were interrupted. What do librarians read?"

"Right now, I'm reading *The Count of Monte Cristo*. But don't be impressed. I usually stick to the bestseller rack."

"I saw the movie once. I remember being disappointed that Dantes and Mercedes didn't get back together."

"Now you've spoiled it for me."

"I'm sorry."

"Don't be." Sarah laughed. "I've seen the movie too."

Moments later, they arrived at Eastgate. "You're sure you'll be all right?" Paul asked.

"I'll be fine. I wish there was something more I could do to thank you," Sarah replied, standing up to get off the train.

Paul smiled. "Don't worry about it. I'm glad I was able to help."

"Well, thank you again."

"Good-bye, Sarah."

"Bye," Sarah replied softly as the doors closed behind her. She assumed that she'd never see Paul Taylor again and felt strangely disappointed.

． ． ． ． ． ． ．

Sarah walked the three blocks home without incident. Her one bedroom apartment was on the top floor of an old three-storey walk-up. It was distinctly modest, but the rent was cheap and she could walk to work.

Once inside, Sarah bolted the door and dropped onto the worn couch, still shaken from the experience. After a few minutes, she forced herself to get up. She went into her tiny kitchen, wondering what to make for dinner and decided on chicken soup, a toasted peanut butter sandwich and a glass of milk. As she prepared the simple meal, she realized she was still trembling. She rarely drank but there was a bottle of wine in the cupboard. She opened it and poured a glass, immediately downing half of it. The wine soothed her and she poured a second glass. After finishing her dinner, she poured a third glass of wine and fixed a warm bath. As she lay there, she felt the warmth of the bathwater and the wine seep through her. An hour later, Sarah reluctantly climbed out of the tub and pulled on pajamas. She settled back on the living room couch, enjoying the mellow, light-headed feeling.

Since her last year in high school, Sarah, an only child, had devoted herself to looking after her parents; first her mother with Alzheimer's, then her father who'd had a severe stroke. She'd been so consumed by caring for them that she hadn't thought much about her own life. Now thirty-four, she really had no life, no close friends, no outside interests, no relationships. She knew her father would be gone soon, which would leave her totally alone. She thought about Paul Taylor. Their conversation had been so commonplace, yet she had enjoyed it. She should have asked him to walk her home, invited him in for coffee. Now it was too late.

· · · · · · ·

After Sarah left the train, Paul Taylor continued to the end of the line where he recovered his Jeep from the municipal parking lot. By the time Sarah climbed out of her bath, he was approaching his driveway. The entrance was barely perceptible - just a slight break in the dense brush that lined both sides of the narrow country road. The winding trail, barely wide enough for his jeep, was heavily rutted with steep inclines and sharp switchbacks and would have been impassable without four-wheel drive. Despite the darkness and treacherous terrain, Paul found his way with effortless familiarity. Still he had to drive slowly and it was another five minutes before he reached his house. He had thought about getting his driveway straightened and paved, but decided against it. He liked the privacy and seclusion its current state provided.

As he pulled up to his house, there was a crashing sound from the nearby brush and out bounded a golden retriever. The dog ran to the car and stood up on his hind legs peering through the window.

Paul gently eased the door open. "Hi fella," he laughed, scratching the dog's ears. "Miss me?"

Delighted to have his master back, the dog followed Paul as he went inside, poured himself a scotch and then wandered out onto the open deck. There was a slight breeze and the air was warm. During the day, the deck provided a spectacular view of Crystal Lake. In the dark, the reflection of a full moon danced across the water. The shoreline was a rugged mixture of trees and rock, now visible only as grey shadows surrounding the glistening blackness of the lake.

Paul had seen the place ten years before and bought it immediately. He owned almost fifty acres of woods and two thousand feet of waterfront, with his nearest neighbor more than two miles away. Easing himself into one of the lounge chairs, he sat there quietly, sipping his scotch and listening to the water lapping the shoreline. The dog curled up contentedly beside him.

Paul Taylor had joined the navy right after high school, getting his degree and becoming a navy seal. When he was thirty, he had left the navy and worked as a mercenary in Latin America and the Middle East. At that time, a growing number of executives and diplomats were being kidnapped by terrorist groups, drug cartels or rogue governments seeking money, bargaining chips or just publicity. Paul saw an opportunity for someone with his skills and he started a business retrieving them. His success rate was excellent. He was soon in considerable demand and priced his services accordingly.

At forty-six, just one month before, Paul closed his business and retired. He had enjoyed the challenge of his work, but he knew that he would eventually make a mistake and wind up dead, or worse, rotting in some foreign jail. Having put away more than thirty-million dollars, there was no need to keep working.

He retired to Crystal Lake intending to spend his days sailing, canoeing, and reading. At the time, it sounded blissful, but only weeks after "retirement," Paul was feeling restless. And, he had to admit, lonely. He'd had numerous relationships with women, but none had lasted. Now, looking at the possibility of living the rest of his life by himself, he wondered what it would be like to have someone to share the years ahead. To share the beauty of the lake. To share his bed.

He thought about Sarah Andrews, her shy smile and gentle humor. He should have insisted on walking her home, should have asked for her number, for a date. Now he would never see her again. Suddenly, he remembered the name of the library where she worked. He needed to go back into the city the next day anyway. It wouldn't hurt to drop by the Glenwood Library and have a cappuccino.

CHAPTER 2

CAPTAIN PETER LINDSAY HAD BEEN IN CHARGE OF THE SIXTH Police Precinct for three years. At forty-two, he was the youngest precinct commander in the Department and many were already predicting he would be the next Chief of Police. Some also said that he would do whatever it took to get there.

The Sixth Precinct had a well-deserved reputation as the toughest in the city. Its territory spanned the Docklands, a dying portion of the downtown core and the Warehouse District, which consisted of run-down tenement apartments and largely deserted warehouses used for crack houses and drug deals. Predictably, the Sixth's rate of violent crime was the highest in the city. The tough environment and the type of criminals being dealt with created a distinct culture within the precinct - a blend of machismo, arrogance, and cynicism; plus a contempt for the criminal justice process, which was seen as being out of touch with reality. As a consequence, the niceties of due process weren't always observed, interrogations were occasionally 'intense' and deficiencies in evidence were 'corrected'. These shortcuts were supported by the perception that Lindsay wanted to improve the precinct's arrest and conviction statistics and didn't care how. Some cops found the Sixth's brutal environment appealing and looked for ways to get into the Precinct. Others did not and took any way out they could find. This self-selection process reinforced the rogue culture.

In addition to running the Sixth Precinct, Lindsay had recently been appointed by the current Police Chief, Ed Moorby, to lead a new city-wide drug initiative, christened the "War on Drugs." Until recently, the drug trade in the city had been limited to the Warehouse District, and nobody cared much. Lately, however, the availability of high quality drugs had exploded into the business area and upscale suburbs, and the City Council was getting pressure to do something about it. Peter Lindsay fully intended to use the appointment and the attendant publicity as a springboard to succeed Moorby as Chief.

When he'd been selected to head the drug initiative, Lindsay had given press conferences and interviews pledging decisive action and quick results. He blamed the drug problem on organized crime, and promised to rout out the leaders and put them behind bars. However, despite the rhetoric, Lindsay had made little progress. A few pushers were in jail but the flow of drugs was undiminished and there had been no high-profile arrests. The media was becoming increasingly critical and Moorby had warned Lindsay that he would have to replace him as head of the War on Drugs unless he delivered results soon. Lindsay knew being dropped would end his chances of getting Moorby's job—and that wasn't going to happen.

Lindsay had a second problem—a hundred thousand dollar gambling debt. His creditors were getting restive and he had to get his hands on the money soon.

· · · · · · ·

The morning after Sarah's incident in the subway, Peter Lindsay was sitting in his office, seething from another tough meeting with Moorby. His assistant buzzed him.

"Yeah?" he snapped.

"Sergeant Gordon said to tell you they picked up Nick Costanza. They've got him in the Backfield Building," she answered. "He asked if you wanted to join them."

"Absolutely. Tell John I'll be there in five minutes." Lindsay hung up before his assistant could respond.

Costanza was just the kind of high-profile arrest he needed. A year ago, Nick Costanza moved from Los Angeles where he had been rumored to be a key figure in LA's drug trade. He'd bought a mansion on the outskirts of the city and lived quietly but well. His move coincided with increased drug trafficking in the city, but they couldn't get a single piece of real evidence on him. Lindsay was convinced that Costanza was the key to whoever was supplying the drugs. Get that name and he could shut down the flow of cocaine into the city. Finally, desperate for a break, Lindsay had him stopped for speeding and the arresting officer conveniently found a large quantity of coke hidden in the trunk of his car.

The Backfield Building was located thirty yards behind the main Precinct building and contained a few holding cells and a couple of interrogation rooms. Originally built to relieve overcrowding, it had become the place suspects were taken if the interrogation was expected to become 'intense.'

When Lindsay arrived, Costanza was fastened to the ceiling by his wrists and naked from the waist up. In his mid-fifties and seriously overweight, he looked awful - pale, struggling to breathe and perspiring heavily. John Gordon was seated on one of several metal chairs, casually drinking coffee and watching Costanza wheeze.

"Has he said anything?" asked Lindsay.

"Says he's retired and doesn't know anything about the drug business."

Lindsay turned to Costanza. "Bullshit."

Costanza looked up at Lindsay. "Well, well - the boss himself. Was it your idea to plant coke in my car? It'll never hold up."

Lindsay smirked. "It'll hold up. Good for three to five. That's if you make it to prison."

"My lawyers will fry your ass. Forget that Chief of Police crap. You'll be walking a beat."

"We know you're behind the drug trade," Lindsay replied, any trace of humor gone. "I want to know who's supplying you. Names and details."

"Don't know what you're talking about. I'm a retired businessman. I spend my time gardening. I was on my way to the nursery to buy some new perennials."

"Real funny."

"Suit yourself."

"Tell you what. You give me the names I need to shut down the drug trade and I'll let you go back to LA and plant all the fucking perennials you want. Otherwise, I'll bury you so deeply in prison you won't see the sun until you're eighty."

"Fuck you."

Lindsay stepped toward Costanza, his fist clenched. "You don't look too good Costanza. And any minute you could look a lot worse."

"My lawsuit's looking better and better," replied Costanza with contempt. "False arrest, assault. Go ahead. Take a swing. It'll be worth it."

"Easy Captain," said Gordon. "The guy's got a battalion of lawyers. One bruise and they'll have a field day."

"Good advice," sneered Costanza.

Lindsay smiled. He went to the filing cabinet and pulled out a taser. Walking back to Costanza, he brandished it in his face. "Know what this is?"

Costanza shrugged. He knew it was a taser. Smaller than a handgun, the taser could be fired or simply held against a suspect. Fifty thousand volts of electricity would surge through the victim, causing intense pain and momentary loss of muscle control. And it left no marks. Intended to subdue violent suspects, the Sixth Precinct increasingly used it as a tool for interrogation.

"A toy gun?" Costanza offered. Despite the bravado, Costanza was unable to conceal his fear.

"Smart ass." Lindsay held the taser against Costanza's bare stomach and pulled the trigger. Costanza's whole body jerked spasmodically. His chest heaved and his mouth opened and closed as if he were trying to scream but couldn't.

Lindsay released the trigger and stepped back, waiting for Costanza to recover. "Not bad for a toy gun," he sneered.

"When I get out of here, you're dead," Costanza croaked.

Lindsay gave him another jolt. "Are we having fun yet?"

Costanza managed a strangled gasp.

"Anything to say?" prodded Lindsay. "We can keep this up all morning."

"Careful, Captain. We don't want his heart to crap out on us."

"Hear that, Costanza?" Lindsay mocked. "John thinks this will kill you. Maybe you better talk."

"There's a deal going down tomorrow night..." wheezed Costanza, beaten.

"That's better, but we need the details."

"In the Warehouse District. 2235 Palmerston."

"When?"

"Ten o'clock."

"What's happening?"

"It's a drug buy—fifty kilos of cocaine."

"What's the pay-off?"

"Three million."

"Who's supplying you?"

"I don't have a name."

"Sure you do. Now let's have it." Lindsay pushed the taser hard against Costanza's gut and pulled the trigger. Costanza's whole body shook violently and then went limp. He looked up at them blankly before his eyes rolled back in their sockets. His body hung motionless.

Gordon went over and felt for a pulse. After several seconds, he shook his head.

"Shit! Get him down," ordered Lindsay. Despite Gordon's earlier warning, he was startled at the sudden outcome.

"Want me to call someone?" Gordon asked.

"Nah. We'd have to explain what was going on here. Take him to one of the holding cells and arrange to have someone 'find' him in a couple of hours. We'll announce that he died of a heart attack while in custody. When you're done, join me in my office. I have a proposition for you."

· · · · · · ·

John Gordon had been a cop for thirty of his fifty-four years, and he was tired of his job. As a Sergeant, he made a hundred thousand a year, but forty thousand went in alimony payments to his wife. In two years, he'd retire on full pension; but his pension was only sixty thousand and he'd still need to pay the forty thousand to his wife. How could he live on what was left? He'd applied for deferred retirement so he could stay on and continue drawing his salary until he was sixty, but knew he had no chance. His service record had some blemishes – drinking while on duty, excessive use of force, plus a few other incidents. In less than a year, he'd be forced out. He'd seen cops take jobs as security guards making little more than the minimum wage after a forced retirement, just to make ends meet. What a way to spend your golden years, he thought bitterly.

John Gordon had always expected bigger things for himself. He'd won a football scholarship to college and hoped to play pro ball. But while he had the size, he didn't have the talent. The competition was tougher than it had been in high school, and he found himself spending more and more time on the bench until he was finally cut from the college team. If his grades had been good, the university would have continued his scholarship; but when he failed his second year, his scholarship was revoked and he had to leave. Gordon applied to the police force and was accepted. He made Sergeant by the time he was thirty, a considerable achievement on a force where years of service was the biggest factor in getting promoted.

A year later, Gordon's partner was killed investigating a report of domestic abuse and it was discovered that Gordon had been in a bar drinking when he was supposed to be on duty. He kept his job but the prospect of any further advancement was over. The fact that his career was over and everyone on the force knew it left him bitter and cynical. He began drinking more heavily, becoming abusive and obnoxious at home. His wife took their daughter and moved out, then sued him for divorce. He hadn't seen either one of them in almost twenty years. He'd written to his daughter a few times but never received a reply.

Gordon had first met Peter Lindsay when Lindsay was a rookie cop. After only three months on the force, Lindsay had mistakenly shot and killed an unarmed suspect. Gordon covered for him, planting a gun, which he carried for just such an eventuality, on the suspect's body. Ambitious and politically savvy, Lindsay's career flourished, but he never forgot what Gordon had done for him. When Lindsay had been appointed to run the War on Drugs, he'd assigned Gordon to the program full-time. It got him away from the day-to-day grind and Gordon was grateful. As he headed to Lindsay's office, he wondered what the newest proposition was going to be.

· · · · · · ·

Lindsay leaned back from his desk. Costanza's death was going to be a problem, but the tip on the drug deal might be an opportunity. A major drug bust would get everyone off his back and the three million dollars could solve his money problems. Gordon arrived a few minutes later and the Captain waved him to a seat.

"Costanza's lead on the drug deal," began Lindsay. "I want you to pick a team and stake it out."

"Will do."

"And set up some video equipment. I want an airtight case. No screw-ups."

"Yes, sir."

Lindsay leaned back in his chair and sighed in irritation. "God damn Costanza, crapping out like that. I'll have the SIU all over my case." The Sixth had had more than its share of in-custody deaths and, much to Lindsay's annoyance, the Special Investigations Unit or SIU was growing more persistent in its investigations.

"What can they possibly prove? Costanza was in his fifties, and overweight. Shit happens."

"You're probably right."

"Rumor has it you've got a lock on the Chief's job when he goes."

Lindsay just shrugged, not wanting to reveal his doubts. "John, I'm looking to add another full-time officer to the War on Drugs, working closely with you. What do you think about Tom Miller?"

Gordon thought for a minute before replying. "Good officer. Keeps to himself, but popular with the men. A bit rough sometimes. Understand he had some trouble in the army, but I don't know the details."

"Didn't even finish high school?" Lindsay queried.

"I wouldn't worry about it. Tough childhood. But he's quick and has street smarts."

"What do you know about his childhood?"

"Nothing official. Just what I've picked up in conversation. He's from some town in the mountains. Father was the mine foreman. Taught him to hunt, trap and fish before he was twelve. Then the mine closed and his father lost his job. His mother ran off with the executive who had closed the mine. Father couldn't handle it and disappeared. Tom never got over it. Faked his way into the army when he was seventeen."

"What happened to the father?"

"Turned out he moved to the city but couldn't find work. Wound up living on the streets. Then somebody found him dead under some bridge. Real tough on Miller. He idolized his father."

"I see he has a couple of official reprimands for rousting vagrants."

"He hates street people. Reminds him of what happened to his father."

"So no problem if I transfer him to work with you?"

Gordon shook his head, wondering if Lindsay was already starting to groom a replacement. "Why the extra manpower?"

Lindsay looked at him. "John, I'm sorry. I just heard yesterday that you're being compulsorily retired next year. I know you want to work past fifty-five and I've been supporting you. I told them I needed someone with your experience on the War on Drugs. You can guess their reasons—your service record, the need to open up some Sergeant positions for the younger men. You know the story."

"That's why you're bringing on Miller?"

Lindsay nodded. "I'm sorry. I'll never forget what you did for me, but I don't have a choice. Don't tell Miller yet. I need to clear it with the Chief."

"Of course and thanks for trying," replied Gordon, wondering how the hell he was going to live on twenty thousand a year.

"I know that leaves you with some financial problems, but I have an idea for you."

"I'm listening."

"You heard Costanza say there was three million involved in the deal tomorrow tonight?"

"Yeah."

"If only two million of that money made its way to the evidence locker, no one would miss the other million."

Gordon nodded, waiting for the rest.

"I'm suggesting a quarter million for each of us. You divide the rest among your team. I assume an extra quarter million would help your retirement plans?"

"For sure."

"Pick guys you trust. You know what I mean. I don't need to tell you the risks if someone talks..."

"No problem. A hundred grand plus buys a lot of silence. And thanks."

· · · · · · ·

Back at his desk, Gordon began to cull through the duty roster to pick a team for the stakeout. He wanted four men plus himself. He soon had a list: Tom Miller, Chris LePan, Frank Carlucci and Ernie Kramer.

The misfit squad, he thought. They all had tarnished service records, but that was what he wanted. Miller had been dishonorably discharged from the army and had several citations for excessive use of force. LePan liked women and lived extravagantly. He was definitely not above skimming off some drug money to support his lifestyle. Carlucci was a bodybuilder—all muscle and no brains. He'd been the subject of numerous complaints for the sexual abuse of female suspects. Kramer had been formally reprimanded twice for drinking on duty. The second time, Gordon's intervention had saved his job.

Gordon was sure that every one of them would be glad to have the extra cash, no questions asked. He instructed each of them to meet him at an upscale strip club called the Purring Kitten the following night at seven. He wanted them mellow and happy when he broached his proposal. With an extra quarter million, retirement suddenly looked more attractive.

CHAPTER 3

THE DAY AFTER THE INCIDENT ON THE SUBWAY, SARAH WAS working on the computer system in the back office when one of the other librarians came to get her. "You've been holding out on us. There's a tall, distinguished looking man out front asking for you."

Sarah was startled. The description could only fit Paul Taylor. How could he have known where to find her? She remembered that she had mentioned the library. But why would he have come all the way down here?

She went out to the front counter.

"Hi, there," said Paul Taylor with a grin. "I happened to be in the neighborhood so I thought I'd drop by and see what a library looks like."

He was dressed in tan slacks and a navy shirt. Sarah hadn't fully appreciated how tall and attractive he was and she was suddenly overcome with shyness.

"Hi," she stammered, unable to think of anything else to say.

"You really do have books here."

"What did you expect?" Sarah laughed, recovering slightly.

"So where's the coffee bar?'

"Over by the window. Here, I'll give you the tour."

"It's certainly not what I expected," Paul commented as Sarah led him around. All I remember about libraries is dusty shelves and crabby librarians."

"I'm only crabby on Tuesdays."

Paul winked at her. "I'll keep that in mind."

They arrived at the small self-serve coffee bar. "The least I can do is buy you a coffee," Sarah offered.

Paul accepted and Sarah fixed him a cappuccino and herself a latte. They sat down in the small seating area. For a moment, Paul just studied her.

"Are you okay?" he asked finally, touching her arm. "I really should have insisted on walking you home. It must have been quite upsetting for you."

His concern and the feel of his hand on her arm sent shivers up her spine. "I'm fine. Thank you again," she replied. She was embarrassed by the tremor in her voice.

He didn't seem to notice. "To be honest, I didn't just come to check up on you or get a tour."

"Oh?"

Paul smiled at her. "I have some meetings in the city this afternoon but I was hoping you'd let me take you to dinner."

For a moment, Sarah was too startled to reply.

Paul Taylor prompted her gently. "I know it's short notice. You probably have other commitments."

Sarah blushed. "Okay."

"Great. Would you like me to pick you up here or at your place?"

Sarah thought quickly. She definitely wanted to shower and change her clothes. "My apartment would be good."

"Sure. Just give me the address and a time that works for you, and I'll be there."

Sarah wrote her address and phone number on a piece of paper and they agreed on seven o'clock. After Paul left the library, Sarah sat at her desk, nervous and excited. At thirty-four, she'd barely had a real date. Where would he take her? What should she wear? Should she even have agreed to dinner? After all, she didn't know him. Sure, he'd saved her in the subway, but what did that really prove? He was a total stranger. She was being ridiculous. How often did she get asked out anyway? Stop worrying. Go and enjoy it.

· · · · · · ·

Sarah got home at six and showered quickly. She settled on a black blouse and a light gray skirt. They were both old. She wished she had something newer, but she almost never went out so she rarely bought clothes. She finished the outfit with black onyx earrings and a matching pendant her father had given her for graduation. She studied herself in the mirror, surprised to see an attractive young woman staring back at her. She took off her glasses. Even better, she thought, slipping them into her purse. She looked at the small chip off the corner of her front tooth, the result of a bike accident when she was ten. Her dentist had offered to repair it, but the thousand-dollar cost seemed like a lot of money. She had kept putting it off. Now she wished she'd had it done.

Other than the chip, she was pleased with what she saw. The black jewelry highlighted her dark eyes and lush ebony hair. She'd never thought of herself as pretty and the fact that she hadn't really had a serious date corroborated this self-perception. Yet the young woman looking back at her from the mirror was definitely attractive.

Sarah had been so preoccupied with her parents' illnesses there were few opportunities for men to get to know her well enough to even consider asking her out. On the few occasions they tried, her shyness was mistaken for lack of interest. With her self-confidence buoyed by seeing her reflection, she even found some perfume.

· · · · · · ·

At exactly seven, there was a knock on the door and Sarah found Paul Taylor standing in the hallway.

"Hi, there," Paul greeted her, handing her a small bouquet of flowers and a bottle of wine.

"Thank you so much." Sarah took them and remained standing at the door.

"Why don't you put them in some water? Have you got a vase or something?" Paul suggested.

"Of course," Sarah replied, jolted from her paralysis. "Come on in."

Paul followed her into the apartment. It was small, a living/dining room, a tiny kitchenette and a couple of doors, leading, Paul assumed, to a bedroom and bathroom. The furnishings were inexpensive, but tasteful and creative.

"It's not much," she apologized, "and I'm sorry about all the stairs. Librarians don't make much money."

Paul laughed. "It's very comfortable and I like the wall hangings."

He watched her as she found a vase and filled it with water. Sarah sensed his eyes on her and felt both self-conscious and flattered. She realized that she had never had a man alone in her apartment before.

"Can I get you something before we go?" she asked hesitantly, wishing she had thought to put out some wine or hors d'oeuvres.

"Sure," Paul replied thinking a drink in familiar surroundings before they left might put her at ease. "If you have a corkscrew, I'll open the wine."

"Coming up." Sarah brought over a corkscrew and a couple of wine glasses and led him to the small couch in the living room. She put the vase on the coffee table and arranged the flowers while he opened the wine and poured them each a glass.

"They're beautiful. Thank you so much."

Paul nodded. "Cheers. Here's to books and librarians surviving the digital age."

Seated beside him on the small sofa, Sarah was acutely conscious of his closeness. Her hands shook as she held her wine glass.

Paul noticed. "You're trembling?"

"I know. It's silly," Sarah replied, flushing with embarrassment. "It's just that so much has happened to me in the last twenty-four hours," she added, unwilling to admit it was just nervousness at being with him.

Suddenly he took her hands in his and held them still. She felt the warmth and the controlled power of his grip. His blue eyes gazed at her with amusement and affection. Her trembling gradually subsided.

Paul noticed a couple of partially disassembled desktops in a corner of the living room. "Looks like you repair computers in your spare time?"

"Actually I do. The library now has more than a dozen PCs. With the constant use, there are a lot of problems and we don't have the budget to send them out. The kids use them to download all sorts of stuff so viruses are a problem too."

"I wouldn't have taken you for a computer geek."

"I'm not sure where I picked it up. Necessity, I guess. But I like it. I developed a lot of the proprietary software we use in the library and I do some contract programming on the side."

"I am impressed."

"Don't be. My only client pays me in stock certificates because he doesn't have any money."

"Can you sell the stock?"

Sarah shook her head. "The company isn't listed. I stick the certificates in the bottom of my desk drawer."

"You're generous."

Sarah shrugged sheepishly. "It was interesting work. It's a start-up security company that designs advanced encryption algorithms. I know the two guys who run it. That is, we've never actually met, but we send emails back and forth."

"Maybe it will be the next Microsoft and you'll be fabulously wealthy someday."

"I doubt it. They haven't made a penny since they started and I don't think they have any customers. But I can always use the stock certificates for wallpaper."

"So how did you get into the library business?"

"I didn't really plan it. I got my degree in History and English. I liked the subjects, but they don't exactly equip you for the job market. The library job was all I could get."

"But you enjoy it?"

"I do. We get a lot of kids coming in. As you saw, we're in a poor part of the city. Most of the kids don't get much support at home. I like helping them. Schoolwork, projects, sometimes just talking to them."

Paul sensed her enthusiasm and dedication. "Sounds like a job where you can make a difference. And I'll bet you do."

"Maybe for a few kids," Sarah replied, touched by his compliment.

"What did you do?" Sarah continued. "That is, before you retired."

"Well, it wasn't your typical job. I kind of drifted into it. I started out in a special branch of the navy where I learned some unusual skills, including how to fight. I left the navy and worked as a mercenary. Not that honorable an occupation, I guess, but I wasn't up for a desk job and it matched my skill set. Then I set up a business rescuing kidnapped executives and diplomats from the world's trouble spots. Kidnappings and abductions of prominent people rarely hit the news, but they happen quite frequently so I got a lot of business."

"It sounds exciting, and dangerous."

"Well, it can be dangerous. And for several years, it was exciting. After a while, pretty much anything becomes routine."

"I assume it paid pretty well, if you're already retired?"

Paul laughed. "Probably better than being a librarian."

"I think pretty much everything pays better than being a librarian."

Seeing her glass was empty, Paul poured her another.

"So what's retirement like?" Sarah asked, trying to imagine what it would be like not having a job to go to.

Paul thought for a moment. "It's been only a month, so I'm not quite sure. My job was pretty intense. When I retired, I wanted to live in the country. Somewhere peaceful. I wanted to hear the water lap the shore, the wind rustle through the trees and the birds sing. I wanted fresh air, space and no crowds. Now that I've got all that, it seems a bit too peaceful."

Sarah sensed that he had shared more than he intended. "Do you live with anyone?" she asked, surprised at her boldness.

"Yes." Then, after a deliberate pause, he added, "a golden retriever named Talisker."

"Talisker?" she asked, relieved at his answer.

"It's the name of a fine single malt scotch whiskey. I like the scotch and they're about the same color, so that's what I call him."

"Talisker," Sarah repeated, thoughtfully. "It's a nice name for a dog."

He laughed. "I think he likes it. At least he comes when I call."

"How about you?" Paul continued. "Any serious boyfriends hanging around?"

Sarah shook her head. She could tell that Paul was pleased with her answer and she was glad.

They talked for almost an hour before Paul split the last of the wine. "Since we've polished off the bottle, I'd better take you to dinner. What kind of food do you like?"

"It doesn't matter."

"Italian work for you?"

"I'd love it."

· · · · · · ·

Paul walked her to a nearby restaurant. The owner led them to a small table in a quiet corner, and was promptly followed by a waiter with a bottle of wine and some steaming garlic bread dripping with cheese. Paul poured a glass for Sarah and offered her the bread.

"I think you're going to get me drunk," Sarah commented.

"I'm just trying to break through that reserve of yours. There's a fantastic person in there and I'm going to get to know her."

"You might be disappointed."

Paul looked into her eyes and smiled with certainty. "No I won't."

The food was plentiful and delicious, and Sarah found herself becoming surprisingly relaxed and engaged. Paul fascinated her with stories about the places he had been. It seemed he had traveled to almost every country in the world. He told her about some of his rescues, "extractions" he called them, and Sarah listened with amazement. They were like stories out of adventure novels.

Later, Paul got Sarah to talk about herself and, before she knew it, she was opening up to him. She talked lovingly about her parents, how devastating it had been for them when her mother was diagnosed with Alzheimer's, her father's stroke and how she had been visiting him the previous night. She described some of the kids she had helped. Afterward, she felt foolish. Compared to the life Paul had led, it must have seemed unbelievably boring and mundane.

"I guess I haven't done too much with my life," she commented wistfully.

"Nonsense. You've looked after your parents with the self-lessness few would have shown. You've put yourself through college and you have a job you love. You're beautiful, intelligent, and charming—and I'm having a wonderful time with you."

For an instant, Sarah thought he must be teasing her, but there was such genuine sincerity and affection on his face, she realized he meant it.

"Thank you," she replied, moved.

The waiter brought the dessert menu and she was about to decline when Paul insisted.

"Now I know that you're trying to get me both drunk and fat."

"Didn't you know that alcohol destroys the calories?" he responded with a grin.

They ordered tartufo and Paul insisted she try a liqueur.

"I shouldn't. I'm really feeling the wine."

"Try it. The glasses are small."

Sarah looked at him quizzically and he winked back at her. They lingered over coffee, and it was almost midnight before Paul reluctantly suggested he get her home. Sarah looked at her watch and couldn't believe that they had been at the restaurant for almost four hours. She didn't want the evening to end.

· · · · · · ·

They left the restaurant and began the three-block walk to Sarah's apartment.

"I feel stuffed, and more than a little drunk," Sarah said contentedly. "Thank you so much."

"Thank you for coming. And for listening to all my war stories."

"They were fascinating."

It was dark and a cool breeze had come up. Paul put his arm around her shoulders and drew her to him. Sarah contentedly rested her head against his shoulder and they walked in silence until reaching her apartment building.

"You don't need to climb all these stairs," Sarah offered when they entered the main floor lobby.

Paul grinned. "It will work off the dinner."

He walked her up the three flights of stairs to the door of her apartment. She stood there not wanting the magical evening to end, wondering what to do or say. Should she invite him in? Would he interpret that as an invitation to stay the night? Was she ready for that? If she didn't invite him in, would he feel she wasn't interested?

Sensing her uncertainty, he took her hand. "Thank you so much. I had a wonderful evening. I haven't enjoyed myself this much in a long time."

"Thank you—for everything."

"Sarah," he continued, looking fondly at her. "I'd like to see you again, to take you out to my house on the lake. Have dinner with you on the deck while we watch the sun set. Can I call you?"

"I'd love that," she replied softly.

"Good. Just so you have it, here's my card. It has my address, email, and phone at Crystal Lake." Paul then took her in his arms and hugged her warmly before kissing her lightly on the lips. "Goodnight, Sarah," he said.

"Goodnight," Sarah replied.

Back inside her apartment, she looked at the card.

> *Paul Taylor*
> *Taylor Security Services*
> *653 Crystal Lake Road,*
> *Birchhill, Vermont,*
> *459-376-8734*
> paultaylor@connections.com

CHAPTER 4

FRED DELL LOVINGLY CRADLED THE NEW BOTTLE OF CHEAP gin, terrified he'd drop it. He unscrewed the cap and took a sip, savoring the burning sensation as the clear liquid ran down his throat. He took another and felt the warmth spread through his body. Then another and another. As always, the magic worked. The six-by-six cardboard box that was his home became a palace. His wasted, sickly body felt young and powerful. His failed and miserable life held renewed promise.

Suddenly Fred heard footsteps. Terrified, he clutched the bottle to his chest. It couldn't be happening again. It couldn't! A feeling of utter desperation overcame him.

"Are you in there?" called out one voice.

"Got a bottle Fred?" called a second.

Fred cowered in silence, praying they would go away. Suddenly his home was lifted off his head and he looked up to see his two nemeses staring down at him. He knew they were going to take his bottle and make trouble. He'd move his house but they always found him. His jaw still ached from the last time. One of them had kicked him in the head, knocking out two of his few remaining teeth. Why couldn't they leave him alone? Why now, when he'd gotten a new bottle?

"Freddy. You're having a party and didn't invite us. That's not very polite."

"Please leave me alone. Please!"

"We can't do that. Our job is to serve and protect."

The first man reached down for the bottle. Fred clutched it to his chest with all his strength, but the man easily pried it free. He held it high above the concrete sidewalk, clearly intending to drop it.

"Please, noooo!"

"But, Freddy, you know it's not good for you."

"Pleeeease!"

The man dropped the bottle and it shattered against the sidewalk. The precious liquid quickly ran down the cracks and seeped into the concrete. Fred stared at the shattered glass in agony. Tears welled in his eyes.

"Oh dear, Fred's crying."

"Do you think it might be something you did?" commented the second man.

For an instant, anger overcame his fear and Fred lashed out with his foot. He was wearing cast-off cowboy boots and caught the first man firmly on the shin.

"Shit! You bastard. You'll pay for that," exclaimed the first man, rubbing his leg.

"Well, well, Freddie," added the second. "I guess that earns you a trip to the swimming hole. Lucky you."

Fred didn't know what the swimming hole was, but he could not swim and it didn't sound good. Already he regretted kicking the man. He realized losing his bottle was probably minor compared to what was in store for him now. "Please! I didn't mean to..."

"On your feet, Freddy," said the first man, yanking him upright while the other one handcuffed his hands behind his back. "We're going for a little drive."

"Where are you taking me?"

"We told you. The swimming hole."

"I can't swim."

"Don't worry about it." They forced Fred into the back seat of their police cruiser and drove off.

"Christ, he smells," said Tom Miller, the cop who had dropped the bottle.

"A swim is just what he needs," replied Chris LePan.

Fred sat trembling in silence as they drove. As they left the city, he grew increasingly fearful. Finally, they arrived at an abandoned gravel pit. They drove down a winding road to the bottom and forced Fred from the car. Nearby was a small pool no more than twenty feet in diameter. The water was black.

"Welcome to our swimming hole," said Miller. "I'm sorry it's not bigger."

"It may not be big, but it's very deep," laughed LePan.

"I don't want to go in there," whimpered Fred, looking at the cold black water in terror.

"What a shame," replied Miller, suddenly pushing him into the pool.

With his hands still cuffed behind him, Fred sank beneath the surface. Instinctively he kicked his feet. The motion brought him back to the surface and he gasped for air.

"How's the water?" asked LePan.

Fred began to sink again and kicked out desperately. He broke the surface choking and coughing. "I can't swim," he sputtered.

"You're doing just fine."

Fred sank again and frantically kicked his way back to the surface, "Please!"

The two cops watched in amusement as Fred struggled to keep his head above the water. For a time, he was able to force his head to the surface often enough to catch a breath; but as cold and fatigue drained his muscles and water weighed down his clothes, he slipped beneath the surface. For several seconds, Fred held his breath as he struggled vainly to reach life-giving air. Finally, reflexively, he inhaled. Water rushed into his lungs. It was unexpectedly painful and he struggled desperately only to see the surface recede far above him. As his consciousness slipped away, Fred Dell began the long slow descent into the blackness below.

"May he rest in peace," commented Miller.

"Amen," replied LePan.

Miller looked at his watch. "Good timing. We can make it to the Purring Kitten by seven."

"Know what this is all about?" asked LePan as they drove back to the city.

Miller shook his head. "Gordon didn't say much on the phone."

"Who else is coming?"

"Carlucci and Kramer."

LePan shook his head. "Interesting group."

"Interesting meeting spot."

"Beats the Precinct squad room," LePan continued. " By the way, you still got that cabin in the mountains?"

Miller looked over at him. "Yup. Go there every chance I can. Want to come up some time?"

"Only if you've got some women, satellite TV and pizza delivery."

"Hardly. There's no running water, no electricity, and no phone."

LePan looked over at Miller in amazement. "So what the hell do you do up there?"

"Hunt, fish, commune with nature."

LePan looked at him skeptically. "You're kidding me. Tell me you've really got a couple of gorgeous mountain girls stashed up there."

Miller laughed. "Ah, Chris. You really have to get a life."

"It's you I'm worried about. Pretty soon those female deer are going to start looking pretty good."

"Does."

"What?"

"Does. A female deer is called a doe."

LePan shook his head in mock frustration. "How'd you come by the place?"

"My father left it to me. He's the one who taught me how to hunt and fish."

"How long ago did he die?"

"A long time," replied Miller vaguely.

"Sorry," replied LePan. Clearly Miller didn't want to talk about it.

• • • • • • •

Frank Carlucci left work at 3 o'clock. He had four hours to kill before meeting John Gordon at the Purring Kitten and, characteristically, he decided to go to the gym. Carlucci spent several hours a day working out, usually going for a couple of hours before his shift started and again for at least three hours after it was over. Meticulous about his diet, he took supplements to help build muscle bulk. He subscribed to three different bodybuilding magazines and belonged to two health clubs. At twenty-nine, he was six-one and weighed 275 pounds - all muscle. Carlucci had once hoped he could build a movie career off his physique. Joining the police force had been a temporary source of income until he became the next Rocky or Conan. After ten years on the force, Carlucci was grudgingly beginning to accept that his dream of being the next Arnold Schwarzenegger would be unfulfilled.

There was a new girl at the gym Carlucci had been eyeing for a couple of weeks. She was pretty, blond and petite. He had overheard her name once. Patti. He had smiled at her several times, but she had always looked away. Once, he'd tried to strike up a conversation but, after several one-word replies, he had given up. She was obviously shy. He would just have to keep working on her. In the locker room, he put on his gym clothes and admired his reflection in the mirror. The new black T-shirt, which he had deliberately bought in large rather than extra-large, was nicely tight and emphasized his shoulders, pecs and biceps.

Carlucci spotted Patti in the free weights section and went to the bench press beside her. He loaded 350 pounds onto the bar and began his routine. Few people in the club could handle more than 200 pounds. As he went through his reps, he looked over at Patti hoping she would notice the amount of weight he was using; but she seemed oblivious to his presence. Carlucci struggled to think of a way to start a conversation; but Patti moved over to the hand weights and he lost his chance.

After a few minutes, he wandered over to the weight rack beside her. Patti looked up and stared directly at him for a moment without saying anything.

"It's quiet here tonight, isn't it?" Carlucci finally managed, still convinced she was just shy.

"Yeah, I guess so." Patti made no effort to look up or give him any encouragement.

"I take it you usually come after work?"

Patti just nodded without looking up.

"You look very fit."

"Thanks," she replied curtly, clearly trying to end the conversation.

Carlucci was oblivious to her rebuff. "How long do you usually work out?"

At that point, Patti stopped her reps and looked directly at him. "Look. You follow me around every time I'm here. I don't mean to be rude but I come to the gym to work out, not to get hit on." She said it loudly enough that a few people nearby looked over at them.

Carlucci was stunned. Angry and embarrassed, he tried desperately to think of something to say. He was acutely aware that people were watching the exchange. "Sorry," he finally muttered, walking away.

He walked to the other end of the gym, fuming. The stuck-up bitch, he thought. He would make her sorry. He went through the rest of his workout mechanically, thinking of what he could do to her and watched her surreptitiously until she left the gym floor. From the window, he saw her go to her car. He memorized her license number. Tomorrow he would look her up on the motor vehicle registry. He'd be able to find out her age, weight, height, address, phone number, social security number, driving record, any criminal convictions, even whether she needed glasses. She would regret embarrassing him. He was still seething when he left for the Purring Kitten to meet John Gordon and the others.

· · · · · · ·

Ernie Kramer finished his shift at the Sixth Police Precinct and drove home. Parking his car in the driveway, he went up the front steps to his house, hoping his wife, Clara, would be home to make him a sandwich. He opened the front door. Damn. The house was empty. She was always out doing something. Why couldn't she stay home? He stomped into the kitchen, got a beer from the refrigerator and crashed onto the worn couch in front of the TV. He pushed the power button on the remote but nothing happened. The batteries were dead. He had told Clara to replace them. God, she was useless. At that moment, he heard the front door open.

"You're early, Ern," called out his wife, apprehensively. She knew he would be angry that she hadn't been there when he got home.

"I thought I told you to replace the batteries in the remote."

"I forgot. I'm sorry. I'll do it right now."

"I've got to go out again in a couple of hours. Some drug stake out."

"I'm sorry. Can I make you a sandwich?"

"I have to eat, don't I?"

A few minutes later, she brought him a ham on rye and put it on the table beside him.

"Where were you?" he groused.

"Sorry. I had to take Tony to piano lessons."

"Piano lessons!" Kramer repeated contemptuously. "He should be playing football."

"His teacher says he's very talented," Clara replied, trying to defuse one more iteration of their running argument about their son's musical inclination.

Kramer looked up at his wife. Despite the heat, she was wearing a long-sleeved blouse. He knew why—to hide the bruises on her arms. She couldn't hide the remnants of the black eye he had given her a week ago. The sight of it made him feel guilty and angry at the same time.

Kramer remembered their last fight. Tony's music teacher had invited a pianist to come in and play for the students. The ten-year-old had been enthralled at the magical sounds the man brought forth from the keyboard and wanted to learn to do it himself. When Clara had told her husband that Tony wanted lessons, he had flatly refused. Boys should be playing sports not studying piano, and besides they didn't have the money. A week ago, Kramer discovered that Tony was taking piano lessons. Furious, he confronted his wife and demanded to know how she was paying for them. He kept her on a very tight budget and knew she didn't have the money herself. Clara admitted that she'd taken a part-time job as a receptionist at a local Ford dealership. Kramer was incensed. Not only had she done it without his permission, she had enrolled their son in piano lessons over his express objections. In a rage, he had swung at her. Reflexively she had blocked his blow with her forearm, but failed to anticipate the second punch, which caught her just under the left eye and knocked her down.

That had not been the first time. They had been engaged only a month when, at the urging of her friends, Clara had called off the engagement. He had begged her not to leave, promising it would never happen again. The second time was a week before their wedding. Kramer pleaded that it was the pressure of the upcoming wedding. Once the wedding was over, he'd be fine. Three months after the wedding, it happened again, and then again. Each time he blamed his temper, her behavior, or the pressures with his job. He would apologize and promise it wouldn't happen again. Lately, he did not bother apologizing.

Kramer gulped the sandwich, downed his beer and left. He had more than an hour to kill before meeting Gordon, but he couldn't stand being alone with her anymore.

"When will you be back?" Clara asked plaintively.

"How the hell do I know?" he growled, as he slammed the door.

. . . .

Ernie Kramer drove directly to the Purring Kitten. The strip club had a reputation for having the prettiest dancers in the city and the fact he was an hour early didn't bother him at all. He settled into a table against the wall and surveyed the large room. There were two stages, each equipped with the brass poles the dancers used in their routines. A well-endowed blond wearing nothing but a thong was dancing on the stage nearest to him. Kramer's concentration was interrupted by a scantily clad waitress and, without thinking, he ordered a beer. After the waitress had gone, he regretted his decision. This would be his second and department regulations prohibited drinking within three hours of going on duty. It wouldn't have been such a big deal except he already had two written reprimands. A third and he could face suspension. Hell, he'd drink Coke after this. What difference could a couple of beers make?

He sat nursing his beer as a succession of girls got up on the stage and gradually shed their clothes. He thought about calling one of them over for a lap dance but considered the twenty-five dollar cost and contented himself with watching the action on the stage. An hour later, John Gordon and Frank Carlucci sat down beside him.

Gordon grinned at him. "You'll burn a hole through them if you keep staring like that."

Moments later, Tom Miller and Chris LePan joined them. Ignoring department regulations, Gordon ordered beers all round and Kramer accepted, reluctant to seem ungrateful.

"So, John, what's goin' on?" asked Miller.

"Lindsay's got the word there's a big drug deal going down at ten in a deserted building in the Warehouse District. We're to stake it out, videotape the exchange as evidence and then arrest them."

"Sounds simple enough," replied Kramer. "What time do you want to leave?"

"Eight-thirty or so. Want to get a couple of cameras and hidden mikes set up and be in position well before ten."

"Damn," commented LePan. "That means we're going to have to stay here and watch the scenery for another hour."

"You'll manage, but easy on the beer—all of you," replied Gordon.

"Such a spoilsport, isn't he?" razzed Miller.

"This one must be important for Lindsay," said LePan. "I hear he's getting heat from both the Mayor and the Chief. A big bust tonight would take some pressure off."

"He wants Moorby's job so bad he can taste it," added Kramer.

"Moorby will be a tough act to follow," Miller commented. "He's popular with the guys, manages the politics well, and he's tough when he needs to be."

Kramer nodded. "I heard a rumor that the Police Commission was considering going outside to replace him."

"That would be a real kick in the head for Lindsay," replied LePan. "By the way, Ernie, how's that gorgeous wife of yours?"

Kramer looked at him puzzled. "Clara?"

"Yeah, Clara. How many wives have you got?"

"She's fine."

"How come you didn't bring her to the Precinct picnic?"

"She's doesn't like that kind of thing."

Miller grinned. "I'll bet she'd love it. You just don't want all your buddies drooling over your knock-out wife."

The conversation continued—typical cop talk—inadequate pay, lousy pension plan, politics on the force, too lenient courts. The discussion was interspersed with comments about the girls on the stage. As time went on, they ordered more beer and began rating the succession of girls on stage as if they were figure skaters. They established several criteria including looks, dancing, costume and hotness. At the end of each girl's shift, they'd write scores up to ten on a piece of paper and then compare them. After an hour, the beer and camaraderie had them all in a good mood, and Gordon decided it was a time to lay out his proposition.

"Guys. Before we go, I have a proposal to make."

"A proposal? Shit. John wants to marry one of the dancers," joked Miller.

"Lay off. This is serious," replied Gordon. "And I need to be able to trust you guys on this. Agreed?"

"We're listening, Sarge," replied Kramer.

"There's supposed to be three million in unmarked bills changing hands tonight. Lindsay has proposed that only two million make it to the evidence room. He wants a quarter of a million. Of the rest, I want a quarter of a million. That leaves a half million for you guys to split. A hundred and a quarter each."

"I'm in," replied Miller. "But how come you get two fifty?"

"Cause I'm the Sergeant."

"Fair enough. But you better pick up the tab tonight."

Gordon nodded his agreement. "And you guys—Frank, Ernie, Chris? Okay with this?"

"I'm cool," replied Kramer.

"Chris?" Gordon prompted again.

"A hundred and a quarter will buy a lot of lap dances," LePan replied with a grin.

"Frank?" There was no response.

"He's too busy watching the dancers," commented Miller.

"I think he's watching his biceps grow," suggested LePan.

"Frank!" shouted Miller. "Say yes."

Carlucci finally turned to them. "Yes?"

Gordon shook his head in frustration, but didn't pursue it. A few minutes later, he settled the tab. As they left, he was conscious that they were all feeling the effects of the beer. Maybe a bar hadn't been the best place to meet. They couldn't afford any mistakes.

LePan drove Miller in his Corolla. Gordon took Carlucci and Kramer in an old gray Pontiac he had taken from the Precinct's collection of nondescript unmarked cars. It was a ten-minute drive to the Warehouse District.

CHAPTER 5

AS GORDON AND HIS TEAM WERE HEADING TO THE STAKEOUT at the Warehouse District, Sarah was working the late shift at the Glenwood Library. She hadn't been able to stop thinking about her dinner with Paul and she wondered how soon he would call. She rebuked herself for acting like a love-struck schoolgirl. It had been one dinner. He might never call. Men often said they'd call—and didn't. However, she had enjoyed herself so much she couldn't bear the thought of not seeing him again. She resolved to buy herself some new clothes. And, if Paul didn't phone, she'd phone him.

It was approaching the library's ten o'clock closing time and Sarah was getting ready to leave when one of the other librarians called her to the phone. It was one of the supervisors at her father's nursing home.

"Ms. Andrews?"

Sarah was instantly alarmed. "Yes?"

"I'm terribly sorry to have to tell you this but your father's been taken to Mercy Hospital."

"My God. What happened?"

"He's all right, but he fell. We think he may have broken his hip."

Sarah was about to ask more questions but realized they could wait. "Thank you. I'll go to the hospital right away."

Sarah called up a map of Mercy Hospital on one of the computers and was relieved to find it was on Bay Street, only a dozen blocks from the library. She thought about calling a cab but decided she could walk it just as fast.

She had gone barely three blocks before she regretted her decision. She often worked until the library closed and always walked home, but Mercy Hospital was in the opposite direction. The stores soon gave way to warehouses, many abandoned, their windows smashed, their doors swinging loose. As the surroundings became steadily more run-down and depressed, Sarah realized she was in the infamous Warehouse District, well known for crime and drugs—definitely not a place for a woman walking alone at night. There were no people or cars anywhere in sight, and most of the streetlights were broken, leaving the sidewalks dark and forbidding. Wind whistled through the empty streets, picking up grit and debris and sending it swirling into the air, stinging her bare arms and legs. Her pink T-shirt and black skirt offered little protection. Nervous, she stepped up her pace.

After going several more blocks without hitting Bay Street, Sarah grew worried. Most of the street signs had been stolen or vandalized and she feared she had taken a wrong turn. She pulled out the map she had printed and paused near an old grey

Pontiac parked under one of the few functioning street lights, completely unaware that it was an unmarked police car.

. . . .

Gordon and his team had set up on the middle floor of a three-story warehouse, and the drug bust went off perfectly. They had eight suspects in custody and were in the process of putting away their equipment. Knowing that Lindsay would want to hear the results as soon as possible, Gordon stepped away from the group and took out his cell phone. He reached Lindsay at home.

Lindsay came on immediately. "I was waiting for your call. How did it go?"

"Went down perfectly. We caught eight of them. They'll be on their way down in the van in twenty minutes, along with a large quantity of coke."

"And the money?"

"Three million as we thought. The 'official' two million is coming in the van. Our cut's in a briefcase in our car. The rest of the guys are just packing up."

"Where's the car?"

"Out front. I can see it from where I'm standing."

"Any problems?" asked Lindsay.

"None. Went down perfectly."

"Good. I'm going down to my office. Meet me there."

"Will do. Let me just go back and make sure things are under control. I'll be there in twenty minutes."

"And bring the money," replied Lindsay.

Gordon was about to rejoin his men when he suddenly froze. "Hey Chris," he called to LePan. "Come here."

As LePan joined him at the window, Gordon said, "Look down there. There's some woman hanging around the car."

"Yeah. I see her. What the hell would she be doing in the Warehouse District at this time of night?"

"I don't know, but I don't like it. I left the money in a briefcase on the front seat. Run down and get rid of her. I'll be down with the others in just a couple of minutes."

"I'm on it."

·······

Minutes later Gordon and the others reached the car to find LePan just standing there.

"So?" Gordon demanded.

LePan looked at Gordon in disgust. "Both the briefcase and the woman are gone."

Gordon looked into the car and then scanned the streets, quickly confirming LePan's statement. His heart sank. Five minutes ago, he'd told Lindsay that the stakeout had gone off without a hitch. Now he was facing a fucking disaster. Lindsay would crucify him, and Gordon could hardly blame him.

"The money's gone?" asked Carlucci.

LePan just nodded.

"Why did you leave the briefcase in the car, John?" Kramer asked with a look of frustration.

Gordon looked at them uncomfortably. "The support team was coming with the van to take the suspects and evidence away. I wanted to get 'our' money out of the warehouse just in case. It was only for a few minutes."

"How the hell could she have got into it so quickly?" Kramer persisted.

"She must have jimmied it," Gordon replied uncertainly, trying to remember if he had actually locked the car.

"Would you recognize her?" Miller asked.

"For sure. Young, dark hair, black skirt, pink top."

"It's only been a few minutes. She can't have gone far," Miller said. "Didn't you say you'd arranged for back-up units nearby? Maybe they can intercept her."

"I'll call them," Gordon replied, brightening.

Gordon got into his car and radioed all units in the vicinity, asking them to be on the lookout for a woman fitting the description, adding, "She may be armed. Approach with caution. Apprehend and call me immediately."

Corporal Trevor Crowe and Officer Stan Peters were sitting in a parked patrol car at Seventh and Jarvis, just four blocks north of the intersection Gordon was calling from.

"Hear that?" commented Crowe.

"Yeah, I wonder what it's about," replied Peters.

"Christ! There she is," yelled Crowe. "Walking right toward us."

CHAPTER 6

OBLIVIOUS TO THE TURMOIL SHE HAD CAUSED JUST A FEW blocks behind her, Sarah hurried on, now completely lost. As she turned a corner, there, unbelievably, was a parked police cruiser with two uniformed police officers inside. She breathed a huge sigh of relief.

As she walked toward the car, the officers got out. To her surprise they both drew their guns. "Don't move. Hands behind your head."

Bewildered, Sarah just kept walking towards them.

"Stop where you are! On your knees. Hands behind your head. Now!"

They couldn't be yelling at her, yet there was no one else around.

In seconds, the cops were on her. They pushed her to the ground and roughly handcuffed her wrists behind her back. Then they yanked her back to her feet, dragged her to their car and forced her to bend over the hood by wrenching her arms upwards. One of them kicked her legs apart. The edge of the car dug painfully into her stomach and her shoulders burned from the pressure.

"Why are you doing this?" Sarah begged, completely terrified. "I didn't do anything."

There was no answer but she felt their hands on her body frisking her—up her legs, under her skirt, over her panties, then her torso and breasts. Sarah was mortified.

"Nothing on her," commented Peters as he lifted her off the hood and turned her to face them.

"Watch her. I'll call Gordon," said Crowe.

Minutes later, the two unmarked police cars pulled alongside the patrol car and five men got out.

"Hi Trevor, Stan," said John Gordon. "That was fast work."

"Hi Sarge," replied Crowe. "She walked right into our arms."

"We'll take her from here," replied Gordon. "She escaped a drug bust we just pulled off. Glad you guys were here."

"Happy to help."

"Come on, young lady," said Miller forcing Sarah toward one of the cars.

"Want us to stay?" asked Crowe.

"No. We're wrapping up. Why don't you guys take off?" replied Gordon. He didn't want them around.

"Thanks. Good luck."

Stan Peters hesitated for a minute. "Sergeant?"

"Yes?" replied Gordon.

"One thing seems odd to me. She walked right to us. If she was trying to get away from you guys, she'd have run the other way as soon as she saw a squad car."

"Thanks, officer. We'll keep it in mind."

As soon as Crowe and Peters drove off, Miller turned to Gordon. "This the woman you saw from the window?"

"It's her. No question."

"Absolutely," added LePan.

. . . .

With her hands cuffed behind her, Sarah looked at the men surrounding her, realizing they must be undercover police officers.

Gordon looked at Sarah angrily. "You were standing near this car earlier, weren't you?" he said, pointing to the same grey Pontiac she had seen in the street a few minutes earlier.

Sarah nodded nervously.

"What were you doing there?"

"I was lost. I just stopped to look at a map. I didn't touch the car."

"There was a briefcase on the front seat. What did you do with it?"

Sarah looked at him blankly. "Nothing. I didn't even see it."

"You must have taken it," Gordon persisted. "I only left it for five minutes and there was no one else around."

"I didn't touch it," Sarah replied plaintively.

LePan shook his head in frustration. "That's bullshit," he said to Gordon. "She took it. There wasn't time for anyone else to have done it."

Gordon looked back at her. "What's your name?"

"Sarah Andrews."

"All right, Sarah. All we want to know is what you did with the briefcase. You're not in trouble. Just tell us and you can go."

"I didn't take the briefcase. Please. You have to believe me!"

Frank Carlucci stepped toward her. "Listen girlie. Talk to us. There's a million dollars in that case and it belongs to us. Now where is it?"

"Jesus, Frank," Miller commented in disgust at the unnecessary disclosure.

"She knows damn well what's in the case," commented Carlucci, not acknowledging his gaffe. "Don't you girlie?" he added with deliberate menace.

Sarah looked at him fearfully. He was huge and utterly terrifying.

Without warning, Carlucci slapped her hard across the face. Her head exploded with pain and she reeled backwards against the fender before crumpling to the ground.

"Where's the briefcase?" demanded Carlucci.

"I don't know. I don't know. Oh God. Please," Sarah whimpered looking up at him in terror.

Carlucci grabbed her hair and yanked her back to her feet. "Are you going to tell us or do I hit you again?"

"Hold it, Frank," yelled Gordon, angrily. "Not here. We'll take her back to the Precinct."

. . . .

At that moment, Gordon's cell phone rang. It was Peter Lindsay. Gordon walked away from the rest of the group so he could talk in private.

"Where the hell are you?" demanded Lindsay.

"Sorry Captain. We ran into a small problem."

"The van's arrived, with your suspects. What's the problem?"

"You remember I told you the briefcase was in my car?"

"Yeah."

"It was stolen." Gordon waited for Lindsay's explosion.

For a moment, there was no explosion. Just silence. Then it came. "Stolen! A million dollars! You leave a million dollars unguarded on the front seat of a car? In the Warehouse District? Fucking idiots."

"We've got the woman who took it," replied Gordon, desperately. "Just picked her up."

"So get it back from her."

"She doesn't have it on her. Must have hidden it."

"So ask her where she hid it," replied Lindsay, his voice dripping with sarcasm.

"We're questioning her now."

"We need that briefcase, John. Whatever it takes."

"I know. I know."

"Where are you?" Lindsay's frustration was evident.

"Where we picked her up. A few blocks from the warehouse where the bust occurred. She must have stashed the briefcase nearby. She only had it for ten minutes, tops, so she didn't have time to be too creative. We're going to look around and then bring her back to the Backfield Building."

"Who have you got with you?"

"Kramer, LePan, Carlucci and Miller."

"Jesus. An all-star team."

"I know what you're thinking, sir, but I needed men who wouldn't be too fussy about intercepting some evidence."

"Or too fussy about losing it, either."

"We'll get it back."

"You'd better."

"Understood, Captain."

"I want you and Carlucci to bring the woman in," continued Lindsay. "When you get back here, have Carlucci to take her to the Backfield Building. I want to talk to you, alone in my office."

"Yes sir."

"Lindsay, I assume?" asked Miller, when Gordon rejoined the group.

"Yeah."

"What did he want?"

"What do you think? He's seriously pissed. Frank, you and I are to take her to the Precinct. Tom, you stay here with Ernie and Chris, and search for that briefcase. Dumpsters, garbage bins, anywhere she could have tossed it. She can't have gone far with it. For Christ's sake, find the damn thing."

. . . .

Twenty minutes later, Gordon had Carlucci drop him at the main Precinct building, before taking Sarah to the Backfield Building. He went straight to Lindsay's office, expecting the worst.

"I can't believe this," Lindsay exploded as soon as Gordon walked into his office. "You leave one million dollars in your car with no one watching it."

Gordon considered explaining that it had only been for ten minutes and the car was locked, but it was pointless. There was nothing to be said.

"You realize, of course," continued Lindsay, "it's not just the money. If that briefcase shows up, we're toast. It probably has your prints on it. So does the money. Someone will figure out what's going on. We're talking careers here, maybe jail time."

Gordon nodded, acknowledging the point.

"Where's the woman now?"

"Carlucci's got her in the Backfield Building."

"You sure she took it?"

"No question. When I was talking to you, I was watching the car out the window. I could see the briefcase on the front seat.

Then I see the woman loitering near the car. I sent LePan down immediately to chase her off. By the time Chris got there, the woman and briefcase were gone. Crowe and Peters picked her up five minutes later, just a few blocks away. But she didn't have the case."

"John, if your guys don't find that case on their own, you need to get her to tell us where it is. Whatever it takes. And then we need to dispose of her."

"Understood, Captain."

. . . .

After dropping Gordon off at the main Precinct building, Carlucci drove around back to the Backfield Building. He grabbed Sarah and pushed her through the doorway.

Still in handcuffs, her head throbbing and her lip bleeding profusely from Carlucci's earlier blow, Sarah struggled to stay on her feet. "Where are you taking me?"

Ignoring her question, Carlucci dragged her down a corridor to a steel door. He opened it and forced Sarah into a room about fifteen feet square. At one side was a battered steel table with several metal chairs. In the center was a single heavy wooden chair, bolted to the floor. The walls, floor and ceiling were gray concrete.

Carlucci led Sarah to the center of the room and pushed her backwards into the chair. Startled, her hip glanced off one corner of the chair and she fell to the ground. With her wrists handcuffed, she could not break her fall. Her head hit the concrete floor. Carlucci reached down and yanked her to her feet, ripping her T-shirt off completely.

"Sit down!" Carlucci yelled

Dazed, Sarah slumped into the chair. Her skirt was hiked up but, with her hands cuffed, she couldn't straighten it. Sensing his sexual interest and smelling the alcohol on his breath, Sarah cowered into the chair.

Carlucci knelt in front of her, his face just inches from hers, and inhaled deeply. He could smell her fear. "If I were you, I'd remember where I put that briefcase," he said softly.

"I didn't take it," Sarah wailed, terrified that he'd hit her again.

He put his massive hand on her bare thigh and began to squeeze. "I said, where is it?"

She cried out in pain. "You're hurting me!"

At that moment, John Gordon entered the room.

Carlucci let go of her thigh and stood up.

Gordon looked at Sarah. One cheek was red and swollen and her lip was split and bleeding profusely. Her T-shirt was lying on the floor and her bra was stained with blood that was still dripping down from her chin. How the hell were they going to explain her appearance, he wondered. He looked at Carlucci suspiciously. "What's been going on?"

"We were just having a chat."

Gordon shook his head in disgust and sat down at the table facing her. "You said your name was Sarah Andrews?"

Sarah nodded.

"Have you got any ID?"

"It was in my purse. I must have dropped it when the other two policemen arrested me."

Gordon studied her skeptically. "What were you doing in the Warehouse District so late at night?"

"I was going from work to Mercy Hospital."

"Where do you work?"

"The Glenwood Library."

"Why were you going to the hospital?"

"My father. He fell. He was being taken there."

"When I saw you from a window, you weren't walking, you were just standing by the car?"

"I told you. I got lost and stopped to look at my map. There was a street light above your car."

"And you didn't see a briefcase?"

"No," Sarah replied firmly.

"Stop lying!" interjected Carlucci. "You took it. Now where is it?"

"I didn't take it," replied Sarah in desperation. "You have to believe me."

. . . .

Just then, LePan, Kramer and Miller entered the room.

"Find anything?" Gordon asked immediately.

"Nothing," replied LePan.

"You weren't gone that long?"

"Jesus, John. Do you know how many abandoned buildings, trash piles and dumpsters there are there? We'd have to be lucky as hell to find one little briefcase."

"Damn."

LePan looked at Sarah. "She'll just have to tell us where she put it."

"She say anything so far?" asked Kramer.

Gordon shook his head.

"We haven't asked her properly yet," Carlucci commented, approaching Sarah once again.

"Hold it, Frank," Gordon ordered.

Carlucci looked at Gordon with annoyance. "Give me five minutes and I'll have our briefcase."

"I said hold it."

"John, can we talk outside?" Miller asked.

Gordon nodded. "Ernie. You and Frank stay here."

Looking at Carlucci, he added pointedly. "Just sit tight, Frank. We'll be back in a minute."

Gordon, Miller and LePan left the room and stepped outside the building.

"John," began Miller. "I know you're not comfortable with this, but we need that briefcase. Now. The longer it's out there, the greater the chance someone finds it. Then we're all in trouble."

"Maybe she really doesn't know anything about the briefcase," replied Gordon.

"I thought you saw her?"

"Yeah, but I didn't actually see her take it. She's scared shitless. If she knew anything, she'd have talked by now."

"She must know," replied LePan, in annoyance. "You and I both saw her and the case from the window. I was at the car less than five minutes later and the case was gone. There's absolutely no way anyone else could have come by, taken the briefcase and got out of sight in five minutes."

Miller looked at Gordon for confirmation.

Gordon shrugged, silently acknowledging the truth of LePan's statement.

"John," Miller continued. "You know she took it. You got us into this. You left the briefcase in the car. Now you need to let us solve it."

Gordon looked at the two men uncomfortably.

"John," LePan persisted. "You're letting her scared innocent routine get to you. She took the damn money. She figures if she keeps her mouth shut, we'll have to let her go. As soon as we do, she goes back to some trash bin—and she's a million dollars richer."

Gordon nodded reluctantly. "Okay. Let me talk to her first."

Back in the room, Gordon turned to Sarah. "Look, Sarah," he began gently, "this is going to be tough on you unless you tell us what we want to know. We're not interested in you. Just tell us where the briefcase is and you can go." A lie, he thought to himself. Thanks to Carlucci, she knew too much.

Sarah was silent, tears rolling down her face. Finally, she asked, "Am I allowed to have a lawyer?"

Carlucci slammed his massive fist on the table. "Com'on, Sarge. We've had enough bullshit."

"All right," replied Gordon, suppressing his discomfort.

"Okay, little lady. Stand up," ordered Carlucci.

"What are you going to do?" Sarah asked in utter terror.

CHAPTER 7

JOHN GORDON LEFT THE ROOM. HE HAD NO TASTE FOR WHAT was about to happen. Roughing up thugs like Costanza was one thing; scared young women like Sarah Andrews were quite another. He sat on a bench and breathed in the night air. Despite his finances, getting out of the police department would be a relief. He was tired, disillusioned and needed a change.

His cell phone rang. Probably Lindsay wanting to know what was going on. To Gordon's surprise, it was Trevor Crowe, one of the officers who had picked up Sarah Andrews.

"Hi, Trevor. Thought you two had gone off duty?"

"Nothing better to do I guess," replied Crowe.

"What's up?"

"You know that woman we picked up for you? It's been bothering us, the fact she walked right towards our car."

"Yeah?"

"Well we found her purse. Must have dropped it when we picked her up."

"And?"

"Belongs to a Sarah Andrews. Picture on the driver's license is a match. She works at the Glenwood Library and lives ten blocks away. There was a map showing how to get to Mercy Hospital—right through the Warehouse District. We checked. Her father was taken there earlier tonight."

"Thanks. I appreciate your help," Gordon replied half-heartedly.

"We also ran a file search on her," Crowe continued. "Nothing. Not so much as a parking ticket. Any chance you've got the wrong person, Sarge?"

"It's possible. We're talking to her. Would you mind swinging by with the purse and anything else you found?"

"No problem."

Gordon hung up and scratched his head in frustration. Crowe's information confirmed his instinct. Whatever had happened to that briefcase, Sarah Andrews hadn't taken it. The evening was going from bad to disastrous. They'd lost the money. Now it looked like Carlucci and his team were working over an innocent librarian — and they couldn't make her disappear because Crowe and Peters knew they had her in custody.

· · · · · · · ·

Gordon returned to the Interrogation Room. "Cut her down, clean her up and take her to one of the holding cells."

"She hasn't talked yet," objected Carlucci.

Gordon looked at Sarah and turned back to Carlucci. "She's unconscious, so she's not going to be too chatty. Cut her down!"

"She'll come round."

Gordon glared at him with disgust. "Dammit. You heard me. Cut her down."

"Lindsay was just here," protested LePan. "He insisted we get that briefcase, whatever it took."

"Lindsay?" replied Gordon, astonished.

"Got here just after you stepped out," replied Miller. "Got right in there himself."

Gordon remembered Lindsay's questioning of Tony Costanza and rolled his eyes.

"So what do you want us to do?"

"Cut her down. I'll deal with Lindsay."

"He'll be pissed," cautioned Kramer.

"Crowe just phoned," Gordon explained, "they found her purse. Just like she said—her name *is* Sarah Andrews and she's a librarian at the Glenwood Library—just blocks from where we picked her up. No criminal record at all. And her father *was* taken to Mercy Hospital earlier tonight."

"So what?" protested LePan. "She took the briefcase."

"Really?" Gordon looked at him mockingly. "A librarian, with no priors, on her way to visit her sick father, sees a briefcase, breaks into a car to steal it, on the chance it has something valuable in it. Then, seeing a police car just a few blocks away, walks right to it."

LePan looked at Gordon without responding.

"But..." Carlucci began.

"God damn it. Cut her down. Now!"

Carlucci cut the rope and Sarah crumpled to the floor. She lay there, motionless.

"Tom. Take her to one of the holding cells."

As Miller carried Sarah's unconscious body out to a holding cell, Gordon stepped outside and dialed Lindsay.

"I was just there," Lindsay replied. "Where the hell were you?"

"I stepped out to make a call."

"Get something?" Lindsay replied skeptically.

"Nothing. Peter, I don't think she took the briefcase after all."

For a moment, there was silence. Then Lindsay erupted. "Christ, John. Where's this coming from? LePan says you both saw her!"

"She was standing by the car. We didn't actually see her take it."

"Who else could have done it?"

"Look, Peter," replied Gordon, trying to calm his boss down. "From the beginning, she's been telling us she's Sarah Andrews, that she works in a library and was on the way to visit her father. One of the cops who picked her up, Trevor Crowe, just called me. They found her purse and checked her out. No record at all."

"She could still have stolen briefcase?"

"It's possible, but she's a librarian, for Christ's sake, with no priors, not even a parking ticket."

"Christ, John. This is getting worse and worse. Where is she now?"

"I ordered Tom to take her to one of the holding cells."

"How is she?"

"You saw her," Gordon replied, not bothering to hide his disgust.

"Wait for me. All of you. I'll be right there."

· · · · · · ·

Five minutes later, Peter Lindsay stood facing Gordon, LePan, Kramer, Miller and Carlucci, barely controlling his anger. "This is one massive screw-up. First you lose a million dollars. And now you beat up a librarian with not so much as a parking ticket."

LePan objected. "She still took the money."

"So where is it?"

There was silence until Lindsay continued. "Forget the damn money. We've got bigger problems than losing the money. With that briefcase out there, we're all exposed."

"We'll make her disappear," Carlucci said.

Gordon shook his head. "This isn't some vagrant no one will miss. Besides, Crowe and Peters know we have her in custody. They'll ask questions."

"Suppose she dies of unidentified causes?" suggested LePan.

"No way," replied Lindsay. "The SIU is already investigating Costanza's death and he was mid-fifties and overweight. I don't need another investigation."

Lindsay continued. "Here's what we're going to do. We plant some narcotics in her clothing and charge her. You picked up a whole group for trafficking tonight. One more won't make a difference. As for her injuries, she had them when we picked her up. We assume she tried to double-cross her partners and skim some of the money for herself. They caught her and whacked her around to make her tell them where she'd hidden it. She got away, and that's when Crowe and Peters picked her up. If the million dollars shows up, our story is she took it."

Gordon shook his head, "Carlucci hit her *after* Crowe and Peters picked her up. They'll know she must have received the injuries while in custody."

"We'll make sure they don't see her again," replied Lindsay.

The men nodded their approval.

Warming to his plan, Lindsay went on. "We recommend leniency. Agree to a plea bargain for a three-month sentence. We'll look like the good guys."

"That stops her claiming we assaulted her?" queried Kramer.

"I'll get Arnold Carney to represent her. He'll convince her if she tries to make trouble, we'll charge her with trafficking, possession, assaulting a police officer and resisting arrest. She'll be in for five to ten years. Play ball and we'll drop everything except a simple possession charge. She's out in ninety days."

"She could make trouble when she's out," warned LePan.

"She won't get out," replied Lindsay. "Women's prisons are tough places. Things happen."

CHAPTER 8

AS CONSCIOUSNESS GRADUALLY RETURNED, SARAH BECAME aware of a soothing female voice and a gentle touch on her back. Where was she? She couldn't remember. She'd been on the way to see her father. Something had happened.

Then it came back. Hanging from the ceiling. The men watching her. Police officers! Grinning, laughing, smelling of beer. Touching her with that little gun thing. It hurt so much. Her heart was pounding so hard, it felt as if it would burst out of her chest. She had begged them to stop, but they touched her again and again. She remembered the lust and excitement in their eyes. She had felt something warm running down her legs. Blood? No. She'd wet herself. They were laughing at her. She wanted to die. The terror came flooding back, drowning out everything else. Frantically, she clung to the darkness, hoping they couldn't reach her there. Yet the soft voice kept pulling her back. She opened her eyes and found herself in a different room. A young woman sat beside her, her touch and her voice gentle.

"Please talk to me," the woman said. "I want to help you."

Sarah turned toward her.

· · · · · · ·

"Oh my God! What happened to you?" the woman gasped, horrified at what she saw. Sarah's face was badly swollen and covered with dried blood. Blood was still seeping from a split lip and there was a visible lump on the left side of her head. Her T-shirt was badly torn and bloodstained, and the rest of her clothes were askew—as if someone else had hurriedly dressed her.

Sarah looked up at her, dazedly.

"My name's Lana. I want to help you. Please talk to me." Lana Crawford was the rookie cop Lindsay had sent to check on Sarah.

"Can you sit up?" Lana took Sarah by the shoulders and eased her to a sitting position. She noticed Sarah wince with pain and wondered if she could have internal injuries.

"I'll be right back," said Lana. "I need to make a call."

From the corridor, Lana called Peter Lindsay. "Sir. I'm really sorry to bother you, but I'm with the girl you asked me to help. I don't know if you actually saw her but she's been really badly beaten and she's obviously in pain. I think she should see a doctor?"

"Look, Officer Crawford," Lindsay replied. "Just do what I told you. Clean her up and get her some fresh clothes. The woman's mentally disturbed. She's exaggerating her injuries and probably making up wild stories. If need be, we'll get a doctor in the morning."

"Yes sir," replied Crawford, completely intimidated.

"When you're finished with her, report back to my office. Understood?"

"Yes, sir."

Lindsay hung up and Lana reluctantly returned to Sarah's cell.

"Why did they do that to me?" Sarah murmured vaguely. "I didn't do anything."

"You're safe now."

"But what if they come back?"

"You're in the police station. There are over two hundred police officers here."

"But it was policemen who hurt me!"

Lindsay was right, thought Lana; the woman was irrational.

"Why don't you tell me about it?" Lana asked, thinking that talking might help Sarah regain her composure.

Sarah looked at her doubtfully. Lana had a police uniform on. Maybe she shouldn't say anything.

Lana touched her arm. "It's all right. Tell me."

Fighting back tears, Sarah began. "They tied my hands up to the ceiling. Then they held this little metal thing against me. Like a little gun with two metal tips. It hurt so badly..." her voice faded off.

"Go on," prompted Lana in disbelief.

"I begged them to stop." Sarah was crying openly now. "But they just laughed at me and kept doing it. I guess I fainted."

Lana couldn't believe what she'd just heard. Sarah must be making it up...but the fear and emotion in her voice were real. "Do you know the names of the police officers who did it?"

"Mostly. There was a John something, they called him Sarge. There was a Chris LePan and Frank something, a huge guy. An Ernie Kramer and something Miller."

Lana was shocked. Sarah's halting but unmistakable identification of the officers involved was convincing. And they all had reputations for being rough on suspects. She'd heard stories about what went on in the Backfield Building.

"And a Peter something was there for part of it. He seemed like the boss."

"Captain Peter Lindsay?" Lana was astonished.

"I guess so. They called him Captain. He came in later. I thought he'd make them stop, but he used that gun thing on me too. When he left, he told them to keep it up until I talked."

"Talked about what?"

"I don't know!" Sarah wailed in frustration. "Some briefcase or something."

Lana Crawford didn't know what to think. What she'd heard was inconceivable. Lindsay had warned her that Sarah was mentally unstable; but, although Sarah was obviously terrified and emotionally exhausted, she seemed rational and sincere. "What happened to your face?"

"The big guy, Frank. He hit me before they brought me here."

Lana had never liked Carlucci. She'd been partnered with him a couple of times. His sheer size was intimidating and he routinely made crude and insulting comments about women.

"I know what you're thinking," continued Sarah, becoming more composed. "You're thinking that police don't arrest people for no reason, don't hit them, or hurt them. But it happened."

Lana was uncertain. "You were picked up as part of a drug bust. Several people were arrested. They recovered two million dollars and a large quantity of drugs from the scene. Captain Lindsay told me they found cocaine in your clothes."

"That's not true at all. I was just on my way to the hospital to see my father. And if they really found cocaine, they put it there. I don't even know what drugs look like."

"We should get you cleaned up. How about that shower?" Lana did not know what else to do. "Then I'll get you something to eat. We can talk more."

Sarah shook her head. "I have to go to the hospital. My father was hurt..."

"You'll have to stay the night. I'm sorry." Lana didn't have the heart to tell her that it would take at least a couple of days to arrange bail.

"All night?" Sarah wailed.

Lana nodded. "Is there anyone you can call?"

Sarah shook her head miserably.

"I might be able to arrange for a lawyer to see you in the morning, if you want me to."

Sarah nodded vaguely, utterly overwhelmed by what was happening to her. After her shower, Lana helped her dress herself in a prison uniform and took her back to her cell. As she dabbed antiseptic on the cuts on Sarah's face, Lana strained to reconcile the evident sincerity of Sarah's story with her own disbelief that such a thing could happen.

"Sarah," Lana began hesitantly, after several minutes of silence. "I don't know if what you said was true. It's hard for me to believe, but..."

Sarah waited, sensing there was more to come.

"Right now, the most important thing for you to do is get out of here," Lana continued. "Telling people you were hurt by the police won't help. Peter Lindsay is in charge of the whole

Precinct. Some people think he'll be the next Chief of Police. John Gordon has been a cop for almost thirty years. The others you mentioned are all experienced officers. Nobody will believe you - and I'm afraid it might make things worse for you."

Sarah studied Lana's face before concluding her concern was genuine. "Okay, thank you." she replied simply.

· · · · · · ·

After leaving Sarah, Lana walked slowly back to Lindsay's office.

"How is she?" Lindsay asked, more gently than he had been on the phone.

"Her face is badly cut and bruised, sir. I got her cleaned up and ordered her some dinner."

"Did she say anything?"

"Nothing much."

"Did she explain how she got her injuries?" Lindsay probed.

"No. She didn't talk much. Still in shock, I guess."

Lindsay studied Crawford, wondering if she were telling him everything. "Thanks, Lana. I appreciate what you've done tonight."

"Sir. She seems completely overwhelmed by what's happened to her and doesn't seem to have anyone to call. Would it be all right if I got her a lawyer? I'd be happy to phone Legal Aid."

Lindsay smiled. "Great idea. Let me get a friend of mine. Arnold Carney. A lot of those Legal Aid lawyers are useless. I can get Arnie to see her first thing in the morning."

"I'm sure she'll appreciate it."

"Happy to do it, Lana. She was making some pretty outrageous accusations earlier, but I think she was just hysterical. She seems to have a clean record and I'd like to help her."

"Thank you."

"Lana. I'd ask that you keep it between us. Can I count on you for that?"

"Of course sir. I'm glad I could help."

Lana Crawford left Lindsay's office, troubled over what had transpired. Sarah's account was unbelievable, but she hadn't seemed hysterical or irrational. And Lindsay's personal interest in the case, his refusal to let her call a doctor, and his offer to get her a lawyer was highly unusual.

· · · · · · ·

As soon as Lana left his office, Lindsay phoned Arnold Carney. Carney was a prominent and well connected lawyer, and a longtime friend. He had founded his own firm, Carney & Associates, which did a lot of work with the police department. He was on retainer to the Police Services Union and had made a reputation for himself aggressively defending police officers charged with criminal offenses in the course of duty.

Despite the fact it was nearly midnight, Carney came on the phone immediately. "Peter, you're working late?"

"Hi, Arnie. I'm sorry to bother you at this hour."

"No problem. I was up anyway. I heard about the big drug bust on the news. Great win for the War on Drugs. Congratulations."

"I didn't realize the media was on it already. It just happened a few hours ago." Lindsay was pleased. He could hardly wait until the Chief and the Mayor saw it in the morning papers.

"I don't know how they find out about this stuff, but from what I've seen it's all positive."

"Thanks."

"I would have thought you'd be either in bed or celebrating, not phoning lawyers."

"It's the bust I'm calling about," continued Lindsay. "I've got a small problem that I need your help with."

"What can I do?" Carney's curiosity was aroused, especially given the hour of Lindsay's call.

"One of the suspects we arrested was a young woman. Very different background from the others. They all had long criminal records, mostly drug related. This woman was a first offender."

"Sure she was involved?"

"We found a large quantity of cocaine hidden in her clothing."

"Interesting." replied Carney, waiting for the rest.

"I don't know how she got involved in this, but it seems out of character," continued Lindsay. "If she cooperates, we're prepared to drop all the charges except for possession. Get her out in ninety days. I'd like you to represent her. I was hoping you could see her in the morning. Her name is Sarah Andrews."

For Lindsay to take such an interest in an individual suspect was surprising and Carney sensed immediately that there was more to it. "Of course. Anything else I should know?"

"She'd been pretty badly beaten when we picked her up. We couldn't get a coherent story out of her, so we're not sure what really happened. I'm afraid she may claim she was beaten by some of the officers involved in the bust. The operation was carried out by veteran officers with impeccable service records. I'd hate to see them have to face a lot of false accusations after having done such a tremendous job."

"How can I help?"

"When you see her, see if you can calm her down. Tell her we'll drop most of the charges if she's cooperative. Three months, if she pleads guilty to simple possession. Otherwise, we'll let the charges stand. Trafficking, assaulting a police officer, and so on. She could be facing five years or more."

"No problem. If you're looking at a single possession charge, any chance you would consider just letting her go? The opportunity to walk out free is a pretty powerful incentive to forget anything that might have happened."

"We're willing to cut her a lot of slack, but I don't think we can go that far," replied Lindsay.

"Understand. I'll see her first thing in the morning. I'll come by your office once I've talked to her. I'm sure we can manage the situation."

"Thanks, Arnie. I appreciate it."

After hanging up, Arnold Carney shook his head. There was no doubt in his mind that Sarah Andrews had been roughed up by the police and that Lindsay needed his help with the situation. And, no doubt, the drugs had been planted in her clothing afterward. Nothing discredited a charge of police abuse more effectively than evidence that the complainant had committed a crime. Carney had helped before. He was always happy to do a favor for the next Chief of Police. And if an innocent bystander did some jail time, what did it matter?

CHAPTER 9

SARAH WAS AWAKENED AT SEVEN-THIRTY IN THE MORNING by a female guard bringing breakfast. It took her a minute to realize where she was, but soon the full horror of the night before came flooding back.

On the wall above the sink was a polished metal mirror. She barely recognized herself in the hazy reflection. Her face was badly bruised and her lip was split. One eye was black and partly swollen shut. Horrified, she sank down on the bed and began to cry. She had never felt so terribly alone.

Thirty minutes later, the guard returned, accompanied by a man in a business suit. The man was led into the cell and the door locked as the guard left them alone. "Mr. Carney. I'll just be outside."

The man sat down on the single metal chair while Sarah sat on the bed. He was middle-aged, paunchy and bald, and he looked harmless.

"Good morning," he said in a kindly voice.

Sarah sensed his shock at her appearance.

"My name's Arnold Carney. I'm a lawyer and I'm here to help you."

Sarah vaguely remembered that Lana had told her a lawyer would be coming to see her in the morning. "Thank you."

"Did you sleep all right?"

"Fine, I guess."

"What do you do?'

"I'm a librarian at the Glenwood Library."

"Have you ever been in jail before?"

"No." Sarah shook her head emphatically.

"I'm afraid it can be a little frightening. Especially the first time. But I'm on your side. We'll get you through this."

"When can I go home?"

"We'll talk about that in a minute."

"But I didn't do anything." Sarah tried not to cry.

"That's not what the police are telling me. You're being charged with possession of narcotics with intent to traffic, assaulting a police officer and resisting arrest."

Sarah sighed. "It's not true. None of it."

"They found a substantial quantity of cocaine in your clothing and they say that you slammed the car door on the hand of one of the arresting officers."

"I have never taken drugs. And one of the other officers slammed the door on the man's hand. I think they were drunk," Sarah objected.

"Maybe you should tell me your side of the story."

Sarah looked at him doubtfully.

"Go ahead. I'm your lawyer. Whatever you tell me is in strict confidence."

Still uneasy, Sarah told him part of what happened. She described walking from the library to the hospital, only to get lost in the Warehouse District, and eventually seeing the police car in which Crowe and Peters were waiting. She described her arrest but left out anything about the briefcase or the questioning she had endured.

"What happened to your face?" Carney asked, sensing she was leaving out a lot.

"I was running to the hospital and fell."

"Must have been quite a fall?"

"I fell into a pile of broken concrete."

"And you've been treated well since you were arrested?"

Sarah just nodded.

"Did they have a doctor see you?"

She shook her head.

Carney didn't believe her explanation for her injuries, and her response to his question on her treatment by the police seemed forced. However, her apparent decision to keep quiet would only make his job easier, so he didn't push.

"What's going to happen to me?" Sarah asked.

"We should be able to get a bail hearing in a couple of days. Let's take it step-by-step after that."

"You mean I have to stay here for two days?"

"I'm afraid so," replied Carney, knowing this was just the beginning.

"But my father was taken to the hospital. I have to visit him."

Carney shook his head. "Sarah. You've been arrested and charged with serious crimes. Your life will be different for a while."

"Isn't there anything you can do?" Sarah begged in desperation. "He's had a stroke and can't speak. He'll need me."

Carney shook his head. "If you tell me what hospital your father was taken to, I can probably find out how he's doing."

Sarah slumped back in defeat. "Mercy Hospital. His name is Martin Andrews."

Carney made a note. "If I can arrange an early hearing, can you get money to put up bail?"

"How much?" asked Sarah.

"Hard to tell. Maybe fifty thousand dollars."

Sarah shook her head in despair. It was an impossible sum. She had at most three thousand dollars in her bank account. Her father's remaining money went to pay the nursing home.

"Maybe we can get it down," replied Carney. Privately he was pleased with her answer. She had no money and no one she could approach to get it. It ensured that she wouldn't be released. While she wasn't making accusations of police brutality now, that might change once she was out. Lindsay would be relieved.

"What happens after the bail hearing?" asked Sarah apprehensively.

"If you can't make bail, you'll be held in custody. After that, it's a bit complicated. There is a hearing to decide whether there's enough evidence to bind you over for trial. If there is, and, unfortunately, there appears to be, a trial date is set. That could be two to four weeks from now, maybe longer. The trial would likely last two or three days. If you are found innocent, that's it. You're free."

A month—even if she was found innocent! "And if I'm found guilty?"

"It depends. Possession with intent to traffic is a lot more serious than possessing a small quantity of drugs for your own use. The prescribed sentence is two to ten years. Assaulting a police officer carries a sentence of one to three. Resisting arrest, up to a year. Given it's your first offense, you won't get the maximum, but you could be looking at five years, maybe more."

Five years! Sarah began to sob.

Carney had achieved the result he wanted. She was terrified. Now to reel her in. "Sarah," he began softly. "There's a chance I can get all the charges dropped, except simple possession, in exchange for a guilty plea. You could be out in three months."

"But I'm innocent," Sarah protested in bewilderment.

"Listen, I'm your lawyer and I want to believe you, but you were picked up within blocks of a major drug bust. Five experienced police officers will testify that you were in possession of a significant quantity of cocaine. Even if I believed you, I couldn't convince a judge in the country that you were innocent."

Sarah remained silent. Two days ago going to jail would have seemed unimaginable. Now it seemed inevitable. "What do I need to do?" she whispered.

"It's called a plea bargain. You agree to plead guilty to a simple possession charge and accept a three-month sentence. It'll be over in minutes. After three months, you get your life back."

She began to cry.

Carney tried to console her. "I know it seems like the end of the world, but we'll get you through this. I promise."

Sarah remained silent, overwhelmed by the terrible choice confronting her.

"Okay?" prompted Carney.

She nodded weakly. She didn't care anymore. Her life was over.

. . . .

Sarah's bail was set at twenty-five thousand dollars. With no possibility of raising that much money, she was forced to remain in custody until her trial. To avoid any awkward questions, Lindsay kept her in the Backfield Building holding cell until her injuries healed, at which point she was moved to the local Detention Center.

Arnold Carney was Sarah's sole contact with the outside world. He had reported that her father had not broken a hip as feared and had been taken back to the nursing home the next day, adding that he'd told the nursing home supervisor that Sarah was traveling on business and wouldn't be able to visit for a while. Sarah knew the story wouldn't work for long, but what else could she do? And what about her job and her apartment? She raised these concerns with Arnold Carney. He promised to call the library and explain that she'd had to leave town suddenly on a personal matter. He also said that he would cover her rent. She could pay him back when she got out.

The trial date was three weeks away. Sarah went where she was told and said what Carney told her to say, barely conscious of what was happening. Her emotional disengagement was so pronounced that Carney wondered about her mental state. As the days passed, her existence was circumscribed by the walls of her tiny cell. Her former life receded so far into the distance that it was hard to believe it had ever been real.

The endless hours alone gave Sarah time to reconstruct what had happened the night she was arrested. Clearly the cops had been on a drug bust and Gordon had left money in a briefcase in his car, which had somehow disappeared. The big cop, Carlucci had said it was a million dollars. But Lana Crawford said they'd recovered two million. Sarah tried to reconcile the comments. The only explanation she could come up with was that the total take had been three million and the cops had skimmed off one million for themselves, leaving it in a briefcase in their car. That would explain why they were so frantic to get it back.

No wonder they had done everything they could to get her to talk and fabricated the evidence to get her sent to prison. The more she thought about it, the more certain she became. Since she hadn't taken the money, she wondered who had. It didn't matter, to protect themselves, they were going to destroy her life. Far beneath her fear and despair, a tiny spark of anger began to smolder.

The Detention Center allowed prisoners one phone call every other day, but Sarah never used it. Her father was not able to talk on the phone and she had no relatives or close friends. Sometimes she wondered about Paul Taylor. She thought about their dinner together, his easy smile and fascinating stories. Being with him had made her feel safe and wanted. She still remembered his response when she commented on how boring her life must seem to him. *"You're beautiful, intelligent, and charming—and I'm having a wonderful time with you."*

She longed to hear his voice again, to feel his arm around her. Someone to know she was there. Someone to care whether she lived or died.

But if she called him, what would she say? *"Hi. Remember me? We had dinner once. Thought you'd want to know that I'm in jail awaiting trial for possession of narcotics. And how are you?"*

But she could not get the idea of phoning him out of her mind, and, finally, she summoned up the courage. After waiting her turn for the communal phone, with hands shaking, she dialed his number. As the phone rang, she struggled to think of what she would say. It rang several times. Disappointed yet almost relieved, she was about to hang up when the answering machine came on. *"This is Paul Taylor. I'm out of the country on business. I may be gone for several weeks and I will not be able to check voice mail. If it is not urgent, leave a message and I'll return your call when I get back. If this is my newfound friend, my Lady of the Books, my sincere apologies for having to leave so unexpectedly. I tried to call you but I just got your machine. I had a great time at dinner and will call you as soon as I am back, I sincerely hope we can pick up where we left off."*

"My Lady of the Books." He must mean her. The few words made her smile. Unable to think of anything to say, Sarah simply hung up. Back in her cell, she wondered where he had gone and how long he would be away. For the first time, she felt that someone was thinking about her, that someone cared whether she lived or died.

· · · · · · ·

On one of his visits Arnold Carney confirmed that he'd been able to get the District Attorney to accept the plea bargain. Three months for possession. Carney expected her to be delighted with the news, but Sarah looked at him blankly.

"You're lucky I've been able to get this deal for you," Carney told her. "You could easily have been looking at five years— maybe more."

"Thank you," Sarah replied dully.

"There was one unusual stipulation."

Sarah waited.

"You need to agree to serve your sentence at a maximum security woman's prison. The conditions are a little more strict, but it's only three months," Carney explained.

She shrugged. Prison was prison. What difference could it make?

• • • • • • •

The day of her trial arrived and Arnold Carney escorted her into the courtroom. At the entrance, Sarah hesitated momentarily, overwhelmed by the sight before her. The room was larger than she'd expected. There were so many people—spectators seated in the gallery, court officers scurrying around preparing for her trial, numerous well-armed and vigilant policemen placed strategically around the room. It was hard to believe that all this was for her. Carney led her to the defendant's table and told her to sit. She watched while Carney approached the judge and the two of them talked quietly together. She looked across at what she assumed was the prosecutor's table and saw two men, presumably attorneys, discussing something. One of them glanced over at her and then quickly looked away. It all seemed so casual, so impersonal, yet she knew they were discussing her future, her life!

Sarah turned and looked behind her towards the spectator gallery. Then she saw them—John Gordon, Frank Carlucci, Ernie Kramer, Chris LePan and Tom Miller. Even Peter Lindsay was there. Gordon was seated by himself toward the back. The others were together near the front, talking and laughing as if her trial were nothing more than a chance to catch up. Memories of what they had done flooded back, the pain, the terror, the humiliation. Their laughter, their breath stinking of alcohol, they'd destroyed her life and they sat there laughing! Sarah turned away, unable to look at them anymore.

The trial was over quickly. The single charge of possession was read out and, before Sarah could react, Arnold Carney stood and announced in a loud voice that the defendant pleaded guilty. There was a brief discussion among the judge, the Assistant District Attorney and Carney. Then the judge pronounced a three-month sentence at the Northbridge Prison for Women. Ten minutes after the trial began, Sarah was led away in handcuffs.

As she was led away, Sarah looked around desperately for Arnold Carney. She thought she would have a chance to ask him to make some arrangements for her father, her apartment and her job. But he had already left the room. It was as if she no longer existed.

As she was led past one of the anterooms, she was startled to see Peter Lindsay and Arnold Carney inside talking. They were smiling broadly and shaking hands. Suddenly they noticed Sarah passing by the doorway. Their smiles vanished and both looked away awkwardly.

Suddenly Sarah understood. Arnold Carney knew! He knew the charges against her were false. Perhaps he even knew what the police had done to her. Arnold Carney hadn't been helping her. He had been helping Lindsay! They were all in on it. They couldn't risk a trial, couldn't risk what she might say in front of a judge. Persuading her to accept a plea bargain ensured there would be no trial.

Within her, the flickering spark of anger burned more brightly.

· · · · · · ·

After the trial was over, Lindsay went back to his office. Gordon, Miller and the others stood together on the broad courthouse steps, enjoying the warmth of the sun and the prospect of having the afternoon off.

"Anyone want to grab a beer?" asked Miller. "I know a pub with an outdoor patio just a block from here."

"Great idea," LePan replied immediately.

"I'm in," said Kramer.

"Sure," added Carlucci.

Gordon wavered for a minute. "Thanks guys, but I think I'll pass."

The others strolled to the pub and settled around an outdoor table overlooking the sidewalk.

"Great idea, Tom. You buying too?" asked LePan.

"My idea. You guys buy. Thought that was the deal."

"You wish."

"What's with John? He never passes up a beer." Kramer asked.

"He's being forced to retire next year," Miller replied. "I think he's worried about money."

"If he hadn't left that briefcase in his car, he'd be a lot richer."

LePan shook his head in frustration. "We'd all be richer."

"Hey Chris," asked Miller. "Speaking of money, how'd you afford that sleek new jag on a cop's salary?"

"Hit it big at the track. It was now or never."

Kramer laughed. "Shit. You must be a high roller. A big night for me is winning enough to take my wife out to dinner."

"That reminds me, Ernie," Miller continued. "I saw your wife at a Honda dealership the other day. Pinnacle Auto. Unlike our friend here, I don't go to jag dealers. We chatted for a bit. She knew more about the cars than the sales guys."

Kramer shrugged. Clara hadn't told him she'd seen Tom Miller. "She wanted a part-time job. Tony's in school all day now."

"Well she's a real nice lady. Looker too." Miller grinned. "Be careful or you'll lose her to one of those smooth-talking salesmen."

LePan noticed their empty glasses. "Frank. Stop staring at the waitress. I want another beer and you're scaring her."

Miller patted Carlucci's massive, rock-hard biceps. "You're getting a little flabby, Frank. Maybe you should join a gym."

Carlucci smiled uncertainly. The others laughed.

"Does all that muscle help you get the girls?" Miller persisted.

"Yeah, but he's not sure what to do with them when he gets them," replied LePan.

"What do you mean by that?" Carlucci glared at LePan, and deliberately flexed his biceps.

Miller intervened quickly to defuse the situation. They'd all seen Carlucci erupt into a rage over some inconsequential slight. "Easy Frank. Chris is just jealous."

"This morning went well," commented Kramer, helping to deflect Carlucci's potential explosion. "If Sarah Andrews had refused to plead guilty, the trial could have been trouble."

LePan nodded, "Who knows what she would have said."

"I wonder how Carney persuaded her to plead guilty?" Miller commented.

"He's smooth, like a snake," LePan replied.

Miller laughed, "Are you speaking from experience?"

"He got me off a perjury charge. Made the key witness look like a pathological liar."

"And was he?"

"She was a nun."

Miller chuckled. "I would've liked to have seen that. He got you off an assault charge too, didn't he, Frank."

"Yeah, but the guy deserved it," Carlucci replied sullenly.

"Look," interjected LePan. "Don't go feeling sorry for her. She took our million dollars and in three months she'll be spending it. Under the circumstances, ninety days in prison isn't that big a deal."

"Except that Lindsay said he'd make sure she didn't get out," commented Kramer.

Miller shook his head. "Doubt he needs to worry about it. Can't see a librarian surviving a high security woman's prison. The other cons will eat her alive."

. . . .

After leaving the others, John Gordon walked slowly back to the Precinct. He'd watched Sarah in the courtroom, so overwhelmed by the tides that now controlled her life. Seeing her had renewed the guilt he had been struggling with since the day they had arrested her. Gordon thought about what awaited her in prison. And he thought about Lindsay's comment: she would never get out. His own daughter, Karen, was about the same age. She even looked a little like Sarah, the same dark eyes and hair. He sighed. Maybe he'd try writing to Karen one more time.

. . . .

Within an hour of the trial, Sarah was on her way to the Northbridge Prison for Women. There were a dozen women on the small bus and she looked around at the others, vainly seeking a friendly face. While diverse in age and race, they all had the same cold, sullen expressions, as if they had ridden this same bus many times before. They looked hard and cruel, and the prospect of living in close quarters with these women horrified her.

As they left the city behind, Sarah looked out the window. There were rolling fields stretching to the horizon. The landscape was dotted with barns and farmhouses, and the sky was incredibly blue, spotted by the occasional fluffy clouds that floated serenely by. So beautiful. So peaceful. Sarah wondered why she had never appreciated the country before. On a fence post near the road, she saw a robin surveying the field. As the bus approached, it flew away slowly. Sarah watched it rise into the sky and fade away into the distance—so effortless, so free. The bus passed over a small bridge and Sarah looked down at the creek beneath. It sparkled in the sunlight and she could hear the gentle whisper of the water as it found its way over the rocks.

Then, in the distance, she saw it — the Northbridge Prison for Women. It was set back from the road and surrounded by a massive concrete wall, like a cancer on the otherwise picturesque countryside. As the bus approached, the gray concrete walls seemed cold, dark and forbidding. She wondered if she would ever see the sky again. It was only three months, but she could not shake the feeling that the prison would swallow her forever.

CHAPTER 10

THE MASSIVE IRON GATE OF THE PRISON SWUNG OPEN AND the bus drove through, coming to a stop in a large asphalt courtyard. Four heavyset women guards emerged from the building. Two of them stood outside with handguns drawn while the other two got on the bus. One by one, the inmates were unshackled from their seats only to have their wrists handcuffed behind their backs and their ankles bound together by a short length chain. Sarah hobbled out into the sunlight. When they had all been removed from the bus, they were marched single file into the prison. As she entered the building, Sarah took a final look up at the sky and a last deep breath of the fresh country air.

"Processing" took about an hour during which Sarah was stripped, searched and forced to take an antiseptic shower. The water was boiling hot and came out with stinging force, scalding her skin. When she attempted to step out from under the searing spray, the guards yelled at her to get back under. After the shower, Sarah was provided with a bright orange dress with "Northbridge Prison" stamped in large black letters on the back. With her skin still stinging from the shower, Sarah was interviewed by a bored guard.

"Name?"

"Sarah Andrews."

"Date of birth?"

When the questions were over, the guard began to explain the rules. "Okay, Andrews. I am only going to say this once, so pay attention. Wake-up call is at six each morning. You'll get dressed, clean your cell and make your bed. There are two wings here, A and B. They have separate mess halls, A and B. You are in A. Don't forget. Breakfast is at seven if you pass cell inspection. If not, you'll remain in your cell all day with no meals. At eight, you'll report to work duty. Andrews, you're assigned to laundry. You'll work in the laundry until noon and return to the meal hall for lunch. From one until three, it's free time in the yard. From three to five it's back in your cell. Dinner is at five, then back to your cell block. Cell doors remain unlocked from six to nine. At nine, the bell will go. Back to your cell. Lights out is at nine-fifteen. No talking after that or you'll be punished. The same the next day and every day after that as long as you are here. You'll follow the instructions of the guards at all times. Disobey and you'll be punished. Any attitude and you'll be punished. Do you understand?"

Sarah nodded.

"I asked you if you understood."

"Yes, ma'am," Sarah replied, realizing a verbal response was required.

"Your prison number is 314159. Memorize it."

Sarah nodded.

"Repeat it for me."

"314159"

"Good."

Sarah committed the number to memory and waited for whatever came next.

"Follow me," ordered the guard.

Sarah was led down the hall into Area A, then down another long corridor with cells on both sides. The Detention Center had been bright, modern and clean, and Sarah had assumed that prison would be similar. It wasn't. Northbridge Prison was almost a hundred years old, poorly maintained and badly over-crowded. As they moved through the corridors, Sarah felt as if she were being led into the bowels of some mediaeval dungeon. The walls were cold and damp and there was a faint smell of sewage mixed with body odor. Through the barred doors, she could easily see into each cell, and she was horrified to see that all of them held two or three women. At the Detention Centre, she'd had a small cell to herself.

The cells were about ten feet wide by ten feet deep. There was a combination sink and toilet at the back and a cot on each side barely three feet apart. In some cells, one of the cots had been replaced by a double bunk so three inmates could be crowded into a cell meant for two. Sarah realized that when she used the toilet, she would be in full sight of the women sharing her cell and within an easy view of anyone who happened to be passing down the corridor. The prospect was mortifying.

About halfway down the corridor, the guard stopped at one of the cells and opened the door.

"Walters. We've got you a roommate. Meet Andrews. She's a newbie. Show her the ropes. Andrews, meet your new roommate Ethel Walters."

Sarah hesitated at the entrance to the cell, but the guard roughly pushed her in and slammed the door behind her. The lock clicked into place with horrifying finality.

Sarah remained standing just inside the door. Prison. No more hearings, no more lawyers, no reason to hope against hope that she wouldn't wind up here. She was locked up with thieves, drug dealers and murderers. How could this possibly have happened to her?

She looked over at the woman who would be her cellmate. Older than Sarah, probably mid-fifties, with gray, stringy hair, she was lying on one of the cots. Sarah waited for some acknowledgement, but there was none. The woman simply stared at her, then rolled over to face the wall. Sarah sat down on the other bunk and looked around the tiny cell. The only light came from a single bulb recessed into the ceiling. The floor, walls and ceiling were made of rough concrete. Her tiny cot was nothing more than a rusting spring platform with a thin, stained mattress. She had been given a pillow, two worn gray sheets and a single blanket. Each bunk had a small steel cupboard attached to the wall for personal belongings. Sarah had nothing to put in it except a couple of changes of prison-issue underwear and a second prison dress that they had given her during processing.

She realized she had to pee, badly. She hadn't been to the bathroom since before she'd been loaded onto the bus. She looked over at the sink/toilet combination. It was grimy and stained, and her skin crawled in revulsion. She couldn't bear the idea of sitting on it, nor of relieving herself in full view of the other woman. But she had to go. Mortified, she squatted over it, careful not to touch anything. When she returned to her cot, she lay down and began to sob into her pillow.

· · · · · · ·

Eventually, Sarah dozed off, only to be awakened by the piercing sound of a bell. Dinner. The cell doors opened automatically and the inmates formed a line down the corridor. The mess hall held twenty tables seating six each. Along one side of the room was a line of counters tended by women in prison uniforms where the inmates would receive their trays of food. There were guards strategically located armed with handguns and nightsticks. Sarah looked around for Ethel but she had disappeared into the crowd.

Sarah picked up a tray and utensils, and got on line. She was handed a large stale-looking bun, a carton of milk, and a bowl of fatty-looking stew. She looked around for a seat. A number of the tables had inmates already seated, and they seemed engrossed in their conversations. Afraid to join any of the groups, Sarah sat down at one of the empty tables and began to eat her dinner. Other inmates, in groups of twos and threes, headed to other tables, leaving Sarah sitting by herself. When she was finished, Sarah looked around wondering what she should do. No one else was getting up so she sat quietly. Suddenly a bell rang and all the inmates stood up. Sarah noticed a few of them gulping the last of their food. Dinner was over whether or not they had finished. Sarah joined the line filing back to the cells. When she got there, the cell doors were open and the inmates were freely walking around, talking, even playing cards. Too timid to start a conversation, Sarah went to her cot and lay down.

At nine, a bell sounded and Sarah heard a guard call out. "In your cells. No more talking. Lights out in fifteen minutes."

The inmates began to shuffle back to their cells. Walters reappeared and lay down without saying a word. A few minutes later, the lights went out and Sarah heard the cell door lock electronically. It was pitch black except for a dim glow from the emergency lights spaced at intervals along the corridor. She lay on her cot, struggling to breathe against the crushing weight of darkness and confinement. It was a long time before she fell into a fitful sleep.

· · · · · · ·

The breakfast routine was the same as dinner and, again, Sarah found herself eating alone. After breakfast, one of the guards made an announcement. "All right, work details. Kitchen, laundry, cleaning, line up at the north, south and west doors. Everyone else to the east door. Now!"

Sarah had no idea which door was which. Hesitantly, she joined the group forming at one of the doors and asked the inmate in front of her if it was the laundry detail. The woman pointedly ignored her, but a second woman pointed to one of the doors. Grateful, Sarah moved to the other group. Two guards also joined that group, one leading the way out the door, the other bringing up the rear. Sarah followed the line of women down several corridors to a large laundry room. The walls were lined with twenty huge washers and dryers. The heat and humidity in the room were suffocating. All the other inmates knew the routine, splitting into small groups. Sarah lingered uncertainly at the doorway.

The inmate who seemed to be in charge yelled over to her. "Hey, newbie, you're on dryer detail. Over here. Put the wet clothes in the dryer. Load each one till it's full. Turn it on. Then move to the next."

Thankful just to be acknowledged, Sarah did as she was told.

"What's your name, newbie?" the inmate asked.

"Sarah Andrews."

"Welcome to laundry, Andrews. I'm Rose Dutton."

Sarah nodded uncertainly. Rose Dutton was a large and powerful woman with bad teeth and an ugly scar on one cheek.

"And, Andrews," she added. "Don't slack off. We have a special punishment for slackers."

The wet clothes were surprisingly heavy, and loading the dryers was tough, backbreaking work, especially in the stifling heat of the room. Sarah was forced to work quickly to keep pace with the damp clothes being stacked on the table. Her arms and back soon started to ache and she was perspiring profusely. Within an hour, she was exhausted. Desperate for a break, Sarah looked up at the clock. It was just after nine. Laundry duty was supposed to run from eight until noon. She couldn't possibly keep it up until noon. She paused momentarily to stretch and catch her breath.

"Hey, newbie," yelled one of the other inmates, a blond woman named Riley. "This is not a country club. Get to work, and don't let me catch you slacking again."

Sarah quickly grabbed another heap of wet clothes. An hour later, her arms seemed to weigh a ton. She kept looking at the clock, and the minutes passed with agonizing slowness. She'd never make it.

"Hey Rose. The newbie's slacking off again," Riley said. "I think she needs to be taught a lesson."

Rose Dutton stopped what she was doing and went over to Sarah. "You know what we do with slackers—we put them in the dryer." She grinned as she said the words.

All the others stopped what they were doing and circled Sarah. "Into the dryer, newbie or we'll throw you in."

Sarah was terrified. Surely, they couldn't mean it.

But one look in their faces and she knew they did. Gratuitous cruelty was a welcome relief from the monotony of prison life. Desperately, Sarah looked over at the two guards for help, but they shrugged and looked away.

"No, please!" Sarah was frantic as the group circled closer. "I'll work harder. Please!"

"Too late, newbie," Dutton shouted.

Sarah struggled frantically, but, against their combined strength, it was futile. She was easily lifted into the air and tossed into the dryer. The door was slammed shut and locked. Sarah looked out the small glass window. Surely, they wouldn't actually turn it on. She watched in horror as Rose Dutton reached up and pressed the button. Seconds later the drum began to rotate.

The drum was about four feet in diameter and had three large fins projecting inwards. As it began to turn, Sarah found herself being lifted up by each fin only to be dropped to the bottom as it neared the top. The next fin would dig painfully into her ribs as she fell again and again. The drum began to rotate more quickly and Sarah found herself being tossed around like a rag doll. Her shoulders were aching from the repetitive blows. As the temperature began to rise the metal sides of the drum scorched her bare skin, and each time she drew a breath, the hot air would sear her lungs.

Frantically, Sarah peered out the door. Surely, they would turn it off any minute. But Rose Dutton and the others stared back at her, their perverse pleasure in her predicament evident. In desperation, Sarah discovered that if she braced her feet on one side of the drum and her back on the other, she could go around without falling to the bottom again and again. It eased the battering. But bracing herself was hard work, and she wondered how long her aching back and leg muscles would hold out. Going round and round, she became dizzy and her stomach began to heave. Finally, she could hold back no longer and she vomited violently, spewing the acrid contents of her stomach throughout the dryer. As she rotated, she vomited again and again until there was nothing left in her stomach. A couple of times her arms and legs gave out and she tumbled helplessly, her body battered and bruised until she frantically braced herself again. Her muscles were screaming in agony. Finally, one of the inmates turned off the dryer and the drum came to a stop. When the door opened Sarah tumbled out onto the floor soaked with perspiration and vomit. Her body was battered and bruised and her hands, knees and back were scorched from the heat of the drum. She lay on the ground, semi-conscious.

"Christ, she stinks," she heard Riley say.

"Cartwright," commanded one of the guards, "take her to the shower and get her cleaned up."

"Why me?" Cartwright grumbled.

"Because I told you to," the guard replied. "You've had your fun. Now do it!"

"Come on, newbie," ordered Cartwright. "Get up!"

Sarah remained motionless. She hurt so badly, she could not bear to move.

Cartwright gave her back a brutal kick. "I said get up," she ordered, "unless you want another spin in the dryer."

Sarah struggled to her feet and let Cartwright lead her to the showers. Still dazed, she stripped off her clothes. The cold water felt good on her battered flesh and she raised her head, opened her mouth and drank copiously. Afterwards, she dried herself and put on the clean dress and underwear that Cartwright tossed to her.

"Glad to see you're still in one piece," said Dutton, when Sarah returned to the laundry room. "We'll go easy on you for the rest of the morning. You get to fold the dry clothes. Tomorrow, it's back to loading. And don't let me catch you slacking again or we'll leave you in for the full cycle."

Compared to loading the wet clothes into the dryer, folding and stacking the dry clothes was easy work, but even that was almost more than Sarah could manage. Every movement was agony. Finally, to Sarah's utter relief, the bell sounded for lunch.

· · · · · · ·

Sarah collected her lunch and, as usual, sat at a table by herself. Her stomach was still heaving so she ate very little. After lunch, she followed the other women outside for exercise period, where she came to the yard—a large rectangle, roughly twenty-five by fifty yards, surrounded by a twelve-foot concrete wall topped with barbed wire. The ground was mostly packed dirt, although, here and there, patches of grass had somehow managed to survive the constant trampling. The sky was blue and the feel of sun on her bruised skin was pleasant. Sarah looked around. Most of the inmates were standing around talking, some were sitting at tables playing cards, others playing catch with an old tennis ball. At one end of the yard, some of the women were working out on an ancient piece of weight training equipment. Sarah walked slowly and stiffly to a deserted part of the wall, gingerly sat down on the ground and leaned back against the rough concrete wall. She remembered the simple things she used to do — eating a pastry from her favorite bakery, sitting in the park watching the children play, exploring the museum. Her life, which had once seemed so mundane, now seemed full and rich compared to the horrors that now surrounded her. She hugged her knees, put her head down and fought back the tears.

CHAPTER 11

AFTER A FEW MINUTES, SARAH BECAME CONSCIOUS OF someone standing beside her.

A slight Asian girl was studying her with concern. "Are you all right?"

Sarah took a moment before replying. "I guess," she said tremulously.

"You don't look all right?" The girl reached over and gently touched the bruises already forming on Sarah's arm. "What happened?"

"They put me in the dryer."

The girl looked at her incredulously. "The clothes dryer?"

Sarah nodded.

"And turned it on?"

Sarah nodded again.

"Jesus," said the girl. "Are you sure you're okay?"

"I hurt all over but I don't think anything's broken."

The girl sat down beside Sarah. "This place seriously sucks, doesn't it?"

Sarah managed a feeble smile. "Seriously."

"How long have you been here?" the girl asked.

"Since yesterday." Sarah made it sound like forever.

"The first few days are the toughest. It's hard to believe, but you get used to it."

"How long have you been in?" asked Sarah, quite certain that she would never get used to it.

"Three months."

Sarah studied her as if surprised anyone could survive that long.

"What's your name?" asked the girl.

"Sarah. Sarah Andrews"

"Mine's Valerie. Valerie Yuen."

Sarah smiled weakly. "Hi."

"How long are you in here for?" Valerie asked

"Three months—if I make it. You?"

"Six months. Three months to go."

"So we get out about the same time."

Valerie nodded. "We should do something to celebrate once we're out."

"What are you in for?" asked Sarah.

"Assault."

Sarah looked at Valerie in astonishment. She seemed too petite to assault anyone. "Really?"

"I dance at this club," Valerie began to explain. "A strip club. Anyway, there was this guy who kept coming into the club. Fancy dresser, lots of money. He had a thing for me. Got me to dance for him, several times a week. For a while it was okay. I made a lot of money off him. Then he started getting possessive.

Started telling me not to dance for other customers. Wanted to date me outside the club. It was getting creepy, so I told him I didn't want to dance for him anymore. He goes berserk, starts screaming, wants to talk to the manager. Finally the bouncers toss him out. I'm walking to my car after the club closes and there he is, waiting for me. Real drunk and belligerent. Tries to lay me out over the car like he's going to take me right there. I manage to grab a brick and nail him one. He drops like a stone and I get in my car and drive off.

"Someone finds him and takes him to the hospital. Just a few stitches and a concussion, but the bastard files assault charges against me. In court he swears he never touched me. Turns out he's a senior executive with some bank. The judge takes his word for it and here I am."

"I'm so sorry. That's terrible."

Valerie just shrugged. "So what are you doing in here?"

Sarah told Valerie most of her story. When she was finished, Valerie looked at her sympathetically. "Oh God, Sarah...I..."

Sarah sighed. "I didn't think things like that could happen to people."

They talked until the bell rang signaling the end of their free time. The inmates began to wander back toward the door and Sarah asked, "Will I see you at dinner?"

Valerie shook her head. "I'm in Wing B. We have a separate mess hall."

Sarah looked disappointed, but Valerie put her arms around her and hugged her. "We can meet here tomorrow though."

They had found a common bond and suddenly Sarah didn't feel so alone.

· · · · · · ·

At dinner that evening, Sarah had just picked up her tray when Alice Cartwright called out. "Hey Newbie. How was the dryer? Did you come out wrinkle-free?"

There were snickers around the room. Flushed with embarrassment, Sarah put her head down and tried to ignore the comment.

"She looks pretty delicate," yelled another inmate. "I hope you girls were nice enough to use the gentle cycle."

There was more laughter.

"She wasn't very dry when she came out," replied Rose Dutton. "Tomorrow, it's the heavy-duty cycle."

Sarah shuddered. She couldn't bear the thought of being put in the dryer again. She would die. With her tray in her hand, Sarah walked toward her table, certain everyone in the room was watching her.

Suddenly she fell to the ground, and her dinner tray went flying. The room erupted in applause.

"Great trick, newbie. Show us again," an inmate jeered.

"Someone teach her how to walk," another added.

Sarah looked to see what she'd tripped over, but saw nothing. She realized that one of the inmates at the table she was passing must have stuck out her leg. For a moment, she just lay there, humiliated.

"Get up newbie!" demanded the inmate nearest to her as she gave Sarah a vicious kick. "You're blocking the aisle."

Sarah struggled to her feet. She stood there for a minute, wondering what to do.

"What are you waiting for? Clean it up!" the guard called out. "There's a mop behind the counter."

Sarah picked up the plates and cutlery and put them with the dirty dishes. Then she got the mop and cleaned up the floor. Finally she went back to get another tray.

"Whoa, newbie, one dinner per person," shouted the guard.

"But..." Sarah stammered.

"Are you arguing with me?"

"No..." replied Sarah, fearfully.

"Good. Now sit down and wait for the bell. Next time, be more careful."

Sarah sat quietly at her table, stung by the total unfairness of what had happened. She was relieved when the bell rang and she could escape back to her cell. She crawled onto her bed and lay there, terrified of what they would do to her tomorrow.

. . . .

The next morning, Sarah awoke a few minutes before the bell. She felt awful. Hunger gnawed at her. Her whole body was sore and she had large ugly bruises on her arms and ribs. There was no way she could manage four hours of the same work in the laundry, and the prospect of being put in the dryer again was unbearable. She lay there in the dark, overwhelmed with fear and despair. She'd never make it out of prison. She wished she could just roll over and die.

The bell rang and somehow she found the strength to get up and tidy her cell before following the line into breakfast. She collected her tray and walked carefully to her table, taking a different route to avoid the inmate who had tripped her. With relief, she reached the table and sat down. Breakfast was a puddle of soggy scrambled eggs, two pieces of under-done toast, and a glass of watery orange juice. But it looked delicious. Sarah was about to take her first mouthful when suddenly her tray went flying off the table, landing upside down on the floor several feet away. The room erupted in applause.

Sarah turned to see Rose Dutton, standing behind her, grinning. "Oh, I'm so terribly sorry. I didn't see you there."

It couldn't be happening again! Frantically, Sarah looked over at the guard. Again, the guard just shrugged. Unable to bear it anymore, Sarah buried her head in her arms and began to sob.

"Oh look," Dutton taunted. "The newbie doesn't like it here."

The whole room took up the chant, "Boo hoo, newbie. Boo hoo newbie."

"Don't just sit there," Dutton screamed. "Get a mop and clean up your mess."

When Sarah didn't move, Dutton punched her viciously in the ribs. "I said get up!"

Slowly, Sarah struggled to her feet, got a mop and bucket, and began to clean up the floor.

"Hope you're ready for the heavy-duty cycle!" Alice Cartwright called out.

"Speed it up newbie," yelled Dutton, still standing over her. "I want to eat my breakfast before it gets cold."

Tears running unchecked down her face, Sarah tried to move more quickly. Then something extraordinary happened. The pain and despair that only a moment before threatened to overwhelm her began to recede, replaced by an eerie stillness. Her mind whirled with a kaleidoscope of images. Rose Dutton peering into the dryer, watching her be battered and burned. Frank Carlucci holding the taser against her body while she writhed in agony. Peter Lindsay and Arnold Carney shaking hands and smiling as she was led off in handcuffs. The small flame of anger smoldering within her suddenly exploded into a firestorm. From the depths of her being, a primeval rage, long dormant and unsuspected, erupted, driving out her fear. Sarah had never felt such a powerful emotion. It was frightening and exhilarating at the same time.

"That's better!" screamed Dutton, taking sadistic pleasure in the fear and humiliation she was inflicting. As she screamed, Dutton vaguely sensed the change in Sarah's demeanor.

Suddenly Sarah stopped cleaning and simply stood there looking at her with an odd expression on her face.

"I said clean it up," screamed Dutton.

Calmly and deliberately, Sarah picked up the metal bucket, heavy with water, and swung it with all her might. Startled by the unexpected attack, Dutton couldn't react fast enough. The lower rim of the bucket caught her squarely on the temple and she crumpled to the ground. The room erupted into pandemonium.

· · · · · · ·

The guards dragged Sarah out of the room and locked her in a small holding cell. Two hours later, she was taken to the Warden's office. Warden Sidney Patterson was pacing angrily behind her desk while the Assistant Warden, Doreen Matlock, was leaning against a table, a smirk on her face.

"Rose Dutton is dead," Patterson announced, looking at Sarah. "Died on the way to the hospital of a cerebral hemorrhage."

Sarah remained silent. She felt nothing. No remorse, no fear. Just a strange sense of peace.

"Nothing to say?"

Sarah shook her head.

"Good move, Andrews," interjected Doreen Matlock. "Looks like you'll be here a lot longer than your ninety days." she added with a malicious grin.

"What happened?" snapped Patterson to the guards.

"Andrews here, picked up a bucket of water and swung it at Dutton. Hit her on the head. She dropped like a like a rock and never moved again."

Sidney Patterson studied Sarah. Pretty, refined, gentle. Her expression showed no emotion, but her eyes reflected intelligence. She didn't look like a killer. In fact, she was not the typical kind they got in prison. She didn't miss the bruises on Sarah's arms and legs. "How long have you been in here, Andrews?"

"Two days."

Two days and she'd killed one of the toughest inmates in the prison! Rose Dutton was a cruel and powerful woman, feared by the other inmates. Curious Patterson turned to the computer on her desk and called up Sarah's file. "Let's see. Sarah Andrews. Ninety days for possession. Pled guilty. First offense. That you?"

"Yes, Warden."

Patterson looked at her in surprise. "How come you're in a maximum security prison?"

"I don't know. It was a condition of the plea bargain."

Patterson looked at Sarah in surprise. She had never heard of such a condition. "Says here you were a librarian and you've got a degree?"

Sarah nodded.

"So what happened?"

"It's like we said," Matlock interrupted.

"I asked Andrews," replied Patterson, giving Matlock a hard look. It seemed unbelievable that Andrews would have attacked Dutton, a woman who probably outweighed her by 100 pounds. She must have been provoked.

"It's like she said." Sarah shrugged.

"Something must have started it?" Patterson probed. Sarah shrugged again.

"Talk to me!" demanded Patterson.

"They wouldn't let me eat," replied Sarah finally.

"How many meals had this happened for?" Patterson was well aware of the games the inmates often played on newbies. She had ordered the guards to intervene when they saw it happening but she knew they usually turned the other way.

"Dinner yesterday and breakfast again this morning."

"Anything else?"

"Dutton and some others put me in the dryer."

"And how many times did that happen?" asked Patterson, with mounting anger.

"Once," Sarah replied. "But they said they were going to do it again."

"It's a common initiation for newbies," Matlock interjected. "Doesn't really hurt them. Just shakes them up a bit."

"In that case, I'm sure you'll be happy to give me a personal demonstration," she shot back at Matlock.

Matlock remained silent.

"So Andrews," continued Patterson. "When all this was going on, why didn't you ask the guards for help?"

Sarah looked over at the guards and back at Patterson without replying.

Patterson turned to the two guards who had brought Sarah to her office. "Well?"

"We didn't see anything, Warden."

Patterson looked at them, wordlessly, with withering contempt.

"I'll inform the police," said Matlock. "There should be a full investigation and possible charges."

"Sounds like self-defense to me," replied Patterson, holding Matlock's gaze, "resulting from negligent supervision. Are you sure you want that investigation?" Privately Patterson was glad that Sarah had fought. She would need to fight to survive. Besides, Dutton was a sadistic bully. It was time she got what she deserved.

Matlock was red with anger, but she did not reply.

"I want Andrews transferred to library duty," Patterson continued, still addressing Matlock.

"But..." Matlock began to protest.

"Do it!" interrupted Patterson. "And I want to know which guards were on duty during the incidents Andrews described. And I want to know why nothing was done. Understood?"

Matlock nodded uncomfortably.

"Andrews," she said to Sarah. "Go back to your cell. That will be all for now."

Word of Rose Dutton's death had spread throughout the prison. In the exercise yard that afternoon and at dinner that night, Sarah was distinctly conscious of the different attitude toward her. There was no more taunting, no more newbie jokes. Instead, there was an unspoken respect, as if she had completed some secret rite of passage. It did not hurt that many of the inmates had been victimized by Dutton and were privately pleased to see someone finally stand up to her.

Lying in her cell that night, Sarah reflected on what she had done. She felt amazed at her rage, her capacity for violence. Where had they come from? She had killed someone! She should be horrified. But all she felt was a quiet sense of satisfaction.

CHAPTER 12

IN THE YARD THE NEXT DAY, VALERIE CAME UP TO SARAH with a grin. "Everyone's still talking about what you did. You're a celebrity."

Sarah smile was sheepish. "I don't know what happened to me. I've never done anything like that in my life. I'm really a bit of a wimp."

"A wimp with an iron fist."

"An iron bucket," replied Sarah, smiling.

"Whatever. From now on, I'll try to stay on your good side."

"Maybe they'll leave me alone."

"It sounds funny, but I'm proud of you."

"Thanks." Sarah smiled wryly. "Were you really a stripper?" she continued, changing the subject.

Valerie smiled. "An exotic dancer, if you don't mind."

Sarah studied her. She would never have guessed. Valerie was definitely beautiful—Asian, with delicate features, high cheekbones and a sensual body. But she didn't have the over-sized breasts and exaggerated figure Sarah vaguely associated with strippers.

Valerie smiled back at her. "What? You don't think my boobs are big enough?"

"Sort of, no...well, you know," Sarah stammered with embarrassment. "I guess I always thought that strippers had to look like Pamela Anderson."

"Have you ever been in a strip club?"

Sarah shook her head.

"The upscale clubs aren't sleazy like you might expect. The clientele is largely professional. `Suits' we call them. The girls are generally intelligent, refined—and often quite well educated. They're pretty, but they're not all over-endowed."

Sarah couldn't contain her curiosity. "What's it like? Stripping, I mean."

Valerie laughed. "At first, I was really nervous. After I got over that, it was a bit of a high, a power trip—all those men staring at you, wanting you, paying you twenty-five dollars just to dance at their table for a few minutes. Then it gets to be just a job. A way to make money. Boring. You go through your routine and your mind's a million miles away."

"How did you get into it?"

Valerie smiled. "Given what I do for a living, you would never guess, but I've got a master's degree in philosophy. When I got out of university, I couldn't get a job. After all, what can you really do with an MA in philosophy? Finally, I got as a job as a sales clerk in a department store, working forty hours a week, on my feet all day, at a salary of twenty-six thousand dollars a year. I could barely pay the rent, and I certainly couldn't afford a car. Then I got laid off. I looked for weeks but couldn't find anything. Finally, I saw an ad for a dancer at the Purring Kitten. I figure, what the hell. I go down in the morning. The manager puts on some music and asks me to get up on the stage and dance. Then he tells me to take off my clothes. It's embarrassing, but I do it. I know what's going through his mind—can't dance, too skinny, no boobs, forget it. Then, to my amazement, he asks me to start that night. At first, I think he must be joking. Anyway, the customers like me. Maybe they get tired of big boobs, who knows. Now I work twenty-four hours a week and make a hundred and fifty grand a year. At least I used to until I wound up in here. Working at night allowed me to go back to school, and I am, or I was, working on my doctorate."

"Wow!"

"So, now you know my life story. What about you? What do you do?"

"I'm a librarian, at least I was a librarian."

"You're joking?"

"No. Why?"

"I don't know. I guess, I always thought of librarians as being old and plain."

"Thanks. I think."

"I meant that as a compliment. You're young and beautiful."

"Hardly. I've had maybe two dates in my entire life."

"Hey, in my business looks count, and I know what I'm talking about. I could get you a job in the Purring Kitten any time you want."

Sarah laughed. "I couldn't do it."

"You'd be a natural. Beats working in a musty old library."

Sarah shook her head, trying to imagine what it would be like. She couldn't.

"So how did you become a librarian?"

"A bit like you I guess. I've got a university degree. English and history. Pretty good marks. Dean's list. But, I had trouble getting a job. Not much demand for English grads. Anyway, I got an offer to work at an inner city library. It wasn't really what I wanted, but I needed a job. Now, I actually kind of like it." It sounded lame and Sarah shrugged apologetically.

"Don't knock it. Not many people can say that about what they do."

Sarah wondered sadly what kind of a job she'd be able to get when she got out, and whether she would ever again have a job she liked.

Valerie sensed her melancholy and regretted her comment. "It will work out," she said. "We'll make it work out."

· · · · · · · ·

As the days became weeks, Sarah settled into the monotony of prison life. The transfer to the library was wonderful. The work was easy—re-shelving books, filing newspapers and periodicals. When the prison officials discovered Sarah's experience with computers, she was also made responsible for maintaining the library network and Internet terminals. She had a lot of free time and spent most of it on the computer.

In the newspaper one day, Sarah saw an article describing Peter Lindsay's appointment to Deputy Chief of Police. It described Lindsay as an extraordinarily dedicated public servant who had served the city with integrity and devotion for almost twenty years. There was a picture of Lindsay shaking the Mayor's hand and smiling broadly for the cameras. Sarah stared at it for a long time, shaking with emotion.

The bright spot in her days was the time with Valerie in the exercise yard. They had become fast friends, their relationship a lifeline for both of them. Sarah opened up to Valerie in a way she'd never done before.

For her part, Valerie seemed to feel the same. Once she had hugged Sarah and, with tears in her eyes, exclaimed. "Oh, Sarah. You're such a great person, and friend. I'm almost glad I'm here, otherwise I'd never have met you."

Profoundly moved, Sarah had hugged her back. "Let's promise that we'll always stay friends."

"When we're out, do you want to share an apartment?" Valerie asked.

"I'd like that," Sarah replied, delighted with the idea.

· · · · · · ·

One day, when Sarah and Valerie were standing together in the yard, one of the other inmates approached them. She was massive. Sarah figured she must be over six feet and weigh two hundred and fifty pounds, all muscle. Sarah could see that Valerie was becoming nervous.

"Hello, Marcia," replied Valerie. Sarah could hear the tension in her voice.

"Hi, Baby Val," replied the woman.

"Who's your friend?"

"This is Andrews."

Not quite sure what to do, Sarah offered her hand. Marcia ignored her hand and hugged her. Sarah felt nauseated by the woman's bulk and pronounced body odor, but suppressed the urge to pull away.

"I heard about you Andrews," said Marcia, finally releasing her. "You're the one who took out Rose Dutton."

Sarah nodded uncertainly.

"Good move, Andrews. That woman was a fucking pain. I was going to have to thump her one day. You saved me the trouble."

Then turning away from Sarah, she went over to Valerie and began stroking her hair. "You thought about what I said, Baby Val?"

Valerie backed away nervously, but did not reply.

Marcia was clearly angered at Valerie's lack of response. "Don't think too long, Baby Val," she said, walking away.

"What was all that about?" asked Sarah, upset at her friend's obvious distress.

"Nothing. Don't worry about it."

"Who *was* that woman? She was huge."

"That's Marcia Madigan. She's doing life for first-degree murder. They say she's killed three inmates since she's been here. She's king shit around here. Nobody fools with Marcia. Even the guards treat her with respect."

Sarah heard the fear in Valerie's voice. She wanted to ask more but sensed her friend didn't want to talk about it.

· · · · · · ·

Sarah often thought about Paul Taylor. She remembered every minute of their dinner together. The way he had listened so intently to everything she'd said. The stories he had told her about the countries he'd been too. She could still remember the feel of his arm around her shoulders when he'd walked her home. Just being with him had made her feel interesting and desirable.

It had been almost two months since she had called him from the Detention Center. Paul's voice message said he would be out of the country for several weeks. She wondered where he'd gone. Was it another mission to rescue some kidnapped diplomat or executive? He had told her he was retired but perhaps he had taken one more assignment. While he described his work casually, it sounded dangerous. What if he had been wounded? Or killed? Sarah could not bear the thought. Yet even if he came back, would he want to see her again? After all, it had only been one dinner and a lot of time had passed. But then she recalled the voice message about the "Lady of the Books". One day, feeling foolish, Sarah confided her feelings and fears to Valerie.

"He sounds like a fantastic guy. And you met him on the subway? I should be so lucky."

Sarah's smile betrayed her feelings for him.

"Jesus, you're in love with the guy, aren't you?"

"How can you be in love after one dinner?" Sarah objected.

Valerie just smiled. "Have you talked to him since your dinner?"

"I tried phoning him after I'd been arrested. His voice message said he'd had to leave the country for several weeks. There was a separate message for 'My Lady of the Books' saying he'd enjoyed the dinner and hoped to get together when he returned. I'm sure he was referring to me."

"See! He wants to see you again. Have you written to him?"

"No. I thought about it. But how do I explain that I'm in prison on a drug charge?"

"Just tell him. If he's the guy you think he is, he'll at least give you a chance to explain."

"Maybe I'll..."

"Just do it!" Valerie insisted.

The inmates were not permitted phone calls but they were allowed to write. Summoning up her courage, Sarah began to write a letter to Paul Taylor. After two hours and a dozen drafts, she had one she was satisfied with.

Dear Paul,

Thank you so much for the wonderful dinner. And thank you again for saving my life on the subway. I tried to call you but your voice message said you'd had to leave the country. I really liked the message for "Your Lady of the Books". I've been having some problems and just hearing that message made me feel better. I hope your trip is going well and you get back safely. I want so much to see you again.

Paul, there is one thing I need to tell you. I hope desperately it doesn't change your opinion of me or cause you not to want to see me. I may as well just say it. I was convicted for possession of narcotics and I am currently serving three months in prison. There, I said it. I didn't do it. I promise you. I don't even know what drugs look like.

I'll call you when I get out. I can only pray you will give me a chance to explain.

Yours sincerely,

Sarah (Lady of the Books)

Reading it, Sarah was surprised she could have written such a letter. Apprehensively, she dropped it into the outgoing mailbox.

· · · · · · ·

As Sarah slipped the letter into the slot, Paul Taylor was sitting in his room in a run-down hotel in a small town two hundred miles northeast of Bogotá, Colombia. He was about to leave on a two-day trek through the Colombian jungle to the camp of a terrorist group believed to be responsible for much of that county's drug trade. It wasn't the drug trade Paul cared about. The terrorists had kidnapped the daughter of an old friend who had asked Paul to try to rescue her.

As he checked through his weapons and gear, Paul reflected ruefully that his retirement hadn't lasted long. This was absolutely the last time, he told himself—no matter who asked him. When he had started in the business, it had been exciting. Now, it was just a job. He'd much prefer to be sitting on his deck sipping a cool beer, or skimming Crystal Lake in his sailboat.

Thoughts of Crystal Lake made him think of Sarah Andrews. He could remember every detail of their dinner, what she was wearing, what she said, and the feel of her head resting on his shoulder as he walked her home. He looked forward to inviting her out to his house on Crystal Lake, taking her sailing, making her dinner on the deck, taking her to his bed.

Feeling foolish, he took a piece of stationery from the drawer and began to write.

> *Dear Sarah,*
>
> *I hope all is well with you. I thoroughly enjoyed our dinner together and I am very grateful for the strange circumstances under which we met. The day after we had dinner, I had to leave the country on an assignment. I hoped that it would be over in a month or so, but it has now been over two months and could last several more weeks. I*

*tried to call you before I left to explain and I hope
you at least got my voice message.*

*I will call you just as soon as I am back and I
can only hope we can still pick up where we left
off. I want so much to show you Crystal Lake,
take you sailing and cook you dinner on my deck
overlooking the lake. I think you would like it and
I know I would love having you there.*

Paul.

Before he could change his mind, Paul took the letter down to
the front desk and paid the clerk to mail it for him.

CHAPTER 13

DOREEN MATLOCK WAS IN HER MID-FIFTIES AND HAD BEEN Assistant Warden at the Northbridge Prison for Women for fifteen years. She had been passed over for warden on three separate occasions, the last time being when the current warden, Sidney Patterson, had been appointed. Patterson was ten years younger, which only heightened her resentment and frustration.

Matlock was sitting in her office when the phone rang. It was Kurt. She had never learned his last name but he paid her well for information about specific inmates and the occasional 'project'.

"Hi Doreen. How's prison treating you?'

"Same old."

"You got a Sarah Andrews there?"

"Yeah. Been here about a month. How come a first offender on a possession charge got sent to a maximum security prison?"

"We don't want her to get out. Figured we could control things better there."

"I see."

"There's a Lillian Thompson coming in tomorrow," Kurt continued. "Transferring from Gravenhurst. Her file will say she's serving twenty years for first-degree murder. She'll look after it."

"What do you want me to do?"

"Not much. Get her a weapon and arrange for her to be alone with Andrews. She'll do the rest."

"Same fee?" asked Matlock.

"Same fee."

"Okay. Tell Thompson to be careful. Your Sarah Andrews killed a lifer her second day in here."

"She's a librarian, for Christ's sake. Are we talking about the same person?"

"Mid-thirties. About five-three, dark hair, quiet."

"That's her. So how the hell did she take out the lifer?"

"Caved in her skull with a bucket."

"Was she charged?"

"No. The Warden decided it was self-defense."

"Too bad. That would have solved our problem. Anyway. Let me know when it's done."

"Will do."

· · · · · · ·

Two days later, as Sarah headed back to her cell after the exercise period, she heard her name called. It was Doreen Matlock. It was unusual for Matlock herself to be in the yard. If she wanted to see someone, she would normally send one of the guards. Matlock was a cruel and vindictive woman and Sarah was immediately anxious.

"Yes, ma'am," Sarah replied, dropping out of line.

"Come with me," Matlock ordered. "The server in the library is down. I want you to have a look at it."

Matlock escorted Sarah to the library and settled into one of the chairs while Sarah began to check out the server. It was definitely down, but it would take a while to diagnose the problem. It could be anything from a loose connection to a software virus.

"It could take me a while," Sarah said tentatively. "You might want to have a guard watch me instead of waiting yourself."

"What the hell. You're out in less than two months," replied Matlock, getting out of the chair, "so I don't figure you'll do anything dumb. I'll be back in an hour. If you're not here, it's the hole."

Sarah knew even the toughest prisoners were afraid of the hole. "I'll be here."

Matlock left, leaving Sarah alone in the library. Ten minutes later, Sarah heard the library door open again and looked up in surprise. A woman entered and carefully closed the door behind her. She wore a prison dress but Sarah had never seen her before. She wondered what the woman was doing in the library by herself when the inmates were supposed to be back in their cellblocks.

"Are you Sarah Andrews?" the woman asked.

"Yes."

"That's unfortunate."

"What do you mean?"

"Someone wants you dead," the woman replied. She calmly produced a knife and began to approach Sarah as if killing her was no more significant than borrowing a library book. The woman was large and powerful and the knife looked deadly.

Stunned and terrified, Sarah cried out. "No! Wait! Please! It must be a mistake!"

"No mistake."

"Please!" cried Sarah, overcome by panic.

"Sorry Andrews. It's not personal."

Frantically, Sarah began backing away, looking around for some way to escape, but the woman was between her and the only door. Certain that in seconds she'd be dead, Sarah wondered how much it would hurt. She hoped it would be quick.

The woman lashed out with the knife. Reflexively, Sarah sidestepped and the blade harmlessly sliced the air. Annoyed, the woman lunged at Sarah. Sarah ducked and the knife missed again. Instinctively, Sarah stepped forward and swung her fist. To her surprise, she connected firmly, crushing the woman's nose. The woman staggered back, momentarily startled by the unexpected attack.

"You bitch," the woman exclaimed, clutching her bloody nose. "Now I'm going to make this hurt." She approached again, more cautiously this time, the knife extended.

Suddenly, Sarah felt a cold rage rise up within her. Rage against this woman. Rage against all that had happened to her. Her terror dissipated like fog before the sun and she stood there, motionless, coolly appraising her adversary. The woman was big, but she appeared slow and overly confident. Sarah wasn't going to die without a fight.

Lillian Thompson hesitated uncertainly. Something was odd. When she'd been told that Sarah was a librarian, she had assumed Sarah would panic at the first sight of the knife; that she'd cower and beg for her life. But instead, Sarah stood there, facing her, calmly and unafraid.

Spotting a loose power cord for one of the computers, Sarah grabbed it. Before Thompson could react, she doubled it over, holding the ends and swinging the resulting two feet of heavy-duty power cord. Thompson eyed the cord warily. They circled each other, Sarah with the power cord and Lillian Thompson with the knife, looking for an opening. Thompson suddenly lunged at Sarah, hoping to startle her; but Sarah easily moved out of the way, simultaneously slashing Thompson's forearm with the cord. The knife clattered to the floor. Thompson looked down, and then at Sarah, knowing that Sarah would be on her before she could pick it up.

Sarah moved forward, the cord swinging in her hand. All thoughts of escape had vanished, she wanted to kill. Thompson saw the anger burning in her eyes and for the first time she felt fear.

Sarah feigned a blow and Thompson stepped backwards into a table. Seeing her momentarily startled, Sarah lashed out savagely. The cord struck the side of Thompson's face. She screamed in pain and fell to the floor. In a flash, Sarah grabbed the knife, intending to jump onto the woman but Thompson rolled to one side and leapt to her feet. Sarah was a fraction slow to react and Thompson was able to grab her from behind. In an instant, Sarah found herself in a chokehold. Feeling her air cut off, she flailed wildly in a vain attempt to break the woman's grip, but the woman's massive forearms only tightened further around her neck. Knowing she was only seconds from uncon-sciousness, Sarah desperately plunged the knife back over her left shoulder. She felt resistance and assumed she had struck Thompson's arm. Feeling the woman's grip weaken, Sarah wrenched herself free and turned toward her. The knife was impaled to the hilt in the woman's left eye. Thompson staggered momentarily and then collapsed. She was dead before she hit the ground. The blade had penetrated far into her brain.

· · · · · · ·

An hour later, Sarah was standing in Warden Sidney Patterson's office, a guard on each side. Patterson was seated behind her desk. Doreen Matlock was leaning against the wall.

They were both visibly angry—for two entirely different reasons. Patterson was angry that someone had been killed in "her" prison. Matlock was furious that Sarah had somehow thwarted the attempt to kill her; which meant she wouldn't be paid.

"Okay Andrews. What happened?" demanded Patterson.

"She attacked me with a knife," replied Sarah, not volunteering any detail.

"What were you doing in the library alone?"

"Assistant Warden Matlock asked me to see if I could fix the library server."

Patterson looked over at Matlock with surprise. "Is that true?"

Matlock just nodded.

"And you left her alone?"

"I didn't think she'd do anything," replied Matlock. "It seems I was wrong."

Patterson studied Matlock. "And who is Lillian Thompson and why was *she* in the library?"

"She was transferred in from Gravenhurst Prison yesterday. She's a lifer."

"Why was she transferred?" asked Patterson, increasingly suspicious.

"File wasn't clear. Apparently some problems with another inmate."

"How come *she* was in the library?"

"No idea," replied Matlock, resentful that she was being questioned.

Patterson looked back at Sarah. "You say she just appeared and came at you with a knife?"

Sarah nodded.

"Did she say anything?"

Sarah shook her head. She remembered the woman's statement about someone wanting her dead, but instinct made her keep quiet.

"Okay Andrews. For now you can go." Looking at the guards, Patterson added, "Take her back to her cell."

"What?" exclaimed Matlock, as Sarah was led away. "Andrews should be charged. She killed the woman! There's not a shred of evidence to support her contention that it was self-defense."

Patterson studied Matlock for a long time. "What reason would Andrews have? Thompson transferred here just yesterday? Pretty damn coincidental. She shows up at the library when Sarah's there alone. Another coincidence? That knife was no homemade shiv. Someone slipped it to her. She outweighs Andrews by fifty pounds. It was a planned hit. I'm just surprised Andrews came out alive."

· · · · · · ·

Back in her own office, Matlock closed the door and placed a call to Kurt.

"Done?" he asked immediately.

"No."

"What happened?"

"Your Lillian Thompson fucked up. Andrews took her out."

"It's not possible. Thompson's an experienced killer."

"*Was* an experienced killer. Now she's a corpse."

"How?"

"Damned if I know. I set it up like you asked. I get Andrews alone in the library. Tell her the server's down. Then I slip Thompson the knife and send her in. I don't hear anything. An hour later, I go back to the library. Thompson's dead on the floor—the knife buried in her eyeball. Andrews is sitting there calmly, waiting for me. Tells me she's fixed the server."

"That's impossible!"

"Thompson's dead. Andrews is alive."

"Shit. Can you get her charged?"

"I tried. Patterson's having none of it. She's suspicious. Realizes Thompson's transfer was odd. Knows someone must have arranged for them both to be in the library at the same time. Figures that someone slipped Thompson the knife. I think she suspects I had something to do with it. Looked at me real strange."

"Don't worry. Sit tight and let it blow over. We've got time."

· · · · · · ·

The next afternoon, Sarah's killing of Lillian Thompson was the topic of discussion throughout the exercise yard. Even Marcia Madigan came over to her. "Well, Andrews. You're big news today. How the hell did you do it?"

Sarah shrugged. "I guess I got lucky."

Marcia looked at her quizzically. "You could say that again. Thompson's killed a lot of people—tougher than you."

Sarah just shrugged.

"So why does someone want you dead?"

"What do you mean?"

"The word is that Lillian Thompson was deliberately put in here to take you out."

Sarah recalled Thompson's comment that someone wanted her dead. "No idea," she replied calmly.

Later, Sarah asked Valerie about it. "Why would someone want to kill me?"

For a while, Valerie did not reply. "You know how you were framed by those cops?" she said finally. "What they did to you while you were in custody. What you know about their taking the money. Remember how you told me you had seen Lindsay and Carney talking after the trial? Maybe they're afraid you might talk when you get out? Maybe... Oh God, Sarah."

Sarah remained silent. Was it possible they were trying to kill her? She hadn't thought about it before but it made sense. She was still a threat to them. It was a terrifying thought.

Valerie looked at her with an expression of concern. "What were you doing in the library?"

"Matlock sent me there. Said the server was down and wanted me to look at it."

"And that's when Thompson showed up?"

"Oh God!" Sarah replied, realizing the implications. "You think Matlock's involved?"

"I don't know," replied, Valerie hugging her. "I hope not."

Sarah shivered. If the cops were trying to kill her and the Assistant Warden was involved, what could she possibly do? If they wanted her dead, they'd find a way. When she had first been brought to the prison, she'd wanted to die. Now, to her surprise, she found she had a fierce will to live.

CHAPTER 14

TWO DAYS LATER VALERIE WAS NOT AT THEIR USUAL MEETING place in the exercise yard. Puzzled and concerned, Sarah walked around the yard looking for her. While the yard was roughly rectangular, a subsequent addition to the main prison building had created a projection that partially blocked off a back corner. Because of its seclusion, Marcia Madigan and her friends usually hung out there and staked claim to the area. The occasional newbie who, unaware of this custom, wandered into "Marcia's territory" emerged badly beaten for her blunder.

As Sarah approached the corner, she heard screams. Valerie! She ran around the corner and saw Valerie lying on the ground. Two of Marcia's friends were holding her legs apart and Marcia was kneeling between them.

Without thinking of the consequences, Sarah ran toward her friend. "Let her go!"

Startled and angered at the interruption, Marcia stood up. "Move along Andrews. This is none of your business."

"Let her go," Sarah replied firmly.

"Big mistake Andrews." Marcia and her two friends left Valerie lying on the ground and moved toward Sarah, clearly intending to inflict some serious pain. From the corner of her eye, Sarah saw Valerie struggle to her feet and stand there uncertainly.

"Run, Valerie!" Sarah ordered as the three women advanced toward her, their eyes gleaming with vicious excitement.

Just then, attracted by the screams, two guards came around the corner with their guns drawn.

"Move along, Madigan," ordered one of the guards, guessing roughly what was occurring. "You too," she added to Marcia's friends.

As Marcia slowly walked past Sarah, she whispered in her ear. "You'll regret this Andrews. And so will your friend Yuen. Nobody messes with me. Not even the guards."

After Marcia left, Sarah went over to Valerie. "Are you okay?"

"I think so," replied Valerie forcing a weak smile. "Another few minutes and I'm not sure I would have been. God I hate that woman."

"What happened?"

Valerie sighed miserably. "She wants me to move into her cell. I'm sure you can guess why. My cellmate was transferred and hers was just released. We both need new bunkies. If I request it, they'll move me, but I don't want to move in with her. Marcia knows that and is trying to 'persuade' me."

"Jesus. Can't you get the guards to help?"

"You've been here long enough. The guards don't give a shit. It's the law of the jungle."

"Is there anything *I* can do?" asked Sarah, worried for her friend.

"No. I'll just have to do what she wants. It's the only way I'll get out of here alive."

Sarah had an inspiration. "My cellmate, Ethel Walters is getting out in a couple of days. What if you moved in with me?"

Valerie brightened slightly. "Maybe that would work. If I bunk with you, Marcia would be pissed, but there is nothing she can do. She'd probably give me a hard time for a while and then go pick on someone else."

"It would be so great to have you," added Sarah, excited at the prospect. "I don't think Ethel has said more than ten words since I've been here."

Valerie hugged Sarah. "I'd love it. By the way, thanks for what you did back there. It was very brave. I just hope Marcia doesn't do anything."

"Don't worry about it. I'll just carry around my bucket."

They both laughed.

· · · · · · ·

That night, just before lights out, two guards appeared at Sarah's cell and unlocked the door. "Okay Andrews, come on out!" they ordered.

"What's going on?" Sarah asked anxiously.

"It's the hole for you, Andrews. Five days!"

Sarah was terrified. Officially known as solitary, but unofficially known as 'the hole', it was the most severe punishment that could be meted out. The hole was a tiny unfurnished cell in the sub-basement, without heat or light. The usual sentence to the hole was forty-eight hours. Five days was unheard of. "I didn't do anything!" Sarah begged frantically.

"Matlock's orders. Fighting in the yard," the guard replied indifferently.

"Does the Warden know you're doing this?" asked Sarah in desperation.

"Just move it, Andrews! The Warden doesn't need to know about every con that gets the hole."

The guards forced Sarah down three long flights of stairs into the sub-basement where they entered a narrow corridor that sloped further downwards. The floors and walls changed from concrete to stone. The stone was cold and wet and the air was dank. Northbridge Prison had been build almost a hundred years ago on top of the ruins of an eighteenth-century prison. They were now in the foundations of the original jail.

They went down still more stairs to another corridor. The silence was broken only by the sound of their shoes echoing through the narrow musty corridor. It was obvious no one ever came down here. Finally, they reached a small iron door only four feet high. One of the guards unlocked the heavy bolt and opened the door.

"Here's your new home, dearie," said the guard. "Have a look before we close the door because this is the last light you'll see for five days. See that hole in the floor, that's the potty. Don't fall in. There's a bucket of water by the door and you'll find some hunks of bread in a box near the water. Use it sparingly. That's all you get until you're out."

Sarah looked through the door, horrified by what she saw. The room was tiny, barely four-feet by five-feet and less than five feet high. Apart from the hole in the floor and the bucket and box by the door, the room was totally empty. No bed, no blanket, nothing. Oh God, she couldn't survive in there for five days.

"Please," she begged futilely. "I can't go in there."

"Sure you can," replied one of the guards. "Now your clothes."

"What?" asked Sarah in alarm.

"No clothes are allowed in solitary. Don't want you hanging yourself. But don't worry, there's no one around to see you."

"You'll find it a little chilly though," sneered the other guard.

Sarah slowly stripped off her dress and handed it to the guard. "And your underwear." demanded the guard. Flushing, Sarah stripped off her bra and panties.

"In you go. Sweet dreams. Just hope we remember to come and get you."

Fearfully, Sarah ducked through the doorway. The guards slammed the door and Sarah heard them draw the heavy bolt across the outside of the door. Everything went black. She straightened up only to hit her head on the low ceiling. Sarah listened for the guards but heard nothing. In the utter silence, she was sure she could hear her heart beating.

Fighting her panic, Sarah felt around the tiny cell to get oriented. The walls and floor were stone, distinctly cold and damp. She found the hole in the floor the guards had told her about. The foul odor of decomposing fecal matter made her stomach churn. By touch, Sarah found the water bucket and box of bread. She felt for the door and found it. She pushed against it. It didn't budge.

When the shock began to wear off, Sarah realized she was cold. The room was barely sixty degrees and damp. With no clothes, Sarah was already beginning to shiver. Surely, they'd give her a blanket. She pounded on the door.

"I'm freezing. Can I at least have a blanket? Pleeeeease!" But there was no response. She was totally alone. She could die in here and no one would know. Sarah sat down, cringing as her naked buttocks came into contact with the cold stone floor. She wrapped her arms tightly around her knees and put her head down in a vain attempt to ward off the chill that was already seeping into her bones.

In time, Sarah fell into a fitful sleep. She awoke later to find her body stiff from the dampness and cold. Shivering uncontrollably, she stood up only to hit her head again. Crouching over, she tried to walk to generate some body heat, but the cell was too small to move around. She wondered how long she'd been there. There was no way of telling but it was probably only a few hours. She couldn't possibly survive five days.

· · · · · · ·

The days passed. With her sleep patterns disrupted by the constant darkness, Sarah soon lost any sense of time. Images passed through her mind, leaving her unsure whether they were dreams or hallucinations. She remembered times from her childhood. Her excitement when her father had bought her first bicycle. Her sadness as she watched her mother's capabilities inexorably diminished by Alzheimer's. She thought of the library and the look of gratitude in some of the children's eyes when she took the interest in their dreams that their parents never had. She remembered the date with Paul Taylor. The look in his eyes that said she mattered to him, the feel of his arm around her shoulders. Then the pleasant thoughts were crowded out by the horrors of her arrest. The paralyzing agony of the taser. The grinning faces of Peter Lindsay, John Gordon, Ernie Kramer, Chris LePan, Tom Miller and Frank Carlucci. She could still see the lust and cruelty in their eyes. Then came more recent memories of prison, Marcia, Valerie, Rose, being put into the dryer, the fight with Lillian Thompson. The images blurred together until Sarah was sure she was going insane.

She eventually exhausted the last of her food and water. Thirst, first just an annoyance, became a constant torment. In desperation, she tried sucking on the stone walls of the cell, hoping to extract some relief from the dampness. She listened constantly for some sound outside the door. They must be coming to get her soon! But there was only unending silence. Sarah became convinced that she had been there much longer than five days. They must have forgotten about her. Suddenly, a horrible thought occurred to her. Since the attempt by Lillian Thompson had failed, perhaps they were just going to leave her there to die. If that was to be her fate, she hoped death would take her soon—and bring an end to the cold, the thirst and the devastating isolation.

Yet she wanted to feel the warmth of the sun once more, to hear the birds sing. She wanted to see her father again, laugh with Valerie, feel Paul's arm around her and look into his blue eyes. Somewhere deep within her, Sarah found a reservoir of strength and determination that she had never known existed. With renewed resolve, she fought against the growing delirium and despair. She would survive.

· · · · · · ·

Five days later, the two guards went back to release her. Two days in the hole was usually enough to break the toughest inmate; they would crawl out broken and whimpering. They reached the tiny door and unlocked it, peering into the darkness. To their absolute astonishment, Sarah stepped out as soon as they opened the door. She straightened up slowly and blinked momentarily from the sudden light. Then she looked at them and smiled, before calmly following them back to her cell.

In the yard the next day, the inmates gathered around Sarah, astonished at her seeming lack of any ill effects.

"How was it?" asked one of the inmates

"It wasn't so bad," replied Sarah. "No bells, no work period, it was actually kind of peaceful."

Sarah immediately looked for Valerie. When she didn't see her in their usual spot by the wall, she asked one of other inmates.

"Didn't you hear?" the woman replied with surprise. "Her cell was torched two nights ago. When they finally put the fire out, she was dead."

Valerie Yuen was the best friend she'd ever had in her life. She couldn't be dead! "Valerie?" asked Sarah in anguish.

"I'm so sorry," the woman replied, sympathetically. "I know you two were friends. I thought someone must have told you."

Sarah staggered over to an isolated part of the prison wall, slumped down onto the ground and sobbed and sobbed.

After a time, Sarah began to regain her composure. It was Marcia Madigan. It must have been. She remembered Marcia's threat. Her grief turned to an icy anger. Getting to her feet, Sarah went to the secluded corner where Marcia usually hung out.

"You murdered her, you fucking bitch!"

Marcia looked up in astonishment. Nobody ever talked to her like that. "Calm down, Andrews. I didn't kill anyone."

"Valerie Yuen. You killed her because she wouldn't move in with you, because she was my friend. You had me put in the hole and then you killed her!"

By now, the whole prison yard was watching the exchange in disbelief, even the guards. No one had ever stood up to Marcia that way.

"If you don't watch your mouth, baby, you'll get the same."

"We'll see," replied Sarah in an icy tone. "We'll see."

• • • • • • •

At two the following morning, Marcia Madigan awoke in her cell with a start. Certain that something had wakened her, she raised her head and looked around. Nothing. Then she became conscious of a strong smell of gasoline. She realized her bedclothes, mattress and nightgown were soaked and there was a quarter of an inch of gasoline on the floor of her cell. That instant she knew! Then she saw her. Sarah was standing outside the cell door holding a lighter in her hand.

"Whoa, baby, don't do this." Marcia cried out frantically.

Sarah simply looked back at her with an eerie calm. She flicked the lighter and held it, watching the flame flicker, so tiny, so deadly. Madigan too watched the flame, knowing with horrible certainty what was going to happen. Suddenly Sarah tossed the lighter through the bars and, instantly, the cell became an inferno. Marcia screamed in agony as her nightclothes caught fire. She lurched desperately toward the cell door, frantic to escape the raging flames. But the lock held firm. As she lost consciousness, the last thing Marcia saw was Sarah Andrews standing there, watching, a gentle smile on her face.

• • • • • • •

By the time the guards arrived, Marcia's body was just a charred hulk still huddled against the door and Sarah Andrews was fast asleep in her cell with the door locked.

Because of the incident in the yard, Sarah was the prime suspect in Marcia's death. However, the investigation concluded that Sarah could not have done it, as she hadn't been out of her cell all night. The cell doors were controlled by the prison computer that produced an automated log of all activity. According to the computer, Sarah's cell door had not been opened from nine the previous night until seven that morning.

What they did not know is that weeks ago, Sarah had figured out how to hack into the prison network using the computer in the library. The day of the fire, she had simply slipped into the library before dinner and modified the program it so both her cell door and Marcia's would automatically unlock for twenty minutes at 2 a.m. without being logged. Earlier, she had taken the gasoline from the generator room attached to the laundry and hid it behind the boxes of laundry soap in the laundry.

. . . .

While the prison officials concluded Sarah couldn't have been responsible, the inmates all knew she'd done it. Those in the cell opposite Marcia's had seen Sarah standing there watching the flames. Others had seen her in the corridor that ran outside the cells. However, no one said anything. Not only was there an unwritten but inviolate rule never to squeal, but Marcia had been feared and hated throughout the prison and they were happy to see her gone.

In the two months she had been in prison, Sarah had killed Rose Dutton, Lillian Thompson and Marcia Madigan. Three months ago, the thought that she could kill anyone would have seemed absurd. Now it seemed almost normal.

The fact that Andrews had killed three people and survived the hole was well-known among the inmates. In the prison hierarchy, that put her on top. The other prisoners would nod as she passed or offer a, "How's it goin, Andrews?" Even the guards acknowledged her presence.

Sarah sensed the respect and subconsciously enjoyed it. She had changed a lot from the terrified young woman who had entered the prison gates two months ago. Deep within her, she was conscious of a simmering anger. Powerful, explosive and barely controllable. She wasn't sure where it had come from. Perhaps it had always been there. Perhaps it had been newly formed in response to the horrors she experienced. Whatever the source, it gave her a sense of inner confidence and strength she had never known.

CHAPTER 15

BEFORE SHE KNEW IT, SARAH'S SCHEDULED RELEASE DATE was only two weeks away. When she had first arrived, the three-month sentence seemed like an eternity. She never thought about what awaited her on the other side. Now she began to reflect on the world beyond the prison walls and wonder what life held for her. What would she do? She couldn't imagine going back to the Glenwood Library. *I've been in prison for narcotics possession, but now I'd like my job back.* What work could she get with a criminal record? Would her apartment still be there? How would she pay the rent? Would her father still be alive? How could she possibly explain her absence to him?

Sarah wished with all her heart that Valerie was still alive. They'd had such plans; they were going to get an apartment together, take courses together. She remembered Valerie's quick smile and gentle laugh. The memories made her happy and sad at the same time. She missed her terribly.

Every day, Sarah checked the mail for a reply from Paul Taylor—but it never came. Had her letter gone astray? Was he still out of the country? Did he ever think of her? Had he been frightened off by her disclosure? The uncertainty was unbearable. Summoning up her courage, Sarah wrote another letter.

> Dear Paul,
>
>> I wrote to you several weeks ago and I hoped you would write back. I had such a great time with you at dinner and I want so much to see you again. Perhaps telling you that I am in prison caused you not to write. Perhaps you just don't think it will work between us. Perhaps, and I can only hope this is the reason, you did not receive my letter. If it's my being in prison that concerns you, you just have to give me a chance to explain. If, after that, you don't want to see me again, I will accept it. But could you please write and tell me that so at least I know.
>
>> Your Lady of the Books,
>
>> Sarah

Sarah re-read the letter, closed her eyes and prayed, and dropped it into the outgoing mailbox.

· · · · · · ·

A day later, Doreen Matlock took another call from Kurt. "Any developments?"

"Andrews took out another inmate. A two hundred and fifty pound lifer who had ruled the place since she'd been here—until she messed with Sarah. We found her torched in her cell."

"Jesus."

"Your *librarian* is something else. Looks harmless, but she's deadly."

"Her release date's in less than two weeks. We don't want her getting out."

"Nothing else I can do. The Warden's watching me like a hawk."

"Okay. Okay. We'll deal with her after she's released."

"Good luck. You'll need it."

"Anyone been visiting her?"

"Not a single visit."

"Get any letters?"

"Nope."

"Write any?"

"A couple. I destroyed them, like you asked."

"Good. Do you remember who they were addressed to?"

"No. Some guy I think. You said just destroy them."

"All right. Thanks. If anything develops, call me."

· · · · · · ·

One day, Sarah saw a young girl sitting alone in the yard, crying. Sarah hadn't seen her before and assumed she was new. Remembering her own difficult first days, Sarah went over and sat down beside her. "You okay?" she asked.

The girl looked up hesitantly, but said nothing.

"The first few days are the worst," Sarah offered, putting her arm around the girl. "It will get better, not great, but better."

The girl smiled slightly, grateful for any gesture of friendship.

"What's your name?" asked Sarah.

"Donna, Donna Baker," the girl replied.

"Mine's Sarah." Noting the fresh bruises on the girl's arms, Sarah continued. "What happened?"

"They put me in the dryer and turned it on," Donna replied tearfully.

"Who did?" asked Sarah, holding her.

"There were a bunch of them. Riley, Cartwright and some others."

Sarah nodded sadly. "I know who you mean."

"They said they'd do it again tomorrow. Said they'd put it on the heavy-duty cycle. I couldn't bear it again. It was horrible," Donna blurted out, breaking into sobs.

Sarah remembered the terror she had felt when she had been thrown into the dryer. Her eyes hardened with quiet determination. "Let's go talk to them."

"What do you mean?" asked Donna, looking at Sarah in surprise.

Sarah smiled. "I mean, I'll tell them you're a friend of mine and ask them not to do it again."

"Are you sure?" replied Donna. Sarah did not seem that big or strong. What could she do against Riley and the others?

Sarah stood and took Donna's hand, pulling her to her feet. "I'm sure."

The two of them found Riley and her cronies chatting in another corner of the yard.

"Hi girls," Sarah began.

"Hi Andrews, what's up?" replied Alice Cartwright.

"Just wanted you to meet a newbie here. Her name's Donna."

"Yeah, we already met her," replied Riley, maliciously. "Heavy duty cycle for you tomorrow, Donna."

Sarah looked steadily at Riley. "Donna's a friend of mine."

Riley immediately understood. The other women watched to see how she would respond.

"Everyone goes through the dryer initiation. You did."

Sarah shrugged. "Things change."

"And some things don't..."

"Well this does," replied Sarah coldly, holding Riley's gaze.

"Who says?"

"It stops now, Riley. You too, Cartwright. No more putting newbies in the dryer."

"Hold on, Andrews. You can't…"

"It's over, Riley."

Riley looked at Sarah trying to decide how to respond. Sarah didn't look that formidable, but Riley occupied the cell just down the corridor from where Marcia Madigan had been burned alive. Marcia's screams of agony still haunted her. No one had ever figured out how Sarah had got out of her cell to set the fire, but everyone knew she had. If she'd done it once, she could do it again. As well as Madigan, Sarah had killed Rose Dutton and Lillian Thompson, both large and powerful woman. In all, Andrews had taken the lives of three inmates in less than three months. Andrews may not look like a killer, but Riley was not about to take a chance. "All right, Andrews. You got it."

"Thanks, Riley. I appreciate it."

"No hard feelings, Donna?" continued Riley.

"It's okay," replied Donna timidly.

Sarah led Donna away, back to another part of the wall. "See. That wasn't so hard."

"Thank you so much," said Donna fighting back tears of gratitude. It was the first kindness she had been shown since coming to prison.

"It was nothing," replied Sarah, putting her arm around her. "Let me know if there is any more trouble."

· · · · · · ·

The next day in the yard, Sarah saw Donna sitting alone again by the wall and went over to her. "How'd it go this morning?"

Donna looked up and smiled, pleased at the company. "A lot better. They were even nice to me."

"I'm glad."

Sensing some uncertainty, Sarah continued. "What's up?"

"They told me you've killed three women since you've been here?"

Sarah smiled. "Sounds a lot worse than it was. One tried to kill me first. One was making my life hell when I first got here and the other killed the best friend I've ever had in my life."

"But you killed them?"

Sarah just nodded.

"And you survived the hole for five days?"

Sarah laughed. "You've been checking up on me."

Donna said nothing but looked at Sarah with a mixture of fear and awe.

"Donna, I need to go and talk to some people. Let me know if you have any more problems. Okay?"

Donna nodded and smiled sadly, sensing that Sarah didn't want to be friends.

Privately Sarah worried about what would happen once she left. She knew Riley and Cartwright resented her intervention on Donna's behalf, and once she was no longer around to protect her, they might make Donna's life hell—or worse. Spending time with Donna during her last few days might only make it worse.

· · · · · · ·

With his appointment to Deputy Chief, Lindsay had moved out of the Sixth Precinct to the Police Headquarters Building amid mounting speculation he was in line for Chief Moorby's job.

A week before Sarah's release, Lindsay summoned John Gordon, Ernie Kramer, Frank Carlucci, Chris LePan and Tom Miller to his office at the Police Headquarters Building. When the five of them arrived, Lindsay's executive assistant showed them to an adjoining conference room and asked them to wait until Lindsay could join them.

"Hey John, what do you think Lindsay wants?" asked Kramer.

"No idea."

Maybe he just wants to show off his fancy digs?" suggested LePan, gesturing to the lavish furnishings.

"Think we could steal a couple of chairs for the squad room?" Miller asked.

"Wouldn't match the decor," replied Kramer.

"Didn't know we had decor."

Finally, Lindsay entered, carefully closed the door and sat down at the head of the table.

"So how's the Sixth Precinct?" Lindsay asked.

"Same old," replied Gordon. "How's Police Headquarters?"

Lindsay smiled slightly. "Better furniture."

"We noticed. Any chance you could get me a new filing cabinet?" asked Miller sarcastically. "I've requested one but was informed that the department can't afford it. The drawers stick on the one I've got. Have to use a screw driver to open it."

"Surprised you were able to requisition a screwdriver," commented LePan.

"I wasn't. That got turned down too. Had to bring my own."

"Knock it off," replied Lindsay slightly annoyed. Since his promotion, he had become used to more deference, and their residual familiarity irritated him. "We've got a problem that concerns everyone in this room," he continued.

The others turned serious and waited expectantly.

Lindsay continued. "You men remember a Sarah Andrews you picked up as part of that big drug raid four months ago?"

"Yeah, what of it?" replied Kramer.

"She's about to get out of prison."

Miller looked at Lindsay with concern. "I thought you were going to arrange for an accident."

"I did. Arranged for an experienced killer to take her out. What happens? This Sarah Andrews kills the woman."

"No way," exclaimed Carlucci in disbelief. "She was a fucking librarian, afraid of her own shadow."

"She not only killed the woman who was supposed to eliminate her," Lindsay continued, "she killed two other inmates. One had her head caved in with a bucket, the other was torched in her cell."

LePan laughed in disbelief. "She's one hell of a librarian."

Miller grinned. "Better check your place for any overdue library books."

"At least I can read."

Gordon turned to Lindsay. "There must be some mistake. She couldn't have weighed more than a hundred and thirty pounds. When we brought her in, she was totally petrified. There's no way the woman I remember could take out three cons."

"There's no mistake," replied Lindsay firmly.

"Okay. So she's a survivor," commented Kramer. "What of it?"

Lindsay paused for a moment, looking at each of them individually in turn to underscore the severity of the situation. "She's no dummy. She's a university grad and there's a good chance she's put it all together and realized we were skimming the money. And now, it looks like she's also found some backbone. Once she's out, she's a walking time bomb—for all of us."

"Who's going to believe her?" Kramer replied.

"That's where we have a problem," replied Lindsay. "I didn't know this until I became Deputy Chief, but about five months ago, right after Costanza's death, the SIU installed video cameras in the Backfield Building's interrogation rooms. Everything that goes on is recorded and filed. There are thousands of hours of tape. Actually, it's on disk. It's not reviewed unless there's a complaint; but if our Sarah Andrews makes a stink, the disk will be pulled and everything that happened that night will be on display."

Miller looked at Lindsay in astonishment. "Holy shit!"

"Shit is right," replied Lindsay. "The disk will show not just what we did to her, but all the discussions we had – the money, about framing her for possession, getting Carney to persuade her to plead guilty, about her never getting out of prison."

There was stunned silence around the room as they all realized the exposure was huge. Theft, perjury, falsifying evidence. If this blew up it meant serious jail time. And the life of a cop in jail, if he survived at all, was brutal.

Kramer looked at Lindsay with growing concern. "You're the Deputy Chief. You must have access. Can't you just get the disk and destroy it?"

"Not even the Chief has access," replied Lindsay. "Just the SIU itself, which reports directly to the Police Commission."

"Fuck! We're toast," commented LePan.

Lindsay paused for emphasis before replying. "We're only toast if the disk is pulled. And the disk will only be pulled if Andrews files a complaint. And she can only file a complaint if she's alive."

The room was silent as they absorbed the implication of Lindsay's statement.

"Here's her release date and the address of her apartment," Lindsay continued, handing a sheet of paper to Gordon. "You guys created this little problem. Can I leave it to you to solve it—permanently—and discreetly?"

Gordon didn't take the paper. "Peter. Do we really need to do this?"

Lindsay exploded. "What do you mean? This is your mess in the first place."

"I know. And I'm sorry. I just don't think she is likely to pursue this. She's not the type."

Lindsay stared at Gordon angrily. "And you want to take that chance? You want the rest of us to take that chance — due to your screw-up?"

"Christ John," LePan interjected angrily. "She can destroy us all."

"John," added Miller, more gently. "We got into this together, we have to clean it up together."

"If you hadn't left the briefcase in the car, we wouldn't be in this situation," Kramer added. "What about all that stuff you're always giving us about holding the line."

Gordon sighed.

"John," LePan continued. "Besides. She took the damn briefcase. This will give us another chance to get it back. Maybe you can still buy that retirement home in Florida."

Gordon finally took the paper from Lindsay's hand.

Lindsay put his arm on Gordon's shoulder. "I know this is a tough one, and I respect your feelings. But this is the right thing to do. Let's just get it cleaned up and behind us."

· · · · · · ·

The morning of her release, one of the guards came to Sarah's cell. "Warden wants to see you. Come with me."

Anxiously, Sarah followed the guard to Patterson's office.

"Leave us," Patterson instructed the guard, when Sarah was seated opposite her desk.

"You want me to cuff her?" the guard asked.

"No. Please wait outside," Patterson replied.

Sarah waited, wondering what was happening.

Patterson smiled. "Congratulations. When you arrived here, I didn't think you'd make it to this day."

"Neither did I," Sarah replied, relieved to find there was no problem with her release.

"You've changed a lot."

Sarah nodded. "I guess I had to."

Patterson smiled slightly. "You know, I'm still curious about how someone was able to torch Marcia Madigan's cell in the middle of the night."

Sarah shrugged. "Maybe there's a bug in the computer program that controls the cell doors."

Patterson smiled. "Maybe." Becoming more serious, she continued. "Do you know what you're going to do?"

Sarah shook her head. "No."

"I've read your file. You weren't guilty, were you?"

"No."

"The officers involved—Lindsay, Gordon and the others. And that lawyer Carney—You're not the only one they've done this to."

Sarah looked at the Warden, wondering where the conversation was going. She saw an unexpected trace of sadness and resignation in Patterson's expression. "How do they keep getting away with it?" Sarah asked.

"I don't know. Lindsay's a friend of the mayor and they say he'll be appointed Chief of Police soon. The system isn't perfect. "

"Is there nothing that can be done about it?"

"Sarah," Patterson continued, ignoring the question. "You know something that frightens them. You could still be in danger."

Sarah looked at Patterson curiously. Beneath the Warden's tough demeanor, she realized the woman truly cared. "I know. I'll be careful."

"If you have nothing holding you here, you might move to another state."

"I've thought about it. My father's in a local nursing home. I'm his only remaining family."

"I wish I could do more for you."

"You've done a lot. Thank you."

Patterson nodded.

"There is one more thing you could do," continued Sarah on a sudden impulse.

"What is it?"

"There's a new girl I met in the prison yard, Donna Baker."

"I've seen the name."

"I think Donna's one of those who shouldn't be here."

"I'm sorry, but there's nothing I can do."

"I know. It's not that. It's just that she was having trouble with some of the other inmates. You know, Riley, Cartwright and that group."

"I know them," Patterson replied with a frown.

"I asked them to let her alone, but I'm afraid of what they'll do once I'm gone."

"I'll look after it."

"Thank you."

Warden Patterson rose and reached out to shake Sarah's hand. "Good luck, Sarah."

Sarah took her hand. "Thank you, Warden. For everything."

Sarah was given five hundred dollars and a taxi voucher to anywhere she wanted to go. She told the cab driver to take her back to her apartment. Sitting in the back seat, she looked out the window at the rolling countryside. The sky was blue and the fields were green with ripening crops. The cab passed over the same creek that Sarah had seen on the way in. It had only been three months ago, yet it felt like another time. Things were different now. *She* was different.

As Sarah watched the scenery pass, she reflected on Patterson's warning. She had no way of knowing that Gordon and his men were already preparing to eliminate their "little problem" and that Paul Taylor was back in the country trying to find her.

CHAPTER 16

PAUL TAYLOR HAD ARRIVED BACK IN THE COUNTRY JUST THE day before Sarah was released and didn't reach his house on Crystal Lake until eleven at night. He'd had a local farmer periodically check his house and board Talisker. Paul debated picking him up, but given the hour, decided to wait until morning.

It was good to be back. He wandered down to the dock and looked out over the lake. The water glistened invitingly in the moonlight. Slipping off his clothes, Paul dove into the shimmering blackness, reveling in the silky feel of the water against his skin. He stroked powerfully away from shore, not stopping until he was almost two hundred yards from the dock. He paused, looking back at the lights from his house, glowing gently in the distance. He remained there for several minutes, a tiny figure floating serenely in the vastness of the lake, enjoying the solitude and the feeling of being home. Eventually, he swam back to the dock, hoisted himself up and then lay there, letting the warm night air dry him before putting his clothes back on.

Back in the house, he poured himself a scotch and settled into one of the lounge chairs on the deck. As usual, his thoughts turned to Sarah. He imagined her sitting there with him, watching the stars and listening to the trees rustle softly in the evening breeze. The thought made him go back into the house and check his mail. He flipped indifferently through over three months' accumulation of letters, magazines and flyers, hoping for something from Sarah. Maybe a reply to the letter he had written from Columbia. Nothing. He checked his answering machine that had long ago exhausted the room for messages. Again, nothing. No emails either. Disappointed and vaguely uneasy, he thought about phoning her. Realizing it was almost midnight, he reluctantly decided to wait until the next day.

. . . .

At eight the next morning, Paul phoned Sarah's apartment, wanting to catch her before she left for work. To his surprise, a recorded announcement advised him the number was no longer in service. He re-dialed the number to confirm he had dialed correctly, only to hear the announcement again. He tried the cell phone number he had for her, only to find it had been deactivated. Feeling a deepening sense of concern, he decided to drive into the city. If she wasn't at her apartment, he would go to the Glenwood Library.

Two hours later, he pulled up in front of Sarah's building, climbed the three flights of stairs to her apartment and knocked. After a long interval, he knocked again. Finally, a middle-aged woman opened the door and peered at him, obviously irritated at the interruption. She was wearing a bathrobe and her hair was disheveled.

"Sorry to disturb you. I'm looking for Sarah Andrews."

"Never heard of her," the woman replied in a raspy voice, moving to close the door.

Holding the door open with his foot, Paul continued pleasantly. "Does anyone else live here besides you?"

The woman simply shook her head, pushing the door more forcefully.

"How long have you lived here?" Paul continued, easily holding the door open.

"Two months. And if you don't leave me alone, I'm calling the cops."

Paul studied her for a moment before concluding she truly knew nothing about Sarah Andrews. "Sorry to bother you," he replied, releasing the door.

Paul then went back down the stairs, found the superintendent's apartment and knocked at his door.

"Are you the superintendent?" he asked when an elderly man appeared at the doorway.

"Yes. Steve Harris. Are you looking for an apartment?"

"No. Paul Taylor. I'm a friend of Sarah Andrews. I've been away for several months and just got back. I haven't been able to reach her by phone. I just tried her apartment and there appears to be someone else living there. Do you know how I can get in touch with her?"

Harris shook his head sadly. "I haven't seen her for over three months. She just disappeared one day. I finally had to pack her stuff and rent her apartment to someone else."

Paul couldn't believe what he just heard. "What do you mean disappeared?"

"Just disappeared. Left one day for work and never came back. I phoned the library where she worked. They said she had been at work that day as usual, but had never shown up again. Never called. Nothing. I phoned the nursing home where her father lives. Sarah was always so dutiful about visiting him. I was *sure* they would have seen her; but they said the same thing, that she'd just stopped visiting."

"You said you had to rent her apartment?"

"Yes. I waited more than a month but finally the owner insisted."

"When you cleaned her apartment, did it look like she'd planned to go away?"

"No. There was milk in the fridge and her suitcase was in the closet." Harris looked at Paul with a look of anxiety. "She was such a nice girl. I hope nothing happened to her, but..."

"Did she have any friends or relatives I could check with?"

Harris shook her head. "If she did, I never saw them. She was so devoted to her parents, I don't think she had much of a social life."

"Thanks. I need to find her. If you hear from her, or think of anything else, call me. Here's my card."

Harris looked at Paul Taylor, wondering about their relationship. "Of course."

Paul walked slowly out to his Jeep lost in thought. Sarah had seemed so responsible. It just didn't seem possible that she'd simply walked away from her life, her job, her father. Yet if she had been injured or killed, Steve Harris and the library would have been notified. As he pulled away from the front of Sarah's building, he was vaguely conscious of a cab pulling up and parking in the spot he'd just left, but thought nothing of it. He tried the library where she worked, but the story was the same.

One day she had failed to show up for work and they never heard from her again.

Late that evening, back at Crystal Lake, Paul wandered out to his deck and slumped into one of the lounge chairs, totally dejected. He'd spent the afternoon on the Internet searching for some sign of her. Accident reports, death notices, national online phone directories, popular social networking sites. Nothing. During the months he'd been away, he'd though of her often, and looked forward to picking up where they'd left off. Now it appeared he might never see her again. He resolved to keep looking. Tomorrow, he would go back to the city, talk to Steve Harris again. Maybe Harris had saved some of Sarah's things that might provide a clue. He would go to her father's nursing home, talk to the library staff. People did not just disappear. Whatever had happened to her, he would find out.

Suddenly his phone rang.

. . . .

After the hour-long drive back to the city, the cab driver dropped Sarah at her building. Sarah didn't notice Paul's Jeep pulling out just in front of her. She climbed the three flights to her apartment and pulled out her key. It would be so good to be in her own place again. Of all the things she looked forward to, the biggest was simply the privacy—to shower by herself, to go to the bathroom by herself. In prison, she was never alone. As Sarah went to unlock the door, the key wouldn't turn in the lock. After trying a third time, she went down to the superintendent's apartment and knocked on the door.

"Sarah?" Steve Harris exclaimed in astonishment as soon as he saw her.

"Hi Steve. I had to go away for a while," she replied vaguely.

"Why didn't you tell me? Why didn't you call?"

"Didn't my lawyer call you and pay the rent in advance?"

Harris shook his head sadly. "Nobody called. I tried to reach you. I called your work. They said you hadn't showed up. They had no idea where you were. I tried your father's nursing home. They said you had stopped visiting. Where were you?"

"I'm so sorry, Steve. I couldn't call but I had arranged for someone to contact you and explain and to pay my rent."

"Sarah," Steven Harris replied miserably. "No one called. I waited over a month. Finally, I had to let your apartment go. The owner insisted."

Sarah was shattered. "You mean there's someone living in my apartment?"

"I'm so sorry. If I'd known you were coming back, I would have paid the rent myself. I just didn't know what had happened to you."

"What about my stuff?" Sarah asked desperately.

"The owner insisted I sell the furniture to cover the back rent. I only got five hundred bucks, didn't cover the rent you owed. I put your personal stuff in boxes. It's in the basement. I didn't know what else to do with it. Oh Sarah. I'm so sorry."

"My computer?" she asked, desperately hoping he hadn't sold it.

"Downstairs, too." He smiled, knowing how important it was to her. "The owner would have wanted me to sell it too, but I knew how much you used it. I hoped you might come back someday and I wanted to keep it for you."

"Thank you." Her whole world was on that computer. "You're sure no one called you to explain that I'd be away?"

"No," he replied sadly.

"I need a place to stay. Is there anything you can suggest?"

"There's a cheap hotel down the street. The Colony. I'm sure you could get a room there until you get sorted out. I can keep your stuff here until you find something. I wish I had a vacancy. I'm so sorry."

"It's okay. I'll try the Colony. I might come back tomorrow just to get a few things. Will you be around?"

"All day."

"Thanks, Steve."

"Sarah, I feel so badly. I didn't know what to think."

"Don't worry about it," smiled Sarah. "You saved my computer for me. I couldn't have asked for more.

As she left, he wished he had remembered to tell her about Paul Taylor's visit just minutes earlier. No matter. He would tell her tomorrow when she came back for her things.

. . . .

The Colony was a small, aging hotel just three blocks from Sarah's old apartment. While it had long since lost any pretensions of grandeur, the rooms were clean and cost only forty-nine dollars a night. Once settled in her room, Sarah sat down at the tiny desk and picked up the phone. First, she checked her bank and was relieved to discover she still had three thousand dollars in her bank account, and that her credit card, while overdue to the extent of $500, had not yet been cancelled. At least for a while, money wouldn't be a problem.

She then phoned her boss at the library. George Barnard, the library manager, was pompous and ineffectual and Sarah collected herself for a difficult conversation. When she identified herself, he immediately lectured her for her irresponsibility. He explained she had been terminated for not showing up for work and that the library had magnanimously granted her

a one thousand dollar severance payment that had been transferred with her final pay to her bank account. He emphasized
that in the circumstances, the library didn't really owe her any
severance at all.

"I had to leave town on an emergency," explained Sarah
in vain.

"You could have informed us."

"I arranged for my lawyer to call you and explain the circumstances. He must have forgotten. I'm very sorry."

"It was totally irresponsible behavior. We were short-staffed
for a week," Barnard huffed.

Sarah pondered asking if she could get her job back, but
knew the answer would be no and she didn't want to give him
the satisfaction. She apologized again and hung up.

Arnold Carney! He had promised to phone her landlord,
her work, and her father's nursing home. He hadn't done the
first two and she was certain she would find he hadn't phoned
the nursing home either. The only possible explanation for his
not making the calls was that he never expected her to get out
of prison.

Apprehensively, Sarah dialed the number of her father's
nursing home. As soon as she identified herself, the receptionist asked Sarah to hold while she got the supervisor.

"Is this Ms. Sarah Andrews?" asked the supervisor coming
on the line.

"Yes," Sarah replied nervously.

"And your father's name is Martin Andrews?"

"Yes."

"I'm terribly sorry to have to tell you this, Ms. Andrews
but your father passed away two months ago. He had another
stroke. He knew he was dying. He asked for you. He couldn't

speak, but several times he wrote your name on a piece of paper and thrust it at the nurses, as if begging them to find you. We tried your apartment, your landlord, your employer. No one knew where you were. I'm so terribly sorry. "

The image of her father begging the nurses to find her one last time before he died tore her apart. What had he thought? That she'd been hurt or killed? That she just didn't want to see him anymore? She couldn't bear the thought that he had died that way, alone, frantic, and not knowing. Sarah began to sob uncontrollably.

"I'll have to call you back," she choked into the phone. "I'm sorry."

Sarah lay down on the bed and cried. She cried like she'd never cried before. Her whole body heaved as great wracking sobs overcame her. After a long time, emotionally exhausted, she slipped off her clothes and crawled into bed in her underwear. In moments, she was asleep.

Two hours later, Sarah was jolted awake by the sound of the door being smashed open.

CHAPTER 17

SARAH SAT UP IN FRIGHT AS THREE MEN CHARGED INTO HER room. Before she could react, they had pushed her face down onto the bed and taped her wrists and ankles. Her cry for help was quickly smothered with duct tape. She was then flipped over on her back, and left lying there, helpless and wearing only her underwear.

She recognized them immediately. Frank Carlucci, Ernie Kramer and Chris LePan.

Kramer studied her uncertainly. "Sure it's her?"

"It's her," replied LePan.

"Okay. Let's get her out of here before someone checks on the noise."

Carlucci easily picked her up, slung her over his shoulder, and carried her down the three flights of stairs to the back door of the hotel. The door opened into a narrow laneway where a cargo van was waiting. Sarah was dumped roughly into the back of the van. Carlucci, Kramer and LePan climbed in after her. There were two other men sitting in the front seat. Sarah recognized them instantly—Tom Miller and John Gordon!

"We got her!" yelled Kramer to the men in front. "Let's go."

Sarah lay there helplessly, being bounced around on the hard metal floor as the van sped away. There was no doubt in her mind that they were going to kill her. Having failed to have her killed in prison, they had simply waited until she was released. She was doubtlessly being taken to some remote place where they could dispose of the body.

· · · · · · ·

They traveled for about thirty minutes before coming to a stop. Carlucci opened the rear door and hopped down before picking her up and flinging her over his shoulder. Looking around, upside down, Sarah was sure she must be back in the Warehouse District where she had first been arrested. Carlucci carried her into the nearest building and dropped her onto the floor. Looking up, she saw the five of them, standing there, staring down at her.

"Well, well," began Kramer. "You're quite a survivor."

Carlucci reached down and tore the tape from her ankles before yanking her to her feet. He then ripped the tape from her mouth, leaving her standing before them, still in her underwear, wrists taped behind her back.

Sarah looked around. They were inside a small warehouse consisting of a single large room, roughly fifty feet wide by seventy feet long and at least twelve feet high. The room was empty except for a pile of abandoned equipment along the back wall. There were several windows but they were all boarded over and the only door was the one they had come in through.

"Bet you hoped you'd never see us again?" Carlucci grinned maliciously.

Sarah just stood there silently.

"Nothing to say?"

Sarah simply looked at them with a mixture of fear and hatred.

"I hear you killed three inmates in prison," commented Miller. "Hard to believe, a little thing like you."

"Too bad we didn't bring a taser," Carlucci continued. "You were so cute when we plugged you in. All that dancing and screaming."

"If you're going to kill me, just do it," said Sarah coldly, her anger overcoming her fear.

Carlucci grinned at her. "There's lots of time. Be patient."

Gordon scowled. "Let's do what we came to do and get out of here."

Miller stepped forward and grabbed her chin, forcing her head up. "I think we should ask her where the million dollars went first."

"Good point," added LePan. "How about it, little girl?"

Sarah looked at them all, standing there, leering at her. She hated them. "Fuck you," she replied savagely.

Kramer grinned. "Well, well. Our librarian's getting an attitude."

Suddenly headlights flashed through one of the windows.

"Who the hell could that be?" exclaimed LePan

"Someone's probably just lost," replied Kramer.

"Check it out," ordered Gordon.

As LePan and Kramer moved toward the door, a second set of lights flashed by the window.

"Tom. You watch her!" Gordon commanded. "The rest of you outside and circle the building. Ernie and Chris go left.

Frank and I will go right. I want to know who those lights belong to."

· · · · · · · ·

As the others left, Tom Miller prodded Sarah toward the back of the room with his gun. "Move!"

Sarah walked slowly toward the pile of equipment, assessing her options. If she ever had a chance to escape, it was now while the others were outside; but her hands were taped and he had a gun on her. What could she do?

"Sit down!" ordered Miller when they reached the back of the room.

Sarah sat with her back to one of the pieces of equipment while Miller leaned against the wall.

She studied him. He was a big man, dirty blond hair and blue eyes. His eyes crawled over her naked flesh and she shivered with revulsion. Yet there was some uncertainty in his eyes too. She wasn't sure why—perhaps he was uncomfortable with what they were doing to her.

Looking around, she saw a large wrench lying under some of the equipment. A possible weapon, if she could get her hands free. She discreetly ran her fingers over the equipment behind her, feeling for sharp edges that she could use to cut the tape binding her wrists. Yes! She felt some sort of blade. Now to distract him while she worked her hands free.

"Why are you doing this?" she asked.

"What do you mean?"

"Why are you going to kill me?"

"Dead is dead. What difference does it make?"

"So tell me why."

"You know perfectly well. You're probably a very nice lady. Just shouldn't have been walking around the Warehouse District."

"You don't really think I took that briefcase, do you?"

"Doesn't really matter, does it?"

"Yes it matters. Your friends are going to kill me, and I didn't do anything."

Miller looked at her but did not reply.

"Couldn't you let me go? Tell your friends I escaped."

"Forget it."

"Please." persisted Sarah, sensing a momentary hesitation in Miller's response.

"Stay still!" Miller ordered, detecting the movement as Sarah rubbed her wrists against the equipment.

"I'm sorry," Sarah replied contritely. "The tape is too tight. It's cutting off the circulation in my hands."

Miller shrugged indifferently. "That will be the least of your problems."

"Please. I don't want to die." Sarah felt her wrists come free.

"Enough lady. Not another word." To end the conversation, Miller got off the wall and turned to the door, looking for the others.

Sarah saw her chance. Jumping to her feet, she picked up the wrench and leapt toward Miller. Sensing the unexpected movement, Miller started to turn back to her, but he was too slow. The heavy wrench glanced off his temple and he crumpled to the ground.

Sarah looked around desperately for some route of escape. Going out the door was too risky. The others would be right outside. Then she saw it—a small window at the very top of the back wall. It wasn't boarded over like the others. If she could climb up on the machinery stacked beneath it, she might be able to reach it. Quickly, she ran back to the pile of machinery and began to climb.

She was barely halfway to the window when she heard the others return.

"So who were they?" asked Gordon, not realizing anything was wrong.

"Just a group of teenagers looking for some place to party," replied Kramer. "Told them if they weren't out of here in thirty seconds, they'd spend the night in jail. You should have heard those tires squeal."

Suddenly, Gordon spotted Miller lying on the ground. "What the hell?"

Miller groaned as consciousness returned.

"You idiot!" Gordon yelled. "We leave you alone for two minutes and you let her get away!"

"There she is!" shouted Carlucci, pointing to the stack of equipment at the back of the room.

"Get her!" yelled Gordon.

Carlucci sprinted to the pile of equipment and began climbing. Hearing Carlucci behind her, Sarah scrambled up as fast as she could, desperate to reach the window at the top. Suddenly she felt a searing pain on her left arm. She looked to find she had brushed against a cutting blade on one of the machines and sliced her arm open. No time to worry about it. Carlucci was closing in fast behind her. Sarah gritted her teeth against the pain and continued to climb.

Reaching the window, she pulled on the latch. To her immense relief, it swung open. She climbed out onto the tiny ledge and looked down. It was twelve feet to the ground, too far to jump. She looked back. Carlucci was climbing quickly, sensing she was trapped. It was either jump or let him catch her. Sarah jumped.

She hit the ground heavily. A stabbing pain shot through her right ankle and she crumpled to the ground. Knowing she had to get out of sight before Carlucci reached the window, Sarah struggled to her feet and hobbled painfully across the laneway, continuing around the back of the warehouse on the other side of the lane.

By now, the rest of them were out in the street. She heard Gordon call up to Carlucci, now at the window. "See which way she went?"

"No," Carlucci replied in frustration. "It's a twelve-foot jump. I can't believe she made it and kept going."

"Maybe *you'd* better *climb* down," suggested LePan with a grin.

"Split up," ordered Gordon. "We've got to find her."

Sarah struggled to keep going. Each step on her right ankle was agony and there was no way she could outrun them. She had to find a place to hide. Spotting an old brick office building, she limped toward the door, hoping it was unlocked. It was. She slipped inside and quietly closed the door behind her. In the darkness, she felt a bolt lock and quickly slid it closed just as she heard one of the men outside the door and felt him try to open it.

Sarah heard Carlucci call back to the others. "She couldn't have gone in here. It's locked." Despite the circumstances, Sarah smiled at the spurious logic.

"Try the next building," replied Gordon.

Relieved, Sarah slumped to the ground, resting her ankle and breathing deeply to control the pain. Something warm and wet was running down her leg. She realized that her arm was bleeding badly.

After a few moments, her eyes began to adjust to the dark. There was a small office on the other side of the room. Through the open door, she could see a desk and a phone. She stumbled over to the desk. It was covered in dust and clearly hadn't been used in months. She picked up the receiver and, to her astonishment, heard a dial tone. Her instinctive relief at finding a working phone quickly paled. Who could she call? Certainly not the police. Then she thought of Paul Taylor. She could still remember the phone number from his card. It was a ridiculous idea. She'd had one date with him over three months ago and he'd ignored two letters from her. What would she say? What other options did she have? Sarah dialed Paul's number.

· · · · · · ·

The phone rang several times with no answer and Sarah was about to hang up in despair. Then she heard a familiar voice. "Paul Taylor here."

Sarah was suddenly unable to think of what to say. Calling him at all had been silly.

"Paul Taylor," he repeated.

"It's Sarah Andrews," she stammered. "I don't know if you even remember me...."

"Sarah! Of course. I've been trying to find you. Where are you?"

"Paul," Sarah began frantically. "I'm in trouble. I need your help."

"Anything! Just tell me where you are."

The quiet assurance in his voice and his obvious determination to help filled her with renewed hope.

"Some men are chasing me. They are trying to kill me. I'm hiding in a warehouse."

"And I thought you were going to tell me that you had an overdue library book."

"Paul! I'm serious." Sarah replied in frustration—but she couldn't resist a smile. His banter made her feel better.

"Sorry. Where are you?"

"I don't know. I was kidnapped and thrown into the back of a van. When I got out, I was in front of an old warehouse. I think I'm somewhere in the Warehouse District."

"Sarah. I'm almost two hours away. It would be faster to call the police. Or I can call them for you?"

Sarah hesitated. There was no way she could explain. Not now anyway. Closing her eyes in silent prayer, she replied. "The men who are chasing me *are* policemen."

There was silence from the other end of the line and Sarah was terrified he was going to hang up.

Paul paused for a moment. If the cops were after her, there must be a reason. He barely knew her and it would be foolish to get involved. Yet, he trusted his instincts about people and Sarah Andrews was no criminal. Paul's jaw clenched with steely determination. He'd figure out the rest later, but now he would help her. "Sarah, for a librarian, you live a most intriguing life. Now let's find out where you are and get you out of there."

Sarah breathed a deep sigh of relief. "Thank you."

"Can you describe the place?"

"It's just an old abandoned office building," Sarah replied, knowing the information was virtually useless.

If Paul was frustrated by the vague answer, he didn't show it. "Is there a desk there?"

"Yes, I'm sitting at it."

"Look around for something with an address on it. Incoming mail, the letterhead on blank stationery, shipping labels, anything."

Brightening at the insight, Sarah looked around. There *was* some unopened mail, all addressed to 4610 Latimer. There was also some unused letterhead that read *Gutberg's Printing Equipment, 4610 Latimer.*

"Yes. I've got it—4610 Latimer," Sarah replied, excitedly.

"Hang on," Paul replied. "Let me see if I can find it on my GPS. Yes, I see it. It's going to take me at least ninety minutes to get there. Are you all right for the moment?"

She was feeling faint and her ankle throbbed painfully. With five of them searching for her, they'd surely find her before Paul could make it. "They're searching for me now, but I'll try to hide."

"Are you hurt?" asked Paul, sensing her fear.

"A little. I cut my arm pretty badly and I hurt my ankle jumping out of a window."

"Can you walk?"

"Slowly. It hurts when I put weight on it."

"How bad is the cut?"

"Pretty bad I guess. It's bleeding a lot. Almost gushing."

"Sounds like you've cut a small artery. You've *got* to stop the bleeding. Is there anything there you can wrap around it? A cloth, old clothing?"

"I see an old towel."

"Good. Wrap it around the cut and find something to tie it with."

"There's some string on the desk."

"Good. Tie it tight. If you lose too much blood, you'll pass out."

"Thanks for the morale boost."

Paul smiled. She had spunk. That would help. "How is it?"

"Give me a minute. I have to put the receiver down."

"Okay."

Sarah came back on the line. "Seems to be working."

"Good. Now, you have to get farther away. They will tend to search around the place they last saw you. Every block helps. Do you think you can get yourself a few blocks farther away, maybe into another warehouse?"

"I'll try."

"Go as far as you can and then hide. The more creative the better. Think about false ceilings, air ducts, garbage bins. Don't come out until you hear someone whistling *Jingle Bells*. That will be me."

"Okay. And thanks." Sarah was frightened, but it felt so good to have an ally—even one ninety minutes away.

"See you soon." Paul replied, hanging up.

CHAPTER 18

KNOWING PAUL WAS COMING, SARAH FELT SHE HAD A chance, but she had to hide. Limping to the door, she opened it a few inches and looked out. There was no one in sight. She slipped outside and hobbled down the alley as fast as she could before turning down the next street. After two blocks, the pain and exhaustion forced her to stop. She was weak and dizzy from the loss of blood and needed to find somewhere to hide and rest.

In front of her was small concrete building. It would have to do. Finding the front door locked, Sarah worked her way around the back, looking for another way in. At the rear of the building was an old iron fire escape leading to a door on the third floor. Feeling increasingly faint, she began to climb the narrow stairs, praying that the door at the top was open, knowing she wouldn't have the strength to climb down again.

As she climbed, each step was an effort. She reached the top landing and collapsed. Everything went black.

· · · · · · ·

Paul Taylor drove as quickly as he could to the address Sarah had given him. It was past nine in the evening so the traffic was light and he made it in just over an hour. As he drove, he reflected on the mystery surrounding Sarah Andrews. Why would a librarian who appeared to live a simple and sheltered life suddenly walk out on her father, her job and her apartment? Where had she been for the last three months? Why would a bunch of cops be trying to kill her? A mystery he was determined to solve.

Paul retrieved the Glock handgun from the special compartment under the dash and shoved it into his belt, wondering whether he would need it. Parking a couple of blocks away, he covered the rest of the distance on foot, keeping to the shadows and laneways. The area was filled with run-down warehouses, most of them deserted and disintegrating. The streets were empty. No people, no cars. He spotted a lone van parked outside one of the warehouses. It must be the one they'd used to bring Sarah. Cautiously, he entered the dilapidated building. There was no one inside but the lights were on and he could see footprints in the dust. One set was smaller and barefoot. Sarah's! Looking around, he saw a pile of machinery at one end of the room and spotted a trail of blood leading up the machinery to a small window near the ceiling. She must have climbed the machinery and escaped out the window. She was bleeding badly. He went back outside and around to the back of the building. The window was at least twelve feet above the ground, which explained how she'd hurt her ankle.

Sarah had left a path of bloody footprints and Paul was easily able to follow her trail, knowing that if he could track her, the cops could too. Paul found the office from where she'd called him but, after that, the footprints stopped. She'd been able to stop the bleeding—but where had she gone?

· · · · · · ·

Sarah regained consciousness to find Carlucci kneeling over her, with a sinister grin. "Nice try, but you'll pay for it."

Knowing that her slim hope of rescue had slipped away, she was overcome with despair. By the time Paul arrived, she'd be dead, her body stuffed into some dumpster. With neither the strength nor the will to fight, she submitted passively while Carlucci re-taped her wrists and ankles.

"I've got her," Carlucci yelled to the others. He then slung her over his shoulder and carefully descended the fire escape to rejoin LePan and Kramer who were waiting on the ground.

LePan radioed Gordon. "We got her."

"Thank God. Where are you?"

"A couple of blocks south."

"Stay put. We're on our way."

Sarah was still lying limply over Carlucci's shoulder as Kramer approached and lifted her head by her hair. "She doesn't look too good."

LePan shrugged. "Doesn't matter much, does it?"

"Evening, gents. Working late are we?" Although half-conscious, Sarah recognized the voice immediately. It was Paul! From the corner of her eye, she saw him walk casually out of the nearby warehouse building. How had he gotten there so fast? Maybe she'd been unconscious longer than she realized. It didn't matter. He was there!

The cops looked at him in astonishment.

"Nice night for a walk, isn't it?" Paul Taylor continued cheerfully.

"Who the hell are you?" demanded Kramer.

"Andy Smith, the night security guard. From Control National. Maybe I should ask who *you* are."

"Look Andy Smith," replied Carlucci in a threatening tone. "If you know what's good for you, you'll go back into that building, close the door and forget what you saw."

"Kind of hard to forget you saw three men carrying a woman's body in the middle of the night, don't you think?"

"A wise guy eh? Well, we'll see if a little encouragement might help," replied Carlucci. He dropped Sarah's body to the ground and moved toward Paul, welcoming the excuse to cause some pain. At 275 pounds of solid muscle and facing a man he figured must be in his fifties, Carlucci was not anticipating any serious resistance. Sarah landed heavily on her injured arm and gasped in pain. Paul breathed a sigh of relief. She was alive!

From long experience, Taylor quickly sized up his opponent, detecting the bulging muscles under his clothes. He would need to be careful. Carlucci approached quickly and swung a ham-sized fist at Taylor's head, but his fist hit nothing but empty air. Paul had moved aside quickly and, at the moment Carlucci's arm was extended he jammed his foot down on the side of his leg. Carlucci fell to the ground screaming, his lower leg bent sideways at an unnatural angle, his knee dislocated. Paul then delivered a quick kick to the side of his head, knocking him cold. Surprised to see Carlucci so easily dropped, Kramer moved in quickly. Taylor easily ducked his first blow and landed two quick successive punches to his chin and gut, knocking him to the ground. A kick to his head rendered him unconscious. Seeing his companions so quickly dispatched, LePan went for his gun. Taylor was on him before he could draw it. A feint with his left hand followed by a chop with his right to the side of LePan's neck and LePan crumpled to the ground near his colleagues.

With all three cops lying unconscious on the ground, Taylor went over to Sarah. She looked up at him, still dazed, but overcome with relief.

"Hi there," Paul said simply.

"Hi."

"You're a long way from the library, aren't you?" Paul asked with a grin.

Sarah smiled weakly. "In a lot of ways. Thank you for coming."

Paul pulled a knife from his belt, reached down and cut the tape binding her wrists and ankles. While freeing her, he examined her quickly. She was pale and weak. The cut on her arm was still bleeding through the towel and her ankle was badly swollen. Sarah was conscious of his gaze and remembered with embarrassment that she had nothing on but her underwear. Paul sensed her thoughts and smiled. "Right now we've got bigger problems than dress code. Can you stand?"

Sarah struggled to her feet, gasping as her right foot touched the ground.

"Good girl. Have you got any more friends around?"

Sarah nodded. "There are two others."

"I thought so. Lean on me. We need to get around the corner of this building."

They had just moved out of sight when Gordon and Miller appeared. At first, they didn't see their three colleagues lying unconscious in the street.

"Where they hell could they have gone to?" grumbled Gordon.

"Probably stopped for some play time," replied Miller.

"They better not have."

"Holy shit," exclaimed Miller, spotting Carlucci, LePan and Kramer lying unconscious on the ground.

Gordon surveyed the scene in bewilderment. He approached the bodies carefully, assuming they had been shot and surprised they hadn't heard the gunfire. To his astonishment, none of them had gunshot wounds. Someone had taken them out by hand. Carlucci, especially, wouldn't be easy to take down.

Suddenly, Taylor stepped out from behind the corner. "Evening gentlemen."

"Who the hell are you?" demanded Gordon.

"Andy Smith, the night watchman," replied Taylor casually. "These gentlemen on the ground were trespassing."

"I don't know what the hell you think you're doing, but those are police officers and you're in serious trouble."

"Interesting. I'd heard you guys were cops but didn't quite believe it. Hardly seems like standard police operating procedure, kidnapping women and sneaking around dark alleys—does it?"

Miller pulled his gun. "Lose the mouth and show us some ID."

Taylor moved on them with such speed and assurance that they had no chance to react. Miller's gun was knocked from his hand and a quick kick under his chin jerked his head up which such force he crumpled to the ground. Gordon reached for his gun but was too slow. A powerful blow to the stomach doubled him over only to catch Taylor's knee in his face crushing his nose and knocking him unconscious.

Taylor went back to retrieve Sarah. "That all of them?"

Sarah nodded.

"Good. Just the same, let's get out of here. My Jeep's two blocks away. If you don't mind, I'm going to carry you. It'll be faster and easier on that ankle of yours."

Before Sarah could respond, he picked her up in his arms and strode easily away. Moments later, he reached his car and deposited Sarah gently in the front passenger seat. He then retrieved a blanket from the back and wrapped it around her before climbing into the driver's seat.

Paul then reached over and pulled a first-aid kit from the glove compartment. "Here. Let me do something for your arm. I wouldn't want to go to all this trouble just to have you bleed to death on the way home."

She held her arm out toward him. It was caked with dried blood and blood still oozed from the long jagged cut.

"You really did a job on this," Paul grinned. "I'll have to give you some stitches later, but for now I'm just going to stop the bleeding." He wrapped gauze around the wound and then bound it with adhesive tape.

"Thank you."

Paul looked over at her, squeezed her hand and smiled. "I'm afraid we've got a ninety minute drive back to my house over some rough roads, and you look like you've had a long evening. Why don't you try to sleep?"

Sarah felt battered, sore and very weak; but as she looked at Paul and saw the affection shining in his eyes, she felt a sense of belonging, and a new beginning.

CHAPTER 19

AFTER DOZING FOR MORE THAN AN HOUR, SARAH WAS JOLTED awake. The Jeep was moving slowly and pitching violently from side to side. Sarah grabbed the door handle to steady herself.

"Sorry about the ride," Paul said, seeing her awake. "We're on the private road leading into the back of my house. I deliberately left it rough to discourage visitors. We'll be there in about five minutes."

Sarah stretched. She still felt weak and sore; but the nap had refreshed her. She looked out the window. It was completely black outside; but as her eyes adjusted to the darkness, she could see they were surrounded by dense forest. The road was barely wider than the car. Massive trees loomed on both sides and closed in above them, blocking out the night sky. Branches brushed against its windows as the Jeep slowly but powerfully navigated the rugged trail. It was an eerie sight and Sarah instinctively pulled the blanket around her more tightly. She looked over a Paul Taylor. He was watching the road intently as he guided the Jeep forward with relaxed confidence.

Sensing her glance, he looked over and smiled reassuringly. "Almost there. How are you doing?"

"A little tired but a lot better than I was, thanks to you."

"How's the arm?"

She had almost forgotten. Sarah inspected her arm to find that blood was seeping steadily through the bandage. She was surprised the sight didn't bother her more. "It's still bleeding a little."

"I'll put some stitches in as soon as we get to my house."

"I've never had stitches before."

"My. You *have* lived a sheltered life, despite much evidence to the contrary."

"Until a few months ago, I'd have agreed with that."

Finally, they reached a gravel driveway behind the house and Paul parked the Jeep near the back door. "Why don't you let me carry you in?" he suggested. "The gravel will be tough on your bare feet."

Before Sarah could reply, he easily picked her up and carried her toward the door. She was acutely conscious of his closeness, the strength in his arms and the warmth of his body against hers.

Paul carried her through the back door and past the kitchen into the living room. Built of pine logs, the house was large and attractive. The living room projected out from the front of the house with vaulted ceilings and floor-to-ceiling windows on three sides. At first, Sarah could see nothing out the front window, but then she made out a lake shimmering darkly below them. Sarah was struck by how black the sky was. In the city, the night sky reflected a faint but constant haze of light—pollution and the refraction of city lights. Here the sky was totally black. Against the darkness, hundreds of stars flickered, like tiny diamonds floating on a midnight sea. For a sight so commonplace, it was hauntingly beautiful.

Paul gently lowered her onto a couch facing the front window. "Welcome to my country sanctuary."

"It's beautiful."

A golden retriever appeared and padded cautiously over to Sarah. She scratched its head. "Talisker?"

"Good memory."

Paul fetched a small first-aid kit from which he produced a needle and thread. "Give me your arm."

It looked like a normal sewing needle and Sarah looked at him dubiously.

Paul smiled. "Trust me. I may not be a doctor, but I've sewn up more than my share of battlefield injuries, including several of my own."

"You saved my live, so I guess you're not going to kill me now."

Paul laughed. "This may sting a little. Sorry. I don't have any local anesthetic."

"Have you got any scotch?"

"I didn't imagine you as a scotch drinker."

"I'm not, usually; but if you're going to stick that needle into me, I thought I'd go for the strong stuff. Besides, it's been a tough day."

Paul laughed at the understatement. "Scotch coming up."

He returned with two glasses of scotch on ice. Sarah took a sip and enjoyed the characteristic taste and the slight sting in the back of her throat.

"Okay. No more stalling. Hold out your arm," Paul ordered.

Obediently, Sarah held out her left arm, while taking another large sip of scotch with her right.

Paul removed the bandage and inspected the long, deep cut. "It's nasty, but clean. Shouldn't leave much of a scar."

He gently washed the wound and dabbed it with antiseptic. It stung fiercely and Sarah gasped.

"Sorry. I forgot to warn you. But the stitches will be a breeze after that."

Sarah looked at him skeptically. "Maybe I should have held out for a real doctor."

"Don't get finicky on me now. Have another sip of scotch."

As Paul began to sew the edges of skin together, Sarah turned away, unable to watch the needle piercing her skin. It hurt and she bit her lip in pain.

"Sorry," Paul said, feeling her tense up. "Just a few more." He finished stitching and put a bandage on her arm to cover them. "There. Now let me check out that foot of yours."

He knelt in front of her, running his hands expertly over her ankle. "It's not broken. Just a sprain. It will heal on its own. We'll just have to keep you off it off it as much as possible."

Sarah downed the rest of her scotch and settled back into the couch. Her arm stung, her ankle throbbed and she was exhausted, but it was good to be cared for.

Paul looked at her, pleased to see her relax. "Tell you what. I've got a guest room with its own bathroom for you. If you're beat, you can go right to bed. If you would rather, you can have a bath while I make you some soup and a sandwich. Or...you can have another scotch."

Despite her exhaustion, the bath sounded wonderful and the food even better. "I'll take the bath and the soup."

"Coming up. Stay here while I get things ready."

Paul disappeared into the bathroom, leaving Sarah to her thoughts. Talisker had settled peacefully at her feet and Sarah reached down to pat him. The dog rested his head against her leg enjoying the attention. Everything seemed so unbelievably peaceful. It seemed a million miles and a million years from the prison—and from the cops who were trying to kill her.

Paul reappeared and helped her into the bathroom. The tub was filled, soap and shampoo were on the ledge and a towel and a bathrobe lay on a chair near the tub. "Anything else you need?"

"No. It looks wonderful. Thank you."

"I'm sorry I don't have much for you to wear. I've left you one of my bathrobes. It will be a little big on you. If you're feeling up to it, I'll take you shopping tomorrow."

"You're doing too much for me," Sarah replied gratefully.

"Don't fall asleep in there. I'm putting the soup on."

When Paul left, Sarah slipped off her underwear and slowly eased herself into the bathtub. It felt delicious. All she'd had in prison were the weekly lukewarm communal showers. The opportunity to luxuriate in hot water and complete privacy was heaven. Sarah washed and rinsed her hair, soaped her body and then simply lay back in the tub savoring the warmth and feeling of peace.

· · · · · · ·

Suddenly Sarah became conscious of a gentle knocking on the door and realized she must have dozed off.

"Soup's ready. Just making sure you haven't drowned," Paul called through the door.

"I'll be right out." She reluctantly got out of the tub, put on the robe and limped to the living room, settling back onto the couch.

Paul appeared from the kitchen with a tray, putting a large steaming mug of vegetable soup and a toasted ham and cheese sandwich in front of her, before sitting on the other end of the couch with his scotch.

Looking at the food in front of her, Sarah realized she had not eaten all day. She dug in ravenously.

He watched her eat with amusement. "I can see your appetite hasn't suffered."

"It's delicious. Thank you."

Paul grinned. "Not at all. I told you after our first dinner, I wanted to get you out to see this place. I just never imagined it would be such an adventure."

She laughed softly. "Neither did I, but it's nice to be here."

"I *am* curious how a librarian comes to be chased by five cops, but I'm sure it's a long story, so you can save it."

Sarah nodded gratefully. She wondered what he knew. Had he received her letters? Did he know she'd been in prison? If not, would his attitude change once he found out? She was too exhausted to deal with it; but she knew she would eventually have to tell him everything.

Sarah finished the simple meal and leaned back in the couch, fighting off the fatigue that was descending over her. Paul saw her struggling to keep her eyes open. "You look beat. And you've had a long day. Why don't you go to bed?"

"I *am* fading," Sarah replied drowsily. "Sorry I'm not better company."

Paul stood, picked her up in his arms and carried her into the guest bedroom. "In the circumstances, you're forgiven," he said as he depositing her onto the bed. "I'm sorry I don't have anything to suggest for pajamas. We'll get you something tomorrow."

The bed looked warm and comfortable and the prospect of crawling under the covers and letting sleep overtake her was irresistible. Sarah smiled at him gratefully. "Thank you again—for everything."

"Sleep tight," Paul replied, bending over and kissing her lightly on the forehead.

As Paul left, she slipped off the robe and crawled under the covers. It was the first time in over three months she hadn't slept in a prison cell. The sheets felt rich and smooth, and the mattress soft and welcoming. Within minutes, Sarah was sound asleep.

· · · · · · ·

It was almost eight the next morning before Sarah awoke to sunlight streaming into the room from a sliding glass door. She wasn't used to waking up in a comfortable bed in a bright airy room and, for an instant, she thought it must be a dream—a beautiful dream that would soon vanish, to be replaced by the grim reality of prison. Then the extraordinary events of the day before came back to her.

She stood up only to gasp as she put weight on her ankle. She'd totally forgotten about it. Slipping the bathrobe on, she limped to the sliding glass door, discovering it opened onto a balcony that ran along the front of the house overlooking the lake. She opened it and stepped outside.

The view over Crystal Lake took her breath away. The water shimmered gently, shrouded by the morning mist. The pale blue sky was spotted by wisps of cloud. Tall pines lined the shores of the lake, soaring majestically into the air. Here and there, massive granite outcroppings broke through the trees and angled steeply into the water. She listened to the silence and drank in the fresh morning air, letting it fill her lungs. To

Sarah, used the city's noise, grime and squalor, it seemed like another world.

There were two deck chairs outside her door facing the lake and she settled into one of them, feeling the warmth of the morning sun on her face and enjoying the simple splendor and tranquility of the scene before her.

Ten minutes later, Paul stepped onto the balcony from the door off the living room. "Good morning. I saw you come out here a while ago, but you looked so peaceful I didn't want to disturb you."

"It's wonderful, but you're not disturbing me. It must be marvelous to wake up to this every morning."

"It is. I never get tired of it. I made some coffee. Can I get you some?"

"Thank you." Fresh coffee in the morning was a luxury she'd never had in prison.

Paul brought them each a coffee and eased into the chair beside her. Talisker appeared from the woods beside the house and sauntered up the stairs to the deck. Seeing their new guest, he trotted over to Sarah, licked her ankle and settled down at her feet.

Paul grinned. "I think you've made a friend."

Sarah reached down and scratched his ears.

"Two friends, I hope," Sarah replied, softly.

"Two friends," replied Paul, quietly, taking her hand and squeezing it gently. "So how are your war wounds?"

"Much better."

Paul leaned down and felt her ankle. "Swelling's already down a bit. You'll limp for a few days but you'll be fine. I'll check the stitches tonight."

"Tell you what," Paul continued. "You can't wear that robe forever. First, I'll make us some breakfast. Then we'll drive into town and get you some clothes and anything else you need. When we come back, I'll give you a boat tour of the lake. That is if you think you can walk well enough."

"I don't have any money or credit cards."

"You worry too much. My treat."

"I couldn't."

"I'm not talking about designer fashions. I'm talking about shorts, T-shirts and a couple of pairs of jeans. Now unless, you want to keep wearing my bathrobe, you'll say yes."

"Yes," Sarah conceded.

"Good girl. Now will it be pancakes or bacon and eggs for breakfast?"

"It doesn't matter," replied Sarah, suddenly feeling hungry again. Either sounded delicious.

Ten minutes later, Paul served up pancakes at the table on the deck. After three months of prison food, it was delicious. Mounds of pancakes drenched in syrup, sausages, orange juice and coffee. Sarah couldn't stop making a pig of herself.

After they finished breakfast, Paul got her a pair of his own jeans and a T-shirt. "Here. If we are going to take you shopping, you can't very well wear a bathrobe. These will be big but see what you can do, just until we get you something."

Sarah took the jeans and top back to her room. The T-shirt came almost to her knees and the jeans were hopelessly too long and baggy. She had a thought. She took off the jeans and used the sash from the robe as a belt for the T-shirt. Checking herself in the mirror, she decided it would pass nicely as a casual dress. Pleased with her ingenuity, she returned to the living room, handed the jeans back to Paul and, somewhat self-consciously, modeled her creation.

He laughed. "I'm not sure you'll start a new fashion trend, but you look adorable."

"I'm not sure what to do for shoes?"

"Hadn't thought of that. Tell you what. There's a general store just as we enter town. I'll run in and get you some sandals. There's not much walking until then."

As they got in the Jeep, Paul handed Sarah several hundred-dollar bills. "Get yourself some shorts, jeans, T-shirts, shoes and anything else you need."

"It's too much," Sarah protested. "I just need a pair of jeans and a top so I can give you back your T-shirt. I really should go back to the city in a day or so and let you have your peace and quiet. "

Paul looked at her, a grave expression on his face. "Those cops who were trying to kill you won't give up. Having been knocked around a bit, they'll probably be angrier than ever. I don't know why they're trying to kill you or where you've been for the last few months. But you're staying here until we're sure it's safe for you to go back."

Sarah looked at Paul. He was right. She had been so tired and relieved to escape, that she hadn't thought about the implications.

"Besides," he added more gently. "I like having you here."

Sarah saw the affection and concern in his eyes and knew he wasn't going to give her a choice. "Thank you," she whispered gratefully.

CHAPTER 20

ELMWOOD, THE NEAREST TOWN, WAS A FORTY-MINUTE DRIVE. Once they had emerged from the rugged trail that led to the back of Paul's house, the Jeep pulled onto a paved road that wound leisurely through the undulating countryside. The land was mostly virgin forest, broken periodically with rocky outcroppings and small lakes. Here and there, a farm had been carved from the wilderness, its fields dotted with sheep or cows. Sarah watched enthralled as the scenery rolled past, each curve in the road revealing an intriguing new vista.

When they finally entered the small town of Elmwood, it looked like something from another time. There was a main street, predictably called Main Street and, at the principal intersection, Sarah saw a general store, a gas station, a hardware store and a bank. Farther up, set back from the street was a little church built of stone.

Paul glanced over at Sarah, enjoying her fascination. "The town of Elmwood has been here for over three hundred years. It was built on a river that feeds Crystal Lake so you can actually get here from my place by boat. It takes a couple of hours, but it's a nice trip. We'll do it some day."

"It sounds fun."

"It's hard to believe," Paul continued, "but there is actually a small shopping plaza on the other side of town. It was built last year. Nothing fancy, maybe a half dozen stores; but there's a women's clothing store and a drug store. I think you'll have better luck with your shopping there. However, tell me your shoe size and I'll jump out and get you a pair of sandals at the general store."

Paul parked and returned moments later with a pair of black leather sandals. Sarah slipped them on. "Perfect," she smiled.

They reached the shopping plaza and Paul stopped to let her out. "There you go. You should be able to get everything you need. I need to buy some parts for my boat at the marina about a half-mile away. What if I meet you back here in an hour? There is an ice cream store on the right and a small park beside it. If you finish early, buy yourself an ice cream cone and I'll meet you there."

· · · · · · · ·

Sarah finished her shopping with ten minutes to spare and changed into a pair of white shorts and a black T-shirt. Taking Paul's suggestion, she bought herself an ice cream cone, wandered over to the park and sat on one of the benches, simply enjoying the sun and fresh air.

Paul arrived right on schedule and smiled when he saw her new outfit. "Looks like you made out all right."

Sarah gave him a satisfied grin. "They had a lot of nice things. I even bought a dress and a bathing suit. I hope you don't mind."

"Not at all. I should have suggested it. I'll have to take you out to dinner so you can wear it."

"Did you get what you needed for your boat?"

Paul nodded and sat down beside her, wiping a dab of ice cream off the corner of her mouth with his finger and then sucking his finger clean. "Delicious."

Sarah laughed. "It is. I haven't had an ice cream cone for so long, I'd forgotten how good they are. Want one?"

Paul shook his head. "I have a proposition for you. There is a nice restaurant just outside of town. It has an outdoor patio overlooking some locks on a river connecting two lakes. Why don't we have lunch there before going back?"

"It sounds lovely."

They drove to the restaurant and found a table at the edge of the patio. While Sarah watched the boats move through the locks in fascination, Paul studied her. He wondered what extraordinary circumstances could have led to this woman being chased by five cops—seemingly intent on killing her? He sensed a difference in her from their first dinner. She'd been hurt somehow and it had changed her. He wondered where she had been, what had happened, how she had come to be chased by a bunch of cops; but he wasn't going to press her. She looked up, saw him watching her and smiled. Her smile broke through her natural reserve like a ray of sun through an overcast sky. Paul knew he would do anything to protect her.

After lunch, they drove back to his house. He suggested a boat tour of the lake and Sarah willingly accepted. She put away her things and then joined Paul at the dock where he kept his twenty-foot powerboat. He helped her in and maneuvered the boat away from the dock.

"Hold on," he said opening up the throttle.

The boat leapt from the water and was soon skimming along the surface of the lake. Sarah felt the wind in her hair and the occasional spray thrown up as the boat flew over the waves. She looked down to see the water racing past and forming a long wake behind them. The sensation of speed and power was exhilarating. Paul followed the shoreline, giving Sarah a view of the surrounding forest, interrupted periodically by rocky cliffs that rose out of the water.

"This lake and the others in the area were carved out by glaciers during the ice age. You see that cliff ahead of us?" Paul had to shout to be heard above the sound of the boat's engine.

Sarah nodded, awed by the sheer cliff rising abruptly from the water, soaring three hundred feet in the air above them. It was a spectacular sight.

"The water just off that cliff is almost a thousand feet deep. It is the deepest part of the lake by far. Usually glaciers scrape out the lakes with a fairly even bottom. Below the cliff, there is a deep trench. No one knows how it was formed."

Sarah nodded again, not sure she could be heard over the engine.

Past the cliff, Paul slowed the boat and maneuvered into a small bay. "The Trialyn River enters the lake from this bay. If you're up for a side trip, I can get about a half-mile up the river before it becomes too shallow for the prop."

"Sure, sounds interesting," Sarah replied, thoroughly enjoying herself.

They reached the mouth of the river and Paul slowed the boat to a crawl. Trees on both banks rose above them and arched over the river, largely blocking out the sun. The water was smooth and black, almost opaque. It was eerily beautiful. Paul touched her arm and pointed to a beaver dam just up a creek that joined the river. A beaver was crouched on the dam, gnawing at a sapling, unconcerned by the unexpected audience. Farther up, he pointed out a heron perched on an overhanging branch. It was so still, it looked like part of the tree and, for a moment, Sarah couldn't see what he was pointing at. As the boat drew closer, the heron took off and flew languidly upstream. Ten minutes later, they reached a spot where the river narrowed.

"I have to turn around here," Paul explained. "If you want, we can come back in a canoe and work our way several miles farther up the river."

"It's beautiful. I'd love to."

Paul carefully steered the boat back down the river and out into the lake. There he opened the throttle again and continued skirting the shoreline. Turning to Sarah, he asked, "Want to drive for a while?"

"I don't know how."

"It's easy. You just steer. Here, I'll slow it down a little."

Paul eased back on the throttle and guided Sarah into the driver's seat. Apprehensively, she took the wheel, turning it slightly to get a feel for how the boat responded. After a moment, she began to relax and enjoy herself. Suddenly she felt the boat accelerate. Paul had opened up the throttle again.

"Hey!"

Paul grinned at her. "There's nothing you can hit. Go for it."

After a moment's hesitation, her confidence returned and she reveled at the speed and power she controlled, looking over at Paul with a delighted smile. Sarah continued along the shoreline until they had circled the lake and she saw Paul's house up ahead of them. She could see the cathedral windows and the deck where they had enjoyed breakfast. It was an impressive sight from the water.

As they approached the dock, she turned to Paul. "Maybe you better take over."

"This time. Tomorrow, I'll teach you how to dock it yourself."

Afterward, they went swimming. Sarah had learned to swim in city pools and had never swum in a lake before. At first, the darkness of the water and the vastness of the lake unnerved her, but once she was in, she delighted in the cool, silky feeling of the water against her skin. Then, they lay together on the dock letting the sun dry them.

Paul reached out and removed a damp strand of hair from her face. "I'm glad you're here. It makes me appreciate things I tend to take for granted."

"I don't think I could ever take all this for granted."

"Tell you what," Paul continued. "Let's go back to the house and change. I bought some streaks in town today and I have lots of wine. We'll barbeque the steaks on the deck. Then, we'll eat and drink and watch the sunset.

· · · · · · ·

Sarah took a quick shower and changed. When she returned, Paul was already on the deck with a glass of wine. He poured her a glass and put a couple of steaks on the barbecue. Sarah relaxed on a lounge chair, sipping her wine and watching him tend the barbecue. The sun was slipping below the tree line on the other side of the lake creating a red-orange glow in the sky that was reflected across the water. Sarah watched the reflection, mesmerized by the ever-changing beauty of Crystal Lake.

When the steaks were done, they sat together at the small pine table. Sarah suddenly found herself acutely conscious of Paul's closeness and the fact that they were alone together, miles from anyone. She sensed he liked her and wanted to help her, and it was nice to feel cared for. But it was more than that. While they had been lying on the dock, she sensed he wanted her. It scared her a little, but she liked the feeling.

Unaware of her thoughts, Paul described how he had first seen the house many years ago and immediately bought it. He had researched the history of the area and fascinated Sarah with descriptions of the Indian tribes that had originally occupied the land, the coming of the first English settlers, and the founding of the town of Elmwood over three centuries ago. After dinner, he fetched another bottle of wine and refilled her glass. Then he led her to a double swinging lounge and they sat down together, rocking gently. Paul put his arm around her and gently pulled her toward him. Feeling mellow from the long day, the dinner and the wine, Sarah rested her head on his shoulder, enjoying their closeness. The wind dropped and the lake became as smooth as glass. The air was warm and still, and the crickets chirped from the bushes.

Paul kissed her lightly on the temple. "Well, my Lady of the Books, I've rescued you from the evil trolls, bought you exotic gifts from the magical town of Elmwood, plied you with a wondrous grape elixir and dazzled you with a glorious sunset. Are you going to tell me where you've been and why the evil trolls were hunting you in the first place?"

Sarah looked at him with a mixture of sadness and concern. "Paul. I want to tell you, but I'm afraid."

"Sarah," replied Paul, holding her and looking into her eyes. "When I was away, I couldn't stop thinking about you. The first thing I did when I got back was call you. When I couldn't get you, I called your landlord and the Glenwood Library. That's when I learned you had just disappeared. Something's happened in your life. You're in some kind of trouble. I want to help you and I *can* help you, but I need to know what's wrong."

"You didn't get my letters?"

He shook his head.

She looked up at him, and pulled his arm around more tightly around her. "Paul. Something *did* happen. Something bad. I'm afraid of what you'll think. Afraid you won't want me to stay."

It poured out with such heartfelt anguish that Paul hugged her tightly. "Sarah. There is absolutely nothing you could say that would cause me to think less of you."

She looked at him uncertainly. Who was this man she barely knew but who had changed her life? This man who could effortlessly overcome five armed cops and who now looked into her eyes with anxious affection. "You promise?"

"I promise."

· · · · · · ·

Sarah began her story the day after their first dinner. She told him about the call from her father's nursing home telling her he'd been taken to the hospital, about finding herself in the Warehouse District, getting lost, and being arrested. She told him about being taken to the police station, tied up and worked over with a taser. She tried to keep her narration dispassionate, but as she described the events of that terrible night, she was overcome with emotion and had to pause. Paul cradled her to his chest and stroked her hair as she struggled to recover.

After she composed herself, she went on to describe her meeting with Andrew Carney, how Carney persuaded her to plead guilty to drug possession charges, how she'd later seen him laughing with Peter Lindsay. She explained why she believed the cops had skimmed the million dollars from the cash recovered from the drug bust and thus why they were so frantic to find the briefcase. She briefly described her time in prison, being released only to find her apartment taken and her job gone. Fighting back the tears, Sarah described how she learned her father had died alone while she was in prison. She told him how the very same cops had kidnapped her and taken her to a deserted warehouse clearly intending to kill her, and how she had escaped long enough to call him. "Oh Paul! I just prayed you would answer. Prayed you would come. You did. The rest you know," she concluded, softly.

When she was finished, Paul sat silently for a long time holding her close. It was an incredible story and Paul also knew it wasn't over. She knew too much and the cops would keep looking for her.

Sarah misinterpreted his silence to mean that he didn't believe her. "You don't believe me?"

Paul looked into her eyes before replying softly. "I believe every word you've told me. You probably left out the worst parts. I'm just so sorry. Sorry for what you've been through. Sorry I wasn't there for you. Oh, Sarah.... " He broke off and hugged her, not knowing what else to say.

Sarah heard the anguish in his voice and realized how deeply he cared for her. "But it's over. I'm here, in your arms, eating too much and drinking too much, and feeling more content than I ever have before."

They sat together in silence, enjoying the warm evening air and each other. Sarah snuggled into his chest and closed her eyes. She too, knew her problems were far from over, but for now, she wanted the moment to last forever.

CHAPTER 21

THE MORNING AFTER PAUL TAYLOR HAD RESCUED SARAH from the warehouse, Gordon, Miller, Carlucci, LePan, and Kramer had met Peter Lindsay in his office. Carlucci was wearing a knee brace, Gordon a bandage over a broken nose, and the rest of them all showed signs of the encounter.

"Jesus!" exclaimed Lindsay when he saw them. "What the hell happened to you guys?"

Gordon looked sheepish. "It was bizarre. We pick her up easily and take her to an old warehouse. We're about to waste her and lose the body, when this old white-haired guy shows up. Says he's the night security guard. But man, does he know how to fight."

"I can see that," replied Lindsay sarcastically. "So where are they now?"

"They got away," replied Gordon, uncomfortably.

"Christ!" Lindsay pounded the table in frustration. "I can't believe this. I arrange to get her killed in prison and she takes out the woman who is supposed to make the hit. Then all *five* of you go after her and come back beat to shit. A librarian for Christ's sake!"

"She had help," protested Carlucci.

"Yeah," replied Lindsay with disgust. "One old white-haired guy."

"We'll get her," LePan said.

"And what about this white-haired guy," continued Lindsay. "Who is he?"

"We don't know," Gordon replied. "As expected, the name he gave us was phony. All we have is a general description. We're looking, but it will be tough."

Lindsay shook his head. "This is unbelievable. Find her! And this time make her disappear. And while you're at it, lose the white-haired guy too."

· · · · · · ·

The morning after Sarah had told Paul about her ordeal, she noticed that he was unusually quiet. "Second thoughts about harboring an ex-con?"

Knowing that her casual question betrayed an underlying concern, Paul took her hand. "Not a chance. I'm just worried about you. You know enough to send those cops to prison for a long time. They know that and they'll keep looking for you."

"I know," Sarah replied softly.

"I've been thinking about something. You'll find this frightening but hear me out."

Sarah looked at him curiously.

"I want you to change your identity."

Sarah remained silent for a moment, digesting what Paul had said. "How?"

"I have a friend who can create a new identity for you in a few days—new name, new birth certificate, new social security card, new passport, driver's license, everything."

Sarah was silent for a moment. "It sounds weird."

"Think about it. Even if you weren't worried about the cops, every job application you fill out will ask if you have a criminal record. Do you really want that hanging over you for the rest of your life?"

Sarah had already thought about it. It *was* true. How would she ever get a good job again? "Is it really that easy?"

"If you know how. My friend can access any computer database you could imagine. Want a degree from Harvard? You can have it, and when someone checks, it will show up on their records. You can even pick the hospital you were born in."

"I had no idea. Do people actually do that?"

"More often than you'd imagine."

"Okay," replied Sarah, dubiously.

"Good. I'll call him after breakfast. We'll go into the city tomorrow."

"Can we do something else while we're there?"

"Of course."

"The superintendent at my old apartment building saved a box of my things. I'd like to stop by and pick them up."

"No problem. We'll have to stay for a couple of days anyway while my friend prepares the documents. We'll have lots of time. We can turn it into a mini-vacation."

· · · · · · ·

That morning Paul took her sailing. At first, Sarah was nervous. The boat seemed so small and heeled so easily, but she quickly got the hang of it and thrilled at the sensation of skimming silently across the waves, powered solely by the wind.

"I don't understand how you can make the boat go against the wind."

Paul laughed. "Think about squeezing toothpaste out of the tube. You push against the tube and the toothpaste comes out the top. Imagine your fingers are the wind and the toothpaste is the boat."

Sarah smiled, delighted with the analogy.

They had lunch on the deck and, afterwards, Paul went off for a jog while Sarah settled into a lounge chair with a book she'd found. Talisker lay down contently at her feet. It was hot and, after an hour, Sarah decided to go for a swim. She changed into her bathing suit, went down to the dock and dove in, feeling the cool silky water caress her. She swam out about a hundred feet before stopping and looking back toward the house. Talisker had come down to the dock and was looking out toward her. Suddenly, he jumped in and swam out to her.

She laughed. "What are you? My personal lifeguard?"

Sarah swam back with Talisker right beside her, climbed out and lay face down on the dock, letting the sun dry her. The dog settled down nearby.

Paul arrived at the dock soon after. "I see you two both took a swim. How was it?"

"Wonderful."

"My turn." Paul dove off the dock, entering the water cleanly and swimming at least fifty feet underwater before coming to the surface and continuing at a brisk crawl. For ten minutes, he swam back and forth, parallel to the dock, before climbing out of the water and laying down beside Sarah.

That evening, Sarah made them a pasta dinner and set the table on the deck. She loved eating outside overlooking the lake.

Refusing Paul's offer to help, she fetched him a scotch. "Just sit and enjoy your drink."

Finally, Sarah announced that dinner was ready. She had even made garlic bread and decorated the table with wild flowers.

"This is fantastic," exclaimed Paul.

She smiled, pleased at the compliment.

After dinner, Sarah discovered a large hammock strung between two trees at the side of the house, and carefully crawled into it, rocking gently back and forth. "This is great," she said. "I could stay in this thing forever."

"Hang on," Paul replied. "I'm going to join you."

Careful not to tip them both out, he crawled in with her. Sarah cuddled up beside him and put her head on his shoulder.

· · · · · · ·

As they lay together in the hammock, Paul was acutely conscious of her closeness, her warmth, the smell of shampoo in her hair and the silky smoothness of her skin. He wanted desperately to take her to bed and make love to her, but he resisted the impulse. It was too soon. She had been through so much. They simply lay there in silence, enjoying the evening and the feeling of being together.

After several minutes, Sarah looked up at him. "Paul," she began hesitantly.

He smiled down at her. "I know. You've had a long day and I should let you go to bed."

"No. There's something else, something, I'd like to tell you—to ask you."

"Anything."

"You might find this hard to believe."

He kissed her. "Try me."

"It's silly..."

"Out with it."

"I've never slept with anyone," Sarah blurted out. "But if you want to, I'd like to. Now I mean."

"You are truly a remarkable woman, Sarah Andrews. And there is nothing in this world I would rather do."

Paul picked her up and carried her to his bedroom. There, he gently laid her on the bed and slowly undressed her until she lay there naked before him. He took one of her feet in his hand and, one by one, kissed each toe slowly and tenderly. He moved to her ankle, then her knee, stroking, kissing. Sarah closed her eyes and surrendered herself to him. Her body quivered uncontrollably; her breath came in ragged gasps. Then he entered her. Sarah felt him deep within her, warm, full and urgent. She felt her own body respond. She gasped as the sensation grew within her, radiating from her loins until it suffused her entire body, gripping her with almost unbearable intensity. She arched her back and cried out as it broke over her in a shuddering climax. She heard Paul gasp with simultaneous release.

Afterwards, they lay entwined together in silence as their climax slowly faded into a blissful feeling of peace and fulfillment. Sarah looked up at him and saw the love for her in his eyes. She smiled and wriggled more deeply into his arms. "If I fall asleep, will you promise that you'll still be holding me when I wake up?"

"I may never let you go."

· · · · · · ·

It was morning when Sarah awoke, still in his arms. She looked up to find him smiling at her.

"I told you I'd still be holding you."

"It's a wonderful way to wake up," Sarah replied drowsily.

"If you'll let me go for a minute, I'll shower and make you breakfast."

"Not yet," Sarah replied, pulling him toward her with a mischievous smile. "I have to make up for lost time."

Afterwards, Paul brushed a stay curl from her forehead. "Sarah Andrews. I don't know by what strange twist of fate you came into my life. Perhaps this is all a dream. But if it is, I don't ever want to wake up."

"If it's a dream, it's my dream too and I hope it never ends. Now how about *you* sleep in and I'll make breakfast."

Sarah crawled out of bed only to realize she was completely naked. She looked back to see him admiring her. She flushed with a mixture of pleasure and embarrassment. Smiling, she grabbed her clothes and hurried to the bathroom where she showered and dressed.

After breakfast, they drove into the city to see Paul's friend and pick up the box from the superintendent at Sarah's old building. As the city skyline grew closer, Sarah felt increasingly anxious. Crystal Lake was like another world where she'd been able to forget her problems and the danger she was in. Now she had to confront them.

CHAPTER 22

ERNIE KRAMER SAT IN AN UNMARKED CAR ACROSS THE street from Sarah's old apartment building, reading a magazine and periodically glancing up at the main door. He was bored and frustrated, and his neck still ached from the upper cut that Paul Taylor had delivered. It had been three days since Sarah had eluded them in the warehouse and Kramer couldn't understand why Lindsay insisted they still stake out the place. Her apartment had been rented to new tenants over two months ago and there was absolutely no reason for Sarah to go back.

Kramer's thoughts turned to his wife. Yesterday, Clara had suggested they see a marriage counselor. The nerve! All marriages had their problems. There was no way he was going to see some dopey shrink. He'd been staying out with the guys most nights, even going to the Purring Kitten alone sometimes. But why go home? They only fought anyway. So he'd cuffed her around a few times. The broken arm was *her* fault. She'd tripped on the stairs during one of their fights. She wasn't fun like she used to be when they were dating either. Back then, as well as being pretty, she was outgoing and vivacious. Something had happened to her.

From his rear-view mirror, Kramer noticed an old couple hobbling slowly along the sidewalk toward him. They didn't look like they could make it to the end of the block. Shaking his head in disgust, he looked at his watch. Still another hour before Miller was supposed to relieve him. Several minutes later, the old couple made it past the car and began to cross the street to the apartment. Kramer wondered if they were looking for some place to rent. Hope they signed a short-term lease, he thought to himself.

· · · · · · ·

"Did you get a look?" whispered Paul, careful to avoid his wig falling off. "I think he's one of the cops I hit the night I found you."

Sarah nodded, leaning heavily on her cane. "Ernie Kramer," she replied coldly.

Remembering what Kramer and his buddies had done to her, Paul's first impulse was to go back. There was no one on the street. One quick twist of his neck. It would be all over. He restrained himself.

They entered the apartment building and rang the buzzer for Steve Harris. It was only after they were inside his apartment that Sarah removed her wig and let Harris see who she was.

"My God! Sarah!" Steve exclaimed.

Paul took off his wig and beard and grinned. "Hi Steve."

Steve Harris smiled in recognition. "Paul Taylor. I remember you."

Paul quickly cautioned him. "Just so you know, there's a cop outside in an unmarked car."

"I know. Damn cops. They've been hanging around here and pestering me with questions. I'm glad you came disguised. It all started three days ago. First, you came in the morning, asking me about Sarah. That's when I told you I hadn't seen her for over three months. Then, only a few minutes later, Sarah knocks on my door. I can't believe it. And then I forgot to tell you that Paul had just been here."

"It's okay," replied Sarah gently.

"Then, an hour after Sarah leaves, the *cops* come," Harris continued. "Five of them! Real mean. They almost broke down my door."

"What did they want?" asked Paul.

"They asked if Sarah had been here. I had to tell them..."

"You had no choice," Paul reassured him.

"They asked if I still had any of your stuff," Harris continued. "I told them no. That I'd sold it all. I knew if I told them I still had it, they would want to go through it. Maybe take it. It didn't seem right."

"Have they been back?" Paul asked.

"Yeah. Two of them returned yesterday. Asked me if I'd heard from Sarah. Asked again if I had any of her things. Said they would find out if I was lying and I'd regret it. I still told them no."

"Thank you," Sarah replied, relieved.

"They may come back and search the place, so you should take your stuff now if you can."

"That's why we're here. My Jeep's a block away," Paul replied.

Harris led them down into the basement and showed them two boxes stacked in a back corner. The first box contained her clothes, carefully folded; and other personal belongings, including a picture of her parents. In the second box were her laptop computer, mail and various papers from her desk. Her things had obviously been carefully selected and packed and she was touched by his thoughtfulness.

"Thank you so much," Sarah said gratefully. "I can't tell you how much this stuff means to me."

"Is there a back way out?" asked Paul. "The cop in the car across the street didn't pay us any attention coming in, but seeing us go out with two boxes it might spark his curiosity, disguises or not."

"Sure," Harris replied. "There's a back door into an alley that leads to the street behind the building."

"Good. We'll take the boxes out that way and then come back. If we don't eventually appear at the front door, the cop will wonder."

Paul and Sarah took the boxes out to the Jeep and then returned to the apartment building.

"Thanks again, Steve," said Paul, as they put their disguises back on. "I doubt he'll think anything of it, but if the cop asks about us, just say we were looking for an apartment."

"Steve," Sarah added, kissing him lightly on the cheek. "I don't know if I'll ever see you again, so thank you for everything. Especially today, but also for everything else. You always did so much for me."

Steve smiled sadly. "I'll miss you Sarah, but good luck. I hope everything works out for you." Then turning to Paul, he added. "Look after her."

"I intend to."

Ernie Kramer idly watched the old couple leave the building and slowly shuffle by his car. Ten minutes later, he looked up. Something was bothering him. The old woman. When they had gone in, she had held the cane in her right hand. When they had left, she'd had it in her left hand. Frowning, he got out of his car and went inside to have another talk with Steve Harris.

· · · · · · ·

After leaving Sarah's old apartment building, Paul drove them to his friend's place. From the front, it looked like one of the hundreds of print shops around the city. "Sammy's Print and Copy Shop." Paul gave the bored counter attendant his name and they were promptly ushered into a back room where they were greeted by a middle-aged Asian man.

"Ah, Mr. Taylor. I hear you've retired. What are you going to do with yourself?" Then spotting Sarah, he continued. "Ah ha. Very pretty. Now I see."

Paul laughed. "Good to see you, Sammy. How's business?"

Sammy smiled. "Always good. Especially my specialty business."

"Well. I brought you some specialty business," Paul replied. Pointing at Sarah, he continued. "Sarah here needs to disappear. Can you make her a new identity? Birth certificate, social security card, driver's license? The works."

"For you Mr. Taylor. Anything. Pretty woman sit there," he added, pointing Sarah toward a tall stool.

Self-consciously Sarah perched on the stool while Sammy studied her.

After almost a full minute, Sammy spoke. "Mr. Taylor. Ms. Sarah. With respect, maybe some changes?"

"What do you suggest?" Paul asked.

"Cut hair short. Fix chip on right front tooth. Then Sammy take new pictures."

Paul looked at Sarah. "Okay?"

Sarah had always wanted to get her tooth fixed and she'd often wondered about getting her hair cut short. It was an easy decision. "Okay."

They spent almost an hour discussing the specifics of Sarah's new identity. It seemed she could make up whatever person she wanted to be and Sammy would make it happen. After some discussion, Sarah agreed on "Julia Coulter" as her new name. She decided on a master's degree in history. Paul pushed for a doctorate so she could be "Doctor Coulter", but Sarah decided that was too much. Sammy told them to come back in two days. He would have everything ready. He could take the photographs and apply them to the documents while they waited.

"I'm going to miss that chip on your tooth," Paul said as they left. "It's one of the things I love about you."

"How can you love something that's not there?"

Paul shook his head in feigned exasperation.

• • • • • • •

Paul checked them into the Four Seasons Hotel, requesting a two-bedroom suite.

Turning to Sarah while the desk clerk made the registration, he whispered quietly. "I'm hoping that last night's sleeping arrangements become permanent, but I didn't want to be presumptuous."

She simply gave him an inscrutable smile.

Sarah was awed by the spacious suite and even more impressed when Paul gave her a tour of the hotel including the pool, the spa, and small shopping arcade.

Enjoying her reaction, Paul made a suggestion. "There's a great restaurant on the top floor that overlooks the whole city. We could have dinner there tonight if you'd like."

"I'd love it," she replied happily, "but I'm not sure I've got the right clothes."

"I'm sure you can fix that," replied Paul, pointing out one of the women's dress shops.

At Paul's insistence, Sarah spent the afternoon in the spa, getting her hair cut short, a manicure, a pedicure, and several other treatments she had never heard of. She also went shopping. At first, she was concerned about the money Paul was spending on her, but it didn't seem to be an issue for him and she sensed he was enjoying himself. When she finally got back to the suite, she retired to the second bedroom to get ready for dinner. She emerged wearing a short black cocktail dress, new shoes and her black onyx jewelry. She did a pirouette for his inspection.

Paul took in the new dress, matching shoes and the short hair. "You look absolutely stunning."

"Thank you," Sarah replied, pleased. "I feel very spoiled."

"Good. I like spoiling you. And before I forget, you've got an appointment with a dentist who specializes in cosmetic dentistry tomorrow morning at ten."

Dinner was spectacular. They had small table by the window that provided a panoramic view of the city. The maître d seemed to know Paul and fussed over them all evening. Afterwards, they went for a walk through the downtown streets, holding hands and enjoying the warm evening air.

It was almost midnight by the time they arrived back at their suite. Sarah kicked off her shoes and collapsed on the bed in the main bedroom, tired and happy. She reached up and pulled Paul down beside her. "Thank you for a wonderful evening, Mr. Taylor."

"You're welcome Ms. Coulter. I had a great time."

"You realize this is your last chance to sleep with a woman with a chipped tooth."

"In that case..."

. . . .

The next morning Sarah went to the dentist while Paul dealt with some business.

They met back at the hotel for lunch and Sarah flashed him an exaggerated smile, displaying her 'chipless' tooth. "What do you think?"

"I'm going to miss the chip," Paul replied with a grin.

Sarah laughed. "A thousand dollars in cosmetic dentistry—and you want the chip back."

That afternoon, while Paul went for a jog, Sarah took the boxes she had retrieved from Steven Harris into the second bedroom and carefully unpacked them. It felt good to have some of her things. There was a box of her clothes, pictures of her parents, her university diploma and letters from her father, and her laptop. She connected it to the wireless Internet service provided by the hotel and found everything still worked.

As she continued through the boxes, she found the old share certificates from the IT company she used to do programming for. Probably gone bankrupt by now. On a whim, she checked the company's website, half expecting it to be shut down. Then to her astonishment, she found that its shares were now trading on the NASDAQ—at fifty dollars a share! That would make her forty thousand shares worth two million dollars. It couldn't be! In disbelief, she checked some other websites. It turned out the company had developed some break-though firewall technology, gone public and the stock had taken off. At that moment, Paul wandered in having just returned from his jog. Sarah couldn't suppress her excitement. "Look! I think I'm rich."

Paul came over, sat beside her. Somewhat skeptically, he looked at the certificates, checked some financial websites Sarah had never seen before finally turning to her. "You *are* rich. Congratulations."

"How do I get the money?"

"We'll need to be careful so we don't compromise your new identity. Once you sell the certificates, I can clear the bank draft through an offshore account held by a numbered company I own so it can't be traced."

Sarah looked at him impressed. "Didn't know you were an expert in money laundering?"

He laughed. "I seem to have acquired some unusual skills along the way."

Paul picked up the picture of Sarah with her parents taken when she was about ten and studied it. "I see you were a cute kid too. And there's that chip."

Sarah hit him playfully. "If you go on about that chip, I'm going to get your dentist to put it back."

· · · · · · ·

Two days later, they returned to Sammy's Print Shop. Sammy took Sarah's photograph and disappeared for a few minutes before returning with her new documents. She was amazed. A birth certificate, social security card, passport, and driver's —all with her picture on it—short hair and no chip; and all indicating her identity as Julia Coulter.

"They look so real."

Sammy laughed and then added. "Papers not everything. Very important you become Julia Coulter, not Sarah Andrews."

Sarah looked at him puzzled.

Wagging his finger for emphasis, Sammy lectured her. "Sarah Andrews must disappear—bank accounts, credit cards, everything. Then Julia Coulter should open new bank accounts, get credit cards, and a new address. Don't leave trail between the *old* you and the *new* you. No transferring balances, no forwarding addresses. Don't pay off *old* bills from your *new* bank account. No connections with your past. Don't see your friends, don't go to the same restaurants, nothing. Most important. You understand, Sarah?"

"Yes. Thank you."

Sammy slapped her gently on the hand. "Make mistake already. You not Sarah! You Julia."

Paul laughed. Sarah smiled sheepishly.

"Go then. And good luck to you Ms. Julia Coulter. And you too Mr. Paul Taylor. Have very pleasant retirement," he added, gesturing at Sarah and winking.

"Thank you, Sammy," Paul replied.

They stayed in the city for five more days. Sarah opened up new bank accounts, credit cards and a discount brokerage account. Taking Sammy's advice to get an address, she bought a condominium. She loved it as soon as she saw it. It was on the 45th floor of a new building with a breath-taking view of the city. The building had a recreation center with a gym and a beautiful pool. Compared to her old place, it was unbelievably luxurious. Then she bought herself a car, a four-wheel drive Subaru, so she could get back and forth on her own to Paul's place. She even had laser surgery on her eyes to correct the mild myopia she'd had since she was in her teens, and threw away her glasses, which she rarely wore anyway. The money gave her a sense of independence and financial security she'd never had before. She really did feel like a new person.

As Sarah and Paul spent their days together, explored the city together, laughed together, their relationship deepened. For both of them, there was a sense of connection and they reveled in it. They made love every night, and usually in the mornings, exploring each other, pleasuring each other and becoming one with each other.

· · · · · · ·

Four days after they had picked up the boxes from her old apartment, Sarah noticed a newspaper report. With tears in her eyes, she handed it to Paul.

> *Apartment Super Found Beaten to Death*
>
> *Steven Harris, who had been the superintendent of the Blackstone Apartment Complex for over twenty years, was found beaten to death in a utility shed behind the complex. He had been missing for four days. Residents of the complex were unanimous in praising Harris who they said was more like a kindly old uncle than a superintendent. Police are investigating but acknowledge they have no leads in the case.*

Paul looked at her. "I know what you're thinking. That it was Kramer."

"It can't be a coincidence. It sounds like he was killed the very same day we picked up the boxes. Kramer must have figured out Harris lied about not having my stuff."

"You don't know that."

"Paul..." Sarah protested.

"Okay, okay."

"Paul. It's so wrong. He was such nice old man. He did so much for me, for everyone in the building. I can't imagine him hurting a soul. And now, because he helped me, he's dead."

Paul hugged her. "I know. It *is* wrong, and I'm so sorry."

That night over dinner, Sarah was unusually subdued.

"Still thinking about Steve Harris?" Paul asked.

She nodded. "It's not just Steve. There was another woman in prison who said she was framed by some cops and persuaded to plead guilty to get a shorter sentence. And what about me? But for you, I'd be lying dead in an alley somewhere.

Paul smiled. "But you're safe. And dining on stuffed trout and French Chardonnay."

"But that's not the point," replied Sarah in frustration. "It seems the cops can do whatever they want."

"It's not all cops—just a few bad apples."

"I know, but it's still wrong. I feel I should do something."

Paul turned serious and looked at her with expression of concern. "Sarah, I know how you feel. What happened to you was terrible. But there's nothing you can do except put yourself in danger again."

"What do you mean?"

"If you file charges, it will force you to reveal your new identity. You'll have to appear as a witness and confront the cops who framed you, across a courtroom. You have no proof. The cops will deny everything. It would be your word against six cops, including Peter Lindsay, Deputy Police Chief. And it's not just about winning your case. They've tried to kill you twice. They'll try again. I don't want to lose you."

Sarah saw the concern in his eyes and touched his hand. "I don't want to lose me either, but if no one does anything, it will just keep happening."

"Sarah. The system is stacked against you. There is nothing you can do."

Sarah nodded sadly, knowing he was right. She had money in the bank, a new life and a man she was in love with. Why put it at risk?

That night Sarah lay awake watching Paul asleep beside her, one arm stretched across her hips, holding her to him. He looked so boyish when he slept. She loved just looking at him. She studied the arm that held her. The muscles were clearly outlined even in sleep. She studied the fine dark hair, which could not conceal the occasional scar. She kissed his arm, feeling him reflexively tighten his grip on her.

Yet memories of the *other* night invaded her thoughts. The pain, the humiliation. And then prison. Finding her father had died alone. Paul's words echoed through her mind. *The system is stacked against you. There is nothing you can do.*

CHAPTER 23

FIVE DAYS AFTER LEAVING, THEY RETURNED TO CRYSTAL Lake. Sarah had her new identity, almost two million dollars in diversified investments, a car, a condo, a handful of credit cards—and no chip. She actually felt like a Julia Coulter.

The first thing she did was go to the deck and look out over the sparkling water. Paul followed her and put his arms around her from behind. Sarah turned and smiled at him happily. "Oh Paul. It's so beautiful. I know I've only spent a couple of days here, but I feel like it's home."

"I'm glad."

The next few weeks were magical. They had breakfast on the deck, took the boat through the local lake system and hiked through the woods. Paul taught her to sail and Sarah reveled in her ability to control the fast little laser sailboat as it skimmed over the waves. At night, they usually barbecued on the deck, and afterwards, sat drinking wine, talking and enjoying the sunset. It was as if the rest of the world had ceased to exist. Paul was the lover, friend and confidant she'd never had. She hadn't imagined it was possible to love someone so much. She loved their lovemaking. She loved the moments after lovemaking, just laying together, cuddling and talking until finally, she would fall asleep, cradled in his arms. She was so happy. She wanted it to go on forever.

For Paul, who had settled at Crystal Lake seeking only solitude, it was like being reborn. While he had known dozens of women, Sarah was different. With her, the barriers he had thrown up to keep the world at a distance, disintegrated. It didn't matter what she was doing, he couldn't take his eyes off her. She'd catch him watching her and he'd feel embarrassed; but he saw it made her happy and he would just smile and shrug.

Sarah began jogging with Paul. At first, she could barely manage a quarter of a mile, but within three weeks, she could almost keep up with him over his usual five-mile route. She insisted that Paul teach her to use the gym in the basement and took to weight training with a passion, astonished at how much stronger she became in a short time.

One morning, after finishing breakfast, they were sitting on the deck drinking coffee. "You know how easily you handled the thugs in the subway and later the cops that were trying to kill me?" Sarah asked.

Paul looked at her curiously.

"Could you teach me?"

"Why the sudden interest?"

"I'd just feel more confident if I knew how to defend myself."

"It's not that easy. It takes a lot of practice. You'll be bruised and stiff for the first few days."

"I don't care. I want to learn."

"Okay, okay, I'll teach you. We'll start tomorrow."

"No, now! As soon as you finish your coffee."

Paul was becoming used to Sarah's tendency to do things as soon as they occurred to her and ten minutes later they had cleared an area in the basement, put down some mats and begun. After an hour, Paul suggested they knock it off for the day, but Sarah would have none of it. While he tried to be gentle, Sarah was taking a lot of nasty tumbles, but she seemed unfazed. Paul was surprised and impressed at her tenacity. It was another hour before Paul was finally able to persuade her to quit for the day.

Afterwards, Paul suggested the hot tub to ease Sarah's aching body. Sitting beside her in the tub, Paul commented. "Your determination is commendable, but you'll be stiff tomorrow."

"I don't care. We're on again right after breakfast."

The next day, Sarah shuffled to breakfast, stiff and sore.

With an exaggerated display of concern, Paul pulled her chair out for her. "You look awful."

"I feel awful." Sarah slowly lowered herself into the chair. "What did you do to me? I feel like I'm a hundred years old."

"Suppose we skip today."

"No," she replied firmly. "I'll be fine."

Paul was sure Sarah would lose interest after a few lessons, but she stuck at it with determination. Within a week, she had mastered the basic moves in martial arts. Within two weeks, she was proficient, but when Paul suggested she knew enough, Sarah emphatically refused to stop. There was little more he could teach her. All he could do was continue to spar with her so her moves became totally instinctive. Increasingly, he found he needed to concentrate. She was fast and cunning. A momentary lapse in concentration and he would find himself on his back with Sarah standing over him, grinning triumphantly.

Studying herself in the mirror, in the privacy of the bathroom, Sarah marveled at what she saw. The jogging, weight training, and martial arts transformed her body. She was lean and tanned with sculpted muscles and a rippling abdomen. Her newfound physical strength and fitness infused her with a sense of confidence she'd never felt before

· · · · · · ·

While Sarah was happier and more at peace than she had ever been, she still suffered nightmares of her interrogation. She would wake up in the middle of the night, pale and shaking. She thought of the life she had lost, of her father dying alone and not knowing. She wondered too if the cops were still searching for her. Would she ever feel totally safe?

She wanted to do something, but Paul's words echoed through her mind. *The system is stacked against you. There is nothing you can do.* He was right. She had a new life and she should put the past behind her. Yet, the fear, the nightmares—and the rage—formed a caustic brew that simmered within her, eating at her, demanding resolution. She had to do something. She couldn't live in fear the rest of her life. If the system was stacked against her, there had to be another way. As the days passed, the answer slowly formed within her. At first, it seemed absurd, nothing more than a satisfying fantasy. But the idea pulled at her insistently, irresistibly. If the system was stacked against her, she wouldn't use the system! No. She would hunt them as they were assuredly hunting her. One by one, she would stalk them and destroy them. In their wildest imagination, they would never expect it, but she could do it. She had killed three people in prison. She had money, she could fight and, with her knowledge of technology, she could track them, pry into their lives, their secrets, their vulnerabilities. Her 'project' took root within her and grew relentlessly. She took pleasure in imagining their shock and fear when they realized *she* was stalking *them*. To her surprise, she felt no fear, no uncertainty, only excitement, exhilaration—and a burning impatience to begin.

. . . .

Sarah knew she could not tell Paul of her decision. He would be upset and would try to talk her out of it. Furthermore, whatever happened she didn't want him implicated. Sarah had come to share everything with him, but she could not share this. However, she needed him to teach her one more thing.

That evening over dinner, Sarah brought up the subject. "I want you to teach me how to use a gun."

"Whoa," Paul objected. "Martial arts are one thing. Guns are another. What's going on?"

"Nothing's going on," Sarah protested innocently. "It's just that I want to start going into the city occasionally, on my own. I'll be alone at my condo. After what's happened to me, I'm nervous. I want to buy a gun and keep it there. What if the same cops find me? I want to be able to defend myself."

"Why the sudden desire to go into the city?" asked Paul, reluctant to consider the possibility of not having her with him every night.

"I need to start making a life for myself. I haven't been away from the lake for over a month. Remember, Sammy said I should build a life around my new ID. I need to be seen in the condo, go to the local shops, and use my credit cards."

"Fair enough, but you don't need a gun."

"You're a six-foot-two inch male and can defend yourself. I'm a five-foot-three helpless woman who needs some protection."

"Helpless? I'd have to disagree with you," replied Paul, pointedly rubbing his left shoulder where he had fallen during their morning practice.

"Do you want to find me dead in some warehouse?" Sarah persisted.

Paul shook his head in frustration, knowing there was no counter to that argument. "All right. I'll teach you how to use a gun."

"Thank you," replied Sarah, flashing a triumphant grin.

Starting the next day, Paul taught her how to handle and shoot a handgun. Within a week, she was effortlessly killing tin cans at a hundred feet.

As well as practicing martial arts and shooting, Sarah ran five miles every day, swam a couple of miles up and down the shore and then hit the gym for an hour. Paul was puzzled at her intensity, but when he joked with her about it, she just said it made her feel good.

· · · · · · ·

Whenever she could, Sarah would retire to the spare bedroom where she had set up her computer and files to research her targets and plan her "project". Careful to avoid any of her online activities being traced back to Paul, she routed everything through various different offshore service providers in Ireland, the Cayman Islands and Hong Kong. After a concerted effort, she found a way to hack into the police network so she could access their email, assignments and personnel files.

One series of emails between John Gordon and Peter Lindsay made her shiver. Although disguised, there was no question it referred to her.

> To: John Gordon
>
> From: Peter Lindsay
>
> Subject: The Librarian
>
> What is the status of this investigation? As discussed, the identities of the suspect and her accomplice must be determined and the case closed permanently. Failure to resolve this matter represents an unacceptable risk. Please advise ASAP.

> To: Peter Lindsay
>
> From: John Gordon
>
> Subject: The Librarian
>
> We are continuing to work on the case. Unfortunately, the suspect has completely disappeared. Bank accounts have been closed or abandoned, credit cards paid off and closed, driver's license expired. We believe suspect did manage to get two million out of an investment account, however the bank draft was cleared offshore so we were unable to trace it. Still unable to identify suspect's accomplice; however we have

some significant new leads and expect to have the
matter resolved soon.

To: John Gordon

From: Peter Lindsay

Subject: The Librarian

Acknowledged. It is imperative that this matter
be resolved promptly and permanently. Keep me
apprised of your progress.

It was clear they were still searching for her and that they wanted her and Paul dead. Despite her new identity, with the resources of the entire police force at their disposal, it could only be a matter of time. And what were the leads Gordon referred to? Had she left some clue? Maybe forgotten something in the hotel or inadvertently used her real name somewhere? The emails were two weeks old. Maybe they were already closing in. Any residual doubts Sarah might have had about her decision evaporated. It was no longer just a fight for justice, it was fight for her life—and the life of the man she loved.

Sarah prepared a file on each of the six cops as well as Arnold Carney. She knew where they lived, whom they lived with and how much money they made. For all of them except Carney, she even had copies of the psychologist's fitness reports prepared during their initial background checks. They made fascinating and disturbing reading and Sarah wondered if anyone had actually read the reports before hiring them. Mentally, she ran through the list:

1. Peter Lindsay

Ran the sixth Precinct until his appointment as Deputy Chief of Police three months ago. Close friends with the mayor, Patrick Kelton, who serves as Chairman of the Police Commission that will select the next Chief. Currently forty-two, Lindsay joined the force at twenty-two with a degree in criminology. Progressed quickly through the ranks. Described as ruthlessly ambitious and highly political. His father was a street cop who died early from a massive coronary. His mother is still alive. Lives with his wife, eighteen year-old son and sixteen-year-old daughter. Keeps a small suite in The Windsor as well as a home in the suburbs. Gambles and appears to have substantial gambling debts.

2. John Gordon

Sergeant and in charge of the fateful stakeout. Fifty-four years old, he is being forced to retire in a year after twenty-nine years on the force. Went to university on an athletic scholarship, but didn't finish. Joined the police force and initially promoted quickly; but his advancement had stalled when his partner had been killed responding alone to a call and it was discovered that Gordon had been drinking in a bar. Subject of two complaints alleging excessive use of force. Complaints were found to be unsubstantiated. His wife divorced him over ten years ago. Has a daughter, now thirty-one and married. Lives alone in a small house in Rockview.

3.   Frank Carlucci

Carlucci, twenty-nine years old. Failed his final year of high school and applied to the police force. Initially rejected due to concerns over his psychological profile, he reapplied a year later and was accepted. His father ran off when he was five, raised by his mother. A bodybuilding fanatic, goes to the gym twice a day and competes in local bodybuilding events. His psychological profile indicated he had difficulty forming relationships with women. Has been the subject of numerous complaints, all from women – false arrest, sexual abuse, and falsifying evidence – but none of the charges had stuck. Was recently acquitted of assaulting a Patti Constance who he met at a fitness club. Lives alone in a small house in Copperhill. Suffers from severe claustrophobia.

4.   Chris LePan

Thirty-two years old, eight years on the force. Subject of numerous complaints, all dismissed for lack of evidence. Once charged with perjury but acquitted. (Defended by Arnold Carney.) Never married but has had a succession of girlfriends. Lives alone in a big house in Hazelton and drives an expensive Jag. Appears to live well beyond a cop's salary.

5. Ernie Kramer

Thirty-five years old, fifteen years on the force. Wife Clara, ten year-old son Tony. Wife works part-time at Pinnacle Auto dealership. Clara treated at hospital several times for bruises and broken bones, but refused to press charges. Repeated reprimands for drinking while on duty.

6. Tom Miller

Forty-five years old, transferred to the force in his early forties from the Virginia State Police, which he joined after receiving a dishonorable discharge from the army. (Discharge appears to relate to the death of another soldier, but details not available.) Has been the subject of several complaints alleging excessive use of force and false arrest, but none have been substantiated.

7. Arnold Carney

Heads a small law firm which derives most of its income from representing police officers facing civil or criminal charges or complaints brought through the SIU. Fifty-four years old, divorced with grown children who have left home. Lives alone in a large house in Forest Hills. Close friends with Peter Lindsay and many of the judges in the city.

Sarah was stunned. As a group, they had been the subject of over a dozen complaints to the SIU and several criminal charges—perjury, falsifying evidence, assault, false arrest, sexual abuse, theft, the list went on. Unbelievably, in every case, they'd been acquitted or the charges dropped or dismissed. In many cases, Arnold Carney had been the defense attorney. She remembered Warden Patterson's comment that she wasn't the only one, but she had never imagined the extent to which it was happening. No wonder Paul believed the system was stacked against her. How many others had suffered as she had? Where were they now? In prison? Dead?

· · · · · · ·

One night after making love, Paul leaned over and kissed her. Then looking into her eyes, he asked, "Sarah. You're here beside me. We just made love. I love you more than I ever believed possible. I think you love me. But I feel there's a part of you, and a growing part, that's somewhere else."

"Oh Paul. I do love you," she replied in an anguished voice. "I love every minute we spend together. I didn't think it was possible to be as happy as I am when I'm with you."

"But….." prompted Paul.

"Shhh." Sarah put one finger over his lips while probing his groin with her other hand. Paul groaned with renewed desire and they made love a second time.

Realizing that, whatever it was, Sarah didn't want to talk about it, Paul didn't bring it up again. He noticed that Sarah was especially attentive. She fussed over him, picking him wildflowers, buying him gifts when they went shopping, and fetching him his scotch every evening. While he enjoyed the attention, Paul sensed that something was coming—something that could take her from him.

CHAPTER 24

AFTER SIX WEEKS, SARAH WAS READY. SHE COULD FIGHT, SHE could shoot, she could run five miles over rough terrain without tiring, and she was wealthy. One afternoon when they were laying in the sun after a swim, she told Paul she was going to return to the city.

"I was afraid this was coming. When?"

"I thought tomorrow morning."

"So soon?'

"Waiting will just make it harder. Besides, the sooner I go, the sooner, I can come back."

How long will you be gone?"

"I'm not sure. Several weeks."

Sarah saw the hurt in his eyes and it made her heart ache. "Paul. I love it here. I love you. I owe you so much. My life! Everything. But I have to start building a life for myself. I can't live at Crystal Lake forever."

Paul sensed there was more to it but let it go. "Sarah. I love you. I don't think I've ever loved anyone before. Promise me you'll come back."

Sarah kissed him. "Paul. I *will* come back, as soon as I can."

That night, Sarah fixed a special dinner on the deck including candles, flowers and music. Afterwards they made love under the moonlight.

"You're really trying to make sure I miss you, aren't you?" said Paul, as they lay together afterwards.

"I just want to be sure you'll take me back."

"Always." Paul brushed her face lovingly with his fingers and kissed her softly. "Always."

The next morning, Sarah left before breakfast. After six weeks, leaving Paul was harder than she had expected and another meal with him was more than she could face. She was at her condominium before nine. After making herself some toast and coffee, she sat on her balcony looking out over the city. She wondered what they were doing, those cops who had destroyed her life. Perhaps having breakfast, perhaps joking with each other in the police station, or perhaps abusing some other terrified suspect. So confident, so arrogant, so unaware of the coming storm.

First on her list was Arnold Carney. Sarah figured he would be the easiest target. He wasn't a cop. He wasn't trained to fight. She spent the day planning her approach. That evening, she made herself a light dinner, opened a bottle of wine and settled on the couch. She thought she would be nervous, but she found herself surprisingly calm, eager for the hunt to begin.

· · · · · · ·

Arnold Carney's law practice was thriving. Ten years ago, he'd worked alone out of a small office above a grocery store. Now he had ten associate lawyers and fifteen administrative staff working out of expensively furnished premises in a prestigious downtown office building. Most of his practice involved representing police officers facing SIU investigations, disciplinary actions or civil or criminal lawsuits. He'd also represented the city on several wrongful death suits arising from police actions. Carney had developed a reputation for being tough, aggressive, and almost always successful. While it provided a steady stream of fees, Carney was continually surprised by the frequency and severity of police wrongdoing—as well as their seeming belief they were above the law. Perjury, corruption, physical abuse, intimidation—it seemed endemic. However, it was a big city and it wasn't his job to make moral judgments. Cops were human and had a right to effective legal representation just like everyone else. Besides, all going well, he figured he would clear close to a million dollars this year and he'd recently bought himself a three-million dollar beachfront home in the Bahamas.

Carney was still at home at ten one morning when the doorbell rang. He opened the door to find an attractive young woman standing there. He quickly took in the dark hair, expensive navy business suit, white blouse, jade necklace and matching earrings, and noted she was carrying a briefcase.

"I'm Andrea Kelsey," the woman said before he could say anything. "I'm here to pick up the papers. Judge Creighton said you'd be expecting me."

Carney was baffled. "What papers? And who is Judge Creighton?"

"Are you Mr. Carney? This *is* 47 Berkshire Crescent?"

"Yes," replied Carney, perplexed. The woman seemed vaguely familiar. He must have seen her around the courthouse, yet he couldn't place her. He'd also never heard of a Judge Creighton and he knew virtually all the judges that worked out of the city courthouse. "But I have no idea what papers you are talking about."

The woman became visibly upset. "The Judge insisted I come here right away and get the papers. He needs them within an hour. I'm still on probation. If I come back without them, I could lose my job."

"Don't worry," Carney reassured her. "I'm sure there's been some mix-up. Why don't you come inside? We'll call Judge Creighton together and sort it out."

"Thank you so much," the woman replied with relief.

Carney ushered her into the house and led her along a hallway to a large study. A massive and ornate mahogany desk stood near the window. Carney motioned her to one of the seats facing the desk and eased himself into the large leather desk chair. "Don't worry, Andrea. We'll get this all straightened out for you."

"Thank you, again. I need this job."

"Judge Creighton must be new?"

"I don't know. I just started."

"Well. Tell me his phone number. I'll give him a call right now."

"There *is* no Judge Creighton."

Carney looked at her in bewilderment. "I don't understand. You just said..."

"You really don't remember me, do you?" Sarah Andrews interrupted, standing up and staring at him coldly.

"No...Should I...?" Carney replied, startled at the striking change in her demeanor. "Maybe... Maybe I've seen you around the courthouse?"

"Sarah Andrews. You had me sent to prison for three months for drug possession. You bullied me into pleading guilty when you *knew* I'd been framed."

"I..." stammered Carney.

"Think back. Five months ago. The night a big drug bust had gone down. Peter Lindsay called you late at night."

Carney studied the woman standing before him in astonishment. It *was* her. Not the terrified young woman he remembered, but it was definitely Sarah Andrews.

"You know what they did to me in the police station?" continued Sarah. "Tied me to the ceiling and worked me over with a taser until I passed out."

Carney stalled for time. "I really don't remember... I'm sure..."

"And the next morning you came to see me in the Backfield Building. You said you were on my side, that you'd help me; but all the time you were really helping Lindsay. You persuaded me to accept a plea bargain, telling me it was my best option. The truth was you and Lindsay didn't want me in a court telling my story to a judge. You promised you'd tell my father that I'd gone away to help a friend. You said you'd talk to my landlord and make sure my rent was paid. You said you'd call my boss at the library. You never did any of that. And why? Because you *knew* Lindsay planned to make sure I never got out of prison alive."

Arnold Carney studied her, remembering the frightened young woman he'd talked to just a few months ago, so helpless and overwhelmed by her circumstances. The woman standing in front of him was calm and assured, yet he sensed the barely controlled rage seething within her. The transformation was unbelievable.

He smiled at her reassuringly. "Look, perhaps there's been an injustice here, but..."

"Injustice!" Sarah repeated, her voice ringing with contempt. "Is that what you call it? You planned to have me *killed*!"

Carney stood up, trying to establish control. "If you're not prepared to discuss this civilly, I'll have to ask you to leave."

Sarah smiled softly. "I think we're past the discussion stage, aren't we?"

"You're making a big mistake," Carney, said, the tremor in his voice betraying his growing fear.

"You're the one who made a mistake."

"You'll never get away with this," continued Carney, surreptitiously slipping his hand into the top drawer of the desk where he kept a small handgun. Anticipating his move, Sarah moved quickly around behind the desk and slammed her hip into the drawer, crushing his hand.

As he howled with pain, Sarah reached into the drawer and retrieved the gun. "We're going down to the basement. Lead the way."

"What are you going to do?"

Sarah ignored his question. In the basement, she discovered a small cold cellar that would do perfectly. She found a small stool and put it in the center of the room. "Now get up on the stool."

"What..."

"Just do it!" Sarah commanded, prodding him in the stomach with the handgun.

Totally defeated, Carney complied. Once he was standing on the stool, Sarah tied his wrists behind his back and bound his ankles together.

Carney looked at her in terror. "Please. I've got money in the house. Enough for you to start a new life."

"I've got money *and* a new life," replied Sarah as she fastened a noose around his neck and strung the rope over a pipe running along the ceiling. She pulled the rope tight and fastened the other end to a workbench that was anchored to the concrete floor. Carney was forced to stand on his toes to avoid choking.

Pleased with her handiwork, Sarah stood there watching him struggle to breathe. Short, fat, soft and pale, like a giant white toad. Her anger faded into disgust. She could not believe she had ever been afraid of this man or that he had ever held her fate in his hands.

"What are you going to do to me?"

"Nothing."

"You can't just leave me here."

"Why not?" replied Sarah innocently. "I'm going to make sure that no one bothers you for at least a week. That way, you'll have plenty of time to reflect on what you did to me. And I'm not the only one, am I? From what I can tell, you make a good living getting crooked cops off and sending innocent people to jail."

"Please!" wailed Carney.

"I figure you've got a choice. You can wait until thirst or fatigue cause you to fall off that stool – or you can jump and get it over with."

"You can't do this!"

Sarah looked at him and shrugged before leaving the room and slamming the heavy door behind her.

In twenty minutes, Sarah was back in her condominium. She poured herself a glass of milk, walked out to the balcony and looked down over the city. She had vaguely expected to feel horror at what she had done, but instead she was filled with an exhilarating sense of power. For the first time in her life, she was dictating events, not reacting to them. And Carney was only the beginning.

· · · · · · ·

Three days later, Peter Lindsay received an envelope marked "Strictly Personal and Confidential". Inside was a single piece of paper. Curious, he unfolded it and began to read.

A Tale of Retribution

Once upon a time, a shy young girl was walking through a dark and gloomy forest when she was captured by six evil trolls. The girl begged them to let her go, explaining that she was just a poor librarian on her way to visit her ailing father, but the trolls took her to their cave and did cruel things to her. Later, they locked her in a terrible dungeon so she couldn't tell anyone what they had done.

Eventually, the poor girl was set free only to find her father had died and her home was gone. She was very sad. She wished she could punish the evil trolls but she was poor and weak, and there was nothing she could do.

Then, by chance, she met a wizard and discovered some magical powers with which to destroy the trolls. First, she found the wicked dwarf who had helped the trolls and hung him in the basement of his castle. Then, one by one, she slew the evil trolls, making sure they all died a horrible death.

When the trolls were all dead, the librarian felt whole again. They had broken something inside her, but now it was restored.

The Librarian

Lindsay leaned back in stunned disbelief. Sarah Andrews! It had to be. She must have killed Carney. Details of his death had never been released, yet she knew how he'd died. He recalled her arrest. Lindsay remembered her. She had truly *seemed* like a librarian—timid, frightened, overwhelmed by what was happening to her. Yet she had killed three people in prison, and now Arnold Carney. She'd been out of prison for almost two months and eluded every effort to find her. And now she was threatening to kill *them!*

· · · · · · ·

The next day, Lindsay summoned Gordon, Kramer, LePan, Miller and Carlucci to his office. When the group was assembled, he showed them his letter. "I assume you all got the same letter."

All five of them nodded.

"Do you think she really killed Carney?" asked Kramer.

"She knew details that were never released," replied Lindsay. "Someone strung him up in the basement of his own house. Left him standing on a stool, a noose around his neck and his hands tied behind his back. Made sure he wasn't disturbed. Phoned his office and said he'd had to leave on a family emergency and then phoned his cleaning woman and ask her not to come for a week. Coroner thinks he was there at least twenty-four hours before he fell off, or jumped."

"Hard to believe," commented Miller, doubtfully. "She's a *librarian*." The others nodded.

Lindsay looked at the group grimly. "This *librarian* has now killed four people, survived prison and evaded every effort we've made to find her. And now she's got the nerve to send us all a note telling us she's coming to kill *us*."

Gordon looked at him skeptically. "Why Carney?"

"I wondered about that," replied Lindsay. "She saw me with Arnie after her trial. I saw her looking at us curiously, almost sadly. She must have figured out that he was involved."

"How did she get into his house?"

"We're investigating," Lindsay replied. "There's no sign of forced entry. It appears that she just showed up at his door and rang the bell. Looks like Carney had a gun in his desk and tried to use it, but she was able to disarm him. No prints. Nothing. The whole thing was clean and well planned. You'd think it was a professional hit."

"You really think she's going to come after the rest of us?" LePan asked.

"There's no way," replied Kramer scornfully. "She's just trying to scare us."

"Carney's not scared, he's dead," Lindsay replied grimly.

"I just hope she comes after me," commented Carlucci. "I'll break her pretty little neck. But not before I have some fun with her."

Lindsay looked at Carlucci with disgust, but said nothing.

"So what do you suggest?" asked Gordon.

"I expect you guys to find her—and get rid of her."

Gordon shook his head in frustration. "We looked, but nothing. She's vanished. It's been two months. We figured she'd moved to another state, or right out of the country."

"Obviously not," replied Lindsay.

"We'll keep looking."

"Do that. And what about the reference to a 'wizard'?" asked Lindsay. "Could it be the white-haired guy you say helped her at the warehouse?"

"We tried to follow-up on the guy," replied Gordon again. "But all we had was a general description. We couldn't ID him."

"We have to get her, both of them." Lindsay pounded the table for emphasis. "And make her disappear for good. Continue the stakeouts. Keep talking to people who knew her. She'll make a mistake. She'll go back to the same dry cleaner, send an email to her old friends, something. Then nail her."

"We'll get her, sir," Gordon replied.

After the men had left, Lindsay remained in the room alone. The idea of one young woman taking on the entire police force was preposterous; but he couldn't shake the horrifying image of Arnold Carney, standing on the stool in his basement, a noose around his neck, waiting to die.

Gordon and Miller walked back to the precinct together.

"I can't believe this," commented Gordon. "Who would have imagined..."

"A librarian for Christ's sake," Miller replied.

"Tom. Do you think she took the damn briefcase?"

"I don't know, John. Given what we put her through, it's hard to believe—but what else could have happened to it?"

"Don't know, but I just don't think she took it."

"Either way, we need to finish this."

Gordon sighed. "I know. I know."

· · · · · · ·

Having sent the letter to the six of them, Sarah decided to wait before her next move. Let them wonder, worry, and eventually relax. Then she'd strike. Sarah called Paul and asked if she could come back to Crystal Lake for a few days. He was delighted to have her back and they picked up where they left off, running together in the morning, sailing in the afternoon and barbecuing on the deck for dinner.

One particularly hot muggy day, after jogging their usual five miles, they collapsed on the lawn outside the house, panting with exhaustion. They lay together on the grass laughing and trying to catch their breath. Paul looked over at Sarah. She was wearing thin jogging shorts and a light T-shirt. The T-shirt was soaked and clung to her breasts and torso. Her arms and legs glistened and drops of perspiration sparkled on her forehead. Paul leaned over and kissed them off. "God, you look beautiful," he exclaimed.

"You must have heat stroke." Sarah laughed, pushing him away. "I'm a mess and I probably stink."

Paul rolled on top of her, pinning her to the ground, his intentions obvious. "You've never looked more beautiful," he insisted.

"No." she protested. "Not here! At least, let me have a shower first."

"You can have a shower later. I'll wash every inch of you myself."

"No!" Sarah half-heartedly tried to fend him off as he began to strip off her clothes.

Paul brushed her arms away and ignored her protests. He slipped off her T-shirt and then her shorts, leaving her lying naked in the grass, pinned between his arms. He licked her nipples and then traced a line down her stomach with his tongue. "Mmmm, salty."

Increasingly aroused, Sarah abandoned her protests and surrendered to him.

Paul stripped off his own clothes and pulled her close to him. There in the grass, they made love, their bodies sliding against each other, their perspiration mingling. When they were done, they lay together, naked, contented and fulfilled.

Finally, Sarah got up. "Now can I have a shower?"

Paul looked up at her, standing there, naked and glistening with perspiration. "Yes, but I'm coming with you."

Sarah had forgotten how idyllic their life was together. Even the simple things. Waking up to find Paul sleeping beside her, looking boyish and tousled. Seeing him wake up, smile at her, so obviously glad she was there. Having him pull her body against his in a sleepy morning embrace. Sometimes they would make love as the morning sun streamed in through the window. Then they would shower together, make breakfast together and sit on the deck drinking coffee. With Paul, she felt so connected, so complete.

It would have been so easy to waver in her resolve. She had a wonderful life and a fantastic man who loved her totally. Why put it all at risk? But when those moments came, she recalled the night in the Backfield Building, the horrors of prison, her father's death, and her resolve would harden. If she did not do this, she would never find peace. She would always worry that they were out there somewhere, searching for her, coming to kill her. It would take only a few weeks. Then she would come home—to Paul, and to Crystal Lake.

Sarah stayed with Paul for a week before returning to the city. Chris LePan was next.

CHAPTER 25

PETER LINDSAY LEANED BACK IN HIS CHAIR. IT HAD BEEN A week since they'd got the 'librarian' note and nothing had happened. She was probably just trying to scare them. After all, who in their right mind would set out to take out six cops, and warn them first?

Dismissing Sarah Andrews as a concern, Lindsay began to reflect on his career. Ed Moorby, the Chief of Police, was retiring in less than three months and Lindsay wanted his job. When he was first appointed Deputy Chief, Lindsay was certain that he had the top job locked up. There was only one Deputy Chief—himself. He and everyone else took that as a clear sign that he was the designated successor. Lately however, he was picking up some subtle signs that he might be passed over for someone from outside the force.

Lindsay had been close friends with the Mayor, Patrick Kelton, for many years; and until a month ago, Kelton talked openly about Lindsay becoming the next police chief. But now, he never mentioned it and Lindsay was worried. It wasn't just his ambition. If he didn't get the job, whoever did would want his own team, and Lindsay could be forced off the force completely—and there weren't many job opportunities for ex-Deputy Police Chiefs.

Lindsay's reflections were interrupted when his assistant buzzed him. "Someone from your bank is on the phone. Want to talk to them?"

"My bank?"

"That's what they said."

"Put it through."

"Mr. Lindsay. I'm actually from your *other* bank, if you know what I mean."

"I told you not to call here," Lindsay replied angrily.

"If you'll just pay off your debts, we won't call you at all."

"God damn it! I already paid you."

"That was an interest penalty for late payment. The money was due six months ago. You still owe us a hundred thousand."

"I don't have it. The bank won't increase my mortgage."

"You're Deputy Chief of Police. I'm quite sure you can find a way to get it. We are getting impatient, Mr. Lindsay, and that's not good."

"Alright, alright. I'll think of something. Give me two weeks."

"Two weeks, Mr. Lindsay." The line went dead.

Lindsay leaned back, his hands shaking. He'd already taken out another hundred grand on his mortgage without telling his wife and the bank wouldn't give him any more. He'd been counting on the money from the drug bust. Now he'd need to find another solution.

The intercom buzzed again.

"What?" replied Lindsay tersely, thinking his 'other bank' may be phoning back to reinforce their threat.

"There's a woman on the phone saying she's Communications Director for the Governor. She wants to talk to you."

"Jeremy Roberts, the state governor?" Lindsay asked with surprise.

"That's the one."

"What's her name?"

"Allison Sheffield."

"Put her on."

Allison Sheffield came on the line. "Deputy Chief Lindsay?"

"Good morning Ms. Sheffield. What can I do for you?"

"The Governor asked me to give you a call. He wants me to have a member of my staff work with you on special project."

"I'd be happy to help," replied Lindsay, completely bewildered. "What kind of project?"

"I'm sending her to see you. Her name is Janice Fox. She'll explain the whole thing and will work with you closely. She has the Governor's complete confidence and he specifically picked her for this assignment. Can you meet with her tomorrow afternoon? Say two o'clock?"

"Of course. I'll clear my calendar."

"Thank you. I will report your cooperation to the Governor. I know he will be very appreciative." The line promptly went dead.

Lindsay was perplexed. He had only met the Governor once and he was surprised that Roberts even remembered his name. However, whatever this mysterious project was, it was an opportunity. If Jeremy Roberts made it clear he wanted Lindsay as the next Chief, Patrick Kelton and the rest of the city police commission would fall in line.

• • • • • • •

Chris LePan awoke and squinted at the clock beside his bed. Christ! It was almost nine. He looked over at the girl still sleeping beside him. Sometimes, in exchange for tipping off drug dealers on pending raids by the narcotics squad he arranged for girls rather than money. The girl beside him had been worth every penny. Couldn't be more than seventeen he thought. A looker too—even in the morning. What a waste. In ten years, she'd look forty. Pimps wouldn't touch her then. Be selling it herself on street corners for eating money.

He shook her awake. "Come on gorgeous. Time to go back to work, for both of us."

The girl woke up, rolled over and looked up at him. "Couldn't I stay here for the day? I'm tired and Gino will make me work."

"We got to do what we got to do," replied LePan, unsympathetically. "Hustle, hustle. I want you out of here before I leave. I'll call you a cab. It'll be here in ten minutes. Be ready or you'll walk."

The girl stroked his chest meaningfully. "Let me stay. I'll make you happy when you get home."

LePan whacked her bare buttocks. "I said get up!"

"Ow! You bastard." she yelled, jumping from the bed.

Once the girl had left, LePan grabbed a quick breakfast and then went to his garage, stopping for a moment to admire his midnight blue Jaguar XF. He'd owned it just a few months and still savored the sleek lines, rich leather upholstery and impressive power. Life was good and he lived well—big house, fancy car, crack and girls whenever he wanted. His bank account was growing from money he collected from tipping off drug dealers, and the million he'd taken from the stakeout with Gordon had certainly helped. It had been so easy. When he'd returned to the car, he'd simply moved the briefcase from the front seat to the trunk, telling the others it was gone and that Sarah was the only one who could have taken it. The other guys were schmucks. Wasting their lives working for sixty or seventy grand a year and then retiring on a subsistence pension.

He thought about Sarah Andrews. It had been a week since they'd got that ridiculous 'librarian' note and nothing had happened. Give the girl credit though, she had guts. She'd survived prison and apparently taken out Arnold Carney. But then Carney was a toad.

LePan arrived at the precinct at nine-thirty. As usual, he was late and he hoped Gordon wouldn't notice. He slid into his desk and turned on his personal computer, trying to appear as if he'd been there for a while. All the cops had PCs now. It showed their assignments, case status, court dates, emails, and vacation schedule. He couldn't imagine how they'd managed before. When the monitor came to life, he idly watched the login script. When requested, he keyed in his password and waited for the screen to display his personal home page.

Suddenly the entire screen was filled with an image of flames. Then the words "*Burn in Hell*" appeared in black letters. An instant later, the image disappeared and his home page appeared. LePan stared at the screen in disbelief, wondering if he'd imagined it. He looked around the squad room. No one else seemed to be having problems. It *must* have been his imagination. Too many late nights and too much booze and drugs.

For the rest of the day, LePan tried to dismiss what he'd seen but the incident continued to haunt him. He couldn't have imagined something like that. Andrews? It wasn't possible. The department network had the latest firewall and anti-virus protection. Yet, the image of flames kept flashing through his head.

The next morning, LePan watched nervously as he logged in, but everything was normal. It *must* have been his imagination. However, the following day the image appeared again—this time the message read, *"Your time is near. The Librarian."*

"What the hell!" LePan exclaimed out loud. But by the time the others looked over, his screen displayed the usual home page.

"What's up?" asked Tom Miller, seated at the desk beside him.

"Something's wrong with my computer."

"Looks fine to me," Miller replied skeptically.

"Now. But there was a picture of flames." LePan's voice shook uncontrollably.

"Flames?" Miller replied, smirking. "Chris, your problem is too much high living."

"Yeah. You're probably right," replied LePan struggling to control his nerves, but knowing there was no way this had been his imagination.

All day he was on edge. While angry at letting himself get spooked by some goddamn librarian, he couldn't shake the fear that grew within him.

· · · · · · ·

Janice Fox arrived at Peter Lindsay's office at exactly two o'clock. She breezed in with an air of authority, immediately going to the conference table on the far end of the office, giving Lindsay no choice but to get up from his desk and join her. She was well dressed in a tailored gray business suit, navy blouse and a single strand of pearls. While trim and athletic looking, her hair was completely and prematurely gray. Lindsay guessed her to be in her early forties.

As soon as they were seated, she began. "The Governor asked me to extend his thanks for seeing me. He knows how busy you must be."

"I appreciate the opportunity to provide the Governor with any support I can."

"Then let me get right to the point."

"Please do."

"The Governor and the other leaders of the state Republican Party have identified you as someone they want to groom for senior political roles in the state capital. They feel you share their political perspectives and that you can play a leadership role in the state political arena."

Lindsay was astonished. "I'm honored, but I must say I'm surprised. I barely know the Governor and I'm not very active politically."

Janice smiled tolerantly. "The Governor is constantly on the lookout for rising talent—people with the potential to play a larger political role. You are very much on his radar screen. You're young, charismatic and very marketable."

"I don't know what to say."

"But we have a problem."

Lindsay waited.

Janice continued. "We expected you to be appointed Chief of Police then we were going to approach you to run for mayor. The timing worked perfectly. The Chief Moorby retires in less than three months and the next mayoralty election is in about two years. You would have almost two years as police chief to raise your profile and position yourself to run against Kelton for mayor. Then, as mayor of the second largest city in the state, you'd have state-wide visibility and, with it, a foundation to run for the state legislature."

Lindsay was astounded. He'd hoped to become police chief but he had never thought beyond that. "You said there was a problem?"

"We assumed you'd be appointed Chief of Police when the current chief retires. Now, it doesn't look like you're going to make it. The War on Drugs is viewed as a failure. There's a growing frustration over the increasing crime rate and widespread stories of the police corruption and abuse, particularly in your old precinct. The public wants a real change and the Police Commission members are worried that if they don't appoint someone from outside who would be perceived to have a freer mandate to deal with the issues, it will cost them at the next election. Even Patrick Kelton, who is a friend of yours, is in favor of an outside search. In fact, the commission has already discreetly engaged a prominent search firm to begin inquiries."

Lindsay was startled. He was not surprised at what she'd said and it confirmed his worst fears.

"We can still win this," Janice continued. "But we need to change the momentum and that's why I'm here."

"How do we do that?" replied Lindsay.

"First, we need to raise your visibility. We need to position you as the people's choice. That means you need to make speeches at women's clubs, variety clubs, any venue you can find. You need to come out strongly against police corruption, express your concern over the growing crime rate, especially violent crime and explain what needs to be done about it. By implication you need to portray the current chief as ineffective and out of touch."

"Ed Moorby put me in this job."

Janice shook her head with frustration. "This is politics. There is no time for sentiment or misplaced loyalty. Moorby's going to retire in three months anyway."

Lindsay nodded his acquiescence.

"We also need to get the media in your corner. Right now, they've turned against you. The drug problem, the corruption, the persistent stories of abuse. The media smells a story and is really playing it up. You need to give press conferences, interviews, etc. We've got to subtly convey the message that your hands have been tied; but once appointed chief, you can address these problems."

"You make it sound easy," replied Lindsay.

"It's not easy, but it can be done. The media and the public are amazingly fickle."

Lindsay nodded.

"There's not a lot of time left, so we need to move fast," Janice continued. "The Governor has asked me to move to the city for the next three months and work on this full time. I've booked a suite at The Plaza, just down the street. I am already lining up some speaking engagements for you. You and I will need to meet at least twice a week to discuss status and opportunities. We shouldn't meet here too often so most of the meetings will have to be in my suite or your suite at The Windsor."

Lindsay looked at her in surprise. How did she know about his suite at the Windsor? What else did she know?

"Peter. I've thrown a lot at you quickly, but I've done this dozens of times before," Janice continued more softly. "It's what I do, and I'm good at it. I don't see any problem getting this back on track. But I'll expect your full support and cooperation, and I'll be reporting directly to the Governor regularly on our progress."

Lindsay nodded, suppressing his annoyance. It was clear she expected him to do exactly what she asked, but he reconciled himself to it, realizing it was in his own interest.

"Agreed?" Janice asked pointedly, clearly not satisfied with his nod.

"Agreed."

"Good. Here's my card. You can reach me on my cell phone anytime. I'll be in touch in a day or two."

She rose and saw herself out of Lindsay's office, barely giving him time to say goodbye.

After she left, Lindsay sat at his desk for a long time, reflecting on the extraordinary meeting. He would never have guessed. The Governor himself wanted Lindsay to get the Police Chief's job and had sent one of his people to make sure he got it. That certainly enhanced his chances, and, despite her arrogance, the prospect of working with Janice Fox was not unappealing.

· · · · · · ·

LePan hadn't been sleeping well. The computer images had stopped, but he swore someone had been getting into his house. His sophisticated home alarm system, which logged all entries to the house, showed nothing. Neither did the closed circuit video system that monitored the grounds and the garage. But he kept noticing little things. Papers on his desk seemed to have been rearranged. One morning the alarm went off at eight when he was positive he'd set it at seven-thirty. Was it Andrews? Why change his alarm? Just to show she could? To spook him?

"Jesus, Chris. You look like you've seen a ghost," Kramer ribbed him one day.

Miller shook his head. "It's all that high living. It's catching up to him."

"Knock it off, guys," replied LePan. "Either of you heard any-thing more from Sarah Andrews after that first note?"

"Nothing," replied Kramer, dismissively. "It was just a stupid attempt to scare us. What could she really do?"

LePan looked at Miller for confirmation. "Nothing," Miller confirmed. "Why do you ask?"

"No reason. Just happened to think about it," replied LePan, feigning nonchalance he didn't feel.

Miller looked at him intently, obviously unconvinced. "You sure there's not more to this? You look like shit. Your hands are shaking. Out of the blue, you ask about that librarian note."

"It's nothing. Forget it."

That night, LePan carefully set his alarm clock for seven-thirty. The next morning he awoke on his own. It was seven-forty. Wondering why the alarm hadn't woken him, he looked over but couldn't see the lighted dial of the clock. Maybe the power had gone out. Then the unmistakable smell of burnt plastic hit him. He switched on the light and there it was! His alarm clock was now a melted heap of plastic and electronic components puddled in the middle of the floor. She'd been there! In his bedroom as he slept. Could she still be in his house? He checked every room. Nothing. The home alarm system indicated that none of the doors had been unlocked or opened during the night. How the hell? He *had* to stop this. He'd talk to Gordon and the others that morning. There must be something they could do.

Nervously, he rushed through his shower and breakfast, jerking fearfully at every noise and shadow. Swallowing the last of his coffee, he grabbed his keys and entered the garage through the door leading from the back vestibule. Once in the driver's seat, he reached for the remote to open the garage door and pushed the button. Nothing happened. He tried again. Still nothing. Cursing, he started to get out to open the door manually but the car's doors were locked. He pushed the *unlock* button of the electronic locking system. Nothing. It was frozen! Beginning to panic, he tried opening the windows. The power window control was also frozen. Suddenly his cell phone rang through the car's Bluetooth connection.

"Hello," LePan answered, anxiously.

"Car troubles?" came a woman's voice.

"Who is this?"

"You *know* who it is," Sarah replied.

LePan couldn't suppress a shudder of fear. Sarah Andrews! How the hell was she doing it? Getting into his house, tampering with his car. It seemed she could do anything she wanted.

"Nothing to say, Christopher?"

"You won't get away with this," LePan replied, reaching for the gun he kept in the glove box. The gun was gone.

"Sorry, Christopher. Couldn't let you have a gun."

Startled, LePan looked around. She must be in the garage watching! Yet he saw nothing.

"Great video system you installed. These wireless systems are vulnerable though. Anyone can hack in."

As LePan looked over at the video camera, the monitor nodded up and down as if mocking him. "Hi Christopher," Sarah said.

God. She was not only watching, she was controlling the camera.

"What the hell do you want?"

"I just wanted to chat. Did you miss me?'

"Fuck you!" LePan tried to conceal his growing terror.

"Hope you enjoyed the million dollars," Sarah replied pleasantly. "Is that where the Jag came from?"

LePan was stunned. How the hell did she know he'd taken it? "I don't know what you're talking about."

"Of course you do. The million you and your buddies were trying to steal. The million *you* took for yourself and then convinced your friends that I must have taken it."

"That's bullshit."

"And then you and your buddies worked me over with that taser to get me to talk when all the time you *knew* I had no idea where the money was. I think you can understand why I'm a little annoyed, can't you?"

LePan tried starting the car, thinking he could crash through the garage door and get away, but the engine wouldn't start.

"Sorry Christopher. You're not going anywhere. You know, the electronics in cars these days are really amazing. Did you know I can control everything by remote control?"

"God damn you! You can't keep me in here forever."

"Didn't plan to. Incidentally, your fuel line's got a leak in it. Can't imagine how that happened. I'm afraid when the car starts, it may go up in flames. Could get a little warm in there. Sorry."

"For Christ's sake!" LePan gasped, realizing how she planned to kill him.

"Now don't get upset. I think it's only fair, don't you?"

"Not this way!" LePan begged.

"I begged too, Christopher. Didn't do me any good."

"What do you want?" LePan continued desperately. "I can give you money."

"Don't need money, Christopher."

"What then?"

"Was nice chatting to you Christopher. Goodbye."

"No..!" LePan screamed, but his scream was cut off as his car burst into flames.

· · · · · · ·

Just hours later, Peter Lindsay got a call from John Gordon. "In case you haven't already heard, Chris LePan is dead."

"Christ! How?"

"Trapped in a burning car. In his own garage."

"Andrews?"

"Must have been. The electronics had been tampered with."

Lindsay shook his head in dismay. "God dammit!"

"Miller and Kramer told me that something was spooking Chris," Gordon added, "but he wouldn't tell them what it was."

"We've got to stop her."

"We're looking, Peter, but it's like chasing a ghost."

CHAPTER 26

TWO HOURS AFTER LINDSAY HEARD ABOUT CHRIS LEPAN, HIS assistant put through a call from Janice Fox. She wasted no time on preliminaries. "I just heard the news reports on Chris LePan's murder."

"I didn't realize it was out yet."

"You've got a press conference in two hours to address it. I'll be at your office in twenty minutes to prep you on what you should say. We'll go through possible follow-up questions and prepare answers."

Lindsay was surprised. "Who organized the press conference?"

"I did."

"What about Chief Moorby?"

"I've talked to him. He's agreed to stand down and let you take the lead on this."

Lindsay shook his head in astonishment. Janice Fox seemed to get her way on everything. "Who's coming?" he asked.

"Reporters from the major TV stations, radio and the papers. It's scheduled for two o'clock in the conference room on the second floor of your building. This is a great opportunity for you to demonstrate your control of the situation and steady leadership under fire."

"You don't fool around."

"No. I don't."

Twenty minutes later, Janice arrived, ignoring his assistant and walking into Lindsay's office without knocking. She closed the door and perched on the corner of his desk. "You look like you've seen a ghost."

"I don't like losing men, especially that way," Lindsay replied, hoping the explanation would satisfy her.

Janice looked at him intently. "Did you know Chris LePan?"

"We used to work together."

"Any idea who did it?"

"From the little information I have, it looks like it a professional hit. An investigation is underway and I'm confident we'll find out who is responsible and bring them to justice."

"Great line. Use it in the press conference," replied Janice.

Lindsay couldn't tell if she was being sarcastic and he was becoming annoyed at her arrogance and automatic assumption of authority. Breezing into his office as if she owned the place. Calling a press conference without even checking with him. Presuming to tell him what he should say. Still, she was from the Governor's office and he'd better play along. "Whatever you think."

"And one other thing."

Lindsay concealed his frustration. "What?"

"Here's a bank draft for a hundred thousand. Pay off that gambling debt and don't deal with those guys again."

Lindsay looked at her nonplussed. "How..?"

"How did I know?" Janice interrupted, with a hint of irritation in her voice. "I told you. It's my business to know. We're investing in you, Peter. We have to know what we're getting."

"Thank you," he replied, awkwardly, taking the draft.

At the beginning of the press conference, Lindsay read the prepared statement Janice had given him. He had to admit it was good. He described LePan's death as the cold-blooded execution of a devoted public servant and went on to say he believed it was the work of organized crime syndicates operating in the city. He maintained that this proved the 'War on Drugs' was working and that LePan's murder was a futile attempt to intimidate the police.

Afterwards Lindsay fielded questions from the media. Janice had anticipated almost everything they asked and prepared him with the answers. Lindsay had to acknowledge that the press conference had been a big success. What could have been a public relations disaster had been turned into a successful opportunity to raise his profile.

· · · · · · ·

Two days after LePan's death, Lindsay met with Gordon, Kramer, Carlucci and Miller. Their tone was subdued.

"What's up?" Gordon prompted after Lindsay had remained silent for several seconds.

Lindsay looked at them. "Andrews. This is getting out of hand. Carney. LePan. She's going to keep coming unless we stop her."

John Gordon replied hesitantly. "We're doing everything we can to find her."

"Well, it obviously isn't enough!" Lindsay hoped the others hadn't detected the edge of fear in his voice.

"I'd like to know how she got into Chris's house," Miller commented. "He had an expensive alarm system and steel doors with double bolts."

"We think she hacked into the alarm company's system and found out LePan's security code. Then she was able to deactivate his alarm at will," explained Gordon.

Miller shook his head in astonishment. "Incredible. But it doesn't explain how she undid the locks."

"Apparently, the security system can be used to lock and unlock the doors and windows electronically."

"Jesus!" Miller exclaimed. "Now that I think of it, Chris mentioned problems with his computer at work too."

Lindsay looked at him sharply. "What kind of problems?"

"A couple of days ago, he said there was a picture of flames on his PC screen."

"Flames. Like she was warning him how he was going to die," Kramer commented.

"Jesus!" Lindsay leaned back in his chair in utter frustration. "How the hell is she doing this?"

"According to the manager of the library where she used to work, she's quite a computer geek," Gordon explained. "Set up the network in the library and an automated notification system for regular patrons. Her set-up is now being used as the model for all the libraries in the city. Said she also did contract programming on the side."

"John. I want you to put more men on it," continued Lindsay. "Make up some cover story. Tell your precinct captain it's coming from me. I want every part of her past life staked out, right back to her friends from high school. She's probably changed her identity, but she can't avoid making some connection with her past forever. We need to be there waiting, and then we'll nail her. And find the white-haired guy! If he knows how to fight, maybe he's got a military background."

"Good idea," Gordon replied.

"One other thing," continued Lindsay. "The murders of Carney and LePan were meticulously planned. She knew where they lived, knew their routines. She'd been watching them. She's out there somewhere, watching us, planning her next move."

The group remained silent. Lindsay's observation that she must be stalking them struck home. Privately, they each wondered who was next.

· · · · · · ·

A day later, Lindsay got a call from Janice Fox requesting a meeting that evening at her suite. Predictably, she didn't ask whether he was free. Lindsay arrived at six as she had suggested. To his surprise, she greeted him at the door wearing a low-cut blouse that revealed a lot of cleavage and pajama pants that clung to her hips and legs. A very different image than the professional wardrobe she wore when she met him in his office. Again he was struck by her lithe and toned body, which belied her gray hair. He wondered why she didn't color it. It would make her look ten years younger. It was almost as if she used it as a personal statement, 'I'm gray and I don't give a damn.'

"Thank you for meeting me here," she greeted him. "I don't want to be seen at your office too often."

"No problem. It's nice to get away."

"Can I offer you a drink? I'm having wine."

"Sure. I'll have the same."

Peter Lindsay settled himself on one end of the couch and watched as Janice went to the sideboard, poured him a glass of wine and then refilled her own. She returned to the couch and settled herself facing him with her knee almost touching his. Lindsay was acutely conscious of her closeness, her cleavage and the smell of her perfume.

Janice smiled warmly and touched his knee. "Cheers. You handled the press conference on LePan very well. I'm sure you noticed that a number of the papers commented favorably on the strong leadership you demonstrated."

"I did. Thanks for setting it all up."

"I've arranged for you to speak at a Chamber of Commerce dinner next Wednesday," Janice continued. "It's an influential group and it will be a great chance for you to raise your profile in the business community. Here's a copy of the speech I'd like you to give. It stresses the importance of low crime rates and safe streets in attracting new business to the city. It's tailored to appeal to a professional audience. Read it tonight. By all means add your own touches."

"Thanks." replied Lindsay, again irritated by her presumption that he'd read *her* speech.

"I've persuaded Mayor Patrick Kelton to introduce you," she continued. "He didn't want to do it. Felt it would look like he was endorsing you as the next Chief. But I was able to arrange for a call from the Governor's office. That did the trick."

Lindsay was amazed. Getting the Mayor to introduce him was a huge coup and Kelton wouldn't miss the fact that the Governor's office had called on his behalf. Janice definitely appeared to have easy access to the Governor. "Thanks. That *will* look good."

She talked further about her strategy. More speeches, dinners with key leaders, participation in community events. Periodically she touched his knee or arm to emphasize a point. It seemed unconscious, but Lindsay wondered.

Noticing their glasses were both empty, Janice went to refill them. When she returned, she sat even closer to him.

"So tell me. How did you get into this business?" Lindsay asked, trying to shift the conversation.

Janice smiled at him warmly, seemingly pleased at the personal question. "I sure didn't plan it. Graduated from Lennoxville University with a degree in political science. Got a job at GE in their Public Relations Department. Spent four years there, then ten years at Citi before moving to the Governor's office four years ago. Lindsay quickly did the math. Assuming she'd graduated from university at twenty-two, that made her about forty.

"Ever think of running for politics yourself?"

"I hate kissing babies."

Lindsay laughed. "I take it you have none of your own?"

"No. Never married. Too busy I guess."

"It's not too late."

Janice shrugged. "So what made you decide to join the police force?"

"My father was a street cop. His friends were cops. I just kind of drifted that way. At my mother's insistence, I got a degree in criminology. She never said it, but I'm sure she thought that if I had to be a cop, she didn't want me to be a street cop all my life like my father."

"He must be proud of you."

"I guess so," Lindsay replied. He and his father had never got on well. "He died almost ten years ago."

"I'm sorry."

"Don't be. It was quick. Massive heart attack. It's how he would have wanted it."

They talked for another hour. Janice brought the wine bottle over to the table, refilling their glasses periodically. Lindsay found her exciting and seductive and decided to make an approach.

"It's after eight and I haven't eaten. Can I buy you dinner?"

"Peter. I'd love to," Janice smiled warmly, touching him again. "But I have a conference call with the Governor and a few of his aids shortly. Another time."

"No problem," Lindsay replied, concealing his disappointment. "I've got some reports I should read tonight anyway."

"Read the speech I gave you," Janice added. "I'll call you tomorrow to see if you're satisfied with it."

At the door, Janice suddenly kissed him on the lips. "Good night, Peter. We'll do dinner another night. I promise."

As Lindsay walked back to his office, he reflected on the evening. Having the meeting at her suite, her provocative dress, the wine, how close she sat to him on the couch, the kiss at the door. There was no doubt she was interested in a relationship and the prospect excited him.

· · · · · · ·

The next morning, Lindsay got a call from Tom Miller.

"Sir. John's out on a few days vacation; but I thought you'd want to hear this right away," Miller said.

"Of course. What's up?"

"We found out who the white-haired guy is."

"Great."

"Not so great. His name is Paul Taylor. He's an ex-Navy seal. Expert at martial arts. Several medals. Reached the rank of captain before leaving the Navy. Started his own business rescuing kidnapped executives and diplomats. Has made a lot of money and some high-level connections."

"Shit!"

"Yeah. Shit."

Lindsay paused for a minute. "We *have* to take him out. Andrews may have told him everything. If so, he's as big a risk as she is. Maybe worse."

"This guy's got money and he's connected. If he disappears or shows up dead, there will be questions."

"Where does he live?"

"Got a house in the country, an hour or so out of town."

"Maybe his house burns down and he's trapped in the fire."

"Should work," replied Miller, thoughtfully. "Do you want me to wait for John to get back?"

"No. You handle it."

"Will do."

"And Tom..."

"Sir?"

"Sounds like you better take a lot of men with you."

"I'm already working on it."

CHAPTER 27

JOHN GORDON COULDN'T BELIEVE SHE HAD TAKEN AN INTER-
est in him. At fifty-four, he looked his age and he certainly
wasn't wealthy. One Saturday afternoon, she'd backed into his
car in the parking lot of the local supermarket where he had
gone to get groceries. When he'd felt the jolt, he'd angrily got
out of his car only to confront a stunning blond in her mid-
twenties. Tearfully, she'd begged him not to report the accident, offering to pay for the damage herself. Something about
having previous accidents and being afraid they would cancel
her insurance. Gordon had an old car and there was almost no
damage. When he offered to ignore the whole thing, she was
incredibly relieved and insisted on buying him dinner, suggesting an expensive steakhouse and offered to meet him there.

Gordon found Leila waiting for him in the restaurant lobby,
looking ravishing in a pink mini-skirt and sequined tank top
that left her midriff bare. As the maître d' escorted them to their

table, Gordon enjoyed the envious looks of the other males in the restaurant as they ogled her and then looked at him. Leila was very impressed that he was a cop and bombarded him with questions. What made him decide to be a cop? Had he ever shot anyone? What kind of cases did he work on? She kept him talking throughout the dinner. After leaving the restaurant, he walked her to her car, a late model, green Mustang convertible. When they reached the door, Leila suddenly kissed him firmly on the lips before hopping into the driver's seat. Through the window, she thanked him again and asked him if she could call him. Gordon said yes, but doubted she would.

Two days later, Leila phoned suggesting a picnic lunch the next day. She knew a secluded cove by the ocean just down the coast and offered to pack a lunch, a couple of bottles of wine and pick him up at ten. While excited at the prospect of seeing her again, he was vaguely puzzled at her apparent interest in him, but he put it out of his mind. Maybe she wanted a father figure, maybe she had a thing for cops. He didn't care. She was young and beautiful and he was middle-aged and lonely.

• • • • • • •

The next morning just when Gordon was beginning to think she wasn't going to show up, Leila pulled into his driveway grinning happily. "Hop in. I'm sorry I'm late."

He looked over at her. "Leila, when you were late, I realized I don't even have your phone number."

She shrugged. "I'm in the process of moving. When I get a permanent phone, I'll give you the number. I promise."

"Do you have a cell phone?" Gordon persisted.

"I'm switching carriers. I should have one in a few days."

Dismissing his doubts, he studied her discreetly as she drove. She was wearing a very short beige skirt and a loose blouse. She seemed oblivious to the fact that the skirt was riding up as she drove. She had what looked like a bikini top under the blouse and he wondered if he would get to see the whole thing.

"Did you bring a bathing suit?" she asked. "The water's beautiful." Before he could answer, Leila continued, "I bought a new bikini. I hope you'll like it."

Gordon was quite certain he would. She was tanned and fit and would look awesome in a bikini. He wondered whether he could find a way to avoid putting on his own bathing suit. He had tried it on before he left and was discouraged by the sight. While an athlete in college, he had let himself go for too long. He was soft and pale and there were rolls of fat around his waist. He'd resolved to start watching what he ate and hitting the gym.

"I bought you a present too," Leila continued. "I hope you don't mind. It's just something little, but you've done so much for me. I wanted to do something for you."

"You certainly didn't need to," Gordon replied, flattered at the gesture.

The highway was deserted and Leila drove well over the speed limit. Conscious that he was aware of her speed, she turned to him and smiled. "Relax. You're off-duty."

She chattered cheerfully all the way and Gordon barely noticed the time. After an hour, she turned off on a side road and drove for another mile before parking, explaining that they still had a half-mile walk to the cove.

She smiled excitedly. "You'll see. It's worth it."

The cove *was* beautiful. It was small and secluded, surrounded by rocky cliffs on three sides. The sand was white and untouched, the water an azure blue.

"Isn't it beautiful?" she gushed.

"It's spectacular. How did you find it?"

"Just by chance," replied Leila, spreading a blanket on the beach and laying out the food and wine. "I'm going to have a swim before we eat. Want to join me?"

"I'll get the wine ready."

"So what do you think?

He looked up to see that she had stripped off her skirt and blouse and was standing there, modeling a very skimpy bikini.

"Totally awesome," replied Gordon enthusiastically.

"You're exaggerating, but I'll take it." Leila grinned with pleasure.

She ran out into the surf a few yards and then dove into the water while Gordon watched appreciatively.

After a few minutes, she returned to the blanket. She lay down to dry herself in the sun, drops of water shimmering on her skin. "The water's wonderful. Why don't we eat and then go for another swim."

"Here," replied Gordon, handing her a glass of wine.

"Cheers," Leila replied, toasting him. "To my new best friend."

"To accidents in supermarket parking lots."

Leila laughed and then seemed to remember something. "Before we eat, I have to show you what I bought you."

Reaching into the picnic basket, she pulled out a jeweler's box and handed it to him.

Curious, Gordon opened it to find a gold chain. He was dumbfounded. "This is too much."

"It's eighteen carat gold," Leila announced proudly. "I wanted to give you something nice."

"It's beautiful," he replied, startled at the generosity of the gift. "But you really..."

"Look," she interrupted excitedly. "There's a flat link in the middle. It's engraved."

Gordon read the inscription. 'Forever, Leila' was all it said.

"See," Leila explained happily. "When you wear it, I'll be with you—and you'll think of me."

"It's a wonderful present. Thank you," replied Gordon, both touched and a little perplexed at what she'd done.

"Here, let me put it on for you." She knelt behind him and fastened it around his neck. Gordon was acutely conscious of her warmth and the softness of her breasts pressing against his back. The clasp locked with an audible click.

Admiring her handiwork, Leila began unbuttoning his shirt. "You've got to show it off," she insisted. Gordon was intensely aware of her fingers lingering against his chest.

They ate the lunch and polished off most of the two bottles of wine. Gordon was beginning to feel the effects of the alcohol and was vaguely conscious that Leila seemed totally unaffected. She chattered on cheerfully and he enjoyed just listening to her. He lay back on the sand and looked up at her. Guiltily he let his eyes wander over her breasts and buttocks.

Leila noticed his gaze and laughed. "I think you like my new bikini."

Suddenly, she hopped onto his hips, straddling him with her knees. She took off her top and smiled down at him. "Maybe you'd like me even better *without* my new bikini?"

Gordon looked up at her and sighed with desire. Smooth skin, full breasts, taut stomach, muscular legs straddling his hips. He couldn't believe this was happening. She placed his hands on her breasts and gyrated her hips over his loins. Gordon felt himself stiffen. She leaned down and began kissing his chest, before lying on him and kissing him deeply on the mouth. He felt her naked breasts against his chest and her hips grinding against him. He was also vaguely conscious of her feeling for something in the sand beside his head and he thought he heard a faint click.

. . . .

Suddenly Leila rolled off him and jumped to her feet, putting her top back on. In an instant, her entire demeanor had changed.

"Is something wrong?" Gordon asked bewildered, but Leila did not reply. She simply stood there, a few feet away, looking down at him with a strange expression.

Gordon started to get up, but felt a jerk around his neck. The chain Leila had given him was caught on something in the sand and he couldn't lift his head more than a foot off the ground. He tugged to free himself but it was firmly stuck. He fumbled with the clasp to take off the chain, but it wouldn't release.

Feeling silly lying there while she stood over him, Gordon called to her. "Leila, I'm sorry if I did something. Here, help me get this damn thing unstuck."

"I have to go now," she replied, setting off down the beach.

"Wait! What do you mean you have to go?" Gordon called out, still struggling to free himself.

Leila walked rapidly towards the path they'd come from as he strained to unfasten the chain. Finally, he tried to break it, but the chain wouldn't snap. He yanked at it with all his might but it still held fast. By now, Leila was out of sight and he was alone on the beach. Anxiously, he called after her but there was no response.

Suddenly he became aware that he was *not* alone. A woman was standing there quietly looking down at him. The sun was directly behind her and he couldn't make her out against in the glare. Where had she come from? Who was she?

"Hello, John."

He'd heard the voice before, but couldn't place it.

The woman stepped away from the sun. It was her! The librarian. Sarah Andrews. It had all been a set-up—to lure him here. To kill him. He'd been so gullible. Angrily, he yanked at the chain, but it held fast.

"Save your strength," Sarah said with distain. "The chain isn't gold, it's plated steel. The clasp doesn't unlock without a special key. And the chain is now locked to an old ship-wrecked freighter buried in the sand.

"Where's Leila?" asked Gordon, vainly looking for help.

"She's gone. Twenty-thousand dollars and a new sports car. Easy money for luring you here. Did you really assume a girl like Leila could be interested in you?" Sarah asked scornfully.

"What are you going to do?"

"Nothing."

"Don't bullshit me," Gordon said bitterly, angry with himself for having fallen for the trap so easily. "You've got me here. Alone. You're going to kill me, like you did the others. Where's your gun?"

"Didn't bring one."

"So what are you going to do?"

"I told you—nothing."

"I don't understand."

"You cops really are slow, aren't you?"

"What do you mean?"

"The tide's coming in. High tide where you are lying is about three feet above the level of the beach. The most you can lift your head is about one foot. You figure it out."

Suddenly Gordon realized how she meant to kill him. It would be a slow excruciating death. "For God's sake! Not that way."

Sarah just shrugged, picked up the food and blanket and moved to higher ground, where she sat down, calmly eating an apple and sipping the last of the wine.

Gordon felt the water lapping at his feet and realized the tide was already coming in.

"There *is* something I'd like to tell you, John."

Gordon looked at her blankly.

"The missing million dollars. It was your friend LePan who took it. All he did was move it from the front seat to the trunk. Then he convinced you all that I must have stolen it."

Gordon remembered LePan's insistence that Sarah had taken the money and his eagerness to use the taser on her. He remembered the new jag LePan had bought. God! What had they done?

"I didn't want to do it," he pleaded. "I left the room. Later I made them stop. You must remember that?"

Sarah looked at him with mixture of pity and disgust. "You let it happen and you could have stopped it."

"I'll go to the authorities and confess what we did. I'll implicate all of them. Even Lindsay."

"It's too late John."

"Please!" begged Gordon.

"Relax John. It will all be over in less than half an hour," Sarah replied, picking up the blanket and heading back up the path.

CHAPTER 28

THREE DAYS AFTER THEY HAD TALKED ABOUT THE HIT ON Paul Taylor, Peter Lindsay took a call from Tom Miller. "How did it go?" he asked immediately.

"We burned his house to the ground—with him in it."

"Good. Find out anything about Sarah Andrews?"

"Couldn't. He heard us coming and holed up in the house, with some serious artillery. If we had tried to take him alive, there would have been casualties, and that would have required some explaining."

"So it's not going to look like an accidental fire?"

"No. If there's an investigation, they will find signs of gunfire. Nothing we could do. The guy started shooting at us. Don't think it's a problem. A guy like Taylor makes a lot of enemies."

"I hope so," replied Lindsay, skeptically. "Did you actually see the body?"

"It was too hot to get close. But we know he was inside. We barricaded the doors, dowsed the house with gasoline, and set it on fire. The house was wood and went up like a roman candle. We couldn't get within fifty feet of it. We watched it burn until there was nothing left but a pile of blackened ruble. There's no way he could have survived."

"Good work."

"Thanks. There *is* one other thing you should know," added Miller.

"What's that?" replied Lindsay, sensing trouble.

"John Gordon is missing."

There was a long pause. "Jesus. How long?"

"Just a couple of days. He booked off for a few days. Was supposed to be back last Tuesday."

"No word from him?"

"Nothing. We called his house. No answer. I went by to check it out. His car was in the driveway, but he wasn't there."

"Did you go in?"

"Yeah. I know where he hides a spare key. Nothing was disturbed. No phone messages. No clues as to where he went. Nothing."

"Keep looking." Lindsay hung up, already certain that 'the librarian' had claimed another victim.

· · · · · · ·

Gordon's body was found three days later. Lindsay had the investigating officer brief him directly.

"What happened?"

"He drowned; but it was no accident," the officer began.

"Explain."

When Lindsay finished listening to the explanation, he shook his head in frustration. "Any indication who did it?"

"We're still investigating but nothing so far."

"Could it have been a woman?'

The officer looked at Lindsay in surprise. "Actually we think so. The neck chain had 'Forever Leila' engraved on it. But with no last name, it's not much help."

"Any other leads? Footprints, tire tracks? Anything?"

"Nothing. Looks like whoever did it knew what they were doing."

"Keep looking—and keep me informed," ordered Lindsay.

After the investigator left his office, Lindsay leaned back in his chair. There was no question it was Sarah Andrews. Carney, LePan, Gordon. Each one of them had died horribly. Just like she had said they would. And she was still out there. Taylor's death obviously hadn't stopped her, or perhaps she didn't know yet.

· · · · · · ·

A day later, Lindsay took a call from Janice. "I just heard about John Gordon," she commented. "Any connection with LePan?"

"I doubt it," replied Lindsay evasively. He was surprised that the possibility had occurred to her.

"It will get a lot of press attention, particularly so quickly following LePan's death," Janice continued. "We need to come out quickly and proactively. I'm organizing another press conference."

"Okay," Lindsay replied, half-heartedly.

"The message will be that that Gordon's death is again the work of organized crime and represents a concerted effort to intimidate the police force and discredit the 'War on Drugs'.

You will pledge to stand fast in the face of any intimidation. I'll write something up for you to review."

"Sounds good."

Sensing his lack of focus, Janice continued. "You okay, Peter?"

"Yeah. Yeah. Thanks. Just a bit upset."

After Janice had hung up, Peter Lindsay leaned back in his chair. He suddenly noticed an envelope in his inbox marked 'Personal and Confidential'. He stared at it for several minutes before opening it.

Two Down, Four to Go

> *At first, the evil trolls didn't believe the poor librarian would really try to kill them. But now the wicked dwarf and two of the evil trolls are dead. Soon the other four will die. They deserve to die for what they did. Once they are dead, the poor librarian will live happily ever after. Sleep well, evil trolls. I am coming.*

The Librarian

Lindsay crumbled the note and angrily threw it in the garbage, but his action didn't stop the ball of fear growing in his gut.

· · · · · · ·

Three days after Gordon's death, Sarah was sitting on her balcony having toast and coffee for breakfast. The air was clear and the sky a brilliant blue. She felt good. Strong, confident and in control. She wondered what they were thinking now. At first, they probably hadn't taken her note seriously. Now they would know better. She wanted them to feel afraid, helpless; as she had felt helpless and afraid. There were four to go. Kramer,

Carlucci, Miller and Lindsay. Lindsay would be last. He was the leader, the one who could have stopped it. He was the one who arranged for her to go to prison. She wanted him to feel the fear of anticipation, to see the others killed until he was the only one left, and then to know that he was next.

Sarah's thoughts turned to Paul. She missed him terribly. His touch, his easy smile, the warmth of his body beside her in bed. She wanted so much to share her success with him, but knew she could not. Her 'project' was the one thing she couldn't share.

Strange she thought. She'd called Paul three times over the last couple of days. He hadn't picked up the phone and the answering machine hadn't cut in. She dismissed her concerns. As soon as she'd dealt with Ernie Kramer, she would drive out to Crystal Lake and surprise him.

CHAPTER 29

CLARA KRAMER WAS LATE ARRIVING AT PINNACLE Automobile, the auto dealership where she worked part-time as a receptionist. As she entered the building, she hoped she could get to her desk before the owner noticed. However, Sam Cavell was standing just inside the door talking to a customer. When he finished, he summoned her to his office.

"Clara," he began gently. "You do a great job—when you're here. The sales reps all like you. You're great with the customers and I'd really hate to lose you. But you're constantly late. I need a receptionist who's here when we open, not half an hour later."

"I'm sorry, Mr. Cavell. Something happened at home." What she didn't say was that her husband, Ernie, had slapped her for running out of orange juice.

"Clara, things happen and we can cover for you once in a while, but not every other day."

"I know, Mr. Cavell. You've been very understanding and I appreciate it. It won't happen again." Clara desperately needed the job to cover the cost of her son's piano lessons. which her husband refused to pay for. Tony loved the piano and Clara couldn't bear the thought of pulling him out of his classes.

Noticing the fresh bruise on her cheek, visible under her make-up, Cavell asked, "What happened to your cheek?"

"It's nothing. I bumped into a cabinet at home. I bruise easily."

He shook his head sadly. He'd seen too many bruises to believe her story. Her husband had once come to the dealership and yelled at Clara for something she had supposedly done. Cavell ordered him out of the building and considered calling the police. Clara begged him not to, explaining that Ernie *was* a cop.

"Okay, Clara," Cavell said sadly. "I think I understand, and I'm sorry. Just see what you can do."

"I will, Mr. Cavell, and thank you," she replied gratefully.

Clara went out to the reception desk and sat down. Ernie was getting worse. The slaps and punches, once rare, were becoming a regular occurrence. Ernie hadn't hit Tony yet, but he'd threatened to often enough. She knew she had to do something, but what? Who could she call? Her husband was a cop. If she ran away with Tony, he had the resources to find her.

A few minutes later, a young woman entered the dealership and came over to her. "I'm looking to buy a compact car. Do you think...? Wait a minute. Are you Clara Spinelli?"

"Yes," Clara replied, puzzled. "I'm married now— Clara Kramer."

"And you went to Northumberland High School?"

"Yes," Clara replied, still perplexed. She studied the woman standing in front of her but couldn't place her at all.

"Don't you remember me? Belinda Newton."

"I'm sorry," Clara stammered. "It was a long time ago."

"Don't worry about it. I wasn't as high profile as you," Belinda explained. "I remember you though. You did everything well. Honor list, president of the math club, top scorer on the girls' volleyball team. Right?"

Clara nodded bewildered. How could she not even recognize this woman who knew all about her?

"Clara, I'm new in town. Is there any chance you're free for lunch? I'd love to catch up on old times, and I could use a friend."

"I get off at one. We could go for a sandwich," Clara replied, hesitantly. Ernie wouldn't approve, but he wouldn't be home before four. Although she couldn't remember Belinda at all, the chance to reminisce was appealing and lunch with another woman would be nice.

"That would be great. I'll come back at one. My treat."

• • • • • • •

Belinda returned promptly at one and the two of them went off to a nearby patio restaurant. They ordered wine with lunch and talked about school, their lives, men and their favorite movies. When lunch was over, they ordered more wine and chatted for another hour. Clara found herself laughing and joking, and realized that it had been a long time since she'd had a chance just to talk girl talk with a friend.

"I was in awe of you," said Belinda. "You were so good at everything, yet you were never stuck-up like a lot of the girls."

"I guess I never felt that I was that good," Clara replied. "Just lucky maybe." She *had* been successful at school she thought to herself. Good marks, a talented athlete and popular with the other students. Ernie made her feel so worthless that she'd almost forgotten.

"You said you're married now?" asked Belinda.

"Yes. I married shortly after I graduated."

"Children?"

"One. Tony. He's ten."

"Are you happy?" Belinda asked softly.

"I… yes, of course…" The lack of conviction hung in the air.

Belinda remained silent.

"I don't know," Clara stammered in response to the unspoken question. "All marriages have their problems."

"I noticed your cheek."

"It was an accident…"

Belinda just nodded.

"I… I don't…" Clara stammered and then began to cry softly.

"It's all right. Would it help to talk about it?"

To her surprise, Clara found herself telling Belinda everything. Her first date with Ernie in high school, her infatuation with the tall handsome athlete that Ernie had been at the time, giving in to Ernie's demands for sex for fear she would lose him. She described the death of her parents in an auto accident six months before she graduated, her hurried marriage to Ernie and her disappointment when he had chosen to join the police force rather than go on to college. She described her reluctant acquiescence when Ernie had insisted they start a family rather than let her go to university, despite the scholarship offers she'd received. Sadly, she recounted Ernie's growing discontent with her, no matter how she tried to please him. The verbal abuse that gradually evolved to physical abuse—at first it was just the occasional slap, but now it was becoming increasingly violent. Belinda just listened quietly, letting Clara talk it out.

Simply being able to talk about it made Clara feel better. With her parents dead and no close friends, she'd had no one to share her problems with.

"Oh Belinda," added Clara with tears in her eyes. "I'm so worried about Tony. He's a sensitive boy. Ernie hasn't hit him yet but he's threatened a lot. It isn't right that a boy is afraid of his own father."

"Have you thought about leaving him?" Belinda asked gently, touching Clara's hand in silent support.

"Sometimes," Clara admitted, sadly. "But where would I go? I have no money. I have to look after Tony. I couldn't bear going to one of those shelters for battered women."

"I have a two-bedroom apartment on Pine Street," Belinda replied. "I'm not using it and the lease isn't up for almost a year. You're welcome to use it as long as you want."

"Oh, I couldn't. I barely know you."

"It's nothing. I'd like to do it. Here I'll write down my name and phone number. Think about it. Call me."

Clara took it. "Thank you."

They left the restaurant together and Belinda promised to call her for lunch again.

"I'd like that. It was fun." It was the first time in a long time Clara had been out with a woman friend and she had enjoyed it. She looked at her watch and hurried to get home before her husband.

· · · · · · ·

It was only a few blocks from the restaurant back to her condominium and Sarah decided to walk. So far, she had pulled it off, managing to convince Clara that Belinda Newton really was an old schoolmate. She knew from her research that Ernie

Kramer was abusing his wife and she intended to use Clara to get to him. To her surprise, she genuinely liked her. Clara was intelligent, vivacious and funny; but Sarah could see the pain in her eyes. Her marriage to an abusive and demeaning husband was insidiously crushing her spirit. As well as advancing her project, destroying Ernie Kramer would give Clara a chance at a new life.

Three days later, Sarah phoned Clara again for lunch. They met at another outdoor pub, ordered beer and pizza and easily picked up where they left off.

"How's it going with Ernie?" Sarah asked finally.

"I don't know, Belinda," said Clara sadly. "He's never happy. No matter what I do. I try so hard to please him. But nothing works. He yells at Tony all the time. Makes fun of him. Calls him a sissy for playing the piano."

"Has he hurt you again?"

"Nothing serious. A few slaps. He twists my arm behind my back until I beg him to stop. I think he likes hearing me beg."

"Clara. You *have* to leave him."

"I can't."

"Why not? You can do it right now. We'll pick up Tony and I'll take you to my apartment. The one I told you about."

"I don't have any money. I couldn't pay you. And I'd have nothing to live on."

"You don't need to pay me. I'll give you money to live on until you can find a job and start a new life."

"Ernie would find me. He's a cop. He can track me down. You don't know him. If I ran away, he'd go crazy."

"I'll take care of Ernie," replied Sarah quietly.

Clara looked at her in surprise, and for an instant, she saw the terrible anger in Sarah's eyes. "What do you mean?"

"It doesn't matter. Ernie won't come after you again. I promise."

"I can't," Clara replied forlornly.

"You *have* to. You can't live this way. You need a life. You need to live with someone you love. Tony needs a real father."

"I'll talk to him. I'll tell him things have to change. That he can't hit me any more, that he has to be good to Tony. If it doesn't work, I'll call you. I promise."

"All right," replied Sarah skeptically. "Have you still got my number?"

"Yes, I kept it in my purse."

· · · · · · ·

Late the next evening, Sarah's cell phone rang. It was Clara!

"Belinda?" Clara screamed. "Ernie's gone crazy! He's threatening to break Tony's fingers."

"I'm on my way."

"Hurry! Please!"

"Get off that phone!" Kramer yelled in the background. The line went dead. Sarah would never forget that voice and she felt the latent anger rising within her.

Ten minutes later, Sarah was at the Kramer's house, praying she wasn't too late. The front door was unlocked and she went in. As she entered, she heard a scream upstairs and the sound of a boy crying. She quickly climbed the stairs and found them all in the master bedroom. Clara was cowering in the corner, bruised and bleeding. Tony was vainly trying to protect his mother from his father who was standing over her with a baseball bat. None of them noticed Sarah standing in the doorway.

Ernie Kramer was screaming at his wife. "Who the hell are you to tell me you're going to leave unless I treat you better?

You get treated far better than you deserve, you stupid bitch. You need a lesson in respect," he added, raising the bat over his shoulder.

"No!" Tony screamed. "Don't hurt her!"

"He won't hurt her," said Sarah coolly.

Ernie Kramer whirled around. "What the hell? Who the fuck are you?"

"Put the bat down."

"You must be the new girlfriend who's putting all these crazy ideas in my wife's head. How did you get in here anyway?"

"I said put the bat down," Sarah repeated calmly.

"I'll teach you to interfere," Kramer shouted, moving toward her, still holding the bat.

Sarah made no move to back away or defend herself. She had no weapon and Kramer was puzzled by her apparent lack of fear.

Kramer raised the baseball bat above his head. "I'm going to crack your fucking skull open. This is none of your damn business and you have no right coming into my house."

"We'll see."

"Damn right we'll see!" Kramer replied, viciously swinging the bat towards her head. To his astonishment, he hit nothing but empty air. Furious, he swung again. This time, Sarah grabbed the bat and twisted it from his hands before tossing it out the bedroom door.

"All right, bitch," Kramer yelled, lunging at her throat. "We'll do this the hard way."

Sarah easily sidestepped and Kramer's unchecked momentum caused him to crash into the wall. Enraged he charged her again. "God damn you!" he screamed. This time Sarah stuck out her leg and sent him sprawling into the opposite wall.

Kramer hit his head hard and lay there, momentarily dazed. Clara watched in amazement as Sarah effortlessly handled her six-foot husband.

Keeping an eye on Kramer's moaning figure, Sarah helped Clara to her feet. "Here's the address of my apartment and a key. And here's some cash," she added, handing Clara a thick roll of bills. "Go to a neighbor's house or a nearby store and call a cab to take you there. I'll come by tomorrow."

"You leave this house and you're dead," Kramer shouted at his wife, struggling to his feet.

"Stay down Kramer, and keep your mouth shut!" Sarah hissed savagely.

Clara hesitated, wanting to go, but terrified of what her husband would do.

"Go!" Sarah ordered. "He won't come after you. I promise."

"Don't believe her," Kramer screamed, struggling to his feet. "She can't protect you—or Tony. I'll get you!"

"I told you to stay down," Sarah replied, easily knocking his feet out from under him, sending him crashing back to the ground.

Clara grabbed Tony and ran down the stairs.

"I'll come after you!" Kramer yelled as they fled out the front door.

Sarah looked down at him with contempt. "You're not going anywhere."

"Who the hell are you?" Kramer sputtered.

"After what you did to me, I'd think you would at least recognize me."

Only then did Kramer realize who she was. "Jesus! It's you."

"That's right," Sarah replied. "The woman you tortured and sent to prison."

Kramer said nothing. He thought of Carney and LePan and Gordon. He looked into her eyes and saw the anger—and felt fear. Desperately, he struggled to his feet and stood facing her, his fists clenched. "All right, Ms. Librarian. Let's see what you've got."

Sarah easily dodged his first wild swing, casually feigned a blow to his head, and then kicked his legs out from under him. Kramer crashed back to the floor.

"Is that it?" she asked coldly.

Kramer slowly got back on his feet, only to have her deliver a savage kick to his face that shattered his nose. He crumpled to the ground moaning in pain.

"Are we done?" Sarah asked politely.

Kramer just groaned.

"You know what?" she continued. "I killed the others. But I'm not going to kill you."

Kramer looked at her suspiciously.

"It would be too good for you. Your poor wife has suffered for years—the beatings, the abuse, the degradation. You should suffer too."

"I didn't…" Kramer began.

"Don't bother," Sarah interrupted, suddenly producing a handgun. "Just so you know," she added. "These bullets have hollow points and they do an unbelievable amount of internal damage. If I hit your knee for example, you'd never walk again."

"For God's sake," begged Kramer.

Sarah calmly aimed the gun at his right knee and pulled the trigger.

CHAPTER 30

THE NEXT MORNING, PETER LINDSAY WENT TO THE HOSPITAL where Kramer had been taken and asked to see the doctor responsible for his case. "How is he?"

The doctor hesitated as if deciding how to phrase his answer. "He's still in intensive care. He's stable for now..."

Lindsay sensed the hesitation. "But?"

"It's not good. He took four bullets—one to each shoulder and one to each knee. The bullets must have been hollow point—they shattered on impact. His joints were pulverized. He'll never have use of his arms or lower legs again. Won't be able to walk or even feed himself. I don't know who did this, but it was obviously done deliberately by someone who knew what they were doing."

"Jesus! Isn't there something you can do to reconstruct the joints, or replace them?"

"If just the bones were destroyed, we could replace them with artificial joints; but the bullets not only shattered the bone, they destroyed the surrounding nerves, blood vessels and tendons. He has no feeling in his arms and lower legs, and we're having trouble restoring the blood flow. If we can't, we'll have to amputate."

"Arms and legs?" asked Lindsay, stunned.

The doctor just nodded.

My God!" replied Lindsay. "Is he conscious? Can I see him?"

"Keep it short."

Lindsay entered the private room where Kramer lay. His arms and legs were in casts and his face was badly bruised and swollen. "I've seen you looking better."

"That bitch!"

"So it *was* Sarah Andrews.

"It was her all right. Acted different. Very calm. Knows how to shoot, and fight."

"At least you're alive."

"Shit, Peter! Look at me. I wish she'd killed me. I'd finish the job—except I can't."

"Don't talk like that," replied Lindsay. "These rehab places do wonders. When you're back, we'll get you a cushy desk job.

"Just get her!" replied Kramer. They both knew he would never work again.

"We'll get her," replied Lindsay conveying more confidence than he felt.

After a few moments of small talk, Lindsay found an excuse to leave and walked the few blocks back to his office. He couldn't imagine the life that Kramer was facing. Death would have been more merciful.

There were only three of them left now—Carlucci, Miller and himself; and they still hadn't found a trace of Sarah Andrews. Yet she was hunting *them* down effortlessly. He looked around the crowded streets. Was she out there somewhere, watching him? Lindsay felt a shiver run through him and stepped up his pace.

He was barely back in his office when Janice called. "Peter. I just heard about Ernie Kramer. It was horrible. Are you all right?"

Lindsay fought to keep the tremor from his voice. "I'm fine."

"I had to tell the Governor. He is very concerned. Are you sure there's no connection between Kramer and the others, Gordon and LePan?"

"Just a coincidence. Kramer's assailant was a woman."

"A woman!" Janice replied, incredulously.

"Kramer's conscious and gave us a description."

"Did he recognize her?"

"No," Lindsay lied. "Apparently she was a friend of his wife's."

"We need to talk. How about meeting me for dinner at the Cellar at seven? I'll make a reservation."

"I'd like that," replied Lindsay. Despite the circumstances, dinner with Janice Fox was an appealing prospect.

· · · · · · ·

At the same time Lindsay was visiting Kramer in the hospital, Sarah dropped by the apartment that she had lent to Clara Kramer. "It's beautiful," Clara exclaimed. "I don't know how to thank you."

"There's a pool," chimed in Tony, excitedly.

Sarah smiled at the boy and tousled his hair. "You okay?" she asked Clara, seeing the bandage on her forehead and bruising on her arms and face.

"Yes, thanks to you. I've never seen Ernie so angry. I was afraid he was going to kill me—or Tony."

Clara fixed them both a coffee while Tony went out to play. "I heard what you did to Ernie. It was on the news." There was no judgment in her voice, it was simply a statement.

Sarah looked at her and felt the need to explain. "A long time ago, your husband, along with some other police officers arrested me. They took me to the police station and tortured me with a taser. Afterwards they framed me for possession of narcotics and tried to have me killed while I was in prison."

"My God!" exclaimed Clara. "Why?"

"They'd stolen some money and I found out. They wanted me out of the way."

Clara shook her head sadly. "I'm so sorry."

"I thought I could put it behind me, but I couldn't," Sarah continued. "I kept having nightmares. I don't know if you can understand but I had to do something."

Clara looked at Sarah. "I think I understand. Sometimes when Ernie hit me, I wanted to fight back, but I was afraid he'd only hurt me more."

Sarah nodded. "It was kind of like that, except they hurt me so badly, I wasn't afraid anymore."

"So you're not Belinda Newton?" Clara smiled softly.

Sarah shook her head. "I'm sorry I had to lie to you."

"No wonder I didn't recognize you. Can we still be friends?"

Sarah shook her head sadly. "The police are looking for me. It's better that we not see each other again."

Clara nodded. "I understand."

"I want you to stay here as long as you need to," Sarah continued.

"I couldn't," Clara protested.

"I insist. It's just sitting empty anyway. And here's money for groceries, clothes and anything else you need," she added, handing her another stack of bills.

Clara looked at Sarah with tears in her eyes. "I can't thank you enough. It's like we've got a new start, Tony and I."

"I am glad I could do it."

Afterwards, Sarah went back to her condominium. She still hadn't been able to contact Paul. She picked up the phone to try again, but then put it down, smiling. First thing in the morning, she'd drive to Crystal Lake and surprise him.

· · · · · · ·

That evening, as Lindsay got ready to meet Janice at the Cellar, he reflected on their relationship. They'd seen each other two or three times a week: sometimes at his office, sometimes at her suite in The Plaza and sometimes at his in The Windsor. He found himself intensely attracted to her but he couldn't figure out whether she was interested in more than a business relationship. At times, her dress and behavior were suggestive; at other times, it was strictly business. In any event, since she had begun working with him, his public profile was much higher. He had several speaking engagements a week—community associations, business groups, high schools and so on, and he had been interviewed numerous times for TV and radio. The address he had given to the Chamber of Commerce had gone particularly well. Not only had Mayor Kelton introduced him, but he had been unusually cordial all night, subtly probing him on his relationship with the Governor.

Lindsay arrived at the restaurant first and the maître d' showed him to a small table in a secluded corner. He wondered if Janice had specifically asked for it. It was twenty minutes before she arrived, wearing a tight white dress that revealed a lot of cleavage and leg. Lindsay didn't miss the appreciative glances she got as she was led to his table.

"I'm sorry I'm late," she said, kissing him warmly. "I was about to leave when the Governor called."

"Don't worry about it. I ordered a beer and made myself comfortable."

"I see that." Janice ordered herself a drink and a second beer for Peter. "Here's to the new Chief of Police."

"I'm not there yet."

"Don't worry. Things are going well. You will be."

"I know. Some of the local papers are beginning to talk about me as the next Police Chief as if it's as good as done. All due to you."

"That's my job."

"You certainly do it well."

"To return the compliment, you're very easy to work with. You're a natural public speaker, you're good with people. You're good-looking. Those women's clubs just love you. I've had a request for a return visit from every group you've spoken to."

"You're exaggerating, but thanks."

"Incidentally, one of the things the Governor wanted to know was how things were going. I reported that things were going well and that you were cooperating fully. He was very pleased and said to tell you that."

"I can't believe the Governor himself is taking such an interest."

"Believe me, he is," replied Janice. "It's a two-way street. He's up for re-election himself in a year. The endorsement of the Police Chief of the second largest city in the state can't hurt."

"Tell him he's got it."

"I will. He'll appreciate it."

"The Governor did ask me to ask you about the number of police killings," Janice continued. "LePan, Gordon and now Kramer. He feels it looks like the police force is under attack and is powerless to stop it."

"Tell him not to be concerned," Lindsay replied. "It's a big city and occasionally cops get killed. The fact that there have been three murders in just a few weeks is just a coincidence. The first two may have been connected, probably the drug cartel; but the attack on Kramer was a domestic issue. The assailant was a friend of his wife. Apparently she caught Ernie slapping his wife around and went over the top."

"I'll tell him. Hopefully Kramer is the last. The media is beginning to dig in."

The waitress came and they ordered. The conversation drifted to small talk: friends, hobbies, favorite restaurants. They ordered dessert and then lingered over coffee.

Noticing that she was making no effort to end the evening, Lindsay finally made a suggestion. "We could go back to my suite at the Windsor for a night cap."

Janice looked at him as if trying to make up her mind. Finally, she replied, "Peter. I've had a great evening - and it's a tempting offer. And I think we're good together. However, I can't tonight. May I have a rain check?"

"Only if you promise to use it."

She looked at him meaningfully. "I promise."

CHAPTER 31

IT WAS JUST AFTER EIGHT IN THE MORNING WHEN SARAH eased her Subaru down Paul's long rugged driveway, intending to surprise him, certain he would be drinking coffee on the deck and enjoying the morning stillness. Suddenly and inexplicably, she felt anxious. Something was wrong. It was *too* quiet. Usually, Talisker heard her car and came trotting out to investigate, but today there was no sign of him. Sarah made the final turn into the back of his house, hoping to see that everything was normal. Instead, the sight hit her like a physical blow. Paul's house was a pile of charred rubble. The only thing still standing was the stone chimney.

Sarah got out of her car and simply stood there in shock, unable to accept or react to the scene before her. The silence was oppressive. "Paul!" she cried out, knowing it was futile. Her voice echoed forlornly across the still lake.

Apart from the burned-out house, the scene was eerily normal. Paul's Jeep was still parked out back and his powerboat was still tied to the dock. The lake rippled gently under the morning sun. The beauty and tranquility of the vista contrasted starkly with the brutal destruction before her. Then she saw Talisker, lying on the ground, his body torn apart from a dozen bullet wounds. Any faint hope the fire was accidental vanished. Fighting back the despair, Sarah walked through the rubble, not knowing what she was looking for. The ashes were cold and damp indicating that the fire must have occurred before yesterday's rain. Even Sarah's untrained eye spotted the signs of automatic rifle fire—spent casings and pockmarked tree trunks surrounding the house. It must have been the cops—Lindsay and the others! Somehow, they had identified Paul and found out where he lived. Judging by the number of casings, Paul must have put up a fight. Had he died in the fire? Had they captured him and taken him somewhere else to be killed? If he could, he would have called her, so he was either being held captive—or he was dead. She realized she could be exposed. If they had captured him, they may have forced him to reveal her new identity. Did they know where she lived? Were they coming for her?

Numb with grief, Sarah drove back to the city. It was all her fault. Paul had died because of her. Revenge had been a ridiculous idea. If she'd just put it behind her, she and Paul could be living a wonderful life: sailing, jogging—just being in love. Now Paul was dead and she was in danger. Even if she managed to evade the cops, even if she finished her 'project', what then? She had always assumed Paul would be there for her. Now she'd never see him again.

· · · · · · ·

When she arrived back in the city, Sarah checked into a hotel, worried that the cops might already be staking out her condominium. For two days, disguised with a cheap blond wig, Sarah cased her building, looking for any sign it was being watched. Late the afternoon of the second day, she was sitting at the outdoor patio of the Starbucks across the street from her condo, sipping a latté. So far, she'd seen nothing and she was beginning to believe she was worrying needlessly. The sun was setting, leaving an orange glow in the sky. Sadly, Sarah remembered the many dinners she'd enjoyed on the deck of Paul's house, watching the sunset over Crystal Lake. The sense of loss seemed unbearable and she put her head down on her arms to hide the tears.

Suddenly, she felt a hand on her shoulder. "Lousy wig you've got there, Ms. Andrews."

It was Paul's voice. Could it really be? Hesitantly, she looked up to see Paul standing there, smiling at her, his blue eyes sparkling with amusement.

"Oh God! Paul! I thought..."

"That I was dead? I don't kill that easily. But where the hell have you been? I've been trying to reach you for three days. You haven't been to your condo. You haven't answered my phone messages. I was sure that they had found you and done away with you. Instead, I find you sitting here drinking a latté and wearing a ditsy blond wig. What gives?"

Beneath the humor, Sarah sensed the worry and relief in his voice. Without a word, she got out of her chair and hugged him as if she'd never let go. She felt his arms around her and his body against hers. Tears of happiness streamed down her face.

After a minute, he gently disengaged her. "I really hate to break this up, but in the circumstances, I don't think we should be too conspicuous."

Knowing he was right, Sarah stepped back and wiped the tears from her eyes, laughing and crying at the same time.

Paul took her hand. "Let's go for a walk. I think we have some catching up to do."

They set off toward a nearby park. Sarah squeezed his hand. "Oh, Paul. When I saw your place at Crystal Lake, I was sure you were dead."

Paul laughed. "There's a hidden tunnel that leads from the basement into the woods. Had it built when I bought the place. Thought I might need it someday. With the life I've led, there are a lot of people around the world who don't like me much. Just never imagined it would be police officers from my own country. I actually knew they were coming. I've got alarms and cameras set up along the driveway. I could have easily escaped long before they got to the house, but I wanted them to think they'd killed me. That way they'd stop looking."

"I'm so sorry," Sarah replied. "It's all my fault. Your house is destroyed. Your life is in danger. And Talisker... If you hadn't helped me, you'd be sitting on your deck right now drinking scotch."

Paul stopped, took her shoulders and looked into her eyes. "Sarah. Don't ever think that. If I hadn't helped you, we wouldn't be together. You're the most important thing in my life. Maybe the only important thing."

Sarah reached up and kissed him, her eyes misty with happiness. "Thank you."

"So where have you been for the last three days?"

Sarah laughed when she realized what must have happened. "I was afraid they might have made you give them my new identity before they killed you. I thought I better disappear for a while to be sure."

Paul put his arm around her and laughed. "Well we both seem to be very much alive. To a new beginning."

·······

Back in Sarah's condominium, Paul poured himself a scotch and settled into one of the easy chairs while Sarah moved around the apartment sorting the mail and putting things away.

Sarah looked over, caught him watching her and smiled happily. "Want me to order some Chinese food?"

"Not yet. Come here."

Sarah approached him, at first unsure what he wanted.

Paul took her arms and pulled her toward him. "Closer."

Sarah moved until she was standing between his knees.

"There's something I'd like first," Paul continued, pulling her T-shirt over her head.

He pulled down her shorts and panties, leaving her standing there naked in front of him. Paul put his arms around her hips, pulled her toward him and buried his face in her belly, drinking in her scent and her warmth. "God Sarah. I was afraid I'd lost you."

Sarah put her arms around his head and pulled him against her. "Never."

Paul kissed her bellybutton and then worked his way down. Her knees quivered and she groaned with desire. Paul picked her up and carried her naked into the bedroom, depositing her gently on the bed. He slipped off his own clothes and lay down beside her. Sarah closed her eyes and surrendered her body to him. His lips, his tongue, his fingers seemed to be everywhere. The sensations built within her, becoming overpowering, almost unbearable. She arched her back and gasped, desperate for release.

Finally, when she believed she could stand it no longer, her body erupted into a long and powerful climax. After several minutes, the sensations subsided, leaving her spent and exhausted. When she eventually opened her eyes, Paul was leaning over her, kissing her.

"What did you do to me?' she gasped.

Paul just smiled and kissed her again. For a long time they just lay together contentedly.

· · · · · · · ·

They finally got up, showered together and ordered Chinese food. Sarah opened a bottle of wine and they sat at her kitchen table eating and simply enjoying being together again.

"I never told you but I have a house on the beach on San Alicia, an island in the Caribbean."

"Sounds wonderful," replied Sarah, wondering why he'd brought it up.

"I'd like to show it to you, and you could use the break."

Sarah was about to say no but reconsidered. A week away with Paul would be heaven. And it would give her time to reflect. Believing she'd lost him had shaken her resolve and made her realize what she was putting at risk. Her 'project' could wait. A break would actually be good—put the cops off their guard. It might convince them that the attack on Paul had scared her off. "Okay," she replied.

"Great. I'm sure we can get a flight down in the morning."

"So soon?"

"Why not?"

They arrived at the airport early and Paul took her into the first-class lounge. He was surprised to discover that Sarah had never been on an airplane before, and he enjoyed watching her take it all in. They boarded the plane and were seated in the first-class section at the front of the cabin. The flight attendant brought headphones and a newspaper. Sarah was delighted to find that she had her very own TV built into the back of the seat in front of her. As they took off, she looked down at the ground falling away beneath them. "Look, you can see the whole city," she exclaimed excitedly.

Paul smiled.

"This is so much fun," Sarah continued. "I'm so glad you talked me into it."

He laughed. "We've barely taken off. Wait until you see the ocean around San Alicia. It's even more beautiful than the postcards."

Sarah leaned over and kissed him.

"What was that for?"

"I don't know. For bringing me. For giving me my life. For that look in your eyes that says you love me."

Paul laughed. "I didn't know it was so obvious."

"Only to me," Sarah replied happily. "But don't ever lose it."

The flight attendant came by and offered them champagne. Sarah hesitated. It seemed odd to be drinking champagne so early in the day.

Sensing her thoughts, Paul laughed. "Go for it. You're on vacation."

The flight took four hours and Sarah thoroughly enjoyed herself. She flipped among the movies, studied the duty-free catalogue deciding what to buy on the way back and played with the controls on her seat. The food and drinks kept coming. As they approached San Alicia, Paul told her to look out the window. There it was, an emerald island, ringed by white beaches, floating in a sparkling turquoise sea.

CHAPTER 32

ONCE THROUGH CUSTOMS, PAUL HAILED A CAB AND GAVE the driver an address. Twenty minutes later, the cab turned into a driveway that led to a house set well back from the road.

"Here we are. It's not big, but it's very private."

"Sounds like you. The privacy I mean."

Paul laughed. He paid the driver, collected their luggage and took Sarah inside. Leaving the suitcases in the front hall, he gave her a tour. The house had two stories with three bedrooms upstairs and a living room, dining room and kitchen on the main floor. The master bedroom had a balcony looking down over a large pool and beyond to the beach and out over the ocean. Sarah stood there for several minutes, drinking in the scene before her. The beach was brilliant white sand spotted with palm trees. The ocean stretched to the horizon, a beautiful blue-green color under an azure sky. She could hear the sound of the surf breaking gently on the shore and could smell the fresh scent of the ocean.

Finally, realizing she had been standing there for some time, Sarah turned to Paul to find him looking at her with affection and amusement. "Oh Paul. It's magnificent!"

Paul simply kissed her.

As soon as they had unpacked, Sarah insisted on going down to the beach. They walked along the shore and Sarah was delighted at the feel of the sand between her toes and the gentle ebb and flow of the ocean washing over her feet. She ran in and out of the surf grinning with excitement and then dove into the water, swimming a few strokes before floating lazily on her back. "It's so comfortable, I could lie here all day."

"Don't fall asleep and drift out to sea."

For the rest of the afternoon, they played on the beach like children, building sand castles, searching for shells and chasing each other through the surf. Afterwards, Paul made them dinner on the patio by the pool. Grilled sea bass and vegetables along with a bottle of chilled white wine. It was delicious and Sarah felt content and pampered. Later, they went for a walk along the beach, holding hands and watching the sunset. It was midnight before they went to bed. After making love, Sarah lay awake for a long time, just listening to the waves lap the beach and smelling the sea air through the open door.

"You still awake?" Paul asked gently.

"Yes. I'm tired, but I'm too happy to go to sleep. You're still awake too?"

"Yes. It's just so good having you here," Paul replied, kissing her forehead, gently lifting a stray strand of hair from her face.

· · · · · · ·

The next morning, Paul told her they'd been invited to have dinner with the president.

"You mean the president of the whole country?"

"It's not that big a country. In fact, the population is about a tenth of the city you live in. But yes, I mean the president of the whole country."

"What do I wear?"

"I'm taking you shopping. Nothing fancy, but you can't go in shorts and bare feet."

"What's wrong with my feet?"

"Nothing. Your feet are adorable. But there are still certain protocols that must be observed when you have dinner with the president."

"Okay, I'll wear shoes."

"Sandals are fine."

"Thank you. So how is it that you know the president?"

"His name is Salvador D'Alessandro. Although at least the first time you meet him, you should address him as Mr. President. After that, he'll probably ask you to call him Sal."

"So, how did you meet him?" Sarah persisted.

"It's a long story."

"I like stories."

Paul shook his head in mock frustration. "Sal was once the leader of a band of guerrillas that hid in the mountains in the interior of the island. I helped him overthrow the government and become president.

"Was that a good thing to do?"

Paul laughed. "It depends on your point of view. The previous government was brutal and corrupt. It suspended elections, took over all the newspapers and television stations, and outlawed demonstrations. People were arrested and imprisoned without trial. Many simply disappeared. Once this government was overthrown, an election was held and Sal was elected President. With political stability re-established, Sal was able to attract foreign investment and rebuild the economy. San Alicia now has one of the highest standards of living in the Caribbean. Sal is revered by the people and has been re-elected in every election the country has held since."

"Wow," replied Sarah, impressed.

"I came back to help Sal with something while you were in prison. That's the reason I didn't look for you sooner."

"What happened?"

"Sal called me the day after our first dinner together. His daughter had been kidnapped. He asked me to see if I could find and rescue her."

"Did you?"

"Yes."

"How old is she?"

"Mid-twenties. You will meet her tonight. Her name is Angelina. She's delightful. She's studying physics at MIT but she's home for a vacation."

Sarah looked at Paul with renewed fascination and respect. He didn't talk much about his earlier life and she wondered what other things he'd done. "That's an amazing story."

"It's an incredible family," Paul added. "Sal got his doctorate in economics at Stanford before returning to San Alicia and joining the guerillas. While at Stanford, he met and married an English woman, Angelina's mother, Emily. She has a doctorate in history."

"I hope I'm up for the conversation at dinner tonight."

"You'll be fine."

Later, Paul drove them into the capital city of San Alicia. Sarah thoroughly enjoyed herself, buying a couple of dresses, pantsuits, shorts, tops and bathing suits—and dress sandals. Back at Paul's house, they went for a jog along the beach before showering and getting ready for dinner.

· · · · · · ·

Initially apprehensive, Sarah found dinner delightful. Sal D'Alessandro lived in a beautiful old house set in the hills with a spectacular view of the city and the ocean beyond. He was in his early sixties, vigorous and fun. His wife, Emily, was warm and welcoming, and their daughter Angelina did everything she could to make Sarah feel at home.

To Paul's embarrassment, Angelina insisted on telling Sarah how Paul had single-handedly tracked down and rescued her from the drug cartel, killing at least ten men in the process.

"You exaggerate," Paul protested. "Besides, they were so drunk they couldn't shoot straight."

"Don't believe him, Sarah," Sal added. "Paul has done so much for both my country and my family. Without his support, we would never have overthrown the government forces and I'd probably be rotting in some jail rather than sitting here as president. He saved my life a couple of times as well."

"I just wanted to make sure I got paid," Paul demurred.

After dinner, Angelina offered to show Sarah around the grounds.

"It's so beautiful here," Sarah gushed. "The island, the ocean, the people. It's like another world."

"I know. Growing up here, you tend to take it for granted. My father deserves a lot of credit. He has restored a stable, honest government. He has built roads, and hospitals and schools. He loves the country and the people."

"It shows. When we were driving over, Paul told me a little about him. He seems like a great man."

"*I* think so, but I'm his daughter."

When they arrived back at the living room, Angelina asked Paul, "Would you mind if I took Sarah shopping tomorrow?"

"I think she cleaned out all the stores *today*, but otherwise it's a great idea."

Sarah thoroughly enjoyed the next day with Angelina. Despite their very different backgrounds they quickly bonded and by the end of the day felt like close friends.

· · · · · · ·

The week passed in a blur. It was a magical time and it seemed like the rest of the world no longer existed. Sarah couldn't get enough of the beach, the ocean or the carefree lifestyle. Her 'project' seemed far away and less compelling, and she began to feel that she could happily stay in San Alicia forever. But then she would remember the pain and the humiliation, and the anger would come flooding back. She *had* to go back, to finish what she'd started. She only had three to go—Carlucci, Miller and Lindsay himself. It would be over in less than a month and she could return to San Alicia and put the past behind her forever.

After dinner on their last night together, Paul suggested a walk on the beach. They walked barefoot, along the water-line, enjoying the sight of the ocean shimmering darkly in the moonlight.

"Sarah," began Paul, his tone surprisingly serious. "I want you to do something for me."

"Of course. Anything."

"It's big. But it's important to me."

"Paul. I love you. I'd do anything you asked me to. What is it?"

"I don't think you'll do this."

Sarah laughed in exasperation. "Paul. I can't do it, if you don't tell me what it is."

"I don't want you to go back tomorrow."

"Paul...I..."

"I know what you are doing in the city," he interrupted. "I know what you are going back for."

"I'm not sure what you're talking about," replied Sarah uneasily.

"I know about Carney, LePan, Gordon and Kramer. I know why you had me teach you to fight, to shoot. I know you're going back to kill Carlucci, Miller and Lindsay."

Sarah looked at him in shock and dismay. "How did you find out?"

"It wasn't hard. You told me what had happened to you when I first took you to Crystal Lake. I sensed there was more than you had told me. And your nightmares. You would cry out in your sleep and wake up trembling. Then, the sudden interest in martial arts and guns. And your mysterious decision to return to the city. I happened to see a news story on LePan's death right after you'd gone back to the city. I became suspicious. I checked back and found that Carney's death also coincided with your first trip back to the city. I found some of your notes in your room. That's when I knew for sure."

Sarah looked at him anxiously, unsure whether he was angry with her for keeping it from him or simply worried about her. "Paul. I'm sorry I didn't tell you. I knew you wouldn't approve, and I didn't want to involve you."

Paul stopped, took her shoulders and looked into her eyes. "Sarah, I don't want you to go back. I want you to stay here in San Alicia. You said you would do anything I asked you. I'm asking this."

She remained silent for a long time, agonized by the choice before her. The pain in his eyes, her love for him, their life together. Yet, the rage within her could not be stilled. She would not find peace until they were dead. After almost a full minute, Sarah answered. "Paul, I have to do this."

"It won't change anything."

"It will change me."

"Sarah…"

"When I'm done," she interrupted. "I'll come back to San Alicia, or anywhere you want, and live with you—forever."

"Sarah," replied Paul, no longer able to suppress his anger. "It's too dangerous. You cannot take on the whole police force."

Sarah tried to lighten the mood. "I've done all right so far."

He refused to be mollified. "Be serious, Sarah. Premeditated murder of a cop is a capital offense. You could get life — or worse. Or they'll find you and kill you in some deserted warehouse."

"I'm careful. Nothing's happened so far."

Paul held her shoulders more tightly. "Damn it, Sarah. You've just been lucky. The whole idea is absurd."

Suddenly Sarah went rigid. Savagely pushing him away, she stood facing him, with her hands on her hips. "You're not the one who was strung up and tasered, who lost her father, *her life*. You don't wake up screaming in the middle of the night."

Paul stepped back, stunned by the rage and ruthless determination in her eyes. He remembered the newspaper description of Ernie Kramer's injuries. When he'd read it, he hadn't been able to imagine her standing there, calmly pulling the trigger *four times,* rendering Kramer virtually a quadriplegic. He remembered too that John Gordon had been chained to the beach and left to slowly drown as the tide came in. Now, for the first time, he saw it—the seething fury, the hatred. At that moment, he wondered if he really knew her. Was she the innocent young woman who giggled with delight when she found a pretty sea shell, or was she a merciless, cold-blooded killer? It didn't matter. He loved her.

"Paul. I *have* to do this," she continued, more gently.

"Then let *me* finish it for you. I'll go back. I'll kill Carlucci, Miller and Lindsay. You stay here. I'll be back in less than a week."

Sarah saw the concern and love for her in his eyes and it tore at her heart. "Paul. I can't. I can't let you put yourself at risk. I've already almost gotten you killed."

"I told you, I don't kill so easily."

"Paul. I have to do this myself. That's part of it."

"All right. Then we'll do it together. I'll go back with you. Miller and Carlucci burned down my house, and killed my dog. I want them. You can have Lindsay."

"I can't let you do it."

He looked at her with a gentle smile. "Perhaps, but you can't stop me either."

Beneath his smile, she could see the cold determination in his eyes and knew he'd follow her anyway. He was right—she couldn't stop him. Besides, it would be good to have an ally, especially one as formidable as Paul Taylor. "Okay. You're hired."

The next morning Paul drove Sarah to the airport. They had agreed it would be better if they didn't fly together. Paul would get a San Alicia passport under a new name and follow her three days later. At the airport, he hugged her tightly. "Now promise me, you'll sit tight until I get there. No going after them on your own."

Sarah smiled and kissed him. "I promise. There's something personal I want to do anyway."

CHAPTER 33

THAT NIGHT, ALONE IN HER CONDOMINIUM, SARAH SAT OUT on the balcony, looking down over the city lights. The air was cool and the sky was pitch black as heavy clouds blocked out the moon and stars. She missed Paul already and was glad that he was returning soon. In most ways, she was glad he knew. Keeping her 'project' from him had been hard—and lonely. Having an ally would be nice. Three to go—Carlucci, Miller and Lindsay. Then it would be over. Maybe then, the night-mares would stop and the anger that burned within her would fade away.

After sitting there for a long time, she went back inside, sat down at her desk and flipped on her computer. Her ability to hack into the police network had been invaluable in tracking her targets. She could see when they were on duty and read their emails. She successfully hacked in again and skimmed recent messages. One email particularly amused her.

To: Peter Lindsay

From: Tom Miller

Subject: The Librarian

Suspect's whereabouts still unknown. However, with accomplice decommissioned and no activity or communication for over a week, it appears probable that suspect has been scared off. Realize we still would like a permanent resolution of the problem.

So they still thought that Paul was dead and she had been scared off. Sarah smiled to herself. Soon they would find out otherwise. But Lindsay's response puzzled her.

To: Tom Miller

From: Peter Lindsay

Subject: The Librarian

Imperative you resolve this issue permanently. The SIU tapes still represent an unacceptable risk.

What tapes? It made no sense. Then she had a thought. Was it possible her interrogation in the Backfield Building had been recorded? It couldn't have been or they wouldn't have done what they did. But maybe they didn't know until later, and were now afraid the tapes would surface. She needed to know.

It took her two hours to break through the firewall and hack into the SIU's database. Unbelievably, one of the menu options was a video library. She scrolled down the list of available disks until she came to one marked with the date she was arrested.

Trembling, she initiated a download, certain that some security feature would lock her out, but the download began immediately. Ten minutes later, a message indicated the download was complete. Sarah sat there, paralyzed with indecision. Finally, she clicked 'play'.

At first, she saw nothing but a small empty room with a plain metal table and a few chairs. Then a young woman stumbled in, followed by a man. The woman's hands were handcuffed behind her and her face was bruised and bleeding. Sarah's heart began to pound and she began to tremble uncontrollably. The woman was her! For the next half hour, Sarah watched and listened in horror, transfixed by the images on her monitor. She heard the utter terror in her voice as she vainly protested her innocence. She watched as her wrists were fastened to the ceiling. She heard herself scream and saw her body jerk spasmodically as they held the taser against her.

After she had fainted, she saw her unconscious body carried out of the room and heard them all discuss how to make sure she never talked. She heard Lindsay order them to plant drugs on her and go on to explain that he'd get a lawyer friend of his, Arnold Carney, to persuade her to plead guilty. She heard Kramer ask what would happen if she filed charges after she was out, to which Lindsay replied coldly, "She won't get out. Women's prisons are tough places. Things happen." Moments later, the monitor went blank. For a long time, Sarah just sat there quietly, simply staring at the empty monitor. Instinctively she copied the file to a blank DVD disk.

That night, the images from the video tormented her relentlessly. Her screams, their laughter. Their leering expressions and obscene jokes. The callous discussion over how to deal

with her—"Women's prisons are tough places. Things happen."
Yes, she thought to herself. "Things happen."

. . . .

Sarah's 'personal' errand was a visit to her father's grave. Feeling
guilty that she had not thought of it sooner, she had contacted
the nursing home to find out where he was buried. Early the
next morning, she drove to the small cemetery, parked and
followed a hand-drawn map to the location of the plot. She
felt inexplicably nervous as she approached, almost as if she
expected to meet her father in person. After some searching,
she finally found the small plaque, partially overgrown by
grass. It seemed so inadequate—a life reduced to a metal plate
half-hidden in the ground. Sadly, Sarah cleared away the grass
and placed a small bouquet of flowers on the ground beside
the plaque. She remembered the long walks she'd taken with
her father when her mother was ill; the pride he showed at
her achievements and the support he'd given her when she
met with disappointment. She thought of his last days, so
cruelly crippled and incapacitated by a stroke. How horrible it
must have been for him to die alone in a nursing home—his
wife dead, his only child missing. Tears came to her eyes at
the thought.

"Hi, Dad. I hope you like the flowers. I am going to get you
a headstone with your name and an inscription. I'm sorry I
took so long to visit and that I wasn't there for you the way you
were always there for me. I guess you know what happened, so
I don't need to explain. I'm fine now. Actually, I feel good about
myself. Stronger somehow. I guess you know about Paul too. I
had no idea what it is like to be in love. It's so wonderful. You
must have had that with mom. Maybe you have it now. I hope

you are okay with what I am doing. About the cops, I mean. It's a bit scary. Sometimes I even frighten myself, but I feel I have to do it. Even though he's helping me, I don't think Paul understands. Maybe you do—although I think you would tell me to let it go and build a life with Paul. Anyway, Dad, I love you. Always."

Sarah remained there for a long time. Suddenly, she was conscious of someone behind her. Strange—the cemetery had been deserted when she'd come in. She stood up and turned around. Frank Carlucci was calmly standing there with a gun in his hand!

Sarah stepped backwards in utter shock. How had he found her? Then she realized. The connection with the past! Her father's gravesite. How incredibly stupid! The sense of defeat and despair was so overwhelming that she could barely stand.

"Well, well. You're not a ghost after all." Carlucci smiled and produced a set of handcuffs. "Come here and turn around."

Looking at the gun in his hand, Sarah had no choice but to obey. She felt the cold steel snap around her wrists behind her back.

"Okay, Ms. Librarian. My car's over that hill. Start walking."

When they got to his car, Carlucci put duct tape over her mouth, picked her up and effortlessly tossed her into the trunk before driving off. There would be no arrest, no trial. She would just be taken to some remote location, killed, and her body disposed of. The best she could hope for was that it would be over quickly.

. . . .

Twenty minutes later, Sarah felt the car come to a stop. The trunk opened, Carlucci roughly pulled her out and then simply dropped her on the ground. "Get up!" he ordered kicking her.

With her hands still cuffed, she struggled to her feet. They were outside a run-down warehouse and she was sure it was the same part of town where they had taken her when she had first been released from prison.

A second car pulled up behind them and Tom Miller got out. "If it isn't the librarian," he taunted her. "You don't look that scary."

With her mouth taped, Sarah couldn't answer.

"Any problems?" asked Miller turning to Carlucci.

"Nope. What do you want to do with her?"

"Shoot her and lose the body. Maybe bury it out back. This warehouse's been deserted for years. No one will ever find it."

Sarah felt her heart sink—but at least it would be quick.

Carlucci studied Sarah with a cruel grin. "You remember what she did to Carney? How about we do the same? There is a sub-basement in this warehouse. We'll take her down there, string her up and leave her. Let her stand there in the dark, trying to decide whether to jump or just wait until she faints."

Miller frowned. "Christ Frank. I'm tired of this whole thing. Let's just kill her and get out of here."

"Tom. You've seen Ernie, lying in his hospital bed. He can't even scratch his nose. You want to tell him we just shot her?"

Miller scowled. "Okay, dammit all. Do your thing. And then let's get out of here."

With Miller grudgingly following them, Carlucci prodded Sarah into the warehouse, down two flights of stairs and then along a dark narrow corridor. Finally, they arrived at a steel door and entered a small room. The floor, ceiling and walls were entirely concrete. It was distinctly cool and Sarah began to shiver from the cold.

Taking a piece of rope he'd brought from the car, Carlucci fastened a noose in one end and flung the other over a pipe running along the ceiling. He then put the noose around her neck. He found a small box, placed it under the pipe and began to pull the other end of the rope, forcing Sarah to step up onto the box. Carlucci then tied the other end of the rope to a railing, leaving Sarah standing on the box, her hands cuffed behind her back with the noose tight around her neck. If she stepped down or fell off, she would hang herself. He roughly ripped the tape from her mouth and Sarah had to struggle frantically to retain her balance.

Carlucci stepped back and inspected her appreciatively while Sarah stoically endured his scrutiny. She hated him. Hated him for what he had done to her, hated him for her helplessness.

Miller looked at Sarah, shook his head and headed toward the door. "Okay, Frank. You've done it. Let's just leave her."

"What's the rush?"

"Let's go," Miller replied in exasperation. " I'll buy you a beer at the Purring Kitten. I'll even spring for a lap dance."

"You've got a deal."

The two of them left the room and slammed the door behind them. The echoes of their receding footsteps gradually faded into silence as Sarah stood there on the tiny box, hands still fastened behind her back, concentrating on keeping her balance. The absolute silence and utter blackness were oppressive. Tears held back when Carlucci and Miller were there flowed freely now. It was over. She thought of the beaches of San Alicia, the rocky cliffs of Crystal Lake, the love in Paul's eyes when he looked at her—things she would never see again.

The revenge she had sought seemed pointless now. It had cost her all that she loved. It had cost her her life.

· · · · · · ·

As Sarah was visiting her father's grave, Paul was taking out his windsurfer. The wind was strong and the ocean churned angrily. Dark clouds loomed threateningly on the horizon. He knew it was dangerous but he needed the challenge. The weather matched his mood. He wasn't happy with his agreement with Sarah. There was too big a chance something would go wrong, something even he couldn't handle. He should have made her stay in San Alicia. Yet there was no *making* Sarah do anything she didn't want to do. Beneath her gentle demeanor was a stubborn streak that was both endearing and annoying.

As soon as he left the shore, the sail became taut and the little board fairly flew over the waves, taking all his strength and skill to maintain control. In minutes, the shore was simply a dark line on the horizon. The wind, the speed and the ocean spray made Paul feel better. He stayed out for over an hour, returning to shore only when his arms and legs were exhausted.

Throughout the afternoon, thoughts of Sarah continued to plague him. He was worried about her, but there was something else. Was it something Sarah had said or just his fear that she would be caught? Then it came to him. She'd said she had to do 'something personal.' He wasn't sure why, but he had the nagging sense she'd meant something to do with her old life. He remembered Sammy's repeated admonishment when he gave Sarah the new ID—"No connection with the past!" Was she about to make a mistake? Had she already made it?

Terrified that it was already too late, he immediately phoned her, praying that she'd answer. The phone in her condominium just kept ringing. Same result on her cell. Panicked now, Paul phoned the airport. The first flight was at seven the following morning and he booked himself on it. Throughout the evening, Paul kept calling but there was no answer.

Paul's plane landed at the city airport at eleven. He rented a car and drove directly to Sarah's condominium, letting himself in with his key. There was a newspaper on the table dated the day she'd left San Alicia—two days ago! He checked her mailbox and found it hadn't been cleared for two days. He tried her cell again. No answer. Not knowing where to start, Paul searched through the papers on her desk. Nothing. He noticed an unlabeled DVD. Curious, he booted up her computer and inserted it. It was the video of Sarah's interrogation!

While Sarah had told him about the interrogation, nothing could have prepared him for the horrific images on the disk. Twenty minutes later, Paul Taylor switched off her computer, shaking with rage. He now understood the fury that simmered within her. Any latent ambivalence he harbored over her 'project' evaporated. Miller, Carlucci and Lindsay would die— and die brutally. Let them think he was buried in the ashes at Crystal Lake. They would soon learn otherwise.

Struggling to control his anger, Paul continued to search for some indication of where she had gone. Finally, he found a piece of paper with the address of a cemetery and a map showing the actual layout of the grounds. There was an 'X' in the northeast corner. His initial puzzlement, gave way to the realization it must be her father's grave. He closed his eyes in despair. The connection with the past! His faint hope that there was an innocent explanation for Sarah's disappearance was extinguished. The cops would surely have staked it out. There was no question now. She was either in serious danger—or already dead.

Paul immediately drove to the cemetery and found a small medal plaque buried in the ground with the inscription "Martin Andrews." There was a wilting bouquet of flowers on the ground beside the plaque. She'd been there!

Looking around, Paul saw a small building at the back of the cemetery that looked like a maintenance building. Inside was a man he took to be the groundskeeper. "There's a grave up in the northeast corner," Paul asked urgently. "The plaque indicates it belongs to Martin Andrews. Do you know it?"

"Yeah. Fairly recent. Some guy from a nursing home. Didn't seem to have any family at the time."

"At the time?"

"Yesterday, a young woman shows up to visit the gravesite. Said she was his daughter. Said she'd been traveling abroad and wasn't contacted when her father died. She asked about getting a tombstone. I gave her the names of some companies."

"Mid-thirties, dark hair, pretty?"

"Yeah, that's her. Nice lady."

"Did you see her when she left?"

"No. I must have been out doing something."

"Thanks"

The groundskeeper hesitated, studying Paul.

Sensing he was considering telling him something, Paul prompted him. "Anything else?"

"Several weeks ago, a big guy came by. Said he was a cop and showed me his ID. Told me to call him if anyone ever showed up taking an interest in Martin Andrew's grave. When I asked why, he got real mean. Threatened to charge me with obstructing justice or something."

"Did you call him yesterday?" Paul asked.

"Yeah. Didn't want to, but he was a cop. Didn't figure I had a choice."

"What was his name?"

"Here's his card."

Paul took the card. "Frank Carlucci". The image from the disk of Frank Carlucci holding the taser against Sarah while she screamed in pain flashed before him. He clenched his fists to control his fury. "Thanks," he replied, grimly.

Paul went back to Sarah's condominium figuring she must have Carlucci's address somewhere. Eventually, he found a file on Carlucci with an address, a small house in the suburb of Copperhill. Sarah's file indicated he lived alone.

． ． ． ． ． ． ．

Sarah had been standing on the box for over thirty hours. Exhausted, shivering from the cold, and disoriented by the darkness, she fought to remain standing. Why fight she thought? Why prolong the misery? Just step off the stool. It would all be over. At most, she could only last a few more hours before losing consciousness. No one was going to come.

She began to hallucinate. She imagined herself on the beach of San Alicia feeling the heat of the sun on her body, then in bed with Paul, feeling the warmth of his body against hers. She remembered the day they had made love on the grass after jogging—hot, tired, wet with perspiration, but overcome with desire. Images of the good times with Paul haunted her as if to remind her of what she would never have again. She felt for Paul, too. He loved her and the knowledge that he would suffer because of her stubbornness, tore at her heart. Why had she come back? Why hadn't she listened to him?

In her fading consciousness, Sarah imagined she heard footsteps in the distance. So faint and far away, they must be part of her hallucination. Yet they continued, coming closer. It sounded like Paul's brisk easy strides, but it wasn't possible. Her mind was playing tricks on her. Then, silence. The footsteps were gone. It *was* just a dream. A last cruel joke. Sarah finally lost consciousness and felt herself falling from the box. She didn't care. She just wanted to sleep.

To her surprise, she didn't feel the expected jolt of the rope around her neck. It was as if she was floating in the air. She could still breathe and she felt warmth around her. She dreamed she was in Paul's arms. She heard a voice in the distance, urgently calling for her. Paul's voice! She tried to open her eyes, but she couldn't. Then she felt lips on hers. Paul's lips. Again, she strained to open her eyes. There he was! It *was* Paul! Holding her, kissing her, tears of relief in his eyes.

Sarah smiled weakly. "Paul?" she asked, as if to assure herself that it really was him.

He hugged her tightly. "Sarah. Thank God!"

How did you find me?" she asked as Paul easily picked open the cuffs on her wrists.

Paul smiled. "It's a long story. Got directions from a friend of yours who's tied up in the back of my Jeep."

He helped Sarah back to his car where she saw Carlucci, trussed up in the back. He was a mess. His nose was shattered, his jaw askew, and several teeth were missing. On one cheek, there was a horrible burn mark. It looked like the skin had been peeled back and the underlying tissue and blood vessels cauterized by intense heat.

Sarah pointed to the burn and looked at Paul quizzically.

Paul shrugged. "Blow torch."

"Must have hurt."

"Probably. He didn't want to tell me where you were. Besides, I never liked the guy much."

"Me either. Is he alive?"

"Barely. I wanted to keep him alive as insurance. Just in case you weren't where he said you'd be."

"I guess you don't need the insurance any more."

"Good point." Paul pulled out his gun.

Sarah put her hand on his gun and smiled. "I have a better idea."

· · · · · · ·

After a two-hour detour to drop Carlucci off, Paul drove Sarah back to her condominium where he helped her into a hot bath. When she finally reappeared, Paul had produced a spaghetti dinner complete with wine and candles. "I know you're exhausted, but I thought you'd want to eat."

"Thank you. I'm famished."

Paul studied her. There was bruising around her neck and she looked very tired, but otherwise she seemed fine. "You okay?"

Sarah nodded. "Oh Paul," she exclaimed softly, tears in her eyes. "I was standing there so long. I didn't think I could hold on much longer and I was sure no one would ever find me. All I could think about was never seeing you again."

Paul reached out and took her hand. "Sarah, I saw the disk."

Sarah looked at him uncertainly.

"When I came back from San Alicia to find you, I came here first. I went through your desk to see if I could figure out where you'd gone. The DVD was lying there. I played it. Oh God,

Sarah! It was horrible. I know you sort of told me you about it, but I had no idea. Watching it tore me apart. I'm so sorry."

Sarah saw the anguish, and the anger, in his eyes. "I'm okay now. It brought me to you."

They hugged each other for a long time, silently reaffirming the bond between them. "I think I understand why Carlucci was such a mess," Sarah whispered softly.

Paul smiled grimly. "What you've done to him is far worse. I wonder what the poor guy is thinking now."

"He deserves it all."

"I'm guessing you have some plans for Miller and Lindsay?"

Sarah smiled and for the next twenty minutes, she described her plans and explained where she could use Paul's help. When she was finished, he looked at her in amazement. "Remind me to stay on your good side."

Paul meant his words as a joke, but he could see she was upset by them.

"Paul. Is there something wrong with me? I feel I should be horrified at what I'm doing, but I'm not. I just feel excited, empowered. When I see the fear in their eyes when they know they're going to die, I remember what they did to me and I feel good..."

Paul saw the uncertainty in her eyes and pulled her to him. "It's in all of us—the capacity for rage, the will to survive, the ability to kill. It just takes some event to release it. The human genome hasn't changed since we wandered around bashing each other with stone axes. It's probably why we've survived as a species. When I worked in the Middle East, I saw middle-aged mothers become ruthless terrorists after their families were destroyed by errant drones or random gunfire. Sarah, what they did to you was outrageous. Your reaction is totally human.

You're a good person, Sarah Andrews. You're warm, caring, and generous—and I'm in love with you."

Paul's response brought tears to her eyes. She reached up and kissed him. "Thank you."

After dinner, they sat together on the couch. Sarah put her head on his shoulder and, after a few minutes, Paul realized that she'd fallen asleep. He looked down at her lovingly. She seemed so small and innocent that it was hard to believe she had killed several people. He picked her up and carried her to the bedroom. Feeling his embrace even in her sleep, Sarah snuggled more deeply into his arms.

CHAPTER 34

"I THOUGHT FRANK WAS COMING WITH YOU?" ASKED LINDSAY, when Tom Miller arrived for his scheduled appointment.

"So did I. Must have slept in."

"So what's so secret you two couldn't discuss it on the phone?"

Miller was unable to suppress a look of triumph. "I wanted to tell you that the 'librarian' won't be sending any more notes."

"What do you mean?"

"I mean she's dead."

"How?"

"I thought she might visit her father's gravesite so we arranged for the groundskeeper to call Frank if anyone visited the grave. Nothing for weeks. I figure she's too smart to go back. Then, all of a sudden, Frank gets the call saying someone's there. He drives to the cemetery and there she is, large as life, kneeling at the grave."

Lindsay heaved a sigh of relief. "So she's dead?"

"By now she is *very* dead."

Instantly alert, Lindsay demanded, "What does that mean—'by now'?"

"You know what she did with Carney?"

Lindsay nodded.

"We did the same to her. Left her hanging in the basement of a deserted warehouse. After what she did to LePan, Kramer and Gordon, a bullet would have been too easy."

"So you don't know for sure she's dead?" replied Lindsay angrily. "And you don't know where Carlucci is?"

The possibility of a connection had not occurred to Miller. "Don't worry. No one could possibly find her."

Lindsay looked at him angrily. "Get back to that warehouse. Right now! Make sure she's dead. If she's not dead, kill her. Don't get clever—just kill her. And find Carlucci! Then call me. Understood?"

"Yes, sir." Miller rose to leave. He'd been expecting congratulations. Instead, he was getting yelled at, and Carlucci's absence was now worrying him. What if Sarah *had* got away somehow? He cursed himself for letting Frank talk him out of shooting her.

"And Tom," added Lindsay, as Miller walked toward the door.

"Sir?"

"If you tell me she's not where you left her, I'll hang your fucking asses to the wall. Got that?"

"Yes sir."

On the way to his car, Miller called Carlucci's cell phone. No answer. Anxiously, he drove back to the warehouse and rushed down to the sub-basement where they had left Sarah.

She was gone! The rope they had tied her with lay on the ground, cleanly cut and the handcuffs had been sprung open.

Beginning to panic, Miller drove to Carlucci's house. There was no answer when he rang the doorbell and he let himself in with the key Carlucci kept hidden in the garage. The living room was in shambles. Lamps broken, furniture overturned, holes in the walls. Clearly, there had been a violent struggle, but there was no sign of Carlucci. Whoever he'd been fighting with must have taken him away, and taking out Frank wouldn't be easy. It could only have been Paul Taylor. Taylor must have overpowered him and forced him to tell him where Sarah was. Shit! An hour ago, Miller had been certain both Taylor and Andrews were dead—and their problems were over. Now it looked like they were both very much alive—and their problems more real than ever.

Dreading the reaction, Miller went back to his car and phoned Lindsay.

"So," demanded Lindsay, as soon as he answered.

"I can't find Frank. His living room is pretty badly torn up. Looks like there was a fight."

"Paul Taylor?"

"Must have been."

"And the girl?"

"She's gone too."

For a moment, there was dead silence—then Lindsay exploded. "You fucking idiots. First, you tell me you killed Taylor. Then you tell me you've killed the girl. Now it seems they are both alive—and Carlucci's probably dead. And you can be sure they're coming for you and me."

The line went dead. Lindsay had hung up.

. . . .

Carlucci slowly regained consciousness. He tried to remember where he was. The last thing he could remember was the agonizing pain as Taylor swept the blowtorch over his cheek. He remembered telling him where Sarah was and assumed he must have passed out afterwards. His jaw ached and his shattered nose throbbed. However, compared to the searing pain in his cheek, the other pains were minor.

He opened his eyes. Nothing. Wherever he was, it was pitch dark and completely silent. Eerily silent. It couldn't be a hospital. He gingerly felt his face. His nose felt huge and misshapen and he couldn't breathe through it. His jaw felt crooked and he could open it only slightly before feeling excruciating pain. Must be broken. He ran his tongue around the inside of his mouth and realized he was missing several teeth. On the inside of his right cheek, he felt a hole. His tongue could go right through! The bastard had literally burned a hole through his cheek! Carlucci cringed at the thought of what his face must *look* like. Taylor was a dead man. Next time he'd be ready. Taylor and Andrews would die, and he'd make it slow and unpleasant.

Carlucci tried to sit up but his head hit something. Puzzled, he felt around with his hands. There were walls on all sides. He seemed to be in a box, padded and lined with silk. It couldn't be!

He felt the familiar fear begin to mount within him. When he had been a child, as a punishment, his mother used to lock him in an old steamer chest in the basement. Once she had totally forgotten about him and he'd been left in the trunk for almost 24 hours. Ever since, he had been terrified of being confined in small places. Even elevators frightened him.

Trying to control his mounting terror, he felt around. His hand touched a small cylinder—a flashlight. He turned it on.

It *was* a coffin! He began to panic. He pushed at the lid with all his strength, but it wouldn't budge. He called out, but there was no answer. Then he saw a note taped to the inside of the lid just above his head.

> *Death Comes Slowly*
>
> *In case you are wondering, you are in a coffin. The coffin is buried in a remote corner of a small country graveyard. Scream if you want. No one can hear you. Die slowly, Carlucci. There is no one to hear you, no one to care.*
>
> *The Librarian*

For a moment Carlucci lay still, fighting back the terror that rose like a tide within him. He thought about the earth all around the coffin, pressing in on the walls. He imagined the walls breaking under the pressure and the earth pouring in on him, pressing against his body, filling his nose and mouth. His heart pounded until the sound seemed deafening. His breathing came faster and more shallowly until he could not catch his breath. He had to get out. He had to! With all his strength, he pushed against the lid. Nothing. He pushed harder until his massive muscles screamed with pain. Still nothing. He cried out, listening in vain for some response. There was only silence. The futility of his attempts only magnified the terror that gripped him. He screamed and screamed again until his throat was raw. Nothing. Then Frank Carlucci went mad.

· · · · · · ·

Four days had passed and Tom Miller had found no trace of Frank Carlucci. It must be Sarah Andrews, with help from

Paul Taylor, but it didn't fit the pattern. For the others, she had deliberately left the body to be found so they could see the gruesome way they had died. Why not this time? A day later, Miller received a note.

Tom Miller,

Looking for your friend? Go to the Willow Landing Cemetery. Find the oak tree in the northeast corner and walk twenty feet due south. Beneath your feet you will find what you are looking for. You are next. Sleep well.

The Librarian

Apprehensively, Miller rounded up a couple of off-duty cops, drove to the cemetery and dug in the place Sarah had indicated. Sure enough, six feet down they found a coffin containing Carlucci's battered body. The interior of the coffin was torn apart and covered with blood. Carlucci's fingers were scraped raw from his frantic efforts to escape. He'd been buried alive!

Waiting until he regained his composure, Miller phoned Lindsay. "We found Carlucci."

"And?"

"He's dead," replied Miller, waiting for Lindsay's explosion.

"How?"

"We found him in a coffin, buried in a country cemetery... He'd been buried alive."

"Jesus Christ!"

"She planned it out," Miller continued. "There was an air pump so he didn't suffocate right away. It looks like he lived for two or three days. Frank was afraid of confined spaces and must have gone crazy trying to get out."

"God," replied Lindsay, imagining the horrible struggle that must have transpired, unseen and unheard, as Carlucci frantically tried to escape. And she was still out there! With Taylor! It didn't look like Taylor had been involved in the earlier killings, but he was clearly involved with Carlucci's. Burning Taylor's house did nothing but piss him off. They now had a decorated navy seal coming after them. He cursed Miller's stupidity for not killing her when they had the chance. They might die because of it.

"Peter."

"What?" Lindsay snapped.

"She left a note saying she was coming after me next."

"Yeah?"

"I've got a cabin up in the mountains. Real hard to get to. Not near any major roads or towns. The nearest town is Hawksbury, twenty miles south. Need four-wheel drive for the last five miles and you have to hike in for the last mile. I'm going to take a month off and go up there. Leaving Saturday. I've got the time coming. I grew up near there and know the mountains like the back of my hand. Drink some beer. Do some fishing. They'll never find the place, and even if they do, I don't figure they can get me there."

"You can't stay there forever."

"I know, but I've got to do something. It's better than staying here and being a sitting duck."

"You got a phone up there in case we need to talk?"

"Nothing. No phones. No cell service."

"Shit. Well, email the directions to my secretary."

Lindsay hung up and leaned back in his desk. This was a fucking nightmare. Who would have thought? They had been a little rough with one nerdy librarian—now they were being hunted down, and there didn't seem to be a damn thing they could do to stop it.

· · · · · · ·

The next day, Lindsay called Janice. While they'd exchanged emails, he hadn't talked to her in almost two weeks. He knew he should tell her about Carlucci, and it was an excuse to phone her anyway. He intended to remind her about the rain check.

"Hi, Peter. What's up?" Janice came on the line, seemingly delighted to hear from him.

"Thought I better give you the head's up. Another cop's been killed."

"Christ. What happened?"

"It was Frank Carlucci. Seven years on the force. Found him in a coffin in a country cemetery."

"I don't understand."

"He'd been buried alive."

"How ghastly."

"We're investigating. Looks like someone broke into his house, beat him up pretty badly and then took him up to the cemetery. He may have been unconscious and come to in the coffin after it was buried."

"My God! Any idea who did it?"

"It was clearly a professional hit."

"They went to a lot of trouble if all they wanted to do was take him out," Janice replied, skepticism evident in her voice.

"Probably just trying to shake us up. We're making some real progress on the drug initiative."

"I hope so. It's a good way to spin it for the media and I think we need to organize another press conference. Better to appear proactive and in control. I'll work up something and get together with you later today."

"Let me know."

"Peter. You remember that rain check?"

"Absolutely," replied Lindsay, pleased that she'd brought it up on her own.

"How would you like to take a break this weekend? We can take Friday off to give us a three-day weekend. Drive up the coast together. Find some quiet hotel. It would give us time to unwind. We need to talk about some final strategies to lock up the Police Chief appointment for you anyway. I'll pick you up at your suite Friday morning and have you back early Sunday night. What do you say?"

Lindsay was surprised but delighted at the suggestion. He had hoped his relationship with Janice Fox might develop into something, but her sudden suggestion of a weekend vacation startled him. Three days, and two nights, alone with Janice Fox. The implication was obvious.

"Let's do it," Lindsay replied.

"You'll need to tell your wife something."

"No problem. I have week-end conventions all the time."

"Then it's a date. I'll arrange everything and I'll pick you up at your suite at nine."

CHAPTER 35

PETER LINDSAY WAS WAITING IN FRONT OF THE WINDSOR when Janice pulled up. He had offered to drive but Janice had insisted on taking her car. Tossing his case in the trunk of her Audi A4, he hopped into the passenger seat. "Hi there."

"Good morning," Janice said cheerfully, leaning over to kiss him. She was wearing white jean shorts and a red tank top. "Do I pass?" she added conscious of his scrutiny.

"Absolutely."

"Good."

"So where exactly are we going?"

"It's a surprise, but I'm sure you'll like it."

They were well out of the city by ten and Janice took a scenic route up the coast, while Lindsay settled back to enjoy the scenery—and the anticipation of a weekend with Janice Fox. "Did you need the Governor's permission to take the weekend off?" he joked.

Janice laughed. "Not exactly. But I didn't want him to call me so I told him I was going to visit my mother."

Janice chatted cheerfully along the way, mostly political gossip about the Governor's messy personal life and the sexual indiscretions of one of the state senators. They stopped for lunch at a country restaurant and, by mid-afternoon, Janice pulled into the driveway of a private cottage on a hill overlooking the ocean.

"What's this?" Lindsay asked.

"This is the surprise. It's ours for the weekend. It has its own private beach, a Jacuzzi on the deck overlooking the ocean and a tennis court. I thought it would be more intimate than some big hotel."

"Sounds fantastic. How did you find it?"

"I have my sources."

The cottage was beautifully furnished and Lindsay noticed that the kitchen was stocked with food, beer and wine. "I see you've got us well supplied."

Janice winked at him. "So we don't need to go out all weekend."

"It appears your organizational skills aren't limited to politics."

Janice laughed. "It's been a long drive. I'd suggest a swim, but the ocean's getting a little chilly this time of year. How about a walk along the shore? Afterwards we can warm up in the Jacuzzi before dinner."

"Sounds like a plan."

The sky was overcast and the wind was brisk as they set out along the beach. The ocean heaved and churned, giving quiet warning of its awesome and explosive power. At the shoreline, angry whitecaps, wiped up by the wind, crashed relentlessly against the rocks, sending spray high into the air. They walked away from the cottage for almost an hour before turning back. In contrast to her talkativeness in the car, Janice said little, seemingly entranced by the ever-changing ocean vista. By the time they arrived back to the cottage, Lindsay's legs ached with fatigue, although Janice seemed unaffected.

"How about that Jacuzzi?" Janice suggested.

"Sounds great."

After changing, Lindsay made it back to the deck first and eased into the warm water, enjoying the heat and the feel of the water pulsing against his weary muscles. Minutes later, Janice reappeared wearing a sleek one-piece black bathing suit, bringing them each a cold beer. Lindsay couldn't help admiring her toned body and tanned skin. For forty something, she was definitely fit. "You look like you stay in shape."

Janice laughed. "Thank you. At my age, I think your body starts to disintegrate unless you work at it."

"I don't see any signs of disintegration."

"Sometimes the decay is on the inside."

"Depressing thought."

"Here's to living forever then."

"Much better." Lindsay laughed.

Afterwards, Janice prepared them an elaborate dinner, refusing Lindsay's repeated offers of help.

"I *am* impressed. You can cook too," commented Lindsay as he finished dessert.

Janice smiled. "I'm full of surprises."

"Are there more to come?"

Janice just smiled. "Why don't you make yourself comfortable on the sofa. I'll clean up the kitchen and join you."

"At least let me help you put the stuff away."

"Don't worry about it. You can do breakfast. By the way, there's a fancy coffee maker in here. Makes cappuccinos, espressos and lattes. Want something?"

"Sure. I'll take a cappuccino."

A few minutes later, Janice returned from the kitchen bringing Lindsay a cappuccino and herself a latte. She sat down beside him on the couch. "Here's to stolen weekends," she said proposing a toast.

"To a great weekend then, and thanks again for all your help."

"It's been fun. I think the end is in sight and I'm looking forward to it."

"I'm curious what you do when you're not helping me become Chief of Police."

Lindsay's question launched her into a dissertation on state politics and Lindsay was content to listen, acutely conscious of her closeness and the scent of her perfume. As she talked, Lindsay put his arm around her and drew her against him. Janice settled into his arms and continued her story. With his finger, Lindsay slowly and lightly traced a line starting at her temple down over her cheek, neck and collarbone. Finally, Janice stopped talking. Smiling enigmatically, she took his hand and led him to the bedroom. There, she turned the lights off, quickly undressed and slipped under the covers. Lindsay stripped off his clothes and joined her. The silky feel of her skin and the warmth of her body against his were intoxicating—the realization of his fantasies over the months since he'd met her. With only cursory foreplay, he crawled on top and in minutes, he collapsed beside her, spent and satisfied. He reached over and stroked her hair, but Janice turned away and went off to sleep. By the time Lindsay awoke the next morning, she was up fixing breakfast.

"How do you want your eggs?"

"Thought *I* was on breakfast duty?"

"You can do dinner."

"In that case, however you're having them."

Janice refused to leave the cottage for the entire three days, explaining that she wanted to shut out the world. They took turns cooking, went for long walks along the shore, played tennis on cottage's private court and roasted marshmallows on the beach at sunset. Janice seemed fascinated in everything about him; his parents, his childhood, his early career, and Lindsay couldn't help being flattered by her interest. He found her exciting, intelligent and fun—and she had a knockout body. In bed however, Janice was surprisingly distant. While acquiescent to his overtures, she remained noticeably passive during their lovemaking. Lindsay dismissed it as her natural reserve.

Sunday afternoon they began the drive back. In the car, Janice appeared distracted and, despite Lindsay's efforts to make conversation, she said little. When they reached his hotel, Lindsay thanked her for the weekend and suggested dinner the following evening.

"Peter, I'd love to, but I'll be completely tied up for the next few days. I'll call you as soon as I can."

"You have to eat," Lindsay persisted.

"I'll call you," Janice repeated, vaguely.

· · · · · · ·

The Saturday after telling Lindsay he was going to go up to his cabin in the mountains, Miller loaded up his SUV and set off. After a four-hour drive and a half hour hike in from the end of the road, he reached his cabin. Looking out over the mountains, he drank in the serenity and pristine beauty of the area. He loved it here. It reminded him of the good times with his father. The two of them would come up here on weekends or vacations and hunt and fish and just talk.

Sarah Andrews had been bothering him. When they got the first note, he'd dismissed it as some stupid prank. Now however, LePan, Gordon and Carlucci were dead and Kramer horribly crippled. It was clearly no prank. And worse, that Taylor guy was involved. A librarian was one thing, a decorated navy seal another. He was safe in the mountains though. He knew the land like the back of his hand and he had several high-powered rifles in his cabin as well as hunting bows and a collection of knives. Just the same, Miller spent the next few hours setting out bear traps around the cabin. The jaws could hold a thousand pound grizzly. When he was finished, Miller smiled to himself. Let them come.

That afternoon Miller went fishing in the nearby pond and later sat on the porch eating some of the fish and drinking the beer he'd cooled in the stream. For the first time in more than a month he felt relaxed and safe. He went to bed early and immediately fell into a deep and peaceful sleep.

Just after midnight, he awoke. Certain that something must have wakened him, he lay still, listening. Nothing. Must have been the wind. Then he heard it—a long low moan, faint but definitely real. After a couple of minutes, it was repeated. Strange. It did not come from any animal he knew, nor did it sound human. Puzzled Tom got up, opened the door to the cabin and stood there quietly, studying the woods beyond the clearing around the cabin. Thick clouds blocked out the moon and stars and he could barely make out the shapes of the trees. The soft moaning sound came again. It was barely distinguishable from the sound of the night wind through the trees, but there *was* something out there.

Quietly taking a rifle, Miller slipped out to the rear of the cabin, intending to circle around behind the source of the noise. Crouching low, Miller moved silently and surely through the thick woods. A hundred yards from the cabin, he stopped and listened. Nothing. He moved further. Then he heard it again, closer now and between him and the cabin. He stopped and studied the darkness intently, hoping to detect some movement. Nothing. He moved closer. There! Just a faint outline in the dark, but it looked like a man, standing there, motionless.

Miller moved still closer. It *was* a man, standing completely still, facing the cabin, his back towards him. Miller smiled to himself. Whoever it was, he had him. Holding his gun ready, Miller approached, carefully stepping around an open area covered with leaves, which he knew concealed one of the bear traps. He wondered how the man had avoided it.

Suddenly there was a loud snap. Tom Miller screamed in pain as the jaws of the bear trap closed around the calf of his leg, slicing through the flesh right to the bone. The bones in his leg broke and he fell to the ground in agony, dropping the rifle. He reached down to free himself, knowing it was futile. The jaws could only be opened with a special apparatus that resembled a car jack.

Suddenly the man turned towards him and stepped from the shadows. It was Paul Taylor!

"You!" Miller gasped.

"Nice place you've got," Paul commented, retrieving the fallen rifle. "Bet you don't get many visitors though. Sorry you didn't see the bear trap. When I was looking for the place, I found several. As you've noticed, I moved a few of them around."

"How the hell did *you* get here?"

"It seems the police department network is fairly easy to hack into. All I had to do was follow the excellent instructions you sent to Lindsay's secretary."

"For God's sake," Miller moaned in agony. "Get this off me."

Paul leaned casually on the rifle studying Miller curiously. "You know. I once knew a guy who got caught in a bear trap. Told me about it after. Said it was so bad, he wished he had died. The trap's jaws broke both the bones in his leg, and then the constant pressure gradually forced the bones farther apart, literally stretching his leg. The pain was unbearable. After a day, blood poisoning set in and his leg swelled to twice its normal size. By the third day, it started turning black. At first, it was the pain, but after a couple of days, it was the thirst that drove him crazy. He was lucky. After four days, someone found him. Still lost his leg. Unfortunately, no one is going to find you."

"For God's sake."

Taylor shook his head and his eyes grew hard. "I saw the disk, Tom. The one where you and your pals tied up Sarah Andrews and worked her over with a taser."

Realizing he could expect no mercy, Miller lay back and groaned.

"Tom. It's late and I'm going to wait till morning to go back to the city. You won't mind if I sleep in your cabin tonight, will you? I missed dinner so I'll probably fry up the rest of that fish you caught this afternoon and drink some of that beer you've got cooling in the stream. Sorry you can't join me. Supposed to get pretty cool tonight, but I don't think it will rain."

Miller simply whimpered in pain.

When Paul Taylor returned the next morning, he found Miller shivering in the morning chill. His leg had swollen up grotesquely, and pus and an angry redness were visible around the puncture wounds. Infection was already setting in. "You don't look too good, Tom."

Miller just moaned.

"Brought you the last couple of beers," Paul said, tossing the cans within reach of Miller. "Not sure I'd drink them though. It will just prolong your suffering."

Thirstily, Miller opened one of the cans.

"Suit yourself. Anyway, I enjoyed the visit, but I have to go back to the city now."

"Please," Miller pleaded, trying to raise his head. "Pleeeease."

"Now Tom. We've been through this. Enjoy your time. It will be all over in a few days."

· · · · · · ·

After driving back in the city late Sunday afternoon, Paul went directly to Sarah's condominium. He got there at about five to find her drinking coffee on the balcony. Sensing her somber mood, he went over and kissed her warmly. "Hi there. You okay?"

Sarah rose and hugged him tightly. "Now that you're here, I am. How was your weekend?"

"Better than Tom Miller's. Poor guy got his leg caught in one of his own bear traps. He'll last another few days, whether he wants to or not."

Sarah nodded in silent satisfaction. "And the other stuff."

"All taken care of. What about you?"

"Weekend went as planned. I'm glad it's over."

Paul hugged her. "How about taking off. Right now. We've got a few hours of light. We'll head north, have dinner in some country restaurant and find a B&B for the night. You need the break."

Sarah pulled his arms around her. "Oh Paul. I'd like that, but when we get back tomorrow, I want you to do something for me."

"Of course."

"I want you to go back to San Alicia."

Paul looked at her in surprise. "Why?"

"Paul. I owe you so much. For all that you did before, and now for this. You handled Carlucci and Miller for me. I wasn't sure how I was going to manage Carlucci. The guy's built like a truck."

Paul grinned. "My pleasure."

Sarah laughed, but then turned serious. "They're all gone now except Lindsay, and the trap for him is almost set. There's nothing more you can do and, whatever happens, I want to know you're safe."

"If something happens, I'd rather be here."

"It's only a four hour flight. If something happens you can come back."

Paul hesitated. He knew Sarah's plan for Peter Lindsay and there was nothing more he could do to help. She would be fully occupied for the next several days and the prospect of sitting around doing nothing wasn't very appealing.

Discerning his uncertainty, Sarah pressed. "Paul. Please."

Paul sensed how important it was to her. "Three conditions."

Sarah cocked her head expectantly. "Only three?"

"Firstly, if anything goes wrong, you call me immediately. No matter what. Second, once you spring the trap on Lindsay, you get back to San Alicia. No hanging around to gloat. And thirdly, in two weeks, I'm coming back to take you to San Alicia, for good, whether you're finished with your project or not."

Sarah kissed him. "Agreed. I promise."

CHAPTER 36

IT WAS THURSDAY AFTER THEIR WEEKEND AWAY BEFORE Lindsay finally got a phone call from Janice. He had tried to reach her several times but just got voicemail and she hadn't responded to his messages. "Where have you been?" he asked, unable hide his irritation.

"I'm sorry. I've been busy. I did warn you. Anyway, I have some great news. How about dinner tonight?"

"Sure," replied Peter, brightening at her suggestion. "The Cellar at seven?"

"See you there."

She was already at the restaurant when Lindsay arrived and embraced him warmly. "I've missed you."

Lindsay returned the embrace. "What's keeping you so busy?"

"Just stuff. How's police business?"

"Good. There's been some more favorable press coverage on the War on Drugs."

"I saw it. We need to keep the positive momentum—and the publicity."

"So tell me," pressed Lindsay, unable to restrain his curiosity. "What's the good news you mentioned?"

She laughed. "Be patient. Let me order some wine first."

When their drinks arrived, Janice raised her glass. "A toast to the new Chief of Police."

He looked at her uncertainly and she began to explain. "Chief Moorby went to see Pat Kelton a couple of days ago. His wife has been diagnosed with cancer and he wants to retire as soon as possible to spend more time with her. Pat met with the rest of the Police Commission and you were their unanimous choice to take over as Chief. You can expect a call from the Mayor tomorrow morning to formally advise you. The swearing-in ceremony is scheduled for next Wednesday. In less than a week, you'll be Chief of Police. Congratulations."

Lindsay was stunned. He had been increasingly optimistic that things were falling into place, but he assumed his appointment was still two months away. "I don't know what to say."

"I've informed the Governor. He's very pleased. He asked me to pass on his congratulations."

"Well thank him for me."

"Of course. He also told me to remind you that this is just the first step. He wants you to run for mayor in the next election and asked me to head your campaign."

"You're hired."

When dinner was over, Peter suggested a nightcap back at his suite.

Janice smiled at him. "Peter. Can I pass? The last few days have been pretty hectic. Our weekend was great and we should discuss the future. Give me a couple of days to get back to normal and I'll call you."

· · · · · · ·

At ten the next morning, Lindsay received a call from Mayor Kelton, confirming everything that Janice Fox had said. He could barely contain his elation. He was going to be appointed Chief of Police within a week. He was being groomed by senior party leaders to run for mayor in the next city elections. And on top of that, Janice wanted to discuss their future together. Life couldn't get any better.

As he sat at his desk reveling in his good fortune, he noticed a plain white envelope in his inbox marked "Personal and Confidential." His mood changed instantly and a shiver of apprehension ran through him. He had forgotten all about Sarah Andrews. Lindsay opened the envelope and pulled out the single sheet of paper.

Peter Lindsay,

The others are all gone now.

The Librarian

Miller! If they were all gone except him, Miller must be dead. But how? A cabin in the mountains. No phone, no electricity. It wasn't possible. Lindsay immediately phoned Miller's precinct captain. "Vince. I need a big favor."

"No problem, Peter. What's up?"

"You know Tom Miller's taking a month's leave."

"Yeah. He's at his cabin in the mountains."

"I know. It doesn't have a phone and there's no cell coverage either, and I need to talk to him urgently about a case. Can you have someone drive up there and get Tom to go to the nearest town and call me? My secretary will email you the directions."

"No problem. By the way, there's a rumor you're going to be appointed Chief any day now. Congratulations."

Lindsay smiled. He hadn't realized that his imminent appointment was already getting out, but he was pleased. "I never comment on rumors, but thank you."

Lindsay got a return call from Miller's precinct captain that Saturday at home. "Pete. I'm sorry to bother you at home, but I thought you should hear this as soon as possible."

"No problem. What's up?" Lindsay replied, already certain he knew what was coming.

"Tom Miller is dead. I know he was a friend of yours. I'm sorry."

"How?"

"Looks like a freak accident. He stepped into a bear trap and couldn't free himself. He died of blood poisoning from the puncture wounds. He must have lived for two or three days while the infection set in and spread throughout his body. A lousy way to die."

"Any sign it *wasn't* an accident?"

"We've sent a team up to investigate, but the officer I sent said there was no sign of foul play."

"Thanks, Vince. Keep me informed."

"Will do. And my condolences."

Lindsay leaned back in his chair shaken. It was no accident. They were all dead now—except for him.

As the days leading up to the swearing-in ceremony passed, Lindsay should have been excited over his imminent appointment, but instead, fear gripped him with paralyzing intensity. Like a living entity within him, the fear grew relentlessly, invading his thoughts, constricting his chest—until he couldn't think, couldn't breathe. Sarah Andrews. He recalled the day they had arrested her. So terrified, helpless and alone. He remembered her tied to the ceiling, screaming, as the taser jolted her body. How could it have come to this? He reflected on the terrible deaths she had inflicted on the others. She'd left him to last. Deliberately. What was she planning for him? When would she strike?

· · · · · · ·

As his swearing-in approached, Peter Lindsay was overwhelmed with congratulatory emails and calls. Senior members of the police department found reasons to visit him, hoping to preserve or enhance their positions under the new chief. The media pursued him for interviews. Citizens' groups tried to meet to press their agendas. He reveled in the power and attention and, in the flurry of activity and excitement, his anxiety over Sarah Andrews faded.

The big day arrived. The swearing-in ceremony was to take place at three o'clock in the city hall auditorium. Attendees would include city councilors, members of the police commission, senior officers of the police force, friends and family, and the media—in all, about four hundred people. Following the swearing-in, there was to be a reception in the city hall rotunda to which three thousand people had been invited.

Mayor Kelton and Chief Moorby were waiting when Lindsay arrived at Kelton's office a few minutes before the ceremony. "Congratulations again," said Kelton, shaking his hand.

"My congratulations too," added Moorby. "I couldn't be leaving the force in better hands."

Lindsay shook their hands in turn and smiled broadly. "Thank you both for your support and confidence."

Kelton turned to his assistant. "Well Jean. You better walk us through the process again."

"Of course, sir. Most of the attendees for the ceremony are already seated. Chief Lindsay, your wife, children and mother are in the front row. There's a small head table for the three of you and the three other members of the police commission."

"What's the agenda?" prompted Kelton.

"Mayor Kelton, you'll open the meeting, welcome the guests and give a speech describing Chief Lindsay's career and acknowledging Chief Moorby's long and distinguished service."

Kelton nodded. In fact, Jean had written the speech and reviewed it with him earlier that morning.

"Then, Chief Moorby," she continued. "You'll be asked to make a few comments."

Moorby grinned. "I know. You warned me. I've made some notes. Shouldn't take more than a couple of hours."

Jean smiled. "I'm counting on you to keep it to ten minutes."

"I promise. No point delaying my well-deserved retirement."

"Then, Mayor Kelton, you'll formally swear in Chief Lindsay. Then, Chief Lindsay, you'll make a brief speech. The draft you gave me was excellent. I went over it with the mayor. We think it will play very well with the media."

"Peter," Kelton added. "It really *was* an outstanding speech. It sets exactly the right tone, acknowledging the past and the proud traditions of the police force while setting a new course. If you get tired of being police chief, let me know. I'll hire you as a speech writer."

Lindsay just nodded. Janice had written every word of it. There is no way he could have come up with anything like it himself.

"By four o'clock, we should start moving to the rotunda for the reception," Jean continued. "The Mayor will make a short speech welcoming the guests. The rest of you are off the hook. Just mingle and enjoy."

The men nodded.

"Are we ready gentlemen?" Jean asked.

Kelton grinned. "Some days I wonder who's running this city. Me or Jean."

Moorby slapped his back playfully. "Keep wondering, Pat. The rest of us figured it out long ago."

· · · · · · ·

The auditorium was packed when they arrived. The other members of the Police Commission were already seated at the head table as Jean ushered them to the three remaining seats. As he sat down, Lindsay looked out over the audience, basking in the knowledge this was all for him. His family was seated together in the front row smiling proudly. The most senior officers in the police department, many once senior to him, were seated near the front, hoping for his acknowledgement. It took him a minute to find Janice Fox sitting discreetly five rows back. When their eyes connected, Lindsay nodded imperceptibly and then looked away, afraid his wife might follow his glance. Photographers were hovering around in front of the head table snapping pictures.

After a few minutes, Mayor Kelton rose and the room slowly became quiet. "Good afternoon, ladies and gentlemen. I would like to thank you all for coming."

The ceremony proceeded exactly as Jean had described. Kelton acknowledged Moorby's achievements and described Lindsay's career in glowing terms. Then Moorby said a few words, and finally the Mayor formally swore in Lindsay as the new Chief of Police. As Kelton sat down, Lindsay remained standing, feeling a powerful rush of excitement and pride as sustained applause reverberated though the room.

"Thank you. Thank you so much," he began as the applause finally subsided. "This is a proud day for me and my family. Being appointed Chief of Police of our great city is an extraordinary honor, and one I never dreamed of receiving when I started out as a rookie cop twenty years ago. I would like to thank Mayor Kelton for his support and his confidence. I would like to thank all the members of the Police Commission and, in particular, I would like to thank Chief Moorby for his advice over many years. The fact that I have been considered worthy of this honor is, in no small measure, due to his guidance and wise counsel."

At that moment, Jean re-entered the room through the door behind the head table. She approached the Mayor and whispered something in his ear.

"*Now?*" Lindsay heard Kelton reply in astonishment.

Jean nodded firmly and looked up at Lindsay with a curious expression.

As Kelton left the room, Lindsay continued his remarks.

"I am taking over as Chief of one of the finest police forces in the country," Lindsay continued wondering what could possibly have been so important that Kelton had to leave in the middle of his speech. "Ed Moorby has been Chief for over ten years and has made the force what it is today—highly professional and passionately dedicated."

Suddenly Jean returned and now approached Moorby whispering something to him privately. He looked up in astonishment and then followed her out of the room. Mystified at what could possibly have required both Moorby and Kelton to leave in the middle of the ceremony, Lindsay managed to continue as if nothing unusual had happened.

"But these are changing times and call for new approaches. Using the strong foundation Chief Moorby has created, we need to move forward. While the War on Drugs has been successful, there is more to be done and we need to be resolute in our determination to finish the task before us."

Suddenly Lindsay realized that people were no longer listening. Curious whispers rustled through the room as people sensed something unusual was occurring.

"Let the pushers, the distributors and suppliers find somewhere else to do business," Lindsay continued in a louder voice, trying in vain to recapture the audience's attention. "There is no place for them in this city."

The line was intended to prompt applause; but none came. The buzz in the room intensified. Turning to follow the focus of the audience, Lindsay saw that Kelton and Moorby had returned along with two other men. Lindsay had never seen them before, but he detected the telltale bulge of guns under their suit jackets. The four of them were standing just inside the door in a huddled conversation, periodically looking his way.

Puzzled and increasingly uneasy, Lindsay struggled to continue. "I intend to take back our city from the criminal element which..."

Lindsay stopped in mid-sentence as the two men stepped onto the raised platform and approached him. One of the men took his arm and commanded, "Sir. Would you please come with us?"

Lindsay angrily brushed off the man's hand. "For Christ's sake, I'm in the middle of a speech. Whatever it is can wait."

"I'm sorry sir. It can't wait. Please come with us now."

By now, the room was in pandemonium. The media were hovering around snapping photos and trying to figure out what was going on.

"This is ridiculous!" shouted Lindsay. "I'm not going anywhere until I've finished my speech."

"Please sir," continued the man, gripping Lindsay's arm more firmly, and discreetly producing a badge identifying him as an FBI agent.

"For Christ's sake, let go of me," Lindsay screamed, ignoring the badge.

The man gripping Lindsay looked at the other agent who nodded.

"We didn't want to do this here, Mr. Lindsay, but you leave us no choice," continued the man as he tightened his hold on Lindsay's arm. "You are under arrest for the murder of Tom Miller. You have the right to remain..."

The statement was caught on the microphone and a collective gasp erupted from the audience. The media scrambled closer, flash bulbs popped and microphones were thrust towards the exchange. In seconds the entire room had dissolved into chaos.

"Have you lost your minds?" Lindsay exclaimed in utter disbelief.

"...you have the right to remain silent. Anything you say can and will be used..."

"This is absolutely absurd!"

"...against you in a court of law. You have the right to have an attorney present..."

"I know my rights, you moron. I've read them a million times."

"...during questioning. If you cannot afford an attorney, one will be appointed for you."

"God damn you!" Lindsay exclaimed, as the two FBI agents forcefully pulled his arms behind his back and snapped handcuffs on his wrists. "When this is sorted out, I'm going to hang the two of you out to dry."

As the FBI agents led him out of the auditorium, Lindsay looked around. Janice Fox was nowhere to be seen.

CHAPTER 37

TWO HOURS LATER, LINDSAY HAD BEEN PROCESSED AND LEFT
locked in a holding cell wearing a bright orange prison jumper.
He surveyed the tiny room with disgust: the rusted metal bunk,
the polished metal mirror and the stained toilet—a stark contrast to the lavish office he should now be occupying as Chief of
Police. The whole thing was bizarre. How could he be arrested
for Miller's murder? He'd never been near Miller's cabin. It
was a mistake. A monstrous and absurd mistake. However, his
lawyer was on his way. Within hours, it would all be sorted out
and he would be home, celebrating his appointment.

An hour later, a guard appeared and looked at him curiously.
"Your lawyer's here."

Lindsay was led to an interrogation room where his attorney, Glen Sutton, was already seated at the table with a note
pad ready.

"Glen. Thanks for coming so quickly. This is insane. I'm counting on you to get me out of here. And when I'm out, there will be hell to pay."

Sutton looked at him without smiling. "Pete. You should know right away, this is serious."

Lindsay exploded. "There *was* no murder. Miller stepped into a bear trap. It was accidental!"

Sutton shook his head.

"What do you mean?" demanded Lindsay.

"I know the initial investigation concluded it was accidental, but the FBI got an anonymous tip and went back to Miller's cabin. They concluded that the bear trap was set deliberately and Miller was lured into it by his killer."

"Even if it *was* murder, I've never been near his cabin."

"Peter. Apparently they have evidence that you were at the cabin at the time of the murder."

Lindsay slammed the table in frustration. "What evidence?"

"I'm being briefed tomorrow, but apparently it's extensive."

"That's impossible! I've never been near the place. Besides. What possible motive would I have?" replied Lindsay in exasperation. "Tom Miller was a friend."

Sutton nodded. "They admit they don't have a motive."

"See! The whole thing is ridiculous. And when exactly was I supposed to have driven three hundred miles, hiked to Miller's cabin, killed him and then driven all the way back? It would take a full two days."

"They believe murder took place sometime during the weekend before last. Any chance you've got an alibi?"

Lindsay thought for a moment. That was the weekend he'd gone to the cottage with Janice Fox! He'd been with her every minute. What could be better than an alibi provided by an assistant to the Governor? He'd have to reveal his affair, but he was going to leave his wife anyway.

"I was with someone for the entire weekend."

Sutton brightened considerably. "Who?"

"Janice Fox. Assistant Communications Director in the Governor's Office. We went away for the weekend together."

Sutton looked at him quizzically.

"We were having an affair," Lindsay conceded, "but I guess it doesn't matter now."

"Will Ms. Fox corroborate that?"

"Of course."

"How can I reach her?"

Lindsay gave him her cell number and suite at The Plaza from memory. "I assume this will get me out of here."

"The other evidence is apparently pretty damaging, but a solid alibi from a credible witness would certainly raise some questions. Let me talk to her."

Sutton left and Lindsay was escorted back to his cell. They had no motive and Janice would soon corroborate his alibi. The nightmare would be over. When he was released, he'd insist on a public apology and find a way to destroy those two FBI agents who manhandled him in front of four hundred people and ruined his moment of glory. It wasn't until noon the following day that a guard came to take him back to see Sutton. Lindsay was furious that he'd had to spend the night in jail and Sutton was going to hear about it.

· · · · · · ·

As Lindsay sat down again, Glen Sutton looked at him strangely without uttering a word.

"So! Did you talk to her?" Lindsay demanded impatiently.

Sutton slowly shook his head.

"What do you mean?"

"As far as we can tell, Janice Fox doesn't exist."

Lindsay couldn't believe what he'd just heard. "What do you mean? Did you talk to the Governor's Office? Did you call the number I gave you?"

"The Governor's Office says no one by that name ever worked there. The suite at the Plaza was leased in the name of Janet Smith, who paid her bill in cash and checked out yesterday. The phone number you gave me was one of these pre-paid cell phones, also paid for in cash by a Janet Smith. It was deactivated yesterday."

"That's totally absurd. She must have a driver's license, a social security number."

"We checked all that. There are a few Janice Foxes, but none remotely fitting your description."

"She exists for Christ's sake. She arranged speaking engagements and press conferences for me; got Kelton to introduce me at a Chamber of Commerce dinner. Keep looking!"

Sutton looked at him and sighed. "Peter, of course, we'll keep looking. But I have to tell you it's not looking good. I was briefed this morning. They found your footprints, and your fingerprints on some beer cans around the crime scene."

"That's impossible!"

"Apparently you bought gas in the local town and stayed overnight in a local motel, all using your credit card. The gas station recorded your license number on the receipt."

Lindsay looked at Sutton in astonishment. "Someone must have stolen my card."

"You didn't report it stolen, and it was in your wallet when you were arrested."

Lindsay leaned back in bewilderment. None of it made any sense.

"And they've come up with a motive," continued Sutton.

"What motive?" Lindsay replied contemptuously.

"Blackmail."

"Blackmail! For what?"

"For the murder of Tony Costanza."

Lindsay was silent for a moment. He'd totally forgotten the incident. "Costanza died of a heart attack. The SIU investigated and found nothing."

"Miller apparently had evidence *you* killed Costanza with a taser."

"That's ridiculous."

Glen Sutton looked at Lindsay skeptically. "The FBI took an image of your hard drive. There were emails from Miller on your PC demanding a hundred thousand dollars to keep quiet."

"That's impossible. I never got such an email."

"In fact, the emails indicated you'd already paid him a hundred thousand and he wanted a second hundred."

"I never paid him a cent!"

"According to your bank, you withdrew a hundred grand in cash just a few weeks ago."

Lindsay looked aghast. He'd deposited the bank draft from Janice and then withdrawn the cash to pay off his gambling debts. "That was for some debts I had."

"A hundred grand? And do you usually pay off your debts in cash?"

Lindsay sighed in utter frustration. "They were gambling debts. They insisted on cash."

"I don't suppose you got a receipt."

"Of course not. Whose side are you on?"

"Yours. But I need you to understand what we're up against. And I need you to be straight with me."

"I have been. I don't know what the hell is going on here, but it's all bullshit."

"All the emails were on both your computer and Miller's. How can you explain that?"

"I don't know. This is totally crazy. You have to get me out of here so I can find Janice and get this all straightened out."

Sutton shook his head. "I'll see what I can do, but getting bail on a first-degree murder charge is tough—in the best of circumstances."

· · · · · · ·

Back in his cell, Lindsay collapsed on the tiny cot. What was going on? Someone was framing him. But who? Why? Then, in a flash of insight, he knew. Sarah Andrews! Instead of just killing him as she had the others, she was framing him for murder. But how had she done it all? Then, in a second devastating insight, he realized that Janice Fox must be working with Sarah.

It all fit. Their weekend getaway just happened to be the same weekend Miller was killed. It was Janice's idea to stay in the cottage the entire time, making certain that no one had seen him. She'd insisted on taking *her* car that weekend, which would allow someone to take *his* car to Hawksbury and buy gas for it. He'd once lent her the key to his suite. She could easily have made a duplicate that would give Sarah access to copy his car keys and tamper with his computer. Sarah was a computer geek and must have been able to create the dummy emails from Miller. They could have borrowed his boots and taken some old beer cans that would explain the footprints and fingerprints. They could also have borrowed one of his credit cards and later returned it. He had so many, he wouldn't have noticed. Janice had even given him the hundred grand to settle his debts. Janice Fox had been working with Sarah Andrews all the time! How could he have been so blind?

Two hours later, the guard told him that a legal assistant from Glen Sutton's office wanted to see him. As he was led back into the interrogation room, he saw Janice Fox waiting for him at the table.

· · · · · · ·

Lindsay looked at her uncertainly. "Janice? My lawyer's been trying to reach you. The Governor's Office said they'd never heard you."

Janice looked at him quietly for a long time before replying. "There *is* no Janice Fox."

"What do you mean?"

Silently, Sarah Andrews slipped off the grey wig and ran her fingers through her short raven hair.

Lindsay stared at her in stunned disbelief. "Sarah Andrews!?"

She nodded.

That simple gesture confirmed the entire horrifying truth. All the time they'd been searching in vain for Sarah Andrews, he'd been seeing her regularly, having dinner with her, spending the weekend with her. All the time, he'd been waiting apprehensively for her to try to kill him, and she'd been slowly and meticulously implicating him for Miller's murder. She'd never intended to kill him. It was diabolically brilliant. How could he not have recognized her? How could he, a trained cop, have been so gullible?

Defeat showed in his eyes. "How?" he asked weakly.

"You know how Peter," she replied softly. "You just can't accept it."

"Why this way?"

"Can you imagine what it's going to be like in prison, especially for a police chief? Every con in the place will want a piece of you. You'll probably share a cell with some big biker covered in tattoos. Maybe that's a good thing because he'll protect you—but I don't even want to think about the 'personal services' he'll expect in return. I figure you're in for twenty years of pure hell. Far worse than anything I could do to you. Besides. Perfect justice don't you think? You had *me* sent to prison."

"Why all the work to make me Police Chief?"

"A means to an end. I needed to get close to you. To earn your trust, to get to your computer, your keys, to lure you away for the weekend. Besides, it gave you farther to fall."

"And the Governor?"

"Never met him. It's amazing what people will believe if you flash a fancy business card and speak with authority."

Peter Lindsay studied the confident and self-assured woman before him, trying to see the frightened librarian he remembered. It *was* the same person—yet she was so different. Her eyes reflected not the fear he recalled, but a cold, controlled rage.

"Yes it's me," Sarah replied, sensing his thoughts. "The same shy, frightened librarian you terrorized and sent to prison."

Lindsay remained silent, too shattered to respond.

"It was a room much like this. They tied me to the ceiling and held that taser against me. I screamed and screamed—but they just laughed. When you came in, I was so relieved. You were the boss and you'd make them stop. But you didn't. You took the taser and used it on me yourself."

Lindsay looked at her numbly.

For an instant, Lindsay saw the pain and horror through her eyes. He saw the appalling reality of what they had done to her. But he couldn't deal with it. "You'll never get away with this."

"I already have, Peter," Sarah replied calmly, rising to leave. "I already have."

CHAPTER 38

PAUL TAYLOR SAT ON THE DECK OF HIS HOUSE IN SAN ALICIA, watching the sunset. He was worried. Lindsay's arrest had been reported two days ago and Sarah should have arrived back in San Alicia by now, but she hadn't called and he hadn't been able to reach her cell phone. Something must have gone wrong. He should never have left her in the city on her own. Tomorrow morning, he would fly back to the city and he prayed that he would not be too late.

As he gazed out over the ocean, lost in his thoughts, he didn't see the solitary figure walking along the water's edge at first. Finally the distant movement penetrated his consciousness. Strange he thought. His house was on an isolated stretch of beach, not near any of the big hotels and it was rare to see anyone on the beach—especially in the evening. He watched the figure, nothing more than a dark silhouette against the sunset. Slender—a woman? The stride seemed familiar. Sarah?

It must be his imagination. The figure came closer, and began to run. It *was* her! Paul leapt from his chair and ran toward her. They came together and embraced each other wordlessly, clinging to each other as if they were afraid the moment wasn't real.

"I wanted to surprise you," Sarah finally explained breathlessly. "I got a flight first thing this morning, but it was late taking off and then it was diverted to another airport due to weather. I've been sitting on planes for twelve hours. Finally, I tried to call you, but my cell phone was dead. And when I got to the airport here I couldn't remember your street address. I knew I would recognize your house from the beach, so I had the cab driver drop me half a mile back and I walked along the shore until I saw it. Then I saw you sitting there. Oh, Paul. I'm so glad to see you."

Paul led her up to the deck, holding her tightly, kissing her hair, her neck, her face. "Oh God, Sarah. When I couldn't reach you, I was sure something had gone wrong."

She hugged him with tears of happiness shining in her eyes. "It doesn't matter now. It's over."

Paul laughed. "Can I get you anything? A drink? Something to eat?"

"I *am* hungry. I was in such a rush to get here, I haven't eaten all day."

"Neither have I. Too busy worrying about you. Let's go out and get some dinner."

They walked to a nearby steakhouse and found a table for two on the deck overlooking the ocean. There was a warm breeze and the surf glistened in the moonlight. They ordered a bottle of wine and Paul toasted her safe return. "Any problems?"

Sarah looked at him with a satisfied grin and shook her head.

Reflecting on all that she had done, Paul smiled back. "You are an extraordinary woman."

"Thank you for being here for me. Thanks for understanding. Just thanks." Sarah said softly.

"Always."

Sarah swore she saw tears in his eyes. That she could have such an effect on this man who had fought wars on three continents overwhelmed her. She felt tears come to her own eyes. They held hands and laughed lovingly at each other.

After dinner, they walked back along the beach to Paul's house. When they were inside, Paul offered her a nightcap.

"Paul, I've had a long day. Do you think you could just take me to bed?"

He kissed her and carried her upstairs to the bedroom. "Tell me you're here to stay."

"As long as you want me."

"How about forever?"

"I was hoping for something more permanent, but forever will have to do."

EPILOGUE

PETER LINDSAY WAS CONVICTED ON TWO COUNTS OF FIRST-degree murder and sentenced to consecutive life sentences. For a police chief, prison was absolute hell. In his first month, Lindsay was taken to the infirmary five times: for stab wounds, a broken arm, broken ribs, and a perforated colon. Two months into his sentence, Lindsay tried to hang himself in his cell, but was cut down by the guards before he died. A month later, someone finished the job. Peter Lindsay awoke to find his cell ablaze and died screaming in agony.

Lindsay's conviction sparked a comprehensive investigation by the state Attorney General's office into the Sixth Precinct's methods and procedures. The conclusions were damning. The videos taken in the Backfield Building were reviewed in their entirety providing graphic and irrefutable evidence of the brutal interrogation techniques and sexual abuse that occurred at the precinct. Included in the disks reviewed by the investigators was the one showing Sarah Andrews being tortured with a taser.

A dozen senior officers in the precinct were charged with criminal offenses. Over a hundred court transcripts were reviewed and new trials were ordered in more than half the cases based on indications that evidence had been falsified or police testimony perjured. In all, over forty people had their guilty verdicts overturned and were released. One of those released was Donna Baker, the girl Sarah had helped during her last week in prison.

Clara Kramer left her husband and married Sam Cavell, the owner of the car dealership where she worked. She went back to university, earned a degree in business and then joined her husband's company as chief financial officer.

Ernie Kramer never regained the use of his arms and legs. He was placed in a chronic care facility where nurses had to attend to his every need for the rest of his life.

Lana Crawford, the rookie officer who had helped Sarah, quit the police force, got her law degree and joined the Public Defender's Office.

The investigators connected the murders of Carney, LePan, Gordon, and Carlucci and identified Sarah Andrews as the probable suspect. In reporting to the Governor, the State Attorney-General assured her that Sarah would be found. "She must have established a new identify. We're running a computer algorithm now to try to find her. It will match Andrews' description to all new social security numbers or driver's licenses issued in the last six months and flag those that may be a match."

"Shut it down," replied the Governor.

"I don't understand. This woman murdered several police officers. Whatever the provocation, she should be brought to justice."

"And what justice did *she* get?"

"The system isn't perfect, but that can't justify what she did."

The Governor exploded. "You've seen those disks! What happened to that woman is an absolute outrage. And there were dozens of others. But for her, these abuses would still be going on. There is no public interest served in bringing her to trial and no jury would ever convict her. I can only hope that she can put it all behind her, build a new life and find the peace and happiness that she deserves. Now shut it down!"

Paul Taylor rebuilt his home on Crystal Lake and he and Sarah lived together happily and peacefully, dividing their time between Crystal Lake and the island of San Alicia.